PUFFIN BOOKS

KATY

HAVE YOU READ THEM ALL?

WHERE TO START

THE DINOSAUR'S PACKED LUNCH

THE MONSTER STORY-TELLER

FOR YOUNGER READERS

BURIED ALIVE!

CLIFFHANGER

GLUBBSLYME

LIZZIE ZIPMOUTH

SLEEPOVERS

THE CAT MUMMY

THE MUM-MINDER

THE WORRY WEBSITE

STORIES ABOUT SISTERS

DOUBLE ACT

THE BUTTERFLY CLUB

THE DIAMOND GIRLS

THE WORST THING
ABOUT MY SISTER

HISTORICAL ADVENTURES

OPAL PLUMSTEAD

QUEENIE

THE LOTTIE PROJECT

ALL ABOUT JACQUELINE WILSON

JACKY DAYDREAM

MY SECRET DIARY

MOST POPULAR CHARACTERS

HETTY FEATHER

SAPPHIRE BATTERSEA

EMERALD STAR

DIAMOND

THE STORY OF TRACY BEAKER

THE DARE GAME

STARRING TRACY BEAKER

COMING SOON: LITTLE STARS

FAMILY DRAMAS

CANDYFLOSS

CLEAN BREAK

COOKIE

LILY ALONE

LITTLE DARLINGS

LOLA ROSE

MIDNIGHT

THE BED AND BREAKFAST STAR

THE ILLUSTRATED MUM

THE LONGEST WHALE SONG

THE SUITCASE KID

FIRST-CLASS FRIENDS

BAD GIRLS

BEST FRIENDS

SECRETS

VICKY ANGEL

FOR OLDER READERS

DUSTBIN BABY

GIRLS IN LOVE

GIRLS IN TEARS

GIRLS OUT LATE

GIRLS UNDER PRESSURE

KISS

LOVE LESSONS

MY SISTER JODIE

BOOKS INSPIRED BY CLASSICS

FOUR CHILDREN AND IT

KATY

ALSO AVAILABLE

PAWS AND WHISKERS

THE JACQUELINE WILSON
CHRISTMAS CRACKER

THE JACQUELINE WILSON TREASURY

Jacqueline Wilson

KATY

PUFFIN

PUFFIN BOOKS

UK | USA | Canada | Ireland | Australia
India | New Zealand | South Africa

Puffin Books is part of the Penguin Random House group of companies
whose addresses can be found at global.penguinrandomhouse.com.

puffinbooks.com

First published 2015
003

Text copyright © Jacqueline Wilson, 2015
Illustrations copyright © Nick Sharratt, 2015

The moral right of the author and illustrator has been asserted

Set in 14/17 pt Baskerville MT Std
Typeset by Jouve (UK), Milton Keynes
Printed in Great Britain by Clays Ltd, St Ives plc

A CIP catalogue record for this book is available from the British Library

HARDBACK
ISBN: 978–0–141–35396–8

TRADE PAPERBACK
ISBN: 978–0–141–35399–9

www.greenpenguin.co.uk

For the amazing Nickie Miles-Wildin

*Plus great thanks to Jonathan Pollock
and Elizabeth and Marina*

I

I'm Katy Carr. I'm the eldest.

When I was very small I was given a red car for my Christmas present. Not a little push-along car. A proper car I could climb into and pedal. I pedalled up and down the garden and all over the park and along the road to the shops with my mum. I'd shout out all the time I was pedalling, 'I'm Katy Carr, I'm Katy Carr!'

My mum knew I'd love that car. She understood that I wasn't a girly girl. She didn't give me dollies or dress me in pink. I had red dungarees and a red duffle coat and red wellie boots. I've got photos in my memory box of me in all these little scarlet outfits. The photo I like best is one of me in my car with Mum running along beside me. We're down at the park swings. She's wearing a T-shirt and jeans and her feet are bare. Her hair's in a ponytail and she looks like my big sister, not a proper mum.

Clover's in that photo too. She's my younger sister. She wasn't much more than a baby then, and she's slumped in one of those tiny swings, her fat little legs drooping. She looked a right little pudding, with rosy cheeks and amazing curly blonde hair. Well, she hasn't changed much.

Dad's not in the photo. He must have been the one with the camera.

I remember that day so vividly. Mum and me were having a race. I think she let me win. Then she sat me on one of the big swings and gave me a push, and I remember putting my head back and feeling wonderfully dizzy, as if I were really flying. I laughed and laughed as Mum pushed me higher and higher.

Then we all went to the van to get ice creams. I got my Whippy all down my front but Mum just laughed and called me a mucky pup.

Clover says she remembers that day too, but she doesn't really. She sometimes makes up all sorts of stories about the things Mum did, the things Mum said, but they're not real and true. Clover tells all sorts of fibs when she feels like it.

Dad doesn't get Clover the way I do. He thinks she's this sweet, gentle little girl. She just has to bat her big blue eyes at him and he melts. The teachers at school are like that too. She hardly ever gets into trouble, though she's actually almost as naughty as me.

Even so, I don't mind. I love Clover to bits. She's always understood that I'm the oldest so I get to be the boss. Not in a bad way. It's just that I'm the biggest. Actually, I think I'd be the biggest even if I was the youngest. I'm tall. Not just ordinary tall – really, really tall. And I'm skinny too, no matter how much I eat, so I look lankier than ever.

Izzie was crazy enough to say that I could be a fashion model one day! I just fell about laughing at the idea. Dad did too, though not in an unkind way. I don't think Izzie really meant it. I'm not the slightest bit pretty. I'm hopelessly untidy, always spilling stuff and tearing my jeans, and my hair always straggles loose if I scrape it into a ponytail. I'm also the exact opposite of graceful. In fact, I'm downright clumsy, always tripping over things. And I hate dressing up and can't stick having my photo taken. I've probably got more chance of being a brain surgeon or an astronaut than making it as a model.

Izzie was just sucking up to me. It really creeps me out when she does that. I'd sooner she nagged and moaned the way she usually does. I know that deep down she doesn't really *like* me. I don't care. I don't like *her*. I mean, why would I? She's just my stepmother.

Izzie's *soooo* different from my mum. She's fussy and picky and downright irritating. You could never ever imagine her running races with her little kid or screaming with laughter or acting crazy. She's always immaculately made-up and looks as if she's just come back from the hairdresser's all the time. If she wears jeans they're always carefully ironed and her tennis shoes are snowy white. Why Dad chose her as his second wife I'll never know.

I actually asked him once.

'*Why* did you marry Izzie, Dad?'

Clover looked shocked and I got a bit scared that Dad would be cross or upset. But he sat us down, one either side of him on the sofa, and said gently, 'I married Izzie because I love her.'

'But not as much as you loved Mum,' I blurted.

Dad was quiet for a few seconds. Clover looked as if she might cry. We'd all loved Mum so very, very much. It was the worst thing in the world when she got ill and died. Dad's a brilliant doctor but even he couldn't save her.

'I don't love Izzie the way I loved your mum,' Dad said, very softly, because Izzie was in the kitchen and he didn't want her to hear. That's the good thing about Dad. He always tells us the absolute truth. 'I love Izzie in a different way, because she's kind and caring and she's very creative.'

I sniffed. Izzie designs fancy handbags, for goodness' sake. I don't call that especially creative.

'And I wanted to find someone to help me look after you two girls,' Dad continued.

'We could look after ourselves – you, me and Clover,' I said. 'And now we're lumbered with drippy little Elsie as well as Izzie.'

'Stop being such a meanie, Katy,' said Dad, and then he *did* get cross.

I can't help what I think. Dad's always told us to be absolutely honest. And the plain fact is that Elsie is a total pain.

She's Izzie's daughter from her first marriage, but Elsie doesn't see her own dad. She just hangs round mine. She's nine now, this weird, whiny little girl with a fringe falling over her big brown eyes. She's the spitting image of a long-haired chihuahua, and she yaps like one too.

'I don't understand how you can be so unkind to poor little Elsie,' Dad said, over and over again.

He doesn't understand just how irritating it is, always having to have Elsie join in all our games. Clover and I tried to include her at first, we really did. We just played little-girl games then, Princesses and Pop Girls and Children's Homes, that kind of thing. I made them all up and only had to say a few words to Clover – like 'We're the flower princesses today, and I'm Princess Rose and you're Princess Lily' or 'We've just started a girl group called the Popchicks and I'm the lead singer' or 'We've been dumped in this children's home and

5

we're going to play all sorts of naughty tricks' – and Clover would smile and nod and we'd start the game. Straight away she'd tell me what she was wearing as Princess Lily or start strumming as the lead guitarist of the Popchicks or begin plotting an elaborate food-fight in the children's home. Whereas Elsie would just stare at us with her mouth slightly open, totally incapable of pretending. She'd expect a real Disney princess costume or say she'd never heard of the Popchicks or whine that she didn't want to live in a children's home but wanted to stay with her mum.

We'd get a bit impatient and then she'd always go running *to* her mum. We'd watch her climb on Izzie's lap and cling like a little monkey, and Clover and I would stare at them mutely, because we couldn't ever climb on *our* mum's lap now. It didn't help us to like Elsie any better.

Of course we didn't play those pathetic tiny-girl games now. We still played a few imaginary games in private, where no one could hear or laugh at us, but they were much more elaborate pretends with grown-up content. We made up our own soap called *Victoria Square*, where we were multiple people running a pub and a market stall and having all kinds of affairs. We would sometimes be DI Katy Carr and trusty Sergeant Clover solving complex crimes, but on another day we might easily turn into black-hearted serial killers stalking our prey. We also starred in many of my own horror movies, contending with Blobs and Aliens and Prehistoric Monsters.

We wouldn't let Elsie join in too. We'd tried her out once or twice and she took it all too seriously and then had nightmares. So we left her out, really for her own good. She didn't understand. She was always whining to Dad and Izzie that we wouldn't let her join in.

'We're not being mean. It's just that our games are private,' I told Dad.

'You let Caroline play,' Dad said.

Caroline lives next door. She's my all-time best friend forever. Clover's her second-best friend. We've known her ever since we were babies. We don't call her Caroline. She's actually Caroline Charlotte, so she started calling herself CC in one of our detective games and the name's stuck. She spells it Cecy now and everyone calls her that, even at school.

Of course we let Cecy play. She's great at pretending. She's invented a whole new Celebrity game. Clover and I are a bit rubbish at knowing all the big celebrities because Dad hates that stuff and fusses about what we watch on television and won't let us read any of the magazines. Izzie pretends to disapprove too, but we know for a fact that when she goes to the hairdresser's (which is frequently, because her big blonde hair needs a lot of attention) she buries her nose in *Hello!* and *OK!*

Cecy tells us all the gossip and acts it out and then we play we are the celebrities and we invent crazy weddings

7

and torrid affairs and give birth to babies. We always end up falling about laughing. Then Elsie sees us and thinks we're laughing at *her*.

We couldn't let her join in. She's too little to understand properly and she'd probably blab half of it to Izzie and then she'd tell Dad and we'd all get into trouble.

It used to be difficult meeting up in secret places without Elsie tagging along, but now it's easy-peasy. Both Cecy and I got mobile phones for our eleventh birthdays. Cecy got an ace smartphone. Mine is just an old-fashioned, cheap, distinctly unsmart one. I tried not to mind. I know we haven't got much money as we're such a big family now, and Dad's weird about spending a lot on our presents. He's not mean; he just thinks children shouldn't be spoilt too much, worst luck. But anyway, I can still text on my phone, so Cecy and I can secretly plan where we're going to meet. I flash the text quickly at Clover and then we sneak off.

This really winds Elsie up. She's forever trying to snatch my phone out my school bag and take a peep herself. She thinks we're texting horrid stuff about her. She's cried once or twice and that made me feel all hot and horrible. I don't like Elsie and I don't see why I should just because she's my stepsister, but it's awful when she's really upset. Perhaps Dad's right and I *am* being mean.

Sometimes when I'm awake in the middle of the night I decide I'm going to try to be extra kind to Elsie after all. I'll make a special fuss of her and cheer her up and maybe even invent a new pretend game just for her. I know she'd love that. Then I'll feel good and Dad will be ever so pleased with me. It all seems simple. But then in the morning Elsie will start her little-puppy whimpering about nothing at all and I'll get so irritated I decide that I won't be sweet to her after all.

It's not as if I'm mean to any of the others. I'm a truly good big sister to them all. Even Dad and Izzie say so. They've had three more children. I love Dorry and Jonnie and little Phil, but I do hope there won't be any more babies now. Six children are more than enough. We have to travel in the people carrier if we're going anywhere and that's starting to be a squash. We'll need a coach if Dad and Izzie carry on procreating.

Dorry and Jonnie are six-year-old twins, but they're totally unidentical in every way. Dorry's not a girl; he's a plump little boy with sticking-out ears, very earnest and serious. Izzie and Dad are very careful not to make too much of it but they're worried that he's quite chubby. Izzie tries so hard to fill him up with apple slices and carrot sticks, when all Dorry craves are sweets and crisps and chocolate and cake. He's not supposed to have second helpings either, but he secretly eats half of Jonnie's meals too. She doesn't care. Yes, Jonnie is a girl, though she's as brave and bold as any boy, and her knobbly knees have always got scabs because she's forever doing tricks on her bike and falling off.

Dorry doesn't try to do tricks any more because he's useless at it. I'm trying hard to think of something he's good at, funny little chap. I wouldn't dream of teasing him but I know he does get bullied a bit at school. His real name is Dorian, which doesn't help. Izzie has a lot to answer for. Some of the kids in his class call him Doreen. Jonnie gets mad then and makes up silly names for them in return. Jonnie is really Johanna, with that odd aitch. Izzie's choice again. Typical.

Then there's baby Phil, who's only three. He's astonishingly pretty for a small boy: big blue eyes and soft fair curls and a delicate little face. He has the sweetest merry laugh. I love making him chuckle. It's so easy. I just have to play peep-bo, or suddenly stand on my head or pull a silly face, and he creases up laughing.

At least his name, Philip, is simple enough. His middle name is mad though – Pirrip. He's named after the main character in Charles Dickens' *Great Expectations*. The boy in the book is called Pip for short, and Dad and Izzie sometimes call our Phil that too. Dad loves reading aloud. He has a picture-book session with the littlies at bedtime, and then while Izzie's tucking them up he reads to Clover and me. And Elsie too, though she gets a bit bored and fidgety because she's really too little. Dad reads classic novels, so you'd maybe think we'd get mega-bored and fidgety too, but he's great at reading aloud, doing all the different voices, and he skips the dull passages. He acts things out, throwing his arms about, so that he often forgets he's holding his evening glass of red wine and spills it all over his trousers.

So there we are. That's the whole family. Dad, Izzie, me, Clover, Elsie, Dorry, Jonnie and Phil. We also have our pets: Sally, our serene old lady cat who sits on your lap and purrs to cheer you up when you're feeling miserable, and little Tyler, our rescue terrier. Tyler is little but he thinks he's as big as an Alsatian. Clover and I took him to puppy-training classes when we first got him. I was determined to teach Tyler lots of tricks. I had our future act all worked out in my head. I felt we might easily win *Britain's Got Talent*. But Tyler had other ideas. He didn't want to learn any tricks at puppy training, he just wanted to play with all the other dogs. And he kept doing a wee on the floor, which was seriously embarrassing. I've had to put my plans for *Britain's Got Talent* on hold.

I might just work out some other novelty act. I hoped I might be a singer like my namesake Katy Perry, but then Clover recorded me and when I listened back I discovered I can't actually sing in tune. I wondered about being a dancer instead, very modern and gymnastic, and I tried to build up a routine with Cecy and Clover. Elsie wanted to join in too, and we did try letting her for a bit, but she kept getting her left and right muddled up so we had to drop her. Clover wasn't too great at it either. But Cecy is brilliant. Much better than me, actually. So maybe I'll leave the dancing option for her.

I want to do *something* special and exciting in the future. I'm quite sporty and I'm especially good at being a shooter in netball because it's so easy for me to dunk the ball in the net as I'm so tall. I'm not so hot at running though because my great lanky legs go all gangly. Maybe I'll have to wait till I'm old enough to drive a proper car and then when I get wheels I'll be a brilliant woman racing driver, ever so brave and daring.

Or maybe I'll write seven great magic books like J. K. Rowling, because I'm good at making up stories. Then I'll get very rich and I'll buy a big castle somewhere, and Cecy and all my brothers and sisters can come and live with me there. I'll have a cheery servant or two and pay them so much money they won't mind a bit doing all the chores. They'll fill and empty the dishwasher and sort the rubbish into the right recycling bins and tidy all the bedrooms – all the boring, boring, boring stuff that Izzie keeps nagging me to do.

I'll be famous at something some day, you mark my words.

2

At twelve noon on Saturday we all gathered on the garage roof. Well, Clover and Elsie and I did. Dad won't allow the littlies to climb up the ladder, so they had to wait lolling below us. Izzie says Elsie's not allowed either, but she so wants to be with us that she never takes any notice.

It's a low garage and the ladder's fixed against the wall, so it's really quite safe. Sort of. The garage roof was leaking years ago so Dad had these workmen come to retile it. They put the ladder up and forgot to take it away again. Lots of green moss has grown back on the roof now, which makes it very soft and comfortable, like a green carpet.

I like to sit with my legs swinging down, peering out over next-door's garden. Not number four next door, where Cecy lives. I mean number eight the other side of us – the sad house. Old Mrs Burton lives there. At least I think she does. No one's seen her for years and years.

She used to be this perfectly ordinary old lady when Mr Burton was still around. They invited Clover and me in for tea several times, after Mum died. We didn't really like to go, because we didn't know what to say to them and there was nothing very much to do. Mrs Burton had a collection of little china pots with painted lids and she let us look at each one, but we weren't allowed to touch because they were precious and we were only little.

The tea was very strange too. We had to drink out of cups on saucers, whereas we were used to mugs, so we found it difficult. Then there was a plate of thin bread and butter to eat. Not even any jam. Just a piece of bread and butter. Mrs Burton said if we ate it all up we would be allowed cakes. So we chewed valiantly and then Mr Burton went into the kitchen and came back with a small plate of little iced cakes. He called them fancies. There were two yellow and two pink. I chose yellow and Mrs Burton and Mr Burton took the pink ones. I saw Clover's face. I knew just how much she wanted a pink one too. She didn't eat her yellow one properly; she just bit all the icing off the top and licked the little bit of cream inside.

Mr and Mrs Burton weren't cross with her. They shook their heads and patted her curls and said she was a lovely little girlie.

'A real Goldilocks,' said Mr Burton.

They didn't call me any fairy-tale character. Perhaps they thought I was the wicked witch or the big bad wolf but were too polite to say.

Anyway, it was uncomfortable having tea with the Burtons, so we told Dad we didn't really want to go any more. Then Mr Burton got ill and died and Mrs Burton stopped inviting us. She stayed indoors by herself. Well, she saw a home help every week, and the Ocado van came every Friday with her very small order, but that was all. Dad went to call on her, partly as a neighbour, partly as her doctor, but he said she simply wanted to be left alone.

As we got older Clover and I made up stories about her, seeing her as mad and tragic, like a modern Miss Havisham (she's in *Great Expectations* too). We even dared each other to go and look through her windows or knock on her door. But now I'm older still I feel a bit uncomfortable about her. I don't think she's so much mad as sad. She's still grieving for Mr Burton, who was clearly the love of her life. That seems a bit strange to me, because Mr Burton didn't look anything like a romantic hero. He had false teeth that made him hiss a little and a silly moustache and he always wore cardigans – but perhaps he was Mr Perfect in Mrs Burton's eyes.

I felt truly sorry for her now but it didn't stop me leading the others on special secret expeditions into her garden. It's a very long garden, much bigger than ours. The ordinary back garden is a bit boring. When Mr Burton was alive it used to be bright with flowers in the summer, but now Mrs Burton has a garden firm come once a month and they've planted shrubs that don't need much attention. They just cut them back a bit and mow the lawn. But they only tend the garden as far as the old greenhouse.

It's not a proper greenhouse now; it's all falling to bits. That's a shame because it would make a marvellous playhouse, but some of the glass is broken and all jagged. *I'd* be extra careful, and Clover would too, but it's not somewhere we could ever risk the littlies. Stupid Izzie gave me these sorrowful little lectures about my being the eldest and therefore I should try to set a good example to my brothers and sisters. But I *am* careful and responsible. I won't let the children play *in* the greenhouse. We play *behind* it. The gardeners never go there because it doesn't show from the house. Mrs Burton certainly doesn't go there. No one does. Only us.

It's like another wonderful, wild, secret garden. There are still roses there in summer and lots of buttercups and daisies and dandelions in the long grass. It's so overgrown that it's like a jungle for our dog Tyler. He absolutely loves it in the secret garden. He plays at being a tiger, stalking his prey.

There's a big weeping willow too, which makes an amazing green cave where we can have important meetings and special picnics. Best of all, there's a big tree right at the end by the fence that has brilliant branches for climbing. I can shin up there whenever I want. You can see for miles, all over everyone's back gardens, all the way to the park. It would be the most brilliant place for a tree house. I'm gathering bits of wood out of people's skips and secretly hoarding them. When I've got enough I'll make us all a tree house.

I told all the children and everyone thought it was a brilliant idea – everyone except Elsie.

'What do you mean, make a tree house? You don't know how, Katy Carr. It's not just nailing planks of wood together. You have to make it safe. And how are you going to balance it on those tree trunks? You're all talk, you are,' she said, her voice shrill. 'It won't be safe!'

'Oh yes it will, just you wait and see,' I said airily, refusing to be rattled.

'I suppose it will be as safe as that stupid boat you made when we nearly all drowned!' said Elsie, pink with triumph.

Once, when we were on our way to the park all together, me in charge, I happened to see a piece of someone's fallen-down fence in a skip. I had this sudden brilliant idea that we could turn it into a raft. Clover,

Cecy and I carried it all the way to the duck pond where I launched it on to the water. It was fine when it was just me perched on it. I even risked paddling it from one side to the other and it floated perfectly. But when the others all crowded on to the raft too it tilted violently and suddenly sank. We all got very wet of course, but we didn't nearly *drown*, not when the water only came up as far as Phil's waist.

'You shut up, Elsie,' I said, and I gave her a little push.

She practically made herself fall over and then cried and I got into yet more trouble from Izzie for bullying my little sister. It would be much, much easier if I didn't ever have to include her in our games, but then she'd whine and whimper that we were leaving her out.

So there we all were, Clover, Elsie and me up on the garage roof, Dorry, Jonnie, Phil and Tyler playing digging down below, all of us waiting for Cecy. She goes to dancing lessons now, ballet and modern, on Saturday mornings. Clover's so envious. I don't really want to go and learn dancing, especially not ballet. Oh dear! The thought of looking like a lamp post in a leotard, a metre taller than everyone else, makes me go hot with horror. But I *would* like to go to a Saturday-morning class.

I know you can do drama at the place where Cecy goes. I would so love to do drama! We don't do it properly at school at all. The only play we've ever put on was a Nativity play when we were in the Infants. I wanted to be Mary because it's the main part but our teacher chose one of her tiny girly pets. Then I hoped I'd be the angel Gabriel because he's very important and it wouldn't matter if he were tall, but horrible, simpering Eva got that part. I had to play a shepherd's wife. I wasn't even a shepherd – a shepherd's *wife*. I'd have sooner been a sheep. But even so, I gave the part all I had, beaming at my shepherd husband, startled by the star, overawed by little Baby Jesus, all the while feeding this manky toy lamb with a doll's bottle. I thought I was giving a wonderful performance but my teacher wasn't impressed.

'Calm down, Katy Carr. Stop all the silly faces. You must learn to stand still on stage. You're distracting everyone. The story isn't about you, it's about Mary and Joseph and Baby Jesus,' she said.

I *wanted* it to be about me. I'm sure if I went to a Saturday drama club with a proper drama teacher she'd realize my potential and give me a lead part. And Clover should go to dancing class because she's really quite good at it, almost as good as Cecy. Dorry wants to go to cookery classes because he loves watching *The Great British Bake Off*. Izzie won't let him cook in her kitchen because she says he'd make too much mess. Jonnie could do gymnastics with all the cool little dudes. I suppose Phil's too small for classes. He loves finger painting at nursery though, always bringing home huge great sheets of paper bigger than him, daubed all over with bright poster paints. He did a family portrait of all of us once and it was really good, even though we were all round blobs. He did my legs much, much longer than anyone else's, which was very observant of him. So when he's five or six Phil could go to art classes.

I've left Elsie out. Not really on purpose. I just can't think of her possessing any particular talent. I suppose she'll have to tag along with one of us. This is the point though. Dad won't let us go to any Saturday classes or after-school classes whatsoever. It's so unfair. Almost everyone I know goes to *something*.

Dad just laughs at me when I pester him.

'If you seriously think Izzie and I have got time to ferry you lot around to all these silly classes then you're more of a dunce than I imagined, Katy. Besides, I don't hold with all this hobby-hustling. I think you have far more fun going out to play and making up your own games.'

I suppose this is not all bad news, because Dad does let us roam around and play out lots, whereas some kids I know aren't even allowed to play in their own gardens without supervision. But I still envy Cecy, because she goes to dancing lessons (and piano on Tuesday evenings and junior gym on Fridays) *and* she gets to hang out and play with us too.

'I wish Cecy would hurry up!' I said to Clover now, consulting my watch. It's a very, very precious watch, my favourite piece of jewellery. It's not a very expensive watch, the sort you can buy in any old shop, but it's the best watch ever because it was Mum's. Dad kept it and then gave it to me last Christmas.

I heard Izzie murmur that it wasn't a good idea to give me Mum's watch.

'I know Katy will be thrilled, and it's a lovely thought, but you know how careless she is. She'll lose it or break it within days and then she'll be so upset. Wouldn't it be better to keep it safely and give it to her when she's grown up?' she said.

'I want her to have it now. It will mean the world to her. I'm sure she'll be extra-specially careful with it,' said Dad.

And I am. I can't believe Izzie didn't want me to have it.

My precious watch said it was twenty past twelve now. The littlies and Tyler were getting restless down below. Jonnie and Phil were throwing balls for Tyler and he was leaping about, yelping excitedly. One of them was going to fall over or bite any minute.

Dorry was suspiciously quiet. I leaned right over to see what he was doing, hanging on to Clover for support. I saw my sneaky little brother with his hand in the picnic basket!

'Hey, Dorry, get out of there!' I yelled.

Dorry jumped and immediately stuffed a whole chocolate chip cookie into his mouth.

'Don't you dare start on the picnic!' I said.

'I'm not,' he said, scarcely able to speak for cookie in his mouth. He held up his hands. 'See, I haven't taken anything!'

'You bad, wicked fibber! I've never known such a greedy guts. Right, *we'll* all have chocolate chip cookies when we're in the secret garden, but *you* can't, because you've scoffed yours now,' I said.

Dorry immediately burst into tears, nearly choking himself.

'Oh, do stop, Dorry! You're such a baby,' I said, exasperated.

I ended up having to climb down the ladder to thump him on the back. Then Tyler smelled food in the picnic basket and stuck his little head in and growled and howled when I hauled him out. It looked as if the picnic was turning into a disaster but then – *hurray, hurray!* – Cecy came hurtling over the little garden gate between our back gardens, smiling and out of breath.

'Sorry, sorry! I got held up talking to Miss Lucy. Guess what? She's giving me the star part in the summer show!' Cecy said triumphantly. 'And look! My mum's given us crisps and chocolate for the picnic!'

'Oh, yummy!' said Dorry. 'I'll carry them for you, Cecy.'

'Don't let him get his hands on them! He'll gobble them all up before we've even got to the secret garden,' I said, starting to climb down the ladder.

Clover followed me. We wasted another few minutes over Elsie, who made a huge fuss, saying she felt dizzy and didn't dare climb down herself.

'Then you shouldn't ever have climbed *up*, you little wuss,' I said. '*We* didn't want you up there anyway.'

Elsie's face crumpled and she started crying.

'Oh, do shut up,' I said, but I felt a bit mean. Very mean. Why did I always have to be horrid to Elsie? 'Look, if you can climb up, you can climb down. It's simple.'

Clearly Elsie felt it wasn't simple at all. I sighed and shinned up the ladder again, going one-handed to show how easy it was.

'There now, Elsie,' I said, mopping up her tears with the edge of my T-shirt (I never seem to have a tissue on me when I need one). 'Come on, I'll help you. I'll climb down on to the first rung and then, when you come down, I'll wrap myself all round you so you can't possibly fall. OK?'

'It's not a trick, is it?' Elsie sniffled. 'You truly won't let me fall?'

'No, of course not. Don't be silly, I'm your sister. I won't ever let you hurt yourself,' I said grandly, as if I had all the superpowers in the world.

'Thank you,' said Elsie in a tiny voice. The way she looked at me then made me feel almost fond of her.

'Come on, Elsie-Chelsea,' I said, and I coaxed her gently all the way down.

'There!' I said, when we were safely on the ground and the chocolate and crisps were crammed into the picnic basket. Clover and Cecy carried it between them while I helped the littlies into the secret garden.

It wasn't the easiest job. We'd always had a proper gate between Cecy's garden and ours, because we'd been friends forever and Cecy and I had grown up playing with each other. But the Carrs had never really been proper friends with the Burtons, and now she'd become this weird recluse Mrs Burton certainly wasn't going to have a gate put in just for our convenience. She didn't have a proper fence anyway, just a very big, overgrown, prickly hedge.

I'd found a spot near the old greenhouse where the hedge grew more sparsely. Tyler had helped, digging furiously each day until he'd made a proper little tunnel between the gardens. We could crawl through, just about. It was still very prickly, but I wrapped each small child's head in an old towel so that their faces didn't get too scratched. Our clothes always got filthy, but who cared? Izzie always had the washing machine on the go.

So we all wriggled through one by one. I put Clover and Cecy (plus picnic basket) through first, because they were sensible enough to keep absolutely quiet in Mrs Burton's garden just in case she happened to be looking out of her back windows.

It was always a struggle with the twins. Dorry was getting so tubby it was a real squeeze. Jonnie was thin as a pin, but she always wanted to drag Zebby through with her. Zebby wasn't a cuddly toy; he was a child-sized chair with a zebra head. Jonnie loved Zebby so passionately she frequently tried to take him to bed with her, and he always had to accompany her on expeditions. Zebby got his head stuck in the hedge this time, but after a lot of tugging he struggled through too.

When the last child was in Mrs Burton's garden I let the squirming Tyler go and he shot through like a rocket. I crouched down and crawled through myself. It was getting more and more of a struggle for me as well. I kept thinking of those illustrations in *Alice's Adventures in Wonderland*, where Alice has drunk the magic potion and grown enormous, scarcely able to fit in the house. Halfway through the hedge, almost stuck fast, I had a depressing vision of the future. Perhaps I was going to be a total freak of nature that never stopped growing. I'd end up ten feet tall, Giant Katy, swaying in the breeze like a poplar tree, and the children would have to climb up me with grappling hooks in order to talk to me.

But once I was safely through to Mrs Burton's I cast off this worrying thought and concentrated on getting us safely to the secret garden behind the greenhouse. I kept glancing at her kitchen and living-room windows but there was no sign of any melancholy old woman peering out. I put my finger to my lips even so, and made each child tiptoe across the grass. Tyler went careering off in the wrong direction and I couldn't risk calling him, but – thank goodness – after three mad circuits of the garden he came scurrying back and I grabbed him and carried him down beyond the greenhouse with us.

Then we were safe! The secret garden looked as beguiling as ever. We dumped the picnic basket and circled our special place, admiring every soft, fragrant rose, taking our shoes off to walk in the long grass that tickled our ankles. Dorry even lost interest in the picnic for five minutes and was happy gambolling in the grass with Jonnie, both of them talking their own secret language, while Zebby kicked up his heels and lay on his back. Phil lay nose-to-nose with Tyler conducting a licking contest. This probably wasn't very hygienic but they both enjoyed it very much.

Clover and Cecy dragged the picnic under the weeping willow tree and started setting it out neatly on a plastic tablecloth, dividing everything into seven with scrupulous care. I took the chance to climb my special tree. The knee of my jeans got caught on an awkward branch and there was an ugly tearing sound. They were new jeans too, so Izzie wasn't going to be happy. Oh well, I'd simply have to remind her that ripped jeans were the latest fashion.

I got almost to the top of the tree and clung there, peering down at the tiny world below me. It was particularly weird looking down into my own garden. Dad and Izzie were sitting on the little terrace, drinking cups of coffee. Their heads were close and they were murmuring together. I hated seeing them like that. I looked up at the sky instead. An aeroplane was flying high in the sky. Perhaps I'd be an airline pilot one day and swoop over vast continents on a daily basis. Or maybe I'd be an astronaut and hurtle upwards into space until the Earth itself looked as small as my own back garden.

I went off into a daydream but was soon brought back to earth by the clamour beneath me. The littlies had got tired of playing and wanted their picnic 'now, now, *now!*' So we all ducked under the soft green fronds of the weeping willow and sat cross-legged round the wonderful feast. I pretended it was an exotic gargantuan banquet of champagne and caviar, suckling pig and guinea fowl, and extraordinary sweetmeats, with fine offerings from abroad of crushed cocoa bean and golden slivers of potato, when it was actually lemonade, tuna sandwiches, chipolata sausages and chicken wings, and strawberry cupcakes, with Cecy's contribution of Kit Kats and crisps. I'm sure our real feast tasted just as good as the imaginary one would have done.

We ate and ate, even Elsie, who's ultra picky. Dorry looked at her share hopefully, but she ate it all up, every crumb. Then we lay back with full tummies.

'Start up a game, Katy,' said Clover.

I thought of all my plans for the future.

'OK. What do we all want to do when we grow up? You go first, Cecy,' I said, giving her a gentle nudge.

'Well . . . I'm going to grow my hair right down to my waist – not extensions, my real hair – and I'll have highlights to make it look blonder, and I want to stay quite thin but much curvier, you know . . .' Cecy waved her hand in the air.

Dorry and Jonnie sniggered.

'You shut up, you two! Carry on, Cecy,' I commanded. 'Will you be a dancer?'

'Yes, and a singer, so I'll have several really big hits and I'll be splashed all over the celebrity magazines,' said Cecy.

'Boring!' Elsie muttered, and I glared at her.

'But *then* do you know what I'm going to do?' said Cecy.

'Get married and have five children?' Clover suggested.

'No, I'll have all these film stars and boy bands mad about me and I might have a little fling here and there, but I'm going to use my money to start a special orphanage in some poor country and I'll go there myself and tend all the little babies, just like Mother Teresa,' Cecy said triumphantly.

'You'll be Sister Cecy,' I said. 'That's wonderful! Right, Clover, your turn.'

'Well, I want long hair down to my waist too, and I'll straighten it so there isn't a single curl left, and I'll be very rich too. Maybe I'll work in the City and make pots of money,' said Clover.

'But you're rubbish at maths,' said Elsie.

'I'll be great at finance, just you wait and see. Who's got the most pocket money out of all of us, eh?' said Clover.

Elsie couldn't dispute this, because Clover hoarded her money carefully while we generally spent ours as soon as we got it.

'So, see, I'll be mega rich and live in a huge great mansion with a swimming pool and a helicopter pad, so I'll swim every day *and* go for a ride in my helicopter, and I'll have a brand-new designer outfit every single day – and I'll also buy lovely designer clothes for children and heaps and heaps of toys and mini iPads and small bikes and I'll ship them all out for Cecy's orphans,' said Clover.

'Brilliant!' I said. 'Go on then, Elsie, your turn.'

'Well, I'll – I'll have long hair right down to my feet and I'll be the greatest singer and dancer ever and I'll feed all the orphans in an entire country and I'll make billions and billions of pounds in the City and I'll wear a new set of clothes every hour and I'll be so generous to little children that the Queen will make me Princess Elsie,' she said, waving her arms around emphatically.

'That's just copying Cecy and Clover,' I said. 'But OK, now it's your turn, Dorry.'

'Easy-peasy,' said Dorry. 'When I grow up I'm going to order king-size pizzas every day with ten different toppings on every one, and I'll have giant cupcakes with heaps of buttercream, and ten chocolate bars, and I'll have a huge tub of ice cream every day too and all the fizzy drinks I want, and no one will ever say, "That's enough for a little boy," or tell me I'll get fat.'

We all fell about laughing.

'You little pig, Dorry!' I said. 'What about you, Jonnie?'

'I'll tame a real zebra as my special pet and learn how to ride my bike right up into the sky like in that old *ET* film and I'll play for a Premier League football team,' said Jonnie.

'Cool!' I said. 'And you, Phil?'

'I'll be a big, big lion and I'll eat you all up!' said Phil, and he ran round roaring at us.

Then Dorry and Jonnie started pretending to be lions too and they crawled out of the willow cave and went running round crazily with Phil, playing the Eat You All Up game.

'They're such babies,' said Elsie scornfully.

'They're just having fun,' I said.

'What about you, Katy? You haven't said what you're going to do when you're grown up,' said Clover.

'Yes, go on – tell,' said Cecy.

So I told them all my plans about living in a big house with everyone and being brilliantly famous and winning lots of car races and writing best-selling books. I heard my voice go all wavery while I was telling it, because it suddenly seemed a bit silly. I wanted it to be real, but maybe it was just childish pretend. That was the trouble with getting older. Sometimes I couldn't quite believe things any more. We could be right in the middle of a brilliant new game – all of us playing we were brain surgeons or animal trainers or Russian royalty – and it could seem as real as anything, and then suddenly in a flash I'd see we were just Katy and Clover and Cecy saying silly stuff and getting pink in the face.

But Clover and Cecy still seemed to believe in me, thank goodness.

'Can I have my own room in your house, Katy – a pink room with a giant pink teddy bear and a built-in wardrobe for all my designer clothes?' Clover asked.

'Yes, of course,' I said graciously.

'And will you take me for rides in your cars, if you promise not to go *too* fast?' she said.

'Oh, me too, me too!' said Cecy.

'I'll have a special red Ferrari just for the three of us,' I promised.

'And will you dedicate your first book to me, Katy?' Cecy asked. 'To Cecy, my best friend in all the world.'

'Of course, and it will also be to Clover, the best sister in all the world,' I promised. 'Oh, I forgot! I'm not the only writer in the family! Did you know Dorry's been keeping a diary?'

'*Dorry?*' said Clover.

'I found it this morning, when mean old Izzie was making me vacuum all the bedrooms. He'd hidden it in a sock under his bed. I couldn't help snaffling it to show you. It's hilarious!' I peeped out of the willow fronds, but Dorry was still busy being a lion with the other littlies.

'Look!' I said, fishing the tiny notebook from my jeans pocket. I read it out loud, indicating the valiant stabs at spelling along the way.

Satday – Im going to rite a dairy to tell all the grate
       things I do.
Sunday – Oh yum, pancakes for breakfast and I had
       heeps maypel sirrup. Then rost chiken for
       dinner with 4 potatos and appel crumbel,
       two helps.
Munday – School. Had ice lolly on way home.
Twoday – School. Jonnie gave me half her pizza.
Wenday – School. Nothing day.
Thurday – School. Nothing day.
Fryday – School fish and chips arnt as nice as chip
       shop stuff.
Satday – We had picnic in secret garden and I ate all
       the sossage rolls. Spag bol for supper!!!
Sunday – Rost pork and appel sorse and 4 potatos but
       horid brokalee. Fruit sallad and creem.
Munday – School. Ice creem van not there.
Twoday – School. Nothing day.

Wenday – School. Found old toffee in pocket.
Thurday – School. Nothing day.
Fryday – School. Nothing day.
Satday – Rain. No picnic. Cant be bovverd to keep
          dairy eny more.

We all laughed so much we had to lie down, gasping. We stared up into the roof of our willow cave. I was in the middle, holding hands with Clover one side and Cecy the other.

'I wish every day could be a Saturday,' I said. 'I think I don't want to grow up, even though we're all going to be doing such grand, amazing things. I think being this age is maybe more fun.'

3

I loved Sundays too. Dad didn't have any surgeries or clinics, and there was a locum doctor manning the phone lines so he didn't even get called away to an emergency. We had him all to ourselves.

Well, that's not quite true. We had to share him with Izzie.

When Mum was alive I used to lift Clover out of her cot and carry her in to Mum and Dad's bed and we'd all four have a great big cuddle together.

'I *think* I can remember the cuddles,' Clover says.

I know I can remember. They were the best times ever. And then, after we'd all had a little snooze, Mum didn't mind a bit if we had a proper play. She always joined in, making out we were bears in our cave under the duvet or giving us a ride on her legs or playing peep-bo all together with Clover.

But as soon as Izzie came to live with us Dad said we had to knock on the bedroom door before we came in and we weren't allowed to disturb them until ten o'clock on Sunday mornings. Ten o'clock, when we'd been awake at least three hours!

We were supposed to play quietly in our bedrooms. Izzie left a packet of cornflakes on the kitchen table in case we were hungry. Well, we weren't going to go along with that! We pattered downstairs and I stood on a chair and managed to reach inside the cupboard and we had a proper feast. We ate great spoonfuls of jam and honey and sugar and scooped handfuls of sultanas and raisins and nuts. Clover and I once ate an entire packet of chocolate fingers between us. Elsie trailed after us and sometimes had a little nibble, but she mostly just stared at us balefully and told us we'd get into trouble. Well we did, but we didn't care. We were making a point.

Of course, after Dorry and Jonnie were born no one could have a quiet lie-in till ten o'clock. They started bawling their heads off at six o'clock every single day and went on making a terrible fuss for years. Then as soon as they'd quietened down at last and started sleeping in a bit, little Phil was born. No wonder he likes playing Lions now – he used to roar and roar and roar when he was a baby.

I can reach the food cupboard easily now without standing on a chair. My goodness, I can practically reach up and touch the ceiling! But I'm totally responsible now, boringly big-sisterish. I pour us all a bowl of cornflakes and play a DVD in the living room, something like *Frozen* or *Up* or *Wall-ee* or one of the *Toy Story* movies, and the littlies and Elsie all sit as good as gold. Clover and I sometimes watch too. Or sometimes we go off and chat together or play our own private games.

I should have done the usual thing *this* Sunday. Only I didn't. I was hungry, and reading Dorry's diary yesterday had given me an idea. Why didn't *I* make pancakes? I could make them for all of us, and maybe bring Dad and Izzie theirs on a tray. Then the littlies would be so pleased and Dad would be truly impressed.

So I set to in the kitchen, finding the biggest bowl and a wooden spoon, and setting all the ingredients out on the worktop. I wasn't quite certain how you made a pancake mixture but I was pretty sure you needed eggs and flour. There were lots of us and we all loved pancakes, so I cracked open a dozen eggs and tipped in a whole big packet of flour.

Elsie came trailing into the kitchen in her Hello Kitty nightie.

'What are you *doing*, Katy?' she asked, her eyes round.

'Making pancakes,' I said.

'Do you *know* how to make pancakes?' she asked.

'Of course she does,' said Clover confidently.

'It's easy-peasy,' I said. 'You just stir things round a bit and then fry them in the pan . . . And don't you toss them? That'll be the fun part,' I said.

'Oh Katy! You're so clever,' said Clover.

She looked at me so admiringly that I felt like the greatest cook in the world and beat my pancake mixture with renewed vigour. I had such a huge bowlful that some of the mixture kept slopping over the side. It seemed a bit too wet and slippery, so I found a packet of some other sort of flour and shook some of that in too. Then it became so stodgy I could barely stir it. I'd used up all the eggs, so I poured in some milk and that helped matters tremendously. The mixture stayed pretty lumpy no matter how hard I stirred, but I hoped the pancakes would somehow smooth themselves out when they were cooking in the frying pan.

'Now for the best bit,' I said.

I lit the gas carefully and put a huge knob of butter in the pan, almost half a packet.

'That's much too much,' Elsie said.

'No, it isn't. We don't want the pancakes to stick, do we?' I said.

The butter started sizzling alarmingly.

'Should it make such a noise?' asked Elsie.

'It's got to be piping hot. Stand back though. I don't want you two to get splashed,' I said, determined to be

37

a good, responsible sister. I was getting a bit spattered with butter myself. I decided I'd better start cooking the pancakes quickly, so I poured a dollop of mixture into the pan.

'There!' I said, watching it spread itself out and crackle and spit. 'Look, look! It's turning into a proper pancake!'

'Yes, it really is!' said Clover.

'I think it's burning,' said Elsie, waving her arms about. 'Look at all the smoke!'

'It's fine. I'm sure it's meant to be like this,' I said. 'It's cooked on one side now so I'd better get tossing.'

I seized the pan in both hands and gave a mighty toss. I wanted it to go high in the air for extra effect. I swear I wasn't aiming at anyone. But it sailed through the air with alarming speed and landed right on Elsie's head! She started shrieking. I'm ashamed to say Clover and I burst into helpless laughter because she looked so funny, pancake all over her hair. Then there was a sudden terrible wailing, even louder than Elsie's. All the smoke had set the fire alarm off!

Izzie and Dad came charging into the kitchen in their nightclothes, terrified the house was on fire. Izzie grabbed Elsie in horror while Dad turned the gas off, opened the window and flapped a cloth under the alarm until at last it stopped screaming. Then there was a sudden awful silence, apart from Elsie's snivelling.

'Oh my Lord! Whatever possessed you, Katy?' said Izzie, almost in tears herself. 'Look at poor Elsie! Did it burn you, darling? Does it hurt terribly?'

'Yes!' Elsie wept.

Dad looked at her head carefully. 'No, she's not burned. Come here, poppet. Let's run the tap and get this nasty sticky gloop off you. Katy, how *could* you?'

'I – I'm sorry, Dad. I was just making pancakes as a surprise,' I said.

'Don't be cross with her!' Clover begged.

'She could have seriously injured Elsie and set the whole kitchen on fire!' said Izzie. 'Look at the state of the stove – and my worktop! And what are all these eggshells? You surely haven't used *all* the eggs – and all my flour too? And the butter? Oh, it's just too much! Here, I'll take Elsie and wash her hair in the bath.'

She picked Elsie up and made off with her. They were both in tears now. It was awful – and yet somehow so comical too: poor Elsie still such a sight, now dripping water as well as covered in pancake, and Izzie with her hair all tousled for once and her long face distorted with distress. I caught Clover's eye and the most terrible snorty giggle erupted out of me before I could stop it.

'It's not remotely funny, Katy,' said Dad, in such a sad and weary voice that I sobered up instantly.

'I know, Dad. I'm not really laughing. Look, I didn't *intend* the wretched pancake to land on Elsie. I didn't *mean* to make such a mess. I was just trying to give everyone a lovely surprise,' I said.

'That's really, really true, Dad. Katy just didn't think,' said Clover earnestly.

'Exactly. You never think of consequences, Katy, and I'm getting tired of it,' said Dad. 'Run away and get dressed, Clover. Katy and I need to have a little private talk together.'

My stomach turned over. I hated private talks when Dad told me off. He always made me feel so dreadful. Clover knew, and hesitated, hoping Dad might change his mind.

'Go on, Clover. You can help the little ones get washed and dressed,' said Dad.

She had to go and I was left, waiting for the telling off. Dad doesn't shout like some fathers. He just speaks quietly and seriously and tells you how disappointed he is in you. It's far worse than shouting. He stood there in his old-fashioned stripy pyjamas, his feet bare, yet he managed to have an air of chilly dignity.

'It's about time you stopped these silly pranks, Katy,' he said. 'You're getting much too old for this nonsense. I know you probably meant well – I'll give you the benefit of the doubt. But I'm so tired of you doing silly childish things without thinking first. You're eleven now. You're old enough to know better. You're the eldest. All the others look up to you.'

'Elsie doesn't,' I interrupted.

'And that's another thing. We've had so many conversations about Elsie and you've made so many promises. It upsets me that you continue to be so unkind to her.'

'I don't mean to be –'

'Katy! Just listen to yourself. You've got to learn to *think* first. Be aware of all the consequences. You're not a stupid girl – even though you *behave* stupidly. Now start clearing up this kitchen while I try to concoct some kind of breakfast for us,' said Dad.

'I'm sorry, Dad,' I said, and I leaned against him miserably.

He patted me on the back and I knew I was more or less forgiven, but I felt bad. I resolved to try harder to make Dad truly proud of me.

I was positively saintly all the rest of Sunday, making a special effort with Elsie. It was a struggle. I wasn't sure if Dad was noticing how good I was being, but when he came upstairs to kiss us all goodnight he gave me a special hug.

'There. You're my good girl now,' he said, and I went to sleep happy.

But somehow everything went wrong again on Monday. I overslept for a start. Well, I heard Izzie shouting at me to get up, but I didn't want to. I was having a wonderful dream about Mum. I was little again, and she'd taken Clover and me to the park, and we were having such fun. It was so real. I could feel the hard seat of the swing underneath me, feel the gentle push of Mum's hands behind me, see the clouds swirling dizzily up above . . . I wanted to get back into the dream and stay there forever.

But then Izzie was suddenly in the bedroom, pulling my covers off me.

'For goodness' sake, will you get *up*! Didn't you hear me calling? Clover's washed and dressed and having her breakfast already. So are all the others. What's the matter with you, Katy?'

'*You're* what's the matter with me,' I mumbled, but not quite loud enough for her to hear.

I stumbled out of bed, and managed to go to the bathroom and get dressed in five minutes – a world record. I poured orange juice down my throat and crammed two pieces of toast and peanut butter into my mouth in another five minutes and was more or less ready when Izzie went to the garage for the car. She takes Clover and Elsie and Dorry and Jonnie and me to school and drops Phil off at nursery and then takes Tyler for a walk. Dad can't take us because he likes to be at his surgery at eight sharp. It's ridiculous that Izzie has to take us. I could walk us all to school easily, as I've said time and time again, but Izzie won't hear of it. She seems to think I'd go into a daydream and let Dorry and Jonnie wander off by themselves.

I hate her taking us and nag, nag, nagging all the way. She started a royal nag before we were even in the car because I couldn't find my wretched maths book and had to hunt high and low for it.

'I know I had it somewhere,' I wailed. 'I took it out of my school bag to do my homework last night.'

I hadn't actually *done* my homework because I'd got distracted making up a magazine with Clover. We'd designed the cover, I'd got started on a dramatic serial story, Clover had drawn some fashion pictures and it was coming along splendidly. But then suddenly it was time for Dad to read to us and obviously I didn't want to miss that. I thought I might be able to do my homework in bed by torchlight but I couldn't actually be bothered. I thought I'd wake up early and get it done then, only that plan hadn't worked either.

I decided not to get too fussed. I was sure Cecy would let me quickly copy out all her answers when I got to school. Cecy wasn't actually too brilliant at maths, but wrong answers were better than no answers at all and Mr Robinson, our Year Six teacher, could get a bit narked if you didn't do your homework. But I still had to find my maths *book*.

I thought it must be in my bedroom somewhere but I couldn't find it anyway. I wondered if it had somehow got shoved under my bed, so I crawled underneath. I found two odd socks, a hairbrush, an apple core, a doggy chew and a lot of dust – but no maths book. The doggy chew gave me a clue, however.

'Tyler? Tyler! You haven't had my maths book, have you?' I said.

This was brilliant deduction. I found my maths book in his puppy crate, the back cover completely torn off and a corner comprehensively nibbled. I stared at it a little anxiously, wondering what Mr Robinson was going to say. I wasn't sure he'd appreciate a literal example of that old joke about the dog eating my homework. Still, at least I had the book, so I went charging downstairs where everyone was waiting for me.

'Got it, got it, got it!' I said triumphantly.

'For goodness' sake! What sort of state is it in?' said Izzie. 'How can you be so careless with your school-books, Katy? Now, come on! Let's get in the car or we'll all be horribly late.'

So I got in the car, wondering why Clover was making very weird gestures at me. She was pushing her two hands together through the air and then waving them round in a semicircle, almost as if she were swimming. *Swimming!* Year Six had swimming first thing on Monday mornings. And I didn't have my swimming stuff packed.

'Just one tiny second,' I said, jumping out of the car again and running back to the house.

'Katy! I don't believe this! Get back in the car at once,' Izzie shouted, but I took no notice.

I grabbed the emergency key from under the potted plant in the porch, let myself in and went charging upstairs. Swimming costume and towel. Now where would they be? I looked in the airing cupboard. There were plenty of old towels there, and Clover's pink costume and Elsie's silly little blue costume with Hello Kitty on the front, but I couldn't see my red costume anywhere. What had Izzie done with the wretched thing? If she'd washed it, why wasn't it waiting for me in the cupboard? If she'd washed it . . .

I looked in the dirty-clothes basket, stirring my way through various crumpled garments large and small, but no costume there. I *had* put it in the dirty clothes, hadn't I? Oh dear . . . Perhaps I'd forgotten.

I looked in my wardrobe and there, right at the back, was a little soggy clump of costume and towel, exactly where I'd idly chucked it a week ago. It reeked to high heaven, like the dirtiest old dishmop in the world. I could barely pick it up, it smelled so disgusting. I tried running it under the bathroom tap to see if the smell would wash off, but it stayed resolutely revolting.

I couldn't arrive at the swimming baths without a costume *again*. I'd done it twice already this term. I would be in big trouble with Mr Robinson if it happened a third time.

In desperation I grabbed a clean towel and Clover's costume. Yes, it was a very girly pink, and yes, it would be far too small, but it was better than nothing. I could squeeze into it somehow. Clover was only a year younger than me after all.

I went charging back downstairs and out the house. Izzie had the car all revved up and ready to go.

'I give up on you, Katy Carr. You play this trick again and we'll go without you,' she snapped as we drove off.

'Good! Why don't you? I'd love to walk to school by myself,' I said.

'Oh yes! Could Katy and I possibly be allowed to do that?' Clover asked eagerly.

'No, you could not! *You* might be almost responsible enough, Clover, but Katy certainly isn't,' said Izzie.

I couldn't help blowing a little raspberry at her. It made Dorry and Jonnie and Phil giggle.

'You're making my point, Katy,' said Izzie icily. 'Do you have to behave so stupidly in front of the little ones?'

She nagged on like this all the way to school. I stared out of the window and ignored her. When I was in the Infants, I used to pretend Mum was running along beside the car, her feet barely skimming the pavement. She'd be reaching out to me, wanting to hold my hand. I'd press my own hand against the window, imagining her fingers clasping mine.

I couldn't help trying to do that now. It was getting harder and harder to imagine Mum. I remembered her, of course I did, but often the only images I could conjure up were the ones based on old photographs. I tried desperately, but I could only see a blurry outline of her.

'Why are you frowning so, Katy?' asked Izzie, looking at me in the driving mirror.

'I'm not,' I said, trying to rearrange my face.

'Yes, you are. I often see you frowning like that when you stare into the distance. Maybe you're getting short-sighted because you've always got your head in a book. I think we'd better get your eyes tested.'

'I don't want to! I don't need glasses. I'm fine,' I protested. I wouldn't tell Izzie in a million years that I only looked like that when I was trying to conjure up Mum.

'Right,' said Izzie, in that tight-lipped way she has.

'Yes, right,' I mumbled, though only Clover beside me heard.

It was a sticky start to the day. And it wasn't going to get any better. It was going to get a lot, lot worse.

4

I flew up to Cecy the minute we got to school.

'Hey, Cecy, could I possibly copy your maths? I didn't get round to doing it last night and then I couldn't even find my wretched book for ages this morning,' I said.

'OK – and you'll get them all right too, because I got stuck and my dad tried to show me what to do and ended up doing them all himself,' said Cecy triumphantly.

We huddled together in the playground and I copied all ten sums and their workings in double quick time, whizz, whizz, whizz, and just finished the last when the bell went. Mr Robinson took the register in the classroom, we all handed in our homework and then went off to the swimming pool.

It sounds very grand, our school having its own pool, but it's not very big and the deep end isn't very deep. I can stand up quite easily right at the end, and the water only comes up to my chin. We don't have proper lockers; we just leave our stuff in the changing cubicles, and these are a bit precarious because they don't have proper doors, just curtains. You'd be amazed how many boys try to tweak the curtains when you're changing, accidentally on purpose. Especially Ryan Thompson. He's the worst boy in the whole class. He gets into more trouble than I do. But I actually quite like him. He's not mean or a bully. He just mucks about for fun. We sometimes have a laugh together.

Everyone likes Ryan – except Martin, but he doesn't like anyone. All the girls particularly like him. Eva Jenkins is always hanging round him, giving her simpering little smile and tossing her long fair hair about. Eva is delicate and pretty and her mum buys her glorious clothes. Just occasionally I can't help wishing I was delicate and pretty like Eva. I'd still like to stay the same me inside though. Eva is almost as mean as Martin and plays games with some of the other girls, forever making them her friend one day and then ignoring them horribly the next.

All the boys are crazy about her – but not Ryan. I'll tell you a secret. He actually asked *me* if I wanted to be his girlfriend! I'm not going to, of course. Quite a few of the girls in my class say they've got boyfriends but

I don't want to be bothered with all that stuff. And even though Ryan's fun and he's got a cheeky smile and I don't even mind his hair though it sticks up all over the place, there is one gigantic disadvantage about Ryan. Well, it's the opposite of gigantic. Ryan is small. The shortest boy in the class. Imagine what a couple of idiots we'd look like if we hung out together. The others call us Little and Large already.

Ryan was made to change in the cubicle right at the end, with Mr Robinson watching him outside. Last week Ryan had been in a bit of a tussle with Martin King. Martin is pretty horrible, a big stocky boy with a red face and a very fierce haircut. He's always trying to bully kids smaller than him. I caught him once barging into Clover in the playground and I had to sort him out myself.

He tries it on with Ryan and he generally wins if it's a fight, because he's so much bigger and stronger. But Ryan usually finds a way of getting his own back. He managed to sneak into Martin's cubicle and chuck his pants into the pool. We all thought this hilarious, but Martin sneaked to Mr Robinson and he was furious.

'I'm keeping a special eye on you today, Ryan Thompson. I want no tomfoolery whatsoever,' he said.

'Not even Thompsonfoolery, Mr Robinson?' said Ryan, which made us all laugh.

'Oh for the long-ago schooldays when cheeky young lads like you could be put in their place with a clump about the head,' said Mr Robinson. 'Now, everyone, get changed and in that pool in five minutes flat!'

I shut myself in the poky little cubicle and pulled off my blouse and school skirt and socks and shoes and underwear. I took Clover's pink costume from my bag and stepped into it with difficulty. I loved Clover to bits but sometimes I wished she wasn't quite so girly. I was going to feel pretty embarrassed bobbing about in the pool in her tiddly pink costume.

I tried to pull the costume up so I could put my arms through the straps. I tried and tried. I heaved and strained and yanked. I got the straps into place at long last, but I couldn't even stand up straight. I had to curve in the middle in the most bizarre way. I peered down at myself. Oh no, oh no, oh no! I knew Clover's costume was going to be on the skimpy side, but this was ridiculous. The bottom part was riding right up in an extremely embarrassing manner, and the top half very nearly exposed my entire chest.

I stood there behind the curtain, panicking.

'Katy?' Cecy called. 'Are you nearly ready?'

My throat had dried with the horror of it.

'Not quite,' I croaked.

'Come on, then. Mr Robinson's looking all frowny,' Cecy hissed.

'I – I don't think I can actually come out,' I whimpered.

'What?' said Cecy.

'Just take a peek round my curtain,' I said.

Cecy peered in and gave a sharp intake of breath.

'Oh Katy! Your costume's much too small!' she told me, unnecessarily.

'I am perfectly aware of that,' I said, with as much dignity as I could muster with ninety-nine per cent of my long, lanky body terribly exposed.

'You can't come out in that!' said Cecy.

'I know,' I said.

'Caroline Charlotte Hall!' Mr Robinson suddenly thundered. 'What do you think you're doing! Get in the pool this instant!'

Cecy pulled an agonized face at me and withdrew.

I stayed still, hunching more than ever. About a minute went by – a minute that lasted an eternity. Then I heard footsteps along the poolside.

'Katy Carr?' said Mr Robinson, right outside my cubicle. 'Whatever are you up to in there?'

'I – I'm not really up to anything, Mr Robinson,' I mumbled.

'Are you changed into your costume?'

'Well. Sort of,' I said.

'Then would you mind emerging from the cubicle and jumping into the pool immediately?' Mr Robinson asked, but it wasn't really a question, it was a command.

I peered down at myself in the dark cubicle. I wasn't actually showing anything I shouldn't be. Maybe I was being silly. Maybe I didn't look too awful.

'Katy Carr!' said Mr Robinson.

I pulled the curtain aside and stepped out. There was a sudden astonished silence as everyone stared at me. And then, appallingly, a snort of laughter. Then more. More and more snorts and sniggers and bellows and guffaws, until the pool echoed to its rooftop. Every child except Cecy was doubled up with laughter, pointing at me. And Ryan was roaring with laughter too, slapping the water in emphasis.

'Oh my God, Katy, you look utterly gross!' said Eva Jenkins. 'Like a giraffe in a thong!'

Everyone rocked with laughter again, several repeating her horrible phrase. Including Ryan.

'That's enough, Eva,' said Mr Robinson weakly. He still looked stunned. He shielded his eyes so he couldn't see me properly. 'Katy, what are you playing at? Where's your proper costume?'

'At home,' I whispered, barely able to talk. I could see in the bright light of the pool I'd gone as pink as the wretched costume.

'Well, you can't possibly wear that one. Get changed again. You'll have to miss swimming this week.'

I slunk back behind the curtain and struggled to get out of the horribly inadequate garment. I was so hot with embarrassment it stuck to me determinedly and it was terribly difficult peeling it off. I was shaking as I got back into my clothes.

Everyone still stared at me when I came out and sat miserably on a bench. Eva and her little gang kept pointing and whispering and nudging each other, then going off into further peals of laughter. I felt myself burning.

It was so lonely watching everyone else in the pool splashing about and having fun. It was particularly painful when Mr Robinson asked Eva to demonstrate her breaststroke style to the whole class. She swam so smoothly and stylishly, her little lithe body gliding through the water like a dolphin. When she got to my end she surfaced and smirked at me. I felt like leaping into the water and ducking her.

Then I had a sudden idea. A terrible mad way of getting my revenge. Mr Robinson was kneeling at the edge of the pool, telling everyone to put their heads under the water to practise breathing out. I knew roughly which was Eva's changing cubicle. I nipped in, grabbed a handful of her pretty little clothes, dunked them in the pool and then shoved them back, sopping wet. It took thirty seconds tops – and nobody noticed!

I sat back on my bench, my heart thumping. Oh, just wait till Eva got out of the pool and tried to get dressed! That would so teach her. Then everyone would laugh and jeer at her, and she would see how horrid it was.

But even as I thought this, grinning in anticipation, I was starting to get worried. Maybe it was a truly mean thing to do, even though she'd been so mocking about me. And what if Mr Robinson twigged it was me? I'd be in truly serious trouble. But he hadn't seen me. He didn't have any proof. All I had to do was sit there on the bench and swear blind I didn't have anything to do with it.

The swimming lesson seemed to be going on forever. I was starting to get really anxious now. I couldn't work out in my head just how many of Eva's clothes I'd dunked in the pool. I hoped it was maybe just her underthings. Then she could put on her blouse and skirt and no one would really know. But try as I could to persuade myself, I knew deep down that I'd seized hold of everything.

Perhaps they might somehow dry out in the cubicle. It was boiling hot here after all. I thought of Eva's clothes and mentally ironed them until they were bone dry, without a crease. I was willing it so hard that I jumped when Mr Robinson blew his whistle at last to tell everyone to get out the pool.

There was a bit of pandemonium when they did this. Three of the boys were jostling each other at the steps and one fell backwards into the water, making an almighty splash.

He didn't surface immediately and several of the girls started squealing that he was drowning. There was a great racket as people grabbed hold of him – and then Mr Robinson made an even louder racket when it transpired that the boy had been deliberately holding his breath under the water to tease his friends.

'I don't know what's got into you today, Year Six,' said Mr Robinson. 'Well, don't all stand there shivering and dripping wet. Go and get changed, and be quick about it. Katy, you help me store all the floats in the kit cupboard.'

I went to help, praying that somehow everything would be all right after all. But then I heard screaming.

'Oh dear Lord, what is it now?' said Mr Robinson. He peered round and saw Eva standing outside her cubicle, holding her still sopping clothes, crying her eyes out.

'What's happened? What's the matter, Eva?' he asked.

'It's my clothes! Look! Just look at them! They're all ruined! Someone's thrown them in the pool, even my new skirt, and Mum's going to be so angry because it's designer and dry-clean only,' Eva wailed.

I waited for everyone to start laughing – but everyone looked shocked. It wasn't funny. It was awful. Eva was distraught. And it was all my fault.

Mr Robinson looked horrified. He whirled round.

'Ryan? Was this you? Have you been up to your stupid pranks again?' he thundered.

Ryan put his head round his curtain.

'Me, Mr Robinson?' he said, his eyes open wide, acting innocent.

'Yes, you! I've had just about enough of you. How dare you! Get changed and then go straight to Mrs Henry and tell her exactly what you've done,' said Mr Robinson.

56

'But I haven't done anything!' said Ryan.

'Be quiet and do as you're told!' Mr Robinson said furiously.

My heart was beating so fast I thought it might burst straight out of my chest and lie thumping bloodily at the poolside. I hadn't wanted Ryan to get blamed!

I told myself that I didn't like Ryan any more because he'd been one of the first to laugh at me in my ridiculous costume – but that didn't matter now. Oh, my trick had gone so horribly wrong. There was Ryan in serious trouble and Eva was still in hysterics.

'Katy, go to the secretary's room and see if she has any spare clothing for Eva,' said Mr Robinson. 'Go on, don't just stand there!'

I ran off. I wanted to run right out of the school, out of the town, run away forever because I felt so ashamed. As I hurried down the corridors I felt that all the passing kids were staring at me and pointing. Even the photos and pictures on the wall were peering at me. *There goes Katy Carr,* they were thinking. *The mean girl who plays spiteful tricks and then gets other people into trouble.*

I knocked on Mrs Henry's door and then blurted out that Eva Jenkins' clothes had got soaked during our swimming lesson.

Mrs Henry sighed and started piecing together an outfit from Lost Property. The knickers were easy enough. Mrs Henry kept several spare pairs in case any of the little ones wet themselves. She had a school blouse too, more or less the right size, but no skirt at all, big or small. She handed me a crumpled pair of boy's trousers.

'She'll have to make do with these,' she said.

'But she'll look silly,' I said despairingly. I'd *wanted* her to look silly, but now I just felt terrible.

'I can't help it if she looks silly,' said Mrs Henry. 'She shouldn't have dropped her clothes in the pool.'

'But she didn't,' I mumbled.

I took the odd assortment of clothes and trailed back to the pool. Eva was wrapped up in a towel, still in tears. They increased in volume when she saw the trousers.

'I can't possibly wear them! They're boy's trousers and they won't fit properly. And they're all creased and crumpled anyway!' she wailed.

'For goodness' sake, Eva, you haven't got any alternative,' said Mr Robinson. He glared over at Ryan, who was standing in disgrace.

'Do you feel happy now, Ryan? Does it make you feel great to see poor Eva so upset?' he asked.

'No, Mr Robinson! But I didn't throw her clothes in the pool, I swear I didn't,' said Ryan.

'You're only making things worse for yourself by lying, Ryan, do you realize that?' said Mr Robinson. 'I've always known you were an idiotic prankster, but I didn't think you were a downright liar too.'

Ryan flinched as if he'd been hit. It was too much. I couldn't bear it any more.

'Ryan isn't a liar, Mr Robinson,' I said. 'He didn't dunk Eva's clothes. *I* did. And I wish I hadn't now. I'm so, so sorry.'

'Katy Carr! Whatever's got into you today? Ryan, I apologize. Katy, *you* go straight to Mrs Henry and tell her what you've done,' said Mr Robinson. 'I give up. I don't understand you children. I think I'd have more success teaching a class of chimpanzees.'

Some children giggled uneasily. I had to fight not to cry. I felt the tears pricking in my eyes and my chin starting to wobble. Eva was glaring at me, but it was Cecy's expression of shock and sympathy that made the tears spill over. I ran out, away from the pool again, back down all the corridors, and forced myself to knock on Mrs Henry's door.

'Come in!'

Oh dear, she sounded irritated already.

I took a deep breath and shuffled into her room. She was at her desk, peering at me over her glasses in a frowny sort of way. She was wearing one of her bright suits, yellow today. They always looked rather too tight, and showed too much of Mrs Henry's tummy and bottom.

'Hello Katy. What is it? I'm very busy, as you can see,' she said, shuffling paperwork.

'Mr Robinson sent me, Mrs Henry,' I mumbled.

'About what?'

'About . . . me.'

Mrs Henry sighed and sat back, looking at me through her glasses now.

'What have you done? I gather from your general demeanour Mr Robinson hasn't sent you because you've completed an outstanding piece of work.'

'No, I – I've done something dreadful,' I said.

'I see. Well. Spit it out then,' said Mrs Henry calmly. 'I don't expect it's as dreadful as all that.'

'It is,' I said, and I felt another tear slide down my cheek. 'I dunked Eva Jenkins' clothes in the pool.'

'Oh goodness, yes, that's very dreadful,' said Mrs Henry, her face stern – though her lips twitched. 'What is it with you children and the swimming pool? I had Ryan in here only last week for dunking someone else's clothes.'

'That was Martin – and it was only his pants – and I won't tell tales, but Martin deserved it, believe you me,' I said.

'Did you feel Eva deserved it then?' Mrs Henry asked.

'Well, I was mad at her, because she said I looked like a giraffe in a thong.'

'She said *what*?'

'But I suppose I did look like that, because I was wearing my little sister's swimming costume.'

'You were wearing *Elsie's* costume?'

'No, Clover's. But even that was far too small. I suppose I did look pretty ridiculous. Everybody laughed at me. Especially Eva. And Mr Robinson said I had to change back into my clothes and miss swimming.'

'I get the picture now. Oh dear, Katy. I understand how you were feeling – but it was still a mean, silly trick to play on Eva, wasn't it? Especially mean when it's clear Eva cares very much about the way she looks,' said Mrs Henry.

'Eva always looks stunning. I bet she even looks stunning in the borrowed clothes from Lost Property,' I said.

'Yes, probably,' said Mrs Henry.

We looked at each other, and for one moment we weren't just fierce head teacher and schoolgirl in trouble. We were a plain fat woman and a plain gawky girl sympathizing with each other.

But then Mrs Henry frowned again.

'It still was a very mean trick, Katy,' she said. 'And I expect *Mrs* Jenkins will be very upset when she finds out.'

'Yes. But – but that wasn't quite the meanest thing I did,' I said, needing to tell her everything now. 'Mr Robinson thought Ryan had dunked Eva's clothes. And so he got mad at him and – and for a little while I didn't own up. I let Ryan get a big telling-off. Mr Robinson said Ryan had to go and see you straight away, and after a bit I couldn't bear it and confessed.'

'Oh dear. Is being sent to see me such a terrible punishment then?' Mrs Henry asked, resting her chin on her linked fingers.

'Well, I don't want to sound rude, but yes, we all dread it because you can make us feel really bad,' I said truthfully.

'So I should hope. And you *have* been really bad this morning, Katy. But I know you're not usually a mean girl, so as long as you promise to behave in an utterly exemplary fashion for the rest of the day we'll let it go at that. Now run along,' she said, picking up her paperwork again.

'Thank you, Mrs Henry,' I said, and scuttled from the room.

I stood outside, shaking my head. That hadn't been *so* bad. In fact, she'd really been quite nice about it, all things considered. But I was careful to look suitably subdued, if not downright mournful, when I went back to class. Mr Robinson shook his head at me but didn't say any more. Cecy looked at me super sympathetically. Eva Jenkins flashed me a look of pure hatred. Not that I cared.

Ryan was looking at me too. Perhaps he was remembering what a total idiot I looked like in Clover's costume. I felt my cheeks going hot. I sat down and tried to concentrate on my Victorian project. Cecy was writing about Victorian clothes. So was Eva Jenkins and half a dozen other girls. *I* was doing Victorian funerals because they were so interesting and elaborate.

I didn't get to go to Mum's funeral. I suppose Dad thought I was still too little. I've made him tell me all about it. He said there was just a simple ceremony and then Mum was cremated, and he scattered the ashes on top of Box Hill, her favourite place.

I think this was ridiculous. If I want to have a special private chat to Mum I can't climb all the way up Box Hill, always supposing her ashes haven't completely blown away in the wind. Why on earth couldn't Dad have buried her in the graveyard where I could have visited her every day? And why a *simple* ceremony when she was the person we loved most in the world? I'd have given her an ultra-elaborate ceremony.

I took great comfort in writing about the Victorians, with their funeral processions and horse-drawn carriages and their black mourning clothes and their beautiful stone angels.

Mr Robinson came and had a stalk round in the middle of his marking session and actually nodded approvingly at my passage about Highgate Cemetery, where heaps of important Victorians were buried.

Eva Jenkins glared even more. She came rushing up to me at break. She couldn't stop looking pretty, but the boy's trousers were a little too short so her bare ankles looked silly, and the part by her bottom was much too big.

'I hate you, Katy Carr!' she hissed. 'You are so, so, *so* going to regret this.'

'See if I care, baggy bottom,' I said, and barged past her.

'Careful, Katy,' said Cecy. 'We don't want Eva and all her crowd ganging up on us.'

'I'll soon settle them,' I said airily.

But I went hot all over again when Ryan came up.

'Hey, Katy, thanks for getting me out of trouble with old Robinson,' he said. 'You didn't need to have owned up. No one would ever have guessed it was you.'

'Well, it wouldn't have been fair. And I didn't own up right away,' I said.

'Even so. Thanks,' said Ryan, and he smiled at me.

It wasn't a bit like the awful grin he'd given me when he saw me in the minute swimming costume. This was a proper friendly smile.

'You've gone all pink,' said Cecy, when Ryan walked on.

'No, I haven't.'

'You have so. You really like Ryan, don't you?'

'No, I don't,' I insisted – though I did like him. A lot.

5

Our last lesson of the day was maths. Mr Robinson gave us back our homework. I'd done splendidly and got ten out of ten. Good for Cecy! Well, good for Cecy's dad. Mr Robinson hadn't put any comment, just given me ten ticks. Cecy's was the same.

'He could have put *Well done* at the very least,' I whispered.

When the bell went we grabbed our bags and started making our way out of the classroom.

'Just a moment, Katy Carr and Cecy Hall. I'd like a word with you,' said Mr Robinson.

We peered at each other. Little warning bells clanged in my head.

Mr Robinson sat leisurely at his desk, leaning back with his chin in the air, almost as if he were sunbathing. He waited until everyone had cleared the room and then he sat up properly.

'Well?' he said. He didn't sound friendly.

'Well, what, Mr Robinson?' I said.

'You know very well what I mean, Katy. It's a matter of maths homework, yours and Cecy's,' said Mr Robinson.

Oh dear.

'But – but I got all the maths right for once, Mr Robinson,' said Cecy.

'Yes. And as if that wasn't miracle enough, your very best friend got all her maths right too,' said Mr Robinson. 'How do you explain that, Cecy?'

Cecy swallowed. 'Coincidence?' she suggested unwisely.

Mr Robinson suddenly beat the desk. We both jumped as if he'd beaten *us*.

'Do you take me for a fool?' he thundered.

Cecy wasn't silly enough to answer him. We both stood there, hearts thumping.

'You copied Katy's work, didn't you?' he said.

This time I didn't hesitate.

'No! No, Mr Robinson. I copied Cecy's homework. It wasn't her fault at all,' I said.

'So who did *you* copy, Cecy? Because you and I know very well that you've never got more than six out of ten right ever since you've been in Year Six, and I rather think it's highly unlikely your brain has suddenly gone click, click, click like a Rubik's cube and developed the ability to master all mathematical problems instantaneously,' said Mr Robinson.

'I didn't exactly *copy*, Mr Robinson. I – I got my dad to help me,' Cecy quavered.

'Well, that's excellent. I don't mind dads helping, giving a little advice, going over a particular problem. But in this case I suggest your dad did most of the work himself. Or indeed ended up doing *all* of the work, seeing as his method isn't at all the method I taught you in class.'

Cecy nodded sadly.

'How do you think you can learn to do maths for yourself if you simply get your well-meaning parent to do the work for you?'

'He did try to help me, Mr Robinson. But, as you know, I'm a bit thick where maths is concerned, and so he got fed up and just did it all for me,' Cecy said.

'And I'm afraid I didn't quite have time to do my maths homework last night, so I copied all Cecy's answers,' I said.

'And both of you thought I would mark your identical pieces of work without getting at all suspicious?' said Mr Robinson.

'I suppose it was a bit optimistic of us,' I said.

'Understatement of the century,' said Mr Robinson. 'Now, I want you to do the further ten questions you will find on page 32 tonight. Working separately and unaided. Do you understand?'

'Yes, Mr Robinson,' we said miserably.

'Now come along. We're all late home. Chop-chop.'

Mr Robinson grabbed his briefcase and we went out of the classroom together. Cecy's mum and Izzie, with Clover, Elsie and the littlies, were standing at the gate looking worried.

'Oh dear,' said Izzie, when she saw Mr Robinson. 'Are they in trouble?'

'Just a little matter of too much conferring over homework,' said Mr Robinson. 'Oh, Mrs Carr, while we're on the subject of Katy's pranks, I wonder if you could make sure she always has the right costume for her Monday swimming lesson.'

He walked on, not saying anything else. He didn't need to. Izzie got most of it out of me on the car ride home.

'You wore *Clover's* costume? But she's half your size! Why didn't you take your own?' Etcetera, etcetera, etcetera.

And then the moment we were indoors there was a phone call from Mrs Jenkins. Eva had blabbed the whole story – though I bet she hadn't told her mum she'd said I looked like a giraffe in a thong. It was all poor little Eva and wicked bad Katy and Eva's designer skirt absolutely ruined because it was dry-clean only

68

and the precious darling totally humiliated because she had to wear ill-fitting boy's clothes all day long.

Izzie was absolutely furious with me, and even more so when she saw and smelled my own swimming costume. Dad was out late. For once I hoped he'd be stuck on a difficult house call and wouldn't get home till after we were in bed.

I *was* in bed reading the first volume of *The Hunger Games* when I heard his key in the door. Then I heard Izzie muttering away, and I was pretty sure my name was mentioned. Oh no. I'd have sooner endured all Katniss's trials than face my own father.

Clover was already fast asleep. I switched my lamp off and huddled under the duvet, pretending to be asleep too. I even started making little snorty snoring noises when Dad opened the door.

'Katy? I know you're awake. Oh dear, oh dear! I hear you've been in big trouble today,' he said quietly, sitting on the edge of my bed.

'Oh Dad!' I said, and I sat up and threw my arms round his neck. 'Dad, it wasn't really all my fault. Well, maybe the maths homework was. But all that swimming stuff – they were all laughing at me, Eva most of all. She said hateful things. She was practically *asking* for me to do something to get back at her.'

'Oh Katy, stop the nonsense. And why couldn't you wear your proper costume?'

'Because – because I forgot to put it in the wash.'

'Poor Izzie. She's sure Mr Robinson thinks her a bad mother for not seeing you've got the right costume – and she tries so hard too.'

I fidgeted. I didn't want this to turn into a poor old Izzie conversation.

'Katy, how about *you* trying a little harder?' Dad asked softly.

'I do try, Dad. I truly want you to be proud of me. But somehow everything always goes wrong,' I said, clinging to him.

'I don't expect you to be absolutely perfect. But if you'd just learn to *think* first, it might help,' said Dad, sighing.

'I'll try, Dad, I promise,' I said.

I really, really meant it. Only somehow I got into serious trouble the very next day.

6

School was fine on Tuesday. I made a serious effort to join in every lesson and make Mr Robinson like me again. I even volunteered to be a litter monitor, and spent my entire lunch break trundling round the school with a black plastic rubbish bag, picking up chocolate wrappers and crisp packets. Cecy did it with me, so at least we could have a good talk.

I rather wanted to pick Eva Jenkins up and stuff *her* into my rubbish bag. She was back in her own dinky little designer clothes but she still hadn't forgiven me for yesterday. She'd drawn a stupid picture of a giraffe in a thong on the whiteboard before school started and everyone giggled at it as they came into the classroom.

It was a shock when I saw it. I did my best to keep my face expressionless, because I knew Eva and her little gang wanted me to burst out crying. The trouble was, I *felt* like crying. Eva was good at drawing and she'd somehow made that hateful giraffe look horribly like me, with my turned-up nose and hair all over the place. The giraffe was standing bent over and knock-kneed with embarrassment, wearing its ridiculously minute thong. You couldn't help laughing at it if you were anyone else – so of course the whole class were chuckling away.

Except for Ryan. He came into the classroom immediately after Cecy and me, while we were still standing there, dumbstruck. He marched over to the board and rubbed the giraffe out vigorously, turning it into an inky blur.

I breathed slightly more easily.

'Wasn't it lovely of Ryan to rub the board clean and stop them all sniggering?' Cecy said while we were rubbish collecting.

'I suppose so,' I said, trying to sound cool and unimpressed.

'Just like a hero being gallant in a story,' said Cecy. 'You know, like the prince hacking his way through a hundred-year-old forest to awaken Sleeping Beauty with a kiss.'

'Rubbing a board clean isn't exactly hacking his way through a hundred-year-old forest,' I said, though I was loving this conversation.

'I can see you and Ryan hooking up together,' said Cecy.

'Well, we'd look pretty stupid, wouldn't we? Seeing as I'm so tall and he's a little titch,' I said.

'Size shouldn't be important in a relationship,' said Cecy, sounding like an advice auntie in a magazine column.

'But we *would* look stupid, wouldn't we?' I said, really wanting to know.

'Well . . . maybe,' said Cecy.

I didn't want her to say that, even if she thought it! I was all set to shut her up by saying something snubbing – but I didn't really want to quarrel with Cecy because she was my best friend in all the world.

I kept my mouth shut and started humming a song instead. Cecy began humming along with me, and we continued collecting rubbish together until the bell went.

See, Dad! I said inside my head. *I'm thinking first, OK?*

I even managed not to fall out with Izzie in the car going home. She started nagging at me because I'd got ink all down my school blouse. It wasn't my fault that my silly rollerball pen had suddenly exploded. Well, I suppose I had been chewing it a little tiny bit, but that was just to help the creative process when we had to do a piece of extended writing for Mr Robinson. But did I protest at this? No, I sat there meekly and said, 'I'm sorry, Izzie, truly. I do hope it comes out in the wash.' I *might* have pulled a funny face at Clover while I was saying it, but Izzie was in the driver's seat and couldn't see, so it didn't matter.

We had an early supper, cheesy jacket potatoes and baked beans and then strawberries with squirty cream. We all love squirting the cream out. Dorry and Jonnie and Phil squirted and squirted and squirted, squealing all the while.

Izzie and Dad didn't have any supper. They were going to some fancy medical dinner up in London. Dad looked more handsome than ever in his white shirt and bow tie and dinner suit. I felt so proud that he was my dad. No wonder Mum fell in love with him. And Izzie snapped him up quick as a wink, worse luck.

Izzie was all dressed up too in a dull black dress and silly high heels. She was fussing terribly about leaving us.

'I know Eleanor said she's happy to look after all of you, but I don't know how she'll cope. She's used to just looking after Cecy – and *she's* such a good, sensible child,' said Izzie, with feeling.

'I don't know why you have to bother Cecy's mum. We'll be OK by ourselves,' I said. 'I'll take care of everyone.'

'Katy, you can't even look after yourself, let alone look after the others,' said Izzie. 'Maybe I ought to give the dinner a miss. Though I really was looking forward to going.' She gave one of her little martyred smiles.

'*Go*, Izzie. We'll be fine, fine, fine,' I said impatiently.

We'd have far more fun with Cecy and her mum but again I didn't say it. I was trying so hard to be tactful I practically burst.

Izzie still dithered, but Mrs Hall did her best to reassure her when she came round with Cecy.

'We'll all have a lovely time together. It will be great fun. I've always longed to have a big family,' she said enthusiastically. 'I'm so lucky to have my Cecy, but I wish she had brothers and sisters.'

Izzie smiled at her weakly. I'm pretty sure she was thinking back longingly to the time when she just had Elsie to look after.

'Well, if you're really sure, Eleanor. I took the dog for a long walk this afternoon, so he shouldn't be any trouble. The children have all had supper and in an hour or so Phil and Dorry and Jonnie can go to bed. The older girls go at nine, but they generally read for half an hour or so. We'll be back by midnight at the very latest. Thank you so much. You know I'll return the favour any time,' said Izzie.

'My Cecy practically lives at your house as it is,' said Mrs Hall. 'Off you go then, both of you.'

Izzie wasted another ten minutes telling us to be good and to remember to brush our teeth and to make sure all lights were out upstairs by half past nine, etcetera, etcetera. She even reminded the littlies to have a final wee before they got into bed, which offended the twins terribly. But at long last she went off in a flurry – and there we were, the seven of us and Mrs Hall.

'There now!' she said, falsely bright. 'What shall we do, hmm?'

'Can we watch cartoons?' said Dorry and Jonnie in unison. Dad always tried to get them to play something rather than gawp at the television.

'I don't think your parents like you to watch too much television,' said Mrs Hall.

'Can Katy and Clover and I go and play upstairs?' asked Cecy.

Clover and I nodded enthusiastically. We wanted to get on with a particularly outrageous game of Celebrity.

'Can I play with them too? I'm not one of the littlies,' Elsie interrupted. She didn't even know what game we were intending to play but didn't want to be left out.

'I think it might be better if you all play together. Downstairs,' said Mrs Hall.

'Can we do cooking?' asked Phil. His favourite toy of the moment was a little kiddie cooking set: a small bowl and cookie cutters and a plastic knife and spoon. He didn't do *real* cooking with this sparse equipment. Izzie gave him some pink Play-Doh, insisting he only use it in the kitchen because she didn't want pink stains all over the carpets.

'In kitchen?' Phil continued, looking up at Mrs Hall with his big blue eyes. 'I *love* cooking my cakes.'

'Well, I think that's a lovely idea, Phil,' said Mrs Hall brightly. 'We'll all go into the kitchen and make cakes for an hour. You can all eat one as a special treat before you go to bed.'

We stared at her. Cecy and Clover and I might play our exciting grown-up imaginary games, but we didn't consider pretend-munching a pink Play-Doh cake a special treat. Even Dorry and Jonnie looked baffled, though Dorry's ears pricked at the mere mention of cake.

'Come along then. Into the kitchen. Now, Katy, where does Izzie keep her flour and icing sugar?' asked Mrs Hall.

Oh my goodness, she was intending to make real cakes with us! Izzie rarely let us help in the kitchen because she said we made too much mess. She did let Clover and Elsie and me try making toffee once, only I tried to read *Rooftoppers* while it was my turn to stir and I got too engrossed. The toffee burned so badly Izzie had to throw the saucepan away. And then of course there was my recent debacle with the pancakes.

But now here was Mrs Hall positively encouraging us to bake. I gave my littlest brother a great big hug.

'Brilliant idea, Philly,' I said, rubbing my cheek on his curly head.

Then we all set to. We assembled the ingredients for the cake, plus icing sugar for the topping. Mrs Hall wanted little sprinkles and silver balls, but Izzie didn't seem to have any of those.

'Never mind, we'll make do. There's a packet of walnuts here. We'll use a whole walnut to decorate each cupcake and we'll chop a few to flavour the mixture,' she said. 'Now, you can all take turns weighing out the ingredients, a rounded spoonful each.'

This was democratic but a little unwise. I did my spoonful perfectly and so did Cecy and Clover. Elsie's hand wobbled and most of her spoonful spilled. Dorry and Jonnie argued about who should go next and nudged each other and got flour all down themselves. And Phil got so overexcited at cooking with real flour that he took hold of the packet, going, 'Me do it, me do it, me do it!' and shook flour all over the worktop.

'Whoops,' said Mrs Hall, determined not to be fazed.

'Whoops!' Phil echoed, chuckling.

'I'm afraid he can be a bit clumsy at times, but he is only little,' I said.

'*You* were ever so ever so clumsy with that pancake and threw it all over me. And you're not little; you're big, big, big,' said Elsie.

I managed not to retaliate. I listened to Mrs Hall instead, really keen to learn how to make cakes. It was fascinating creaming the butter and the sugar, mixing them round and round. We all had a go, but I was the one who managed it best. Dorry deliberately got butter and sugar all over his fingers so that he could lick them. When the mixture was a perfect consistency we let Phil have several stirs so he could feel he'd contributed too.

'That's it, Phil, mix away,' said Mrs Hall.

'Mix, mix, mix!' said Phil happily.

Then we stirred in the flour and added the eggs. It looked and smelled wonderful now.

'You have a stir too, Phil,' said Mrs Hall.

'Stir, stir, stir!' said Phil.

'Can we see what it tastes like?' said Dorry, finger hovering above the bowl.

'Not just now,' said Mrs Hall gently. 'You can all scrape out the bowl when we've got the cakes in the oven. Now we need to chop a few walnuts for flavouring.'

She chopped one into tiny pieces with a sharp knife.

'Can we have a go now, Mum?' said Cecy.

'Maybe just you and Katy, if you're very careful,' said Mrs Hall.

So we chopped ultra carefully, with Clover and Elsie and the littlies breathing hard, watching us.

'Chop, chop, chop,' said Phil enviously.

We stirred the tiny pieces of walnut into the mixture and then poured it into the little crinkly cake cases, filling each one almost up to the edge but not letting it slurp over.

'That's it. Well done!' said Mrs Hall. 'You're all great little cake-makers!'

We put the cakes in the oven and then had a wonderful time scraping out the bowl with our fingers. I'm ashamed to say Dorry tried to put his head in the bowl to give it a good lick. He is such a greedy boy.

Mrs Hall didn't tell him off. She just laughed.

'Let's wipe round your face, Dorry. Then we must get a move on making the icing for the topping.'

'Oh, I just love baking cakes!' said Dorry.

Phil was desperate to weigh out the icing sugar too, so I held his hand steady and he managed his spoonful without spilling this time.

Mrs Hall smiled at me. 'You're so good with the little ones, Katy,' she said.

I liked Mrs Hall so much. Cecy was very lucky. Her mum wasn't quite as lovely as *my* mum – no one could be that special – but she was *soooooo* much nicer than Izzie. And somehow she made *me* be nicer too. I wasn't naughty, wild, careless Katy any more. I was kind, caring, capable Katy, the girl I always wanted to be.

We stirred the icing sugar carefully, mixing it with water and a little lemon juice to stop it being too sweet.

'How could anything be *too* sweet?' said Dorry, breathing in the heady smell of sugar.

'Can't I mix too?' Phil said plaintively.

'No, because you're too little and would spill, not like us big ones,' said Elsie.

'*You* spilled, Elsie. Look, you can be a big one too, Philly,' I said, fetching the little metal steps in the corner. 'Up you come. But be careful!'

'I be very, very careful,' said Phil, and he was as good as his word, stirring really gently, his tongue sticking out because he was concentrating so fiercely.

'Mix, mix, mix,' Phil said happily.

'Now we want to get it to exactly the right consistency,' said Mrs Hall. 'We'll leave it until the cakes are out of the oven before giving it a final stir. Then we'll put the walnuts on top.'

'Chop, chop, chop,' said Phil.

'No, darling, we'll put a whole walnut on each cake,' said Mrs Hall, still stirring the icing.

'Chop, chop, chop,' Phil repeated insistently.

We all looked at him and saw he'd grabbed the sharp knife and was trying to chop the remaining walnuts.

'No!' I screamed, and made Phil jump. He went chop, chop, chop right into his finger.

Then he screamed too, louder and louder, as blood seeped from his chopped finger.

'Oh Philly, I'm so sorry! Look what I've made you do! Look at the blood!' I gasped.

'You didn't mean to make him do it, Katy,' said Clover, loyal to the last.

Cecy burst into tears.

'And now he's bleeding to death!' said Elsie.

'Of course he's not,' said Mrs Hall, holding Phil's hand under the cold tap to try to stop it bleeding so.

She seemed nearly in tears herself as she tried to comfort him.

'I'm bleeding!' he wailed.

'It's stopping now, see?' said Mrs Hall.

'I'll get the antiseptic cream and a plaster!' I said, desperate to help.

'Yes, do – but – but I think someone ought to look at the cut. It is quite deep. Oh, if only your father were home! I'll phone Izzie.' She tried phoning on her mobile but Izzie didn't answer.

'It's gone straight to her voicemail,' said Mrs Hall.

She examined Phil's finger again. 'Oh no, it's started bleeding again. He probably needs stitches. I'd better take him to A & E.'

She picked Phil up and hugged him hard. Then she looked at all of us. 'You'd – you'd better all come with us,' she said. 'Oh goodness, how am I going to fit all of you into my car?'

'No, no, you can't take all of us. Look, I'll be in charge at home here,' I said, frantic to impress her.

'But you're far too young, Katy.'

'Cecy and me will look after all the others. I'll give them all cake and then we'll go to bed, I promise,' I said.

Mrs Hall dithered. Phil was threshing about in her arms, wailing and kicking.

'You get Phil to the hospital,' I said.

'Not going hospital!' Phil howled. 'It hurts!'

'No, they'll make it better, Phil. A kind nurse will stop it bleeding and then give you a wonderful big grown-up bandage,' I said.

'A bandage?' said Phil, sniffing.

'Yes, you'd like a bandage, wouldn't you? Just like a wounded soldier,' I said.

'Yes!' said Phil, almost smiling.

'And look, let's find Bunnyhop and he can have a bandage too,' I said, running to fetch him from Phil's bed upstairs.

Phil always slept clutching a strange greyish soft toy with droopy whiskers and one big ear. We'd all cuddled this grubby little animal when little. I had given him his name, insisting he was a rabbit, though perhaps he'd once been a koala bear.

'Bunnyhop!' said Phil, clutching him as if he hadn't seen him for weeks.

'Well, if you're sure, Katy? You have looked after the children yourself before, haven't you? Your dad and Izzie have left you in charge?' Mrs Hall asked.

'Heaps of times,' I said. This was rather an exaggeration. For the last six months Dad has let me take them over to the park. There's only one little side road to cross and I'm very careful. Then I'm always in charge when we sneak off to the secret garden next door. Dad and Izzie had never actually left me looking after everyone while they went out – but I was sure I'd be fine.

'I'll be fine,' I said out loud. 'And you'll be very good and do what I say, won't you?' I looked imploringly at all the children, and to my relief they nodded solemnly.

'Well, if you're really sure . . .? And you won't forget to take the cakes out of the oven?' said Mrs Hall, still looking desperately uncertain.

'My cake! I want my cake!' Phil said, forgetting all about his finger.

'We'll save it for you and you can have it tomorrow morning for breakfast,' I said quickly.

'Cake for breakfast,' Philly murmured, enchanted with the idea. 'And cake for Bunnyhop too?'

'Yes, cake for both of you, as long as you're a good boy for Mrs Hall,' I said.

She smiled at me gratefully.

'We'll be off then,' she said. 'Go to bed as soon as you've eaten your cake. Caroline, you'd better snuggle up with Katy and have a sleepover here as Dad's out tonight. Is that all right, darling?' She gave Cecy that special Mum look that always made my heart thump.

'I'll be fine, Mum, honestly,' said Cecy.

Phil looked suddenly uncertain as Mrs Hall carried him towards the door.

'Katy?' he said, holding out his arms to me.

'You be a good boy now,' I said, seizing hold of his little foot and giving it a gentle tug. 'My goodness, you're going to have such a splendid bandage!'

Mrs Hall smiled at me. 'You've certainly got the knack of handling the children, Katy. You're going to be a brilliant mother when you grow up.'

7

I went back into the kitchen feeling flushed with pride. I'd never really imagined myself as a mother. I wanted all my sisters and brothers to come and live with me in my big house when I was grown up – but now I suddenly imagined a baby cooing in my arms, a little toddler clutching my leg, a four-year-old begging me to read her a story. It was a wonderful feeling. There had been such an aching gap in my life since Mum died. Now I saw there would be a way to feel complete again.

I smiled at the children with a new maternal radiance.

'Why are you grinning at us in that creepy way?' said Elsie.

I could have slapped her for spoiling things, but I made a heroic effort.

'Come now, let's get some of the washing-up done before the cakes come out the oven. Dorry and Jonnie, you can both squeeze up on the steps and do the washing together, and us girls will dry things, OK?' I said, trying to sound calm and grown up.

'Aren't the cakes ready to come out now?' asked Dorry, going to the oven hopefully. 'I can smell them. I'm sure they're all golden now.'

'No, they won't be ready for a while. You don't want to eat cake that's all raw in the middle, do you?' I said.

'I like any kind of cake. And actually, raw cake, like the stuff left in the mixing bowl, is utterly delicious. In fact, cooked cake round the edges and soft, gloopy raw cake inside would be my absolutely favourite cake of all time. Go on, Katy, let's take the cakes out now. Jonnie wants raw cake too, don't you, Jon?' Dorry said.

For once Jonnie didn't back him up. She just stood there with her fingers in her mouth, looking agonized.

'Jonnie, what is it?' I said, going to her.

'Phil!' she said, gulping hard. 'Will he bleed too much? Will he bleed to death?'

'No, he'll be fine, I promise,' I said, hoping I was right. I had a sudden vision of my little brother chalk white, with the last drops of blood pumping out of his finger, and I had a little gulp myself. I pulled Jonnie's fingers out of her mouth, wiped them on my T-shirt and then gave her a kiss on her rosy cheek. 'There now, Jonnie. Come on, you two are my chief washers. Up the steps! Dorry, I dare say when all the dishes are done the cakes *will* be ready.'

'You don't know nothing about cakes,' said Elsie. 'You can't even make pancakes.'

'I know a great deal about whiny little children, and if you don't button your lip and get on with helping I'll pick you up and turn you upside down and shake some sense into you,' I said.

Elsie's face puckered ominously.

'I'm joking, silly,' I said quickly. 'Here, you can pour the washing-up liquid into the bowl. The littlies squirt too much in, but I know you'll be careful.'

'Clever Katy,' Clover breathed as Elsie grabbed the bottle.

'Poor Mum,' said Cecy. 'She said at home that she was a bit nervous of looking after all you lot because you get into so many scrapes. She was trying so hard to let us all have fun – and now she'll be beating herself up about Phil, blaming herself.'

'Well, she mustn't. Of course it wasn't her fault! I suppose it was mine, because I let him up the steps, and that's how he grabbed the knife,' I said. 'And then I screamed and made him start and that's why he cut himself. See, it's all down to me!'

87

'Of course it wasn't your fault, Katy,' said Clover, taking a tea towel. 'Come on, you lot, get on with the washing. I'll help with the big bowl if you like.'

They got the washing-up done quickly while I carefully wiped down all the surfaces. Then I had a little peek at the cakes.

'Mmm, don't they smell lovely now! I think they *are* done! OK, everyone, stand back. No touching of the tin! We don't want any burns or else we'll all end up in hospital with poor Philly,' I said, grabbing the oven glove.

'Will he have to stay in hospital long?' Jonnie asked, still very worried about him.

'No, he'll probably just have to have a stitch or two in his finger, that's all. Stitches aren't too bad. I've had heaps,' I said, truthfully enough. When I was little I was forever tripping down steps or crashing my first bike or failing to balance on the top of walls. I have interesting little scars all over me.

I got the cakes out of the oven without burning my own fingers and set them down to cool.

'Can't we eat them now when they're lovely and hot?' asked Dorry.

'No! We want to put the icing on, don't we? They have to be cool or the icing will melt.'

'I like melted things best,' said Dorry. 'Especially ice cream when it goes all slurpy.'

'*You're* the slurpy one,' I said. 'Now, patience!'

Mind you, it was hard for *me* to be patient. I was so wound up about poor little Phil that I was desperate to cram something sweet into my mouth for comfort. Still, I diverted everyone by telling them a story about a little girl called Katerina who made phenomenally good cakes when little more than an infant and who grew up to be become the greatest pastry chef in the entire world. I made up cake after cake: a wedding cake as tall as a tower with sugar roses twining round and round; a huge christening cake with a life-size stork made out of icing feathers with sticks of pink liquorice for legs; a cake for a chess champion with twenty-four chocolate chess pieces, half white and half dark.

Dorry stayed impatient, declaring he wanted real cake, not pretend, but Clover and Cecy and Jonnie marvelled enthusiastically. I made them up a cake each as a reward. Clover's was pink and very creamy, with her name spelled out in tiny green sugar four-leaf clovers. Cecy's was like a bed with a patterned quilt, with lots of little orphan babies tucked up inside. Jonnie's was a round skateboarding area with all kinds of precarious chocolate quarter-pipes and a little marzipan Jonnie skimming the top of the tallest on her slick toffee skateboard.

'What about *my* cake?' said Elsie sulkily.

It was terribly tempting to invent a disastrous cake for her because she hadn't asked nicely at all, but I relented and made up a doll's house cake for her, with little marzipan dolls peering out of the iced windows.

'Oh, my cake's the best of all!' Elsie crowed, as if she'd made it up herself.

'You girls are all so boring! I want real cake you can eat!' said Dorry. 'Those cakes must be cool by now.' He poked at one with his finger. 'It is, it is! See, Katy?'

'Then we'll ice them right this minute,' I said.

I set to, stirring the icing again, getting it to exactly the right consistency, and then I let them all take a turn pouring and spreading the tops of the cakes, studding each with a walnut.

'And now can we eat them?' asked Dorry, holding a cake a centimetre from his mouth.

'We'll keep four,' I said, separating them. 'One for Phil, one for Mrs Hall, one for Dad and I suppose one for Izzie. But we can eat the rest.'

So we started munching. The real cakes weren't as elaborate as my imaginary ones, but they certainly tasted absolutely delicious.

'Right – now bedtime!' I said.

'That's not fair. I don't have to go to bed at the same time as the littlies,' Elsie protested.

'We're *all* going to bed,' I said. I planned that Clover and Cecy and I would all tell more stories in bed in our room.

I tried to encourage Dorry and Jonnie to get into their pyjamas and wash their sticky hands and faces and clean their teeth, I really did, but they were both overexcited, running round in their underwear and refusing point blank to clean their teeth because they wanted to keep the cake taste in their mouths.

'They're being very silly,' said Elsie. 'I shall tell Mum when she gets back.'

'No, you won't, you little tell-tale,' I said. 'Who cares if they sleep in their pants and don't clean their teeth just this once?'

I had to bribe them into bed though, by giving them half a cake each. Izzie wouldn't mind too much if we didn't save one for her. She was always on a stupid diet anyway.

Clover lent Cecy her best pink pyjamas with little bluebirds flying up and down them. I'd have lent her mine, but they'd have been way too big for her. Then all three of us crammed into my bed and we started telling more stories, but Elsie kept trailing into our room, wanting to join in too.

'Let me get in the bed as well!' she said, pushing at us.

'Elsie, don't be mad. There's no room!' I said, but she wouldn't listen.

She shoved and pushed and wriggled and got into the bed somehow.

'There!' she said triumphantly. 'Plenty of room!'

We were all completely squashed, poor Cecy literally clinging to the edge of the bed to stay in it. Then Dorry came trailing in.

'Katy, Katy! Jonnie's crying again and she won't stop,' he said. 'I think she'd feel better if you let her have another cake.'

'Do you think I'm daft, Dorry?' I asked, but I could hear sad little sniffles from the twins' room and knew that she really was crying.

'Come in here, Jonnie! I can't come to you – I'm stuck in my bed with a hundred and one girls squashing me!' I called.

Jonnie came stumbling in, dragging Zebby with her.

'Oh, darling, don't cry! Look, Phil will be all right, I promise you. He's just getting his finger made better,' I said, praying this was true.

'But now we're all alone with no one to look after us!' Jonnie wailed.

'*I'm* looking after us,' I said. 'Look, you get out for a minute, Elsie, and let Jonnie come in my bed for a cuddle.'

'And Zebby!' said Jonnie.

'I want a cuddle too!' said Dorry.

'Well, there's not room for all of us, you sillies,' I said. And then I had a marvellous idea. 'Tell you what! Let's all get into Dad and Izzie's bed, then we'll have heaps of room.'

'Really? Are you allowed, Katy?' asked Cecy.

'No, she's not!' said Elsie. 'Katy, you know you're not! Mum wouldn't like it one bit.'

'I am too allowed! It's not your mum's bed, Elsie. It used to be *my* mum's, and when Clover and I were little we were always climbing in for cuddles. Dad won't mind in the slightest, I'm sure.'

I wasn't one hundred per cent sure at all, but it seemed a totally practical idea. If we were all in the big bed I could cuddle everyone and keep them all happy and be the most brilliant big sister. Then, when everyone got sleepy, I could carry each child back to their own bed and they'd be settled and fast asleep when Mrs Hall and Dad and Izzie got back. I'd smile at them wearily and they'd clap me on the back and say, 'Well done, Katy. You've really saved the day. What would we have done without you!'

So we all went into Dad and Izzie's room. I put the light on so we could see what we were doing. Cecy had never been in their room before.

'Oh goodness, it's so pretty!' she marvelled, going to the glass dressing table and gently fingering all the rose glass ornaments and Izzie's silver hairbrush and her spray bottle of perfume.

'It was much, much better when this was Mum's room,' I said. 'Izzie's spoilt it all. She's made it too fancy and girly.'

'I think it's beautiful,' said Elsie. 'Mum lets me come in here sometimes when you lot aren't around. She lets me try on her jewellery and she gives me a little squirt of her perfume and says I'm her special girl.'

'Oh yuck,' I said.

'She does too. I'm allowed, but you lot aren't.' Elsie picked up the perfume bottle and sprayed herself liberally.

'Mmm, that's lovely. I want some too,' said Clover.

'No, you can't. *You're* not allowed,' said Elsie.

'Of course she's allowed,' I said. 'Go on, Clover, spray away!'

So Clover sprayed and then of course everyone else wanted to have a go, even Dorry.

Elsie glared. 'Well, *I'm* allowed to wear Mum's lipstick and try on all her jewellery. *You're* not!' she said.

So of course they all took Izzie's make-up bag and experimented eagerly and raided her jewellery box and decked themselves with necklaces and bangles and rings. I didn't want to put on any make-up because I hate that sort of stuff, but Cecy persuaded me and made me up very carefully.

'Oh Katy, you look so grown up and glamorous!' she said.

'Don't talk rubbish, Cecy,' I said, but when I peered in Izzie's mirror I couldn't help being thrilled. The other kids had daubed lipstick here and eyeliner there and looked clownish, but Cecy had applied everything very delicately and I looked almost . . . pretty.

'You look lovely, Katy!' said Clover admiringly. 'Practically grown up! Hey, why don't you try on one of Izzie's dresses and her high heels?'

'No fear!' I said, but all the others urged me to do just that. Except Elsie.

'You mustn't touch my mum's clothes. If you do that, I'm telling!' she threatened.

So of course I *had* to do it then, just to show I didn't give a fig about her threats. Cecy selected the mint green suit that Izzie wore when she went to posh shops to try and get them to stock her silly handbags, and Clover found Izzie's highest heels, black and shiny and spiky. They were actually much too small for me, but I crammed my feet in anyway. I pulled the green suit on over my pyjamas, which made it look a bit lumpy, and the skirt didn't look right with wrinkled pyjama legs sticking out underneath, but even so I looked dazzlingly different.

'My goodness, Katy, you look at least sixteen!' said Cecy.

'No, eighteen!' said Clover.

I minced round the room pretending to be Izzie and everyone laughed and whistled at me. Except Elsie.

'You take them off, you mean, nasty girl!' she said, rushing at me.

I dodged her easily, but twisted my ankle rather – and then there was a sudden *snap*. I looked down, my heart thudding. The black heel had broken right off.

'There! Look what you've done! Oh, you wicked, wicked thing!' Elsie cried.

'I didn't mean to. You shouldn't have hurled yourself at me like that. It was just as much your fault,' I said,

taking the shoes off hastily and thrusting them right to
the back of Izzie's wardrobe. I hoped she wouldn't find
them for days and days. I took the green suit off too
and tried to hang it up carefully. I saw a little of my
lipstick had smeared the collar and I felt bad again. I
squashed the suit right to the back of the wardrobe
too, hoping Izzie might somehow forget about it.

'Come on, you lot. Put all the jewellery back quick
and let's jump into bed,' I said.

Dad and Izzie didn't have a sensible duvet like anyone
else. Izzie had pale peach Egyptian cotton sheets, and
a deeper peach satin counterpane she'd found in a
vintage shop. Clover and Cecy exclaimed at it in
wonder, but I rather hated its slippery feel. I jumped
into bed and everyone tumbled in with me. Except
Elsie.

'Um, you're going to be in so much trouble,' she said.
'Just wait till Mum gets back.'

'We'll make sure we're back in our own beds by then,'
I said. 'And Cecy's mum will be ages at the hospital
because you always have to wait hours in A & E. So
shut up, Elsie. Push off, if you're not coming into bed
with us. And switch the light off.'

Elsie did switch the light off and wandered away
down the dark landing. But then she came scurrying
back.

'I heard a noise! I heard a noise downstairs! I think
it's burglars!' she screamed.

'Burglars!' Dorry gasped. 'They'll steal the cakes!'

'Shall we fight them?' asked Jonnie.

'No, hide under the covers!' said Clover.

'I want Mum to come back!' said Cecy.

'Shh, now! I don't think it *is* burglars. Tyler would start barking if it was,' I said.

We all looked at Tyler. He wagged his tail, happy to have our undivided attention. For once I wished he was a much fiercer dog.

'Here, Tyler,' I said firmly. 'Come with me. We're going to look for burglars.'

'Oh Katy, don't!' said Clover. Then she got out of bed herself. 'All right, I'll come too.'

'And I will,' said Cecy.

'We'll all come and we'll all fight them and we'll win,' said Jonnie.

So we crept slowly downstairs in a little gang, most of us holding hands. Tyler skittered along at our feet, still wagging his tail – but then he suddenly started barking at the kitchen door.

We clutched each other, suddenly really scared. Then I heard a triumphant mew. I snapped on the kitchen light – and there was our old cat Sally, now as bouncy as a kitten, chasing a tiny mouse here and there about the kitchen floor.

'A mouse, a mouse, a mouse!' Elsie squealed.

'Yes, a mouse, stupid, not a burglar. Well, a *cat* burglar,' I said, laughing. I grabbed one of Izzie's empty Kilner jars, pushed poor Sally out of the way, and neatly captured the mouse inside the jar.

'Ugh! Oh Katy, you're so brave!' said Cecy, who seemed almost as scared of the mouse as silly Elsie.

'It's only a little field mouse. It's so sweet! And luckily it doesn't look hurt at all,' I said, showing Cecy the glass jar filled with the tiny rodent, but she shrank away from me.

'OK, OK. I'll take it out into the garden,' I said, and did so. 'There you are, little Mousy. Run fast! Keep away from our Sally!'

Sally was mewing crossly, deprived of her fun, so I let the littlies feed her a cat treat each.

'Can we have a treat too?' Dorry asked.

'No, we're all going back to bed. Come on, who can get into bed first?' I said.

We all tore up the stairs, pushing and yelling, making a mad dive for the bed. Elsie got in too, huddling up close.

'There! Everybody's in now,' I said. 'All safe.'

'Everybody except Philly,' said Jonnie.

'Mum will bring him back all better,' said Cecy.

'But he will hurt,' said Jonnie.

'Let's play bears,' I said quickly, because I couldn't stand the thought of dear little Phil hurting either. 'I'm Father Bear and Cecy can be Mother Bear and you're all our little bear cubs and we're safe in our cave. Pull the covers right up over our heads to make the cave.'

There was an ominous ripping sound. Oh no . . . Izzie's vintage peach counterpane. I didn't dare get up and switch the light on and see what we'd done. Perhaps it was just a *little* rip. Maybe I could turn the counterpane round so that Izzie wouldn't notice. I decided to play bears and distract everyone for ten minutes or so, and then I'd put them all back in their own beds and deal with the counterpane. Clover and I were rubbish at sewing, but maybe Cecy could manage a neat repair if necessary.

'We're bears, we're bears! Big fat growly bears. Grrrr! Grrrr!' I said. 'I'm big Father Bear and I've climbed a tree and found honey for all my baby bears. Snuggle up and have some honey, yum yum yum!' I said, trying to distract myself as well as all the others.

'Honey!' said Dorry. 'Where? Bags I have first lick!'

'It's *pretend* honey, Dorry!' I said.

'I want real honey!' said Dorry.

'Oh, for goodness' sake!' I said. 'All right, all right. I'll go and get you some.'

I climbed out of bed and started down the stairs, desperate to keep them all happy. Tyler came with me and I couldn't help tripping over him in the dark.

'Sorry, sorry, Tyler! Are you all right?' I asked anxiously.

Tyler leaped up and licked my face reassuringly. But then he suddenly started to bark loudly.

'No, shh, Tyler, stop that row! Don't be silly. There's nothing to bark at,' I hissed.

Tyler took no notice. And then I heard something myself. A car door slamming outside. Then scurrying footsteps. I ran to the living room, peeped round the curtain and saw Izzie hastening towards the front door!

I gasped and then flew up the stairs as if I had a real family of bears chasing me.

'Quick, quick! Get back to your own beds!' I shrieked. 'Izzie's back already! *Move!*'

I started yanking every child out of bed and giving them a shove. They scattered wildly, stumbling in the dark.

'Ouch! You landed right on top of me, you great lump, Dorry!' Elsie moaned. 'Put the light on, someone!'

'No, no! Izzie will see. Just feel your way in the dark – and *hurry*!' I said.

I pushed Elsie in the direction of her little room and yanked at Dorry and Jonnie, trying to herd them towards their own shared bedroom.

'Quick!' I commanded, now grabbing Clover and Cecy.

The three of us ran along the landing like the wind and then jumped into bed, Cecy in with me and Clover burrowing down into her own bed.

I heard Izzie's key in the lock.

'Shh, now! Everyone pretend to be fast asleep!' I said.

'But she'll wonder where my mum is, and little Phil,' Cecy whispered.

'Oh goodness, yes! Well, act all sleepy and innocent when she wakes us up,' I said.

I started pretend snoring as I heard Izzie down in the hall. Clover tried too, sounding like a little piglet. Cecy giggled nervously and I couldn't help giggling too. Our bed shook we were laughing so much. I pulled the covers over our heads to try to drown the noise.

We heard Izzie run into Elsie's room first and start talking to her urgently. Oh no, Elsie would be bound to tell on all of us. And sure enough, after a minute's muttering, we heard Izzie rush into her own bedroom and snap on the light.

Suddenly I stopped laughing. I thought of the spilt make-up, the discarded jewellery, the clothes and broken shoe shoved hastily back into the wardrobe. I thought of the torn peach counterpane.

'Oh Lord,' I whispered.

We heard Izzie going into Dorry and Jonnie's room and the sound of her raised voice. Dorry and Jonnie tried to stay silent, but soon we heard them mumbling. Izzie seemed terribly cross. It sounded as if both Dorry and Jonnie were crying now.

Then Izzie swept into our room and switched on the light. I don't know about Clover or Cecy, but I kept my eyes tight shut and tried to breathe regularly.

'Don't be ridiculous, girls! I know you're wide awake,' said Izzie.

I sat up reluctantly, thinking fast. *Divert her!*

'Izzie, you mustn't worry. It's only a little cut, but Philly's at the hospital with Mrs Hall,' I gabbled, hoping this would immediately make her charge off to the hospital and forget about rowing us.

No such luck.

'I know Phil's in A & E having his finger stitched, you silly girl. That's why I'm back early. I listened to Eleanor's message. She explained that she'd left *you* in charge!' said Izzie. She might have gone on more about this decision, but she couldn't very well call Mrs Hall an idiot in front of her daughter.

'I can't believe you could all have been so naughty! My bedroom is a wreck!' said Izzie. Her voice sounded strange, as if she were about to burst into tears. 'You've been wearing my clothes, using my make-up – even tearing my silk counterpane!'

'We didn't mean . . . I just wanted . . .' I faltered.

'It wasn't all Katy's fault. It was all of us,' said Clover.

'That's right,' said Cecy bravely.

'I know that,' said Izzie. 'I'm thoroughly ashamed and disappointed in all of you, but especially you, Katy, as you're the oldest and the others look up to you so. I'm sure it was *your* idea to go into my bedroom.'

'Yes, all right, it was my idea,' I said. 'I only wanted to comfort everyone.'

'Well, you've succeeded in getting all your siblings and your friend into serious trouble,' said Izzie. 'Goodness knows what your father will say.'

'Will you have to tell him? Oh please, dear Izzie, I know we've been bad, but could you possibly not tell Dad? It will upset him so,' said Clover, sitting up and looking adorable in her pink budgie-patterned pyjamas.

Most people can't resist Clover when she begs so prettily. But Izzie resisted easily.

'Of course I'm going to tell your father,' Izzie said coldly. 'He's gone straight to the hospital to check on Phil and relieve Mrs Hall. You're to stay here tonight, Cecy. Now, I suggest you all settle down and go to sleep. I dare say your father will have words with you in the morning.'

Izzie stalked off. We heard her back in her bedroom, trying to set things to rights. We heard her wardrobe door opening – and then a sharp exclamation.

'Oh Lordy, she's found her broken shoe!' I whispered.

'Don't worry, Katy. I'll tell Dad you didn't mean to do it,' Clover whispered back.

'Oh dear, doesn't she get cross!' Cecy whispered.

'Just be very, very glad she's not *your* stepmother,' I said. 'And she'd have been far, far meaner if you weren't here. We all hate her.'

I knew this wasn't really true at all. Elsie loved her mum passionately. So did Dorry and Jonnie and Phil, though I think they loved Dad a little bit more. Clover usually got on OK with Izzie, especially if I wasn't around. I was the only one who couldn't stand her. I don't suppose I actually *hated* her. I just hated her being part of our family instead of Mum.

I didn't really care too much if Izzie was mad at me. That was nothing new, after all. But I was dreading Dad being angry with me too.

I couldn't go to sleep. I stayed awake long after Cecy and Clover were genuinely snoring. I couldn't divert myself by making up stories. I just lay miserably, waiting. At last I heard the front door open and Izzie rushing downstairs. I heard Dad with Mrs Hall, and then a little chirrup from Phil, sleepily boasting about his big bandage.

I *knew* he'd like one. Oh, it was such a relief to have Philly back and to hear he was all right. Izzie stayed downstairs talking to Mrs Hall. I heard her putting the kettle on to make tea. Dad came up the stairs, talking gently to Phil, obviously carrying him. I heard him going into the littlies' room to put him to bed.

I couldn't wait any more. I slipped out of my own bed and tiptoed to the door, doing my best not to wake Cecy or Clover.

'Dad?' I whispered, on the dark landing.

'Katy? Shh, now. I'm just tucking Philly up. Be with you in a minute,' Dad whispered.

I sat waiting for him at the top of the stairs. It was a warm night but I was shivering.

'Dad!' I said, when he crept out of the littlies' room. I clutched at his leg.

'Hey, careful! You'll tip me down the stairs, sweetheart,' said Dad. He eased himself down beside me. I flung my arms round his neck and started crying.

'Hey, hey! Were you frightened about Phil? He's fine. He just needed a couple of stitches, and by all accounts he was very brave. He asked for a very big bandage though. I gather you put the idea in his head. Good girl, Katy!' said Dad.

'No, I'm not good. I'm bad, bad, bad – but I didn't mean to be. Oh Dad! Izzie's absolutely furious with me,' I wept.

'Oh dear,' said Dad wearily.

'You see, everyone wanted to get into my bed and there wasn't room, and I just wanted to be a help, act like a mum, so I suggested we all went into your bed, yours and Izzie's –' I wailed.

'Oh dear. I can see where this is going,' said Dad. 'Izzie likes to keep her bedroom as her inner sanctum, you know that.'

'Yes, but it's your bedroom too, and I knew you wouldn't really mind. Only – only we all got a bit carried away,' I said.

'Well I never,' said Dad, with heavy irony.

'Yes, and somehow some of Izzie's things got a bit messed up,' I said.

'Oh Katy!' said Dad. He sounded pretty sad.

'I didn't mean it to happen,' I said tearfully.

'I know, I know. You never mean anything – but it still happens anyway. What am I going to do with you, hmm? And when are you and Izzie ever going to learn to get on together, eh?'

I didn't answer. I couldn't, because the honest reply would be *never*. At least Dad wasn't really furious with me . . . though he did get quite cross in the morning, after Izzie had had her say.

Phil was delighted we'd left him his cake. Dad and Mrs Hall didn't fancy theirs and left them in the kitchen. Dorry found them and secretly polished them off. So at least my two brothers ended up happy.

8

Cecy and I were best friends forever of course. We'd been best friends ever since we were babies. When we started nursery we played in the Wendy house together and finger-painted at adjacent easels. We sat next to each other the first day at school and still did now we were in Year Six. But that didn't mean Cecy was my only friend.

I had had heaps of special friends over the years. When I was very little I didn't understand that you usually had friends in your own age range. I declared that Mr Harrington in the sweetshop was my special friend because he sang a funny song – *K-K-K-Katy, beautiful Katy* – every time he saw me. Mandy, the nurse at Dad's practice, was my special friend because she gave me Smarties from a glass jar and let me draw with her biro. Miss Ranger the assistant at nursery was my special friend because she let me wear silver cardboard armour and rush around waving a plastic toy sword.

Then when I got to proper school age I started to claim animals as my special friends. I loved Sally our cat with a passion. I convinced myself she loved me back just as much, though she generally seemed reluctant to sit on my lap, and only headbutted me and purred when I fed her. We didn't have Tyler when I was younger. We didn't have any dog because Izzie lived with us by then and always whined that she had so much to do looking after all the babies that she couldn't possibly take on a dog as well. So I had to make friends with all the neighbourhood dogs: Monty, the wonderful, wolf-like German shepherd; Sparky, the beautiful white husky; and Ted, the cuddly little schnauzer. I begged their owners to let me take them for walks in the park. I don't know why, but they didn't quite trust me, though they sometimes let me come on walks with them because I was very good at hurling balls and playing tag and running races. All these special dog friends greeted me with loving licks and waggy tails.

It wasn't quite the same as having my own pet. I kept on at Dad until he gave in and let me buy a hamster with my pocket money at Pets at Home. Izzie screamed when she saw it. That was actually very satisfying, especially when she and Dad had a major row. It made me feel little Hammy was even more of a special friend.

I loved him so much and spent hours in our bedroom letting him run up inside my sleeve, across my chest under my T-shirt and out the other sleeve. I was sure he had the potential to perform all sorts of tricks, and I started constructing hamster palaces for him out of cardboard boxes. He loved playing in them, but unfortunately he gnawed his way out when I went down to supper one day.

We hunted high and low for him (Izzie screamed her head off again!) but we never found him. I cried for days. I eventually consoled myself by writing a long story (well, ten pages, but this was a while ago) called *The Exciting Escape of Hammy the Hamster*. I had Hammy find his way into the garden, set up home in a flowerpot and make friends with field mice, shrews and a robin. I imagined it so vividly I couldn't help looking hopefully for him every time I played outdoors.

Now I had lovely little Tyler and of course he was my special friend too. He wasn't *just* mine – Dad had got him for all of us, overriding Izzie at long last – but I was the one Tyler ran to first, the one who got the most licks and loving.

It was because of Tyler that I made friends with Imogen. Clover and I always took Tyler for a walk before supper, just down the road to the park, once round and back again. If we were lucky we saw Monty or Sparky or Ted, and Tyler had a brilliant time chasing and wrestling and larking about. But this time none of our special dog friends were there. Clover and I took turns throwing the ball for Tyler and he ambled about happily enough, but he kept looking around, clearly hoping for company.

Then he suddenly stopped dead, nose pointing, ears pricked – and dashed madly to the other end of the park.

'Tyler! Tyler, come back here!' I yelled.

'Here, boy! Tyler!' Clover called.

Tyler took no notice whatsoever. He was rushing towards a tiny ball of cream fluff which cowered as he advanced.

'No, Tyler! Gently! That's just a little puppy!' I yelled.

Tyler wasn't much more than a puppy himself, but he was a rough and ready, feisty little terrier. The cream fluff was about the size of a guinea pig and squeaking like one too. Its owner snatched him up and cradled him in her arms. Tyler wasn't deterred in the slightest. He jumped up at her, scratching her legs and barking excitedly.

'*Tyler!* Get down! Oh, I'm sorry. Don't be frightened, he's just trying to be friendly,' I said.

The fluff's owner was a girl about my age. She was a posh St Winifred's girl, wearing their distinctive pale green dress and darker green blazer with gold ribbon edging. She wore her weirdly old-fashioned straw boater hat at a jaunty angle as if to stress her superiority.

I had longed to go to St Winifred's myself. The girls there looked like children from an old Enid Blyton book. I imagined them playing lacrosse and learning Latin and having a French teacher called Mam'selle. I liked their church too. I'd once crept inside and loved the strange rich perfumey smell and admired the statue of the Virgin Mary, her face so pale and pure, her bare feet standing on little angel heads and a crescent moon.

We didn't go to any kind of church and I rather wanted to. It would be good to breathe in this holy smell and confess my sins once a week. I realized I'd have rather a lot to confess, so there would be a whole queue of impatient people behind me waiting their turn – but think how wonderful I would feel afterwards, so good and pure and cleansed.

'Why can't we go to church, Dad?' I'd asked.

'I'm not religious, Katy. You can go by yourself when you're older, if you really want to,' he said.

'Could I go to St Winifred's? Oh Dad, could I go to St Winifred's Convent? Then I could go with the school. I'd love to wear that retro uniform too,' I said.

'St Winifred's *is* a very good school,' said Izzie. 'Their girls always look so smart and well behaved.'

I was surprised she was backing me up. Maybe she wanted Elsie to go there because it was posh.

'If they're smart and well behaved I doubt our Katy would fit in,' said Dad, laughing. He put his arm round me. 'Sorry, chickie – I couldn't send you there even if I wanted to. It's a private school and costs a fortune. I couldn't afford to send you there, let alone Clover and Elsie and Jonnie.'

I looked at the cream fluff's owner now. Yes, she looked rich. She had that lovely pink-and-white skin and beautiful long fair hair in two pigtails with green-and-gold striped ribbons. They looked freshly plaited, though it was late afternoon.

I was suddenly conscious of my own wild hair, half-scraped back with an old elastic band, my fringe falling in my eyes. I looked down at my faded school dress, now far too short on me, showing much too much long leg. I saw my own scabby knees and grubby socks and scuffed shoes.

'Oh dear,' I said. 'We're like a silly video or something. Of owners that look just like their dogs. Tyler and I are all noisy and scruffy and untidy, and you and your little puppy look dead posh and immaculate.'

'Katy!' Clover hissed, puffing up beside us.

'Well, they do,' I said. 'What kind of a puppy is that?'

'She's a little bichon frise.' She pulled a face. 'Silly name, isn't it?'

'What's she called?'

'Coco. What about your dog?'

'He's Tyler. He's a rescue dog. We're not sure what breed he is – some sort of terrier anyway. Tyler! Stop being such a pest. Coco doesn't want to play with you,' I said.

'She's a hopeless wuss but I love her to bits,' said the girl. 'I'm Imogen, by the way.'

'I'm Katy.'

'And I'm Clover, Katy's sister,' said Clover.

'Whereabouts do you live? We've just lived here a couple of months, in Jessop Avenue. Do you know it?' said Imogen.

We knew it all right. Jessop Avenue was one of our favourite walks. All the houses were like palaces: huge Victorian villas with turrets and towers. Some had been turned into flats and several were grand nursing homes, but many were still proper family houses. Clover and I often spent ages deciding which house we liked best so we could buy it when we were grown up and rich and famous. One of our special favourites had been up for sale recently, a beautiful pink house with white shutters, and matching pink and white hydrangeas in the garden.

'You don't live in the pink house, do you?' I asked eagerly.

'Yes! How on earth did you know?' said Imogen.

'Oh, just a guess. It's a lovely house,' I said.

'Do you or your brothers or sisters have the round bit on top for your bedroom?' Clover asked.

'*I* have it. I haven't got any brothers or sisters, worse luck,' said Imogen.

'So there's just three of you in that huge great house?' I asked, amazed.

'Katy!' Clover hissed again.

'It's OK. Yep, just the three of us. And Rosa, she's the housekeeper.'

Clover and I exchanged glances. A housekeeper!

'Well, there's eight of us, without any housekeeper,' I said.

'Eight! Goodness!' said Imogen.

'It's a bit complicated. There's Dad and Izzie, she's our stepmother. Our mum died when we were little. Then there's Elsie, our stepsister. And Dorry and Jonnie and Phil, they're halves. And Tyler.'

'And Sally, our cat,' said Clover.

'You sound like a storybook family,' said Imogen.

'No, *you're* like a storybook girl,' I said.

'How old are you, Katy? Thirteen? Fourteen?'

'Eleven. I just seem older because I'm so tall,' I said, pulling a face.

'I'm eleven too!'

'And I'm ten,' said Clover.

'Do you have a doctor here yet?' I asked.

'Yes, though I'm not ill,' said Imogen, looking puzzled. 'I just had to go to Dr Carr to get some Ventolin as I have asthma sometimes.'

'Dr Carr!' Clover and I chorused.

'Yes. Is he your doctor too? He's ever so nice,' said Imogen.

We burst out laughing.

'He's our dad!' I said. 'And he *is* ever so nice. What does your dad do, Imogen?'

'Oh, he's in the music business. It's a bit of a laugh . . . Ages ago he was in this boy band – Lightning Flash?'

Clover and I looked suitably impressed, though we didn't know much about boy bands and didn't know if Lightning Flash were really famous or not. It didn't really matter. Imogen's dad still sounded impossibly cool and glamorous.

'What about your mum?'

'Oh, she used to be a model. She's an actress now.'

'Oh wow! You've got amazing parents,' I said.

'Is your mum in a play now?' asked Clover.

'No, she doesn't work in the theatre. She's in television, mostly. She had a part in *Shopping Mall* for a while.'

We'd never heard of that either but we raised our eyebrows and nodded.

'Does your stepmum work – or is she too busy looking after all of you?' Imogen asked.

'She makes these fancy handbags out of suede and leather. They're very pretty, with little flowers,' said Clover.

'No, they're not,' I said. 'And they're not much use anyway. You can't fit enough stuff into them.'

Long ago Izzie had made Clover and me special school bags. Clover still had hers, but mine tore after only a few weeks. Izzie mended it, but it ripped all over again, just because I took out six books from the library and stuffed them in my bag, along with my history project and a large biscuit tin full of pennies because I was collecting for Battersea Dogs & Cats Home.

'She made Tyler a bed too,' said Clover.

'Yes, and he doesn't think much of it. He's already chewed half of it to bits, haven't you, little boy?' I said. I picked him up and held him close to Coco. 'Now, say hello properly, *gently*, very gently.'

Tyler squirmed and Coco shrank from him, but they gave each other a little sniff. When we tried putting them on the grass Tyler kept his leaping-about in check and Coco had a little delicate sniff at him.

'There! They're friends!' I cried.

'I'm so pleased. Coco's usually hopeless with other dogs. Yes, they really are friends,' said Imogen, as the two puppies ran round in circles together.

'You must bring her round to our house so they can have a proper play date,' I said. 'Come round Saturday morning. We're 38 Roxburgh Road – it's just down the way. You will come, won't you?'

'We'd both love to,' said Imogen.

'But we always go to the secret garden with Cecy on Saturdays,' Clover said to me on the way home.

'Yes, but not till after she's finished her boring old dancing. Imogen can come round before. And if she stays we can always swear her to secrecy and take her to the secret garden too,' I said.

'Yes . . .' said Clover, but she sounded worried. 'What will Izzie say? You know she always goes on about you asking her first before inviting anyone round.'

That was after a huge row because I'd invited this poor homeless guy round for a cup of tea and a sandwich because he looked so cold and hungry. And it was all Izzie's fault that she'd left her purse practically sticking out of her bag.

'Izzie won't mind if it's just another girl I've asked,' I said. 'And anyway, it's not Izzie's house, it's Dad's, and I'm sure *he* won't mind. Look, we won't say anything, just to be on the safe side. Izzie can't turn Imogen away once she's there on the doorstep.'

'I think we'd better ask all the same,' said Clover.

'You ask, then. You'll do it better than me,' I said.

So at supper Clover smiled sweetly at Izzie, told her the shepherd's pie was extra yummy, and then added casually, 'Oh Izzie, Katy and I met such a lovely girl at the park when we were walking Tyler. She's new to the neighbourhood and I don't think she's got many friends yet. Could she possibly come round to ours one Saturday? Well, *this* Saturday?'

Strangely, Izzie wasn't fooled. She glared at me.

'Katy! I've told you not to go round asking complete strangers to our house! And *if* you do it, have the grace to admit to it yourself. Don't try to let your sister take the blame,' she said reprovingly.

'Look, she's Clover's friend too. And she's lovely, isn't she, Clover?'

'Yes, she's friends with both of us, honestly,' said Clover, ever loyal.

'Well, she can't come round, whether she's friends with both of you or not. I've seen the sorts of girls who hang round that park,' said Izzie.

'*We* hang round the park,' I said.

'Well, I wish you wouldn't. I wouldn't let you if it were down to me. You're far too young to be out on your own,' said Izzie. She glanced at Dad, who was tucking into his own shepherd's pie and feeding Phil his, pretending his spoon was a helicopter flying into Philly's mouth. Phil was still wearing his bandage with pride and insisting he was badly wounded.

'Don't worry, darling. The girls are fine as long as they stick together – and the park's only just down the road,' Dad said mildly.

I can't stand the way he calls Izzie *darling*. I can't ever remember him calling Mum that.

Izzie droned on and on about girls at the park, girls who were just there because of the boys, girls who started smoking and drinking cider by the time they were twelve . . .

118

'Well, Imogen would look a bit weird smoking and drinking in her St Winifred's uniform, but I'm sure you're right, as always, Izzie,' I said sarcastically.

Izzie stared at me. 'This girl goes to St Winifred's?'

I nodded.

'Are you sure? Did she say so?'

'She was wearing the fancy hat and the blazer, so she didn't really need to, did she?' I said.

'Less of the attitude, Katy,' said Dad, making the helicopter hover above Phil's head.

'Well, why didn't you *say* so, you silly girls. Yes, of course you can invite her round, if she's a St Winifred's girl. But what was she doing in that funny little park? It's nowhere near her school,' Izzie said.

'She was walking her dog, just like us. She's adorable, so cute and blonde –'

'Imogen or her dog?' asked Dad, landing the helicopter in Phil's laughing mouth.

'Both, actually. So it's really OK? She can come? I said Saturday morning sometime,' I said.

'Oh Lord, then she might be expecting to stay for lunch, when you usually have your picnic. Perhaps I could do some sort of cold chicken dish, with different fancy salads?' Izzie said, obviously mentally consulting her Ottolenghi recipe book.

'No, we'll have just the usual picnic, please. And we'll eat it, er . . . at the end of the garden,' I said.

Dad and Izzie didn't know we always squeezed through to Mrs Burton's secret garden next door, and I certainly wasn't going to tell them now. It wasn't as if I was telling any fibs. I'd said *garden*, I just hadn't specified *whose* garden.

'Katy, if she's a St Winifred's girl she'll be used to all sorts of gourmet food, not kid's sandwiches,' said Izzie.

'If so, I think she'll find a picnic a glorious change,' said Dad. 'I can't wait to meet her. You always pick such *distinctive* friends.'

'Are you laughing at me, Dad?'

'I wouldn't dream of it,' said Dad, smiling.

So it was all wonderfully fixed. I hadn't told Imogen what time to come on Saturday. I wondered if she might come early. We all usually had a bit of a lie-in on Saturdays. Well, the littlies always got up at the crack of dawn, but then they generally pottered around by themselves. I don't know what Elsie did. Maybe she played one of her silly, girly dolly games by herself. Clover and I dozed or sleepily chatted, telling each other about our dreams or making wishes.

But *this* Saturday I jumped out of bed early and grabbed Dad and Izzie's bathroom while it was empty. (Our children's bathroom is always a mess of damp towels and toy ducks and abandoned pyjamas.) Imogen was so pink and white and polished, and her hair was pristine, so I thought I'd better try to make an effort to tidy myself up a bit. I had a quick bath and then washed my hair.

I hated it being such a boring mouse colour. I peered at Izzie's expensive collection of hair products. She didn't have any actual hair dye because she kept proudly proclaiming she was a natural blonde (though she always came back from her trips to the hairdresser's looking suspiciously blonder). She had some special conditioning stuff though, so I ladled that on, rubbing it in furiously. I hoped it might suddenly lengthen and thicken my hair before my very eyes.

It didn't. It didn't make my hair lighter either. In fact, it was considerably darker, and stuck together in clumps very unattractively. I hoped it might look better when it was dry.

Then I went to get dressed. I stood peering in our wardrobe for a long time. Clover's stuff wasn't too bad, but of course wouldn't fit me. My things were mostly shoved at the back and were all creased. Some had even fallen off their hangers and were in sad little heaps among our shoes. Most of my jeans were ripped or needed a good wash or only reached down to my ankles. My T-shirts weren't much better. I was pretty sure Imogen would arrive looking immaculate.

I decided I'd better put on the garment Izzie called my 'halfway-decent' dress. I wore it when meeting old family friends (always an ordeal because they'd declare, 'Good Lord, Katy! You've grown even taller!') or going to posh parties (given by the dreaded Eva Jenkins, and she only asked me because she'd asked every single member of our class). I would doubtless wear it to the terrifying school leavers' disco looming horribly large in the near future.

It was a blue dress, already way above my knees, and sleeveless, exposing all my long thin arms. I looked like a daddy longlegs in it, but at least it was a proper grown-up dress from Topshop. If I screwed my eyes up tight when I stared in the mirror I thought I didn't look too bad.

Clover leaned up on one elbow in her bed.

'I think you look great, Katy,' she said. 'Well, if you're wearing your best dress then I'll wear mine.' Clover's dress was navy with pink butterflies. It was just a little-girly dress, with puff sleeves and a very full skirt, but she did look lovely in it. We swished our way downstairs, trying to do that rolling, mincing walk that fashion models affect.

Elsie and Dorry and Jonnie and Phil were all in the kitchen, taking a handful of Rice Krispies in turn. Dorry seemed to be having twice as many turns as anyone else.

'You're wearing your best dresses! That's not fair! Well, I'm going to wear mine!' Elsie exclaimed.

'I don't have to wear my yucky best dress, do I?' said Jonnie.

'I'm wearing mine with the frills,' said Dorry in a silly voice.

He made Phil snort with laughter just as he was taking a large gulp of milk. This meant he snorted milk too, and then it spouted out of his nose in the most disgusting manner.

'Oh wow, how do you do that? It looks wicked!' said Jonnie admiringly.

'Don't you dare try!' I said, though it had once been one of *my* favourite party tricks.

'Mum, Mum! Can I wear my best dress?' Elsie yelled up the stairs.

'What? No, of course you can't,' said Izzie, emerging from the bathroom upstairs.

She came down into the kitchen, tying her kimono tightly round her waist.

'Who's been in my bathroom this morning? You still can't see for steam and there are soapsuds all over the bath. And goodness me, what have you two girls got on? Your best dresses! Take them off at once, you'll get them spoilt!'

'Mum, I'm wearing my rainbow dress if Katy and Clover are wearing their party dresses!' said Elsie, tugging at Izzie.

'We're wearing our best dresses because Imogen is coming over. You surely don't want us to look all scruffy when she's so rich and she's got famous parents and she goes to St Winifred's,' I said indignantly.

'What's all this?' said Dad, joining us in the kitchen. He reeled back, pretending to be dazzled by Clover and me. 'Who are these two beautiful strange girls decorating my kitchen? My, what visions of beauty!'

'You can't eat breakfast in those dresses. You're bound to spill it all down yourselves,' said Izzie.

'We're not babies!' I said.

'And we never spill!' said Clover.

She wasn't being quite accurate. *She* never spills. I don't know why, but I seem to slurp stuff all down my front on a regular basis. Perhaps it's because I chatter and gesture a little wildly all the time I'm eating.

'We just want to look good for Imogen! I can't believe this! You nag, whine, moan until blue smoke comes out of your ears because I'm so untidy and don't give a stuff about my clothes and yet as soon as I make a big effort you start telling me off,' I said furiously to Izzie.

'It's ridiculous wearing that dress when you'll be playing in the garden with a friend,' said Izzie. 'You'll rip it to ribbons in no time. You can wear clean shorts and one of your better T-shirts. And it doesn't look as if you've made much of an effort. You might have been in my bathroom for hours but it obviously didn't occur to you to wash your hair. Just look at it, all greasy clumps!'

'I *did* so wash it! And I put conditioner on it to make it look shiny!' I wailed. 'Why do you always have to be so horrible to me?'

'Hey, hey. Calm down, Katy,' said Dad, pulling me close. 'I think perhaps you've put a little too *much* conditioner on that noddle of yours. Better wash it off, sweetie.'

'That'll be my Molton Brown conditioner!' said Izzie. 'Of course you're meant to rinse it off! And you're only supposed to rub in a tiny amount. It looks as if you've used a whole bottle.'

'Of course I haven't,' I said – though I *had* sploshed it on, handful after handful.

'Well, go and wash it off at once. *Not* while you're wearing your best dress. Then put your shorts and T-shirt on. You too, Clover,' said Izzie.

'Can I still wear *my* party frock, Mum? I haven't done anything wrong and I'll be ever so careful,' said Elsie. 'I want to look nice for Imogen too.'

'You haven't even met her, you idiot,' I said. 'She's not *your* friend. She's mine and Clover's.'

'Now, now, Katy. Stop harassing your little sister,' said Dad. 'I can't wait to meet this Imogen. She's certainly had a weird effect on all of you. I'm imagining a bizarre amalgamation of Kate Middleton and Beyoncé at the moment.'

'Oh *Dad*!' said Clover and I in unison.

'I don't think we like this Imogen, do we, Dorry?' said Jonnie. 'We don't have to play with her, do we?'

'I want to show her my bandage,' said Phil. His cut was totally healed now, but he insisted on Izzie giving him a fresh bandage every day.

'Look, she's *our* friend. She'll just be with *us*,' I said. 'Well, until Cecy comes.'

'And then will we go you-know-where and have a picnic?' said Dorry.

'Yes, I expect so. *If* you're all good as gold,' I said airily, and sauntered out of the kitchen to take off my dress and give my hair yet another wash.

Imogen didn't come till gone eleven. I'd begun to think she'd changed her mind. I wished I hadn't made such a big deal of things.

'Never mind. Let's just start one of our usual games, like Celebrity,' Clover suggested, sensibly enough, but I couldn't really concentrate.

Then there was a big shriek from downstairs where the littlies and Elsie were kneeling up on the window seat in the living room.

'Oh wow! There's a great big Range Rover pulled up outside and a big girl's getting out!' Jonnie yelled. 'I think we might like her after all if she lets us have a ride in her big posh car!'

'She looks very grand!' called Dorry.

'That's not a girl, she's a lady, silly,' said Elsie.

Clover and I looked at each other. Our bedroom was at the back of the house so we couldn't have a good peer ourselves. We ran out of our room, across the landing, and hurtled down the stairs. I actually slid down the banisters, which is strictly forbidden in case the children copy me and fall on their heads, but this was an emergency. We had to get to the front door first before the littlies did, or Imogen might back away nervously and run right back to her Range Rover. Our siblings en masse can be very unnerving.

I pushed them all out the way and got to the front door just as Imogen knocked. I flung open the door – and then stared open-mouthed in astonishment. At first I thought a complete stranger was standing at the front door, though she was certainly holding Coco. Then I realized it *was* Imogen – but she looked so different!

9

Imogen's hair was piled up elaborately on top of her head, with long tendrils hanging down in a complicated kind of way. She had make-up on too – her eyebrows looked much darker and she had a ring of black round her blue eyes that made her look incredibly knowing and sophisticated. She was wearing a T-shirt and shorts – but they weren't remotely like *my* T-shirt and shorts. My T-shirt was a man's one, big and baggy on me, with a panda on the front, and my shorts were the long loose kind, down to my knees. Imogen's bright white T-shirt was tiny, so that it barely covered her weeny waist, and her shorts were even smaller, alarmingly so. She had jewelled flip-flop sandals and an elaborate bead bracelet round her ankle.

I could see why Elsie thought she was a lady. She looked incredibly glamorous, years and years older than eleven.

'Wow,' I said uncertainly. 'You look ever so grown up.'

'You've got make-up on!' said Clover. 'Are you really allowed to wear make-up?'

'If I want to,' said Imogen, shrugging.

We stood staring shyly at her, not knowing what to say or do next. Luckily Tyler wasn't anywhere near as bashful. He jumped round our ankles, barking cheerfully at Coco, desperate to be friends.

'Down, Tyler! Stop it! Gently!' I said.

The man in the Range Rover wound down the window, laughing. If Imogen looked amazingly old, then *he* seemed startlingly young. He had longish hair and wore a black vest that showed an elaborate tattoo all down one arm.

'Your dog's a happy little chap,' he said. 'Right, I'm off then. Bye, Imo. Phone when you need a lift.'

Imogen gave him a wave and he drove off.

'Is that your *dad*?' Clover asked.

'Yep, that's Sammy,' said Imogen.

Clover and I looked at each other. I tried to think of calling our dad 'Alistair' so casually. I imagined Dad with long hair and a tattoo and giggled a little hysterically.

Elsie and Dorry and Jonnie and Phil were scrabbling around behind us, desperate to see Imogen too.

'Move out the *way*, Katy!' Elsie wailed. She squeezed past me and then stared openly at Imogen.

'These are my sisters and brothers – the littlies,' I said to Imogen, sighing.

'I'm not one of the littlies! I'm nearly as big as Clover,' Elsie said indignantly.

'Shut up and say hello nicely,' I said. 'And stop whispering, you two!' I added sharply to Dorry and Jonnie.

They all three mumbled hello, though Dorry and Jonnie spluttered, very red in the face. Phil was less bashful.

'Oh, you're so pretty!' he said, clasping Imogen's free hand. 'You look just like the princess in the fairy-tale book.'

'Oh, *sweet!*' said Imogen.

'Katy, Katy! Whatever are you doing?' Izzie fussed in the background. 'Invite your friend inside, for goodness' sake!'

'My stepmother!' I mouthed at Imogen, pulling a silly face. 'Come in,' I said out loud.

Izzie looked startled when she had a proper look at Imogen.

'So you're . . . Imogen?' she said uncertainly.

'How do you do, Mrs Carr?' said Imogen smoothly, holding out her hand.

'How do you do?' said Izzie. A smile flickered across her face at Imogen's perfect, old-fashioned manners – but her brow wrinkled when she looked her up and down. 'I – I thought you were Katy's age,' she said.

'I am. Eleven. But Sammy says I'm eleven-going-on-twenty-one,' said Imogen, laughing.

'Sammy's your brother?' asked Izzie.

'No, my dad!' said Imogen.

'Oh!' said Izzie. 'Well, come and meet Katy and Clover's dad. He's in the living room.'

Dad was sprawled on the sofa, shoes kicked off, surrounded by the Saturday newspapers. He was equally startled by Imogen's appearance. He sat up straight and peered at her above his reading glasses. He can't help looking a bit fierce and intimidating when he does that, but Imogen didn't seem at all bothered. She sat down opposite him on the best velvet chaise longue, smiling.

'Hello, Dr Carr. Remember me? And this is little Coco.' Imogen patted the velvet beside her and Coco leaped nimbly into place.

'Hmm!' said Elsie.

We're not allowed on the velvet chaise longue, let alone Tyler, but neither Dad nor Izzie liked to tell her this. I took a deep breath and sat one side of Imogen, and Clover sat the other. Elsie and Dorry and Jonnie and Phil all squashed up on the opposite sofa, staring at us as if we were on television. Tyler barked enviously at Coco, clearly wanting to jump up on the chaise longue too. I reached over to haul him up but Izzie glared at me.

'No, not Tyler!' she snapped. 'You know he's not allowed.'

'Oh goodness, Mrs Carr! Aren't dogs allowed on the furniture?' said Imogen, gathering Coco up in her arms.

'I'm sure your dog hasn't got muddy paws like Tyler,' said Izzie. 'What a sweet little darling!'

I reached out and patted poor Tyler, aggrieved on his behalf.

'Now, let me make everyone a drink,' said Izzie. 'What would you like, Imogen – fruit juice or milk? And a chocolate cookie?'

'Oh, just mineral water, please,' said Imogen. 'Don't tempt me with a cookie. I'm on a carb-free diet.'

Our jaws dropped. Mineral water? Why on earth would anyone in their right mind choose water? And what on earth was Imogen doing on a diet? She was thin as a pin! Dorry looked particularly astonished at the sight of someone willingly turning down the chance of a cookie.

'Can I have Imogen's cookie?' he asked quickly.

'No, Mr Greedy Guts,' said Izzie, and scurried off to the kitchen.

Dad was still peering over his glasses.

'How long have you been on a diet, Imogen?' he asked. His tone was mild, but we could tell what he thought of the whole idea.

'Oh, don't worry, Dr Carr. I promise you I'm not turning anorexic,' she said. 'My mother's dietitian worked it out for me and it's wonderfully nutritious – and I take vitamin supplements anyway.'

'Even so, surely your parents don't think it a good idea?' said Dad.

'Oh yes, they do! I have to guard against getting tubby! I do a little modelling nowadays and so I really have to stay very slender,' said Imogen. She smiled at me. 'I wish I was naturally thin like Katy,' she said.

I wasn't sure whether she meant it or not. Oh glory, fancy someone like Imogen wishing she was like me!

'You do modelling!' said Clover, sounding awed.

'Izzie says *I* might be a model one day,' I blurted.

Dad made a little noise. He stifled it as best he could, but I heard it. He was *laughing* at me! I sat, silent and stung, while Clover and Elsie chattered to Imogen, admiring her greatly. The littlies remained unimpressed, fidgeting and scratching, but they stayed where they were because they wanted their cookies.

Izzie came back with two cups of coffee, one glass of mineral water, six glasses of juice, and a big plate of cookies. They weren't the ordinary shop-bought kind, they were her own home-made sort, with extra chocolate.

'Perhaps you'll change your mind, Imogen?' Izzie said, offering her the plate, but Imogen remained resolute.

We watched her drinking her mineral water, amazed that she preferred it to sweet juice. I wondered about trying it myself sometime, as it seemed such a sophisticated choice.

'Right. Let's go and play in our bedroom,' I said to Imogen and Clover as soon as they'd finished drinking. Then I blushed terribly, because *play* seemed such a childish word. 'I mean, hang out,' I added, feeling a total idiot.

Imogen came with us readily enough. Elsie clamoured to come too, following us up the stairs.

'You can come with us later, when we have our picnic you-know-where,' I said. 'But not now. We want to do big girls' talk, so scram.'

I gave her a little push.

'You *are* a big girl, Katy,' said Elsie. 'A big, big, big, hideous giant girl. You won't even fit in this house soon. You'll keep bumping your ugly head on the ceiling and I shall go ha ha ha!'

'Take no notice of the infant. She's always whining like this,' I said to Imogen in a lordly way, and slammed the bedroom door shut on Elsie. 'Right, here's our bedroom!'

Tyler ran round and round it, wagging his tail. He picked up one of my old socks and started shaking it wildly, as if it were a rat.

Imogen put Coco down on a bed, away from him. Coco sat obediently, not scrabbling at all.

'That's my bed,' said Clover. 'Do you like my patchwork cushion, Imogen? Izzie helped me make it.

And look, see this picture of the two of us on the wall? Katy did it. Isn't she artistic? I did the decorations all round the edge. And look, there's all our old teddies on the windowsill.'

'Of course we don't *play* with them any more,' I lied hastily.

'Hmm, yes,' said Imogen, clearly unimpressed. She looked round in surprise. 'Don't you have your own television? And what about your tablets?'

'We don't have any,' I said, embarrassed. 'But I have a phone, look.'

Imogen looked and raised her eyebrows.

'That's kind of a granny phone, isn't it?' she said.

'It's because of our dad. He hates most modern technology. He's dead old-fashioned,' I said, still stinging from his little snort of laughter.

'Oh, he's sweet!' said Imogen. 'He can't help being an old fuddy-duddy, bless him. He's quite old, isn't he? I mean, old to have so many young children. He's more like a grandad.'

I swallowed. I knew I'd just called Dad old-fashioned, but it seemed worrying that Imogen was talking about him like that. Dad wasn't *old* old, was he?

'Our mother was much younger,' I said. 'And beautiful.'

'Here she is,' said Clover, pointing to her photo in its silver frame. We took turns to have it on our bedside table, one week me, one week Clover. I wasn't sure

I wanted Imogen to look at her. Mum was too precious. If she said something patronizing about her I knew I'd burst out crying.

But Imogen barely glanced at her. 'So what do you two guys do up here then? I'm guessing you don't have iPods either?'

Clover and I looked at each other. What *did* we do? We played all our pretend games – but even Clover knew not to tell Imogen this. I knew that this grown-up, glamorous Imogen would look incredulous if I outlined even Celebrity, our most sophisticated game. She'd put us on a par with little Phil when he played Lions. She'd call us *sweet*.

'Oh, we draw. And do our homework and stuff. And read of course,' I said, indicating our crammed bookcase. 'Who's your favourite author, Imogen?'

Imogen shrugged. 'I don't really read, like, books. I like browsing stuff on my iPad more,' she said. She sat down on Clover's bed beside Coco and looked at her phone. I felt my arms prickling. Oh God, was she bored already and thinking of calling her father back right this minute?

'We have a special secret place,' I blurted out. 'We'll take a picnic and go there for lunch, OK?'

'A secret place?' said Imogen, looking mildly interested.

'It's a secret garden,' said Clover. 'It's the most magical place ever.'

'What, like in that old film, *The Secret Garden*? With roses and a robin and a baby deer? I loved that part,' said Imogen. 'That was my favourite film when I was a little kid.'

Clover and I looked at each other. It was one of our favourite films *now*.

'Well, you don't get deer in our secret garden, but there are lots of old rose bushes and I'm sure I've seen a robin there sometimes,' I said.

'It's truly lovely and Katy's made us a special camp under a willow tree, with rugs and cushions and all sorts,' said Clover.

'Then let's go there now!' said Imogen. She kissed Coco on the tip of her nose. 'You'd like a secret garden, wouldn't you, baby?'

'Tyler just loves it there,' I said, picking him up and kissing him on the tip of *his* nose. He didn't just accept the gesture placidly like Coco. He wriggled and squirmed and licked me thoroughly all over my face.

'Get off me, Tyler. I've already had one bath today, so I don't need another,' I said. 'Come on then.'

'It's – it's a bit early, isn't it?' said Clover.

I consulted my beautiful watch. It was only half past eleven.

'Well, we'll go and sit on the garage and wait,' I said. 'Let's see if Izzie's got started on our picnic.'

'What kind of picnic?' asked Imogen.

'Oh, it's heavenly! Quail and sweetmeats and passion fruit!' said Clover, her face glowing.

'Wow!' said Imogen.

'Well, we pretend it is,' I mumbled, embarrassed. Imogen didn't seem to hear me and I didn't repeat it.

When we got downstairs I told Clover to conduct Imogen and Coco to the garage while I rushed to Izzie in the kitchen. She was busy preparing food.

'Izzie, could you possibly make it a very, very special exotic picnic?' I said. 'With no carbs, whatever they are?'

'Well, I'm doing my best. Your Imogen's not at all the way I imagined a St Winifred's girl! I'm doing a salad specially for her, and there's carrot sticks and the avocado dip I was saving for your dad's and my supper, and I've taken the skin off the chicken so it's as low-calorie as possible.'

'Oh, thanks so much, Izzie!' I said, so relieved I gave her a quick hug.

She went really pink and her face screwed up, almost as if she were about to burst into tears.

I backed away quickly, feeling awkward, and ran to join Imogen and Clover.

'This is where we wait,' I said, taking Imogen's hand and pulling her outside through the French windows, across the garden to the garage. 'We're allowed to climb right up – Clover and me. It's quite easy, just nipping up the ladder. I'll show you.'

Imogen was staring at me as if I were mad.

'Why do we want to go up on the garage roof?' she said.

'Well . . . it's a good waiting place,' I said.

'Who are we waiting for?' said Imogen.

'Our friend Cecy next door. She has dancing on Saturday mornings but she gets back as soon as she can, about ten past twelve. You'll love Cecy. She's very pretty – but not as pretty as you, of course,' I said.

Imogen dimpled when I said that, but she wouldn't be persuaded to climb the ladder.

'It's easy-peasy,' I said, climbing up and down to show her.

'I can do it. Watch,' said Clover.

'But there's no *point*,' said Imogen. 'I don't want to sit on a garage roof. It looks horribly uncomfy – and dirty too. Can't we just go to the secret garden now?'

'Yes, of course,' I said, though I felt anxious about going there without Cecy. I felt in my shorts pocket for my phone, ready to text her, but I saw I'd let the battery run right down, again. I found a scrap of paper and decided to leave her a written message, but didn't have a pen on me. 'Just half a tick, Imogen.'

I dashed back indoors and asked Dad if I could borrow his fountain pen for a minute.

'Katy, I love you dearly, but I shudder to think what havoc you could wreak on the nib if I let you use my precious prescribing Montblanc for a full sixty seconds,' said Dad.

'Oh, you're just an old fuddy-duddy!' I said, exasperated, and I abandoned my pen-seeking, grabbed the picnic from Izzie and rushed back outside. Dorry followed immediately, and Jonnie and Phil followed him. Elsie was still hanging around Clover and Imogen.

'It looks as if we're all going,' I said.

'Except Cecy,' said Clover quietly.

I chose to ignore her.

I led the way to the gap in the hedge. Imogen looked aghast.

'Oh, come on! Isn't there a gate?'

'This is a *secret* garden. Of course there isn't a gate,' said Elsie impatiently.

'There must be a gate at the front.'

'Yes, but it belongs to old Mrs Burton, and she doesn't have a clue we creep into her back garden. Look, we'll put the picnic blanket down on the earth, so you won't get a bit mucky, I promise,' I said. 'You just have to do one quick wriggle and you're through.'

Imogen gave a great sigh.

'All right – but it had better be a good secret garden.'

'It is, it is! It's the most beautiful place in the whole world!' Clover promised, wriggling through the hedge herself.

The others all followed. Tyler went through, and Coco, encouraged, darted through too.

'There! Now you, Imogen,' I said.

So she wriggled through daintily enough on top of the specially laid-down picnic blanket, but when I squirrelled through afterwards Imogen was still ostentatiously brushing herself down and peering round blankly.

'Is this *it*?' she said. 'It's just some old back garden!'

'No, it's a secret, see, and here's our dear old willow – look, it's just like a green cave inside. That's where we'll have our picnic. And this over here is our grand tree. I can climb nearly to the very top. I'm building a tree house on that big branch. I've nearly got enough wood collected. And the trunk's quite hollow, so I've plans to make a slippery-slip slide, like in *The Magic Faraway Tree* –' I hesitated. 'Of course, I only read that when I was a little kid, but the others still like it.'

Imogen still looked blank.

'But it's just an ordinary tree now,' she said. She consulted her phone again.

'Let's have the picnic,' I said quickly.

'Yes, let's!' said Dorry at once.

'But we'll have to save some for Cecy,' said Clover.

'Of course we will!' I said, spreading the picnic blanket under the willow and opening the basket. 'There! Let us commence our grand repast!'

Izzie had truly done us proud. There were the chicken breasts and a large mixed salad beautifully laid out in a pattern on the big plate, and the green avocado dip with the neatest little carrot sticks set all around it. There was an open mixed berry pie, the fruit all glistening, and a tub of Greek yoghurt, and little orange clementines, and a box of rose-pink Turkish delight.

'Oh look! The kitchen maid has been truly diligent!' I said, starting up the game.

'Oh frabjous day!' said Clover, doing the correct response.

'Oh, the feast of kings and queens!' said Dorry and Jonnie together, as they tucked in greedily.

'Wait, wait! We must serve our honoured guest first!' I said.

But the honoured guest wasn't looking impressed.

'That's not quail, that's chicken!' she said.

'Well, of course it's not *real* quail. That's just in old-fashioned storybooks. We're playing, see,' I said, putting my arm round her.

Imogen shrugged my arm off. '*We* have quail sometimes. And I love it. I thought I was going to have it now. And sweetmeats . . . That's just Turkish delight.'

'Yes, I know, but we pretend, you see, to make it more exciting,' I said desperately.

'I don't see the point,' said Imogen.

'That's because you're stupid,' said Jonnie, very rudely indeed. 'But never mind. Dorry will eat your share if you don't want it.'

'*Jonnie!*' I said furiously, but there was a little bit of me that couldn't help agreeing.

I thought Imogen would flounce out of the feasting cave then and there, but she stayed, and she even ate a morsel of chicken and a sliver of salad. We all tucked in properly, but it felt awkward, and even Dorry didn't eat with his usual gusto.

The three littlies crawled out of the cave as soon as they were finished and started up a complicated animal game.

'Oh God, do we all have to bark and moo and hiss?' said Imogen.

'No, of course not,' I said.

'So what *do* we do?'

'We tell stories,' said Clover. 'We make up what we're going to be, like when we grow up.'

'That's more like it,' said Imogen. 'Shall I go first?'

She had it all mapped out, in immense detail. She was going to continue modelling all the way through school, and reckoned that by the time she was fourteen she'd be modelling proper adult clothes.

'That's where the money is,' said Imogen in a worldly wise fashion. 'I'll develop a new look, maybe do something a little weird with my hair, whatever, and I reckon I'll have my face on *Vogue* by the time I'm fifteen.'

'I'm sure you will,' I said. 'But don't you want to do something else too? Maybe travel to all sorts of exotic places?'

'If you're a top model they fly you all over the world,' said Imogen. 'I shall earn a fortune too, but I won't *stay* a model. I'll go to university, maybe somewhere in America – that might be less stuffy. I'll maybe do some acting. Then again, I am quite musical, though practising gets so boring, but Sammy says I've got a great voice, so maybe I'll be a singer with some totally cool indie band.'

Elsie was getting restless through this long recitation.

'*I'm* going to do all that, modelling and acting and singing, *and* I'm going to have a husband and lots of babies,' she announced.

'I'm not sure about a husband – and I don't think I want babies either,' said Imogen, picking up Coco and cradling her. 'I'll have lots of cute little dogs like Coco instead.'

'Won't you be a bit lonely if you live all on your own?' Clover asked.

'Oh, I'm pretty sure I won't be on my own!' said Imogen. 'I shall have lots of lovers!'

Clover and I gasped.

'Shh!' I said, nodding at Elsie.

'Well, I shall. I've had heaps of boyfriends already. Haven't you, Katy?' she said. She was asking in an irritating way, clearly expecting me to shake my head sheepishly.

'Yes, I've got a boyfriend,' I said.

Clover and Elsie stared at me.

'Really? What's his name? What's he like?' Imogen demanded.

'His name's Ryan and – and he's great fun,' I said airily.

'You haven't got a boyfriend called Ryan, you fibber!' said Elsie.

'Yes, she has!' said Clover. 'She told me all about him. She just didn't tell you because you'd blab to everyone.'

I felt like throwing my arms round Clover and hugging her. Besides, I wasn't *really* fibbing. Ryan had asked me if I would be his girlfriend. All right, I'd said no – but he'd *asked*. And all that mattered now was that Imogen was at last looking reasonably impressed. But still suspicious.

'A proper boyfriend? Have you kissed?' she demanded.

'Of course,' I said breezily. I was really fibbing now. I could feel myself blushing, but that made Imogen actually believe me. She started asking me heaps of questions and I had to elaborate as smoothly as possible, though I was getting really scarlet by then. I tried hard to make Imogen think Ryan was a hot-looking teenager, rather than a boy a head smaller than me with freckles and very untidy hair.

'What about *your* boyfriend, Imogen?' I asked as soon as I could.

'Oh, we broke up,' she said. She gave a great sigh. 'I was simply devastated. I don't want to talk about him now, I'll just get all upset.'

I peered at her. I wondered if perhaps she was good at making things up too. She started humming some pop tune about a broken heart, clearly expecting Clover and me to recognize it.

'Oh, I love that song,' I fibbed.

'Isn't she great on the video? That dance!' said Imogen. She stood up and presumably did an imitation. It looked like very X-rated dancing, though she was brilliant at it.

'Hmm!' said Elsie, wrinkling her forehead. 'My mum wouldn't let us do dancing like that.'

'Well, Izzie's an old fuddy-duddy, just like Dad,' I said. 'We can dance any way we want.'

I tried my best to copy Imogen, but I could tell it wasn't working.

'You look *stupid*, Katy!' Elsie cried.

'No, she doesn't,' said Clover, but she couldn't make herself sound convincing.

'Oh well, I know I'm rubbish at dancing. Cecy's the one who's brilliant at it,' I said. Then I stopped dead. I looked at my watch. It was nearly quarter to one now. Where on earth was Cecy? Why hadn't she come to the secret garden? She couldn't still be waiting for us, could she?

'Hang on a minute,' I said, and rushed out of the willow cave. I wriggled under the fence and rushed up to the garage. Cecy was sitting on top of the garage, her chin on her knees, looking agitated.

'Katy! *There* you are! I was getting so worried. Where on earth have you been – and where are the others? I've been waiting *ages*.'

'Oh Cecy! I'm sorry. I meant to leave you a message, but I forgot. We all went to the secret garden early. I thought you'd realize and come and find us,' I said, feeling dreadful.

'But why did you go without me?' said Cecy, climbing down.

'Well, I didn't *want* to, but this new friend Imogen came round. Clover and I met her in the park the other day and we wanted to show her the secret garden. You must come and meet her, Cecy.'

I held out my hand. Cecy slapped it away.

'No thanks,' she snapped.

'But you'd really like her. She's so grown up and ultra cool, and she's got this adorable little dog . . .'

'I don't want to meet her or her wretched dog. I'm going home,' said Cecy, and she marched over to the gate and let herself into her own garden.

Then when I wriggled miserably back to the others in the secret garden I saw Imogen using her phone, texting her dad.

He picked her up ten minutes later. She said goodbye nicely enough, but she didn't say she hoped to see us again. It was obvious, even to me, that she wasn't going to be inviting us round to her house any time soon.

Imogen clearly didn't want to be my new best friend. And it looked horribly as if I'd lost my dearest old best friend into the bargain.

10

I texted Cecy all that afternoon, but she didn't reply even once. So at four o'clock I went round to her house – not nipping through the back garden gate as usual but knocking formally on her front door.

Cecy's dad answered, a can of beer in his hand. I could hear Sky Sports playing loudly on the television in their living room.

'Hi Katy,' he said, not looking particularly welcoming.

'I'm sorry to disturb you, Mr Hall, but can I talk to Cecy please?' I asked humbly.

'Sorry, dear, she's out shopping with her mother,' he said.

'Oh! Do you know *which* shops?' I asked, wondering if I could get a bus into town and waylay them.

There was a sudden shout from the television.

'Oh no, I think I've just missed a try!' he groaned. 'No, I haven't a clue which shops.'

I trailed back home, feeling dejected.

'Never mind, Katy. I'm sure Cecy hasn't really broken friends,' said Clover, trying to be comforting. She was sitting cross-legged on the kitchen floor with Elsie, both of them making bead bracelets. 'Why don't you make her a bracelet to make it up with her?' she suggested.

'Cecy's got a whole armful of those bracelets already and she can make much fancier ones than me,' I said. 'She's the bracelet queen.'

I decided to write her a letter instead. I still couldn't find a proper pen, so I borrowed Jonnie's set of felt tips and wrote in rainbow colours.

Dearest Cecy,

I totally understand why you're cross with me. It was terribly mean to go to the secret garden without you. And it was a waste of time anyway, because Imogen wouldn't play at anything and turned her nose up at the picnic feast. She's nowhere near as nice as I thought she was. And even if she was extra-specially tremendously nice she could never be a patch on you. You're my best friend forever.

Please say you're still my friend too.

Love from Katy xxx

I drew a picture of me on my knees looking extremely contrite, begging Cecy to be friends with me again. I took particular care drawing Cecy, making her look extra pretty to flatter her. Underneath me I printed *Bad stupid Katy* and underneath Cecy I put *Lovely perfect friend Cecy.*

I put it in an envelope for privacy and posted it through her front door. Then I waited. And waited and waited and waited.

'What time do the shops close on Saturday?' I asked, when we were all sitting down to tea. It was our Saturday favourite, sausages and baked beans and jacket potatoes, but for once I wasn't gobbling mine down.

'Half past five – or maybe six,' said Izzie. 'Phil, don't spear your sausage like that. Cut it up properly like a sensible boy.'

'Then Cecy must be home by now! And yet she still hasn't texted! Oh, what am I going to do if I haven't got a best friend any more!' I wailed.

'You apparently acquired a new best friend only today,' said Dad. 'I'm sure Imogen is a charming girl when you get to know her, but she comes across as rather affected, wouldn't you say?'

'She has boyfriends and does very rude dancing,' said Elsie importantly.

'Then she doesn't seem at all a suitable friend, even though she's a St Winifred's girl,' said Izzie.

'Don't worry, I don't want her to be my friend. I want *Cecy* to be my friend and now she's not speaking to me,' I snivelled.

But at that moment there was a knock on the door. I ran to it – and there was Cecy on the doorstep, holding my letter.

'Yes, I *am* still mad at you!' she said, but then she put her arms round me. 'You total bozo. But I'm still your friend. I'm always your friend.'

'Oh Cecy!' I said, hugging her back.

We stayed hugging and exclaiming until Dad called, 'Why don't you two girls come in the kitchen? You need to finish your meal, Katy – and there's plenty for Cecy too.'

'Oh bum, *I* wanted second helps,' said Dorry.

'Dorry, please don't use that silly expression!' said Izzie.

Cecy and I looked at each other and laughed. Cecy stayed till bedtime, and she came over on Sunday too. We went to the secret garden, just the three of us, Cecy and Clover and me. I was a little worried that it would still look sad and ordinary, the way Imogen had made me see it, but once we were inside the willow cave, sitting squashed together in its green wavery light, the old magic worked.

I felt a little weird when Clover was busy telling Cecy all about Imogen, and what a drag she had been the whole time, so I crawled out of the cave and climbed my big faraway tree and sat on the branch. I swung my legs, and thought how wonderful it would be to have a proper swing. As soon as I'd got my tree house sorted I'd make a splendid swing too.

I remembered going to the swings with Mum and stared upwards at the blue sky and white clouds, wondering if there was really a heaven and she was up there somewhere.

She had got ill so quickly. It was hard remembering exactly when she got so sick that she had to stay in hospital. When we were taken to visit her she didn't seem like our mum any more. She'd lost all her lovely long hair and she looked pale and pinched, and she didn't even smell all sweet and rosy like our mum. But when she put her arms round me and hugged me tight I knew she was still our own dear mum inside. She whispered to me, 'I'll always watch over you, Katy.' I'm pretty sure those were her exact words. I remembered, because I was still young enough to get a bit mixed up and think she was talking about her wristwatch.

I fingered it now, then held it to my ear, listening to the steady *tick, tick*. It was easy to imagine it was saying, *I'm here, I'm here, I'm here.*

I stayed up in the tree until Clover and Cecy started calling me. Then I swung down and was ordinary laughing Katy again, though every now and then I covered the watch with my hand, hanging on to it tightly.

So from that day on, Cecy and I were even closer friends. We walked to and from school together and we strolled round at playtime with linked arms, and sometimes I went round to tea at Cecy's but mostly she came to us. Clover was with us too, of course, and part of everything – but the one thing she couldn't be part of was the leavers' disco.

It wasn't going to be a prom. Eva Jenkins and her little gang had campaigned determinedly for a real prom so they could all dress up in huge long frocks and prance around like princesses, but Mr Robinson put his foot down.

'Absolutely not! You're all eleven years old, not high school teenagers. We're having the usual disco. You can dress up a little if you want, but absolutely no ball gowns or fancy suits – and you come to school preferably on your own two feet, or in your parents' car. No stretch limos or Cinderella coaches with white horses or I'll turn you all into pumpkins!'

Eva and the other girls sulked. Even Cecy moaned.

'I've seen this glorious long pink dress, all sparkles, when I went shopping on Saturday. It had proper straps and was quite low cut, just like a grown-up ball gown,' she said.

I pulled a face but managed not to say anything, because I was scared of upsetting Cecy now. I suppose Cecy would look rather glamorous in a long sparkly dress, and maybe even the low neck would work, because she had started to get a little bit of a figure. I knew one thing: I would look totally ridiculous in a low-cut, long sparkly dress. I was flat as a pancake for a start, and I'd even look a sight from the back because my shoulder blades stuck out so sharply. And I was way too tall for a long dress. Even the longest would probably only reach down to my ankles.

'Mum says I can still have a new dress, even if it's just a disco,' said Cecy. 'So I thought I'd go for very short if I can't have long. And tight. And maybe still sparkly, so it looks good under the disco lights. What do you think, Katy?'

'Mmm. Yes. Yes, you'll look great,' I said.

'And what will you wear, Katy?'

'I don't know. My blue dress, I suppose. That's certainly getting very short now!'

'But you've had your blue dress ages. Don't you want something new?'

'I suppose,' I said, though I actually hated going to buy anything new. I could never find anything I liked and it was so embarrassing going in the changing rooms because I was sure everyone was staring at me. And I had to go with Izzie and she always fussed so.

'I don't expect I *can* have a new dress because Dad says we're a bit strapped for cash,' I said, improvising. 'Especially as I'll have to have all the new uniform when we go to Springfield.'

Thank goodness Cecy and I were going to Springfield secondary school together. For a while Eva Jenkins boasted that *she* was going to Kingtown High, a private school for girls, but then she changed her mind. Maybe she didn't pass the exam. But now she was coming to Springfield with all of us, worst luck. Ryan was coming too. I rather hoped we'd be in the same class. And it was a matter of desperate importance for Cecy and me to be in the same class of course.

I didn't even mention the disco to the family, but Izzie brought it up one day at supper time (bubble and squeak and fried egg).

'Only one more week of school,' she said.

'Hurray, hurray!' said Jonnie and Dorry together. They were going through an infuriating phase when they tried to say exactly the same thing at the same time. It was very irritating and also a little unnerving, because we couldn't work out exactly how they did it.

'I'm going to school, I'm going to school, I'm going to school in September!' said Philly. 'I'm a big boy.'

'Yes, you're going to nursery and you'll be a very big boy,' said Izzie fondly.

'Big boy, pig boy, oink, oink, oink,' said Dorry and Jonnie.

'That's quite enough of that. One more word out of either of you and you'll get down from the table and go without the rest of your supper,' said Izzie.

That shut them up. Going without supper was Dorry's worst punishment ever.

'How do you feel about leaving school, Katy?' Izzie asked.

'She's so lucky!' said Elsie. 'Mum, *why* can't I be home-schooled?'

'Oh, don't start, darling, please,' said Izzie. 'You're doing well at Newbury Road, I know you are. Your teacher says you're one of the brightest girls.'

Clover and I kept quiet. *We* knew why Elsie didn't like school. When Izzie married Dad and came to live with us Elsie had to swap schools. She came in the middle of a term, when all the other kids in her class had made friends. Elsie was the odd one out and she'd stayed that way. She didn't seem to know how to make the other kids like her. We sometimes saw her trailing round the playground by herself.

I felt my tummy clench at the thought, feeling sorry for my little sister even though I mostly couldn't stand her. I resolved once again to try to be kinder to Elsie. Perhaps Cecy and Clover and I might let her join in our playground games after all. I could even make up a game specially for Elsie. It would be easy enough to think of something silly and little-girly . . .

'Katy! I asked you a question,' said Izzie. 'How do you feel about leaving Newbury Road?'

I shrugged. I didn't really like discussing my feelings with Izzie. I didn't know how I really felt anyway. I was looking forward to being at Springfield (though a teeny bit apprehensive too). I didn't exactly love Newbury

Road Primary School. I'd been in quite a lot of trouble there over the years, and been sent to Mrs Henry the head in disgrace more than once. But I'd got so used to it too. I was even a little sad at the thought of saying goodbye to Mr Robinson, though he could be dead sarcastic at times and often told me off.

'Are all you Year Six pupils having some sort of leaving party or prom?' Izzie persisted.

'She's going to a prom over my dead body,' Dad said.

'Relax, Dad. You and Mr Robinson could be soulmates,' I said. 'He hates the whole prom idea too. It's a disco on the Friday night. No fuss.'

'I wish I could go too,' said Clover. 'Can't you take me as your partner, Katy?'

'Mr Robinson says we're not going with partners; we're just all going to mix together and have fun. Well, that's *his* plan. Everyone's pairing up anyway,' I said.

'And are you in a pair?' Izzie asked.

'No! I don't want to go with any of those manky boys,' I said quickly. I had rather hoped Ryan might ask me, even though we'd look ridiculous dancing together, with me so much taller than him. But Eva Jenkins had nabbed him for herself already. I certainly wasn't going to act like I cared.

'What are you planning to wear, Katy?' Izzie persisted.

'I don't know. My blue dress. Whatever,' I said. 'Can we change the subject, please? I don't know why everyone seems so fascinated by this whole lame disco idea. I don't care a jot about it.'

'I bet Cecy does. Isn't she going to have a new dress?' said Izzie.

'Yes, but she knows I'm not. I said we couldn't afford it because there are so many of us,' I said.

'Katy!' Izzie sounded outraged.

Dad choked on a forkful of bubble and squeak because he was laughing so much.

'How *could* you!' said Izzie.

'But it's true. Whenever I ask for an Xbox or a new bike or *anything* you always say we can't afford it, and that six children can't expect to have the same as a child in a small family. You *say* that!' I said.

'You do sometimes say that,' Clover agreed.

'We used to be a very small family, just Mum and me, and sometimes – *lots* of times – I wish we still were,' Elsie said.

'We're a small family of two: Jonnie and Dorry, Donnie and Jorry!' Jonnie and Dorry said, spluttering.

'I'm the youngest so I'm the best!' said Phil, banging his knife and fork on his plate.

'Stop it, Phil! You're *all* the best!' said Dad. 'And money *is* tight, I agree, but I still think we've got enough in the coffers to buy Katy a dress for this silly old disco. You look beautiful in your blue dress, Katy, a positive

159

rhapsody, but perhaps it's time to branch out in another colour. You've got a rainbow choice – red, orange, yellow, green . . .'

'Red! I want red! Oh please! Can I have a red dress?' I said.

'I don't think red's a very suitable colour for a young girl,' said Izzie, but she didn't argue any further.

We went looking for the dress after school on Thursday late-night shopping, just Izzie and me. It was strange being alone with her. It must have been so odd being Elsie, without anyone to play with for so long. I wished Clover had come along for the shopping expedition too.

Izzie led us to the Flowerfields shopping centre. She tried a fancy girls' shop first, just in case they had anything in a very large size. They had all kinds of sugary party dresses with great frothing skirts, but none remotely long enough. So then we went into a boutique for adults because they had all sorts of sparkly meringue dresses in the window bedecked in pink streamers, with a notice in gold wavery writing saying GIRLS! FIND YOUR PERFECT PROM DRESS HERE!

We went inside and Izzie asked if they had anything less ornate, and they brought out several slinky, silky numbers. They weren't red, but I rather liked them because they might just make me look grown up rather than simply overgrown.

'No, no, they're far too sophisticated!' said Izzie, horrified. 'She's only eleven years old!'

Then all the dinky little shop assistants tutted and twittered while I went bright red and felt like a freak. Izzie had a peer at the price tag on the least slinky dress and looked appalled.

She pulled us out of the shop and we went round and round the entire centre looking for a suitable dress. We couldn't find one anywhere.

'What are we going to do?' Izzie asked wretchedly, taking off one shoe and rubbing her sore toes on the back of her calf. She'd worn her highest heels and was bitterly regretting it. 'We've got nowhere! And you're going to need new shoes too. You can't wear your filthy shabby trainers or your school shoes with a dressy dress.'

'I won't have to, because I haven't got a dressy dress, have I?' I said. 'I'll wear my blue dress and I'll whiten my trainers specially, OK?'

'Oh Katy, I don't know what I'm going to do with you! I've tried so hard to be a good mother figure to you –'

'Well, don't try. Because you're not my mother and you never will be!' I said, and I stormed off. I ran right down the escalators, desperate to get out of the wretched place. I felt as if I were choking. If only I had my own mum back. She wouldn't drag me round stupid shops and make me feel dreadful. She wouldn't care what I wore. We'd have such fun together . . .

I leaned against the wall and squeezed my eyes shut to stop the tears spilling.

'Katy?' Izzie said, sounding out of breath. She must have run hard in her high heels to catch up with me.

I thought she might be cross, but she just squeezed my hand and said, 'Come on, let's go and have a drink.'

She had a latte and I had a mango and strawberry ice-cream soda, my absolute favourite. It was very soothing.

'You've got froth all round your lips,' said Izzie. 'OK, let's stop looking for party dresses. Let's go for something more casual. We'll try a couple more shops and then if we don't find anything we'll give up and go home. Deal?'

'Deal,' I said.

We went to TK Maxx and spotted a bright red flared skirt that I loved on sight. It came right up above my knees but still looked OK. I twirled round in it happily.

'We'd better buy you a pair of red pants too, just so you match,' said Izzie.

Then we went to Primark. I wanted a new T-shirt to go with the scarlet skirt, though Izzie suggested a blouse would look much better. We compromised on a T-shirt shaped blouse, black and sparkly.

'It's maybe a bit too sophisticated for you, Katy,' Izzie said doubtfully.

'But it will look good under the disco lights,' I said, remembering Cecy.

'Yes, it will,' said Izzie, surprisingly. 'All right. You can have your sparkly T-shirt. And I've had an idea about shoes. Come and look.'

She found a pair of basic black tennis-type shoes sewn with black sequins.

'There! Now you'll sparkle all over!' she said.

'Do you really think I'll look OK?' I asked.

'You'll look fantastic,' said Izzie.

She probably didn't mean it. But it made me feel good all the same. And when I dressed up in my new clothes on Friday evening I felt I truly didn't look too bad.

Of course I wasn't a patch on Cecy. She was wearing her own new outfit, a short shift dress with pink sequin flowers. She had white tights and new white shoes with kitten heels. They made her walk a little stiffly, like a clockwork soldier, but she still looked beautiful. She seemed especially pink and pretty – and then when I looked closer I saw why.

'You're wearing make-up!' I said.

'Only a little. A bit of foundation so I don't look too shiny, and pink lipstick. I've got it in my bag. Do you want to put some on?'

'Better not. I'll probably smear it all over my face.'

'Oh Katy, I'm ever so nervous, aren't you?' said Cecy.

'No, of course not!' I lied. 'It's only a stupid school disco with all our friends. And our deadly enemies! OK, what do you think Eva Jenkins is going to wear? A bikini top and the weeniest shorts and enormous high heels? All designer, naturally.'

We blinked hard when we saw Eva. She was wearing a hyacinth-blue dress, very showy with lace and frills.

She wore silver strappy shoes with proper heels and she had silvery glitter on her eyelids. Her hair was the most extraordinary part – she'd obviously been to the hairdresser's because it was sculpted into a huge mound on top of her head, with little ringlet twirls hanging down in front of her ears.

'OMG,' said Cecy.

'She looks like one of those American beauty pageant kids,' I said. I affected a totter and an American accent: 'Hi, you folks! I'm little Eva, and I'm *soooo* cute.'

It wasn't really funny but Cecy and I fell about laughing, which made us feel a lot better. It was strange going into the school hall and seeing it lit up with fairy lights, streamers dangling everywhere, and a big scarlet sash suspended above the stage saying GOODBYE AND GOOD LUCK, YEAR SIX! There was a proper DJ deck on the stage, and there was Mr Robinson, hilariously dressed up as a 1980s DJ himself, in a mad blond wig almost as bouffant as Eva's hair and a royal-blue sparkly suit with huge shoulders and rolled-up cuffs.

'You look amazing, Mr Robinson!' I said.

'So do you, girls,' he said, waving at us. 'Help yourself to cocktails and then when you've fortified yourselves I hope you'll grace the dance floor.'

Mrs Henry was serving the cocktails.

'Would you like a lemon sling or a yum punch?' she said, wielding a ladle in both enormous bowls.

One was lemonade with slices of baby oranges and glacé cherries, and the other was cola with cherries – both delicious.

'I'm going to make these cocktails for when we go to the secret garden tomorrow,' I said.

'You'll wait for me this time?' said Cecy.

'I will glue my bottom to the garage roof until you're done dancing,' I promised.

Cecy's dancing skills were wonderfully apparent at the disco. She was better than anyone else – *way* better than Eva. Even though lots of the girls and boys had come in pairs, everyone mostly danced in a great gang, which was much more fun. I felt a bit silly at first, wondering if I was shaking my arms and legs about in a mad way, but soon I got so caught up in the music I jumped about wildly and didn't care what I looked like.

The boys were mostly pretty useless dancers, but Ryan proved spectacular, ultra athletic and rhythmic. Several times everyone else stopped dancing to watch him, and then clapped spontaneously at the end of the song. Eva Jenkins smirked and sulked alternately, pleased that everyone was admiring her partner and irritated that he was grabbing all the attention.

Every now and then there was a slower, quieter dance and a few boy–girl couples ambled round the floor together self-consciously. Eva insisted on dancing with Ryan then, even once daringly putting her head on Ryan's shoulder.

'No smooching!' Mr Robinson called. 'Only Mrs Henry and I are allowed to dance cheek to cheek!'

They did actually have one very staid dance together, while we all wolf-whistled. Two boys in our class, called Keith and Alexander, came up to Cecy and me while we were dancing and started cavorting alongside us, so that we were sort of dancing together. I didn't mind too much because Keith's very tall, so we didn't look too ridiculous. It was fine while we were dancing, but in between dances Keith just muttered boring stuff about the bands he liked and where exactly each song had come in the singles chart. I nodded and smiled every now and then without bothering to listen.

The music got a bit wilder as the evening wore on. Mr Robinson played 'Bohemian Rhapsody' very loud, and everyone did the headbanging bit in the middle, which was fun, though we ended up feeling pretty spaced out and dizzy.

'I'm drunk,' said Ryan, staggering about.

'Stop acting stupid,' Eva said snippily. She was irritated because her elaborate hair had started to unravel after she'd tossed her head around to the music. She had to go to the cloakroom with a little gang of girls to try to pin it back into place.

'You come and have a dance with me, Katy,' said Ryan, taking hold of my hand.

'No, we'd look daft together,' I said.

'Who cares? Go on, I dare you,' said Ryan.

'You're Eva's partner, aren't you?' I said.

'Yeah, but she doesn't own me,' said Ryan. 'Come *on*.'

Mr Robinson started playing some old rock and roll number, the music making you want to jump around.

So I got up and started doing a mad jive with Ryan. I didn't really know what I was doing, but he was very good at swinging me round and pushing me into the right place. I felt dreadful for the first minute, scared everyone would stare at us and laugh, and I stumbled a bit and dithered on the wrong foot – but then the music got to me and my feet took over. I stopped caring about everything else and waved an arm and kicked a leg and whirled about, my new red skirt flaring out and my black sequins dazzling. Ryan grinned at me and I grinned back and wanted the music to go on forever and ever.

'That was great! I like the way you dance,' Ryan said, when the song stopped at last.

'I'm rubbish really. But you're good – very good,' I said.

'I'm really thirsty now. Let's go and get a drink,' said Ryan.

I peered round. No sign of Eva yet, thank goodness. And Cecy looked happy with Keith and Alexander. So I shrugged and nodded.

'You two are very good dancers,' said Mrs Henry, as she gave us our cocktails.

'Thanks, Mrs Henry. We are,' said Ryan. 'Come on, Katy.'

We went and leaned against the wall, sucking noisily with our straws. We both kept glancing at the door, watching for Eva coming back.

'I wish I was here with you,' Ryan muttered, not quite looking at me. 'You're much more fun, Katy.'

I *think* that's what he said. I couldn't hear exactly because the music was still so loud. It seemed impossible to ask him to repeat it. We stood there, nodding at each other every now and then.

'It's weird leaving school, isn't it?' I said.

'Springfield, here we come. Still, we've got the whole summer first. You going away anywhere, Katy?'

'Not till the end of August. We're going to this cottage in Wales, as usual. It's OK. Well, a bit boring. Nothing much to do.' I said this because I felt shy of telling him how much I loved waking up to the sound of the sea through my open window. I'd often get up before all the others, shove on a T-shirt and shorts, and then run barefoot along the beach, the very first person to put footprints on the sand that day. I loved swimming in the sea later, though it was always so freezing cold; I loved making sandcastles for the littlies; I loved ice cream every day and sometimes fish and chips out of the packet for supper; I loved looking up at the stars at night and imagining tiny, alien Katys looking back and waving.

'We're going to Spain, but not till August too. I mostly hang out at Baxter Park. Do you go there?' Ryan asked.

'Sometimes,' I said, though it was right the other side of town and I'd only been there once or twice, when I was Jonnie and Dorry's age.

'It's got a new skateboarding bit near the entrance. It's great. Do you like skateboarding, Katy?'

'You bet!' I said. 'I'm ace at it.' I *had* been, until Dad and Izzie confiscated my skateboard simply because I'd careered into Elsie by total accident and knocked her over. I'd meant to swerve at the last second, truly.

'And they've got those recumbent bikes – the ones like little cars that you pedal? Do you know what I mean?'

'No, but they sound really cool. I used to have a real little pedal car when I was small,' I said. I closed my mouth tight to stop myself blabbing about my mum.

'Then come over to the park next week and we'll go skateboarding and maybe have a bike race. Yeah?'

'Sure.'

'Monday, late morning.'

'It's a date,' I said, and we high-fived each other.

Then we saw Eva and her entourage returning, the famous hairstyle resurrected. We raised our eyebrows at each other and sloped off in different directions.

'Get you!' said Cecy, when I joined her. 'What were you and Ryan *saying*? You've gone as red as your skirt!'

'Wouldn't you like to know!' I said, and laughed.

11

We couldn't go to the secret garden on Saturday. We had a visitor. It was Dad's friend Helen.

We'd never met her before, not even Izzie, but we'd all heard about her. She was one of Dad's first patients, ages ago. She was in her teens then, but she couldn't run or dance or do any of the normal teenage things because she had rheumatoid arthritis. Not the ordinary sort of arthritis that old ladies get, when they hobble a bit and say their knees are giving them gyp. This was a full-blown arthritis that attacked her whole body, distorting her and practically snapping her head off her shoulders. She was in and out of hospitals, but when she was home Dad often visited her.

'She was such a fantastic kid,' he'd tell us, eyes shining. 'She'd moan sometimes – she was only human – and she could be bloody-minded in certain moods, but she had the most amazing courage and resilience. It was a privilege to know her.'

We'd listen to Dad's Helen stories, half fascinated, half bored. She was held up to us as an example, because no matter how ill she was she always studied hard and read difficult books and came top in all her exams. This made us thoroughly dislike her. She went to Cambridge University, wheeling herself to lectures and joining all sorts of societies, and she got a first, and stayed on to study further, and now she's Dr Helen Spencer. She's had academic books published, and always sends a copy to Dad: *To dear Dr Carr, with many thanks for all your care and encouragement. Love Helen.*

And now she'd sent an email to say that she'd been having treatment for her lungs at the Brompton Hospital in London, but was feeling much better now, and it would be lovely if she could meet Dad for a coffee before she went back to Cambridge. Just a coffee. But Dad invited her to stay with us for the whole weekend!

For once Izzie was completely thrown.

'For goodness' sake, Alistair, you could have asked me first! I don't know how on earth we're going to manage an invalid in the house,' she said.

'Oh, lighten up, Izzie. Helen's not an invalid! She'd hate it if you tried fussing round her. Just treat her like any normal guest,' said Dad.

'She uses a wheelchair, doesn't she? She won't be able to get upstairs, but she'll have to sleep somewhere. And what about when she uses the bathroom? It's all very well for you to invite her, Alistair, but *I'm* the one who has to rearrange everything and try to cope. You're impossible at times!' Izzie stormed off to see if she could possibly get a single bed into the little library room downstairs.

I didn't know what to think. I was usually pleased the rare times Dad and Izzie quarrelled. I hated it when they were all lovey-dovey together because it seemed such an insult to Mum. But this time I couldn't help feeling on Izzie's side.

We didn't want this saintly academic ill person to come here either, especially as we couldn't go off and play. We all had to have a bath and wash our hair (Clover and me supervising the littlies) and be dressed in our best, waiting for Helen to arrive at eleven o'clock. I wanted to wear my new red skirt and black sparkly T-shirt but Izzie perversely said they weren't suitable and insisted on the blue dress.

Dad rushed off to fetch Helen from the station. We crowded to the living room window to get a first glimpse of her when she arrived.

'She uses a wheelchair. Dad said,' said Jonnie.

'Hasn't she got any legs?' asked Phil.

'Yes, but they don't work,' I said, wondering fleetingly what it must be like to be stuck in a wheelchair all the time.

I tried to imagine what Helen would look like. I pictured her as a little fierce figure with scraped-back hair and glasses, maybe even wearing a black academic gown.

The real Helen was a revelation. She looked wonderful, a little like a tiny Cleopatra, the Egyptian queen. She had long shiny black hair in a pageboy bob and big brown eyes made even larger by dark eye make-up. She wore a green silk dress and silver sandals showing her toenails, which were painted bright blue. She had a silver seahorse pendant round her neck and bangles on each small arm. If you looked closely you saw her fingers couldn't work properly any more, and she was of course in a wheelchair, but she looked so dynamic it was hard to realize she'd been very ill.

'Oh, I've been waiting ages to meet all of you!' she exclaimed. She held out her arms to Izzie. 'Hello! You're just as beautiful as Alistair said!'

Clover and I bristled a little, because Izzie wasn't beautiful at all, nowhere near as naturally lovely as our own mother, but I suppose it was a tactful thing for Helen to say.

Then she looked at me.

'So you're Katy, the eldest!'

I waited for her to say something about my height. Everyone did when they met me for the first time.

'You're the one who makes up stories and gets into scrapes. You're a girl after my own heart! Come and give me a hug,' said Helen.

I was a little afraid of hugging her, just in case I hurt her in some way. But her arms were strong around me so I relaxed and hugged her back. She smelled of wonderful perfume, orangey and exciting. I hoped a little of it would rub off on me.

Dad must have told her all about us, because she didn't once have to be told who we were.

'Hello Clover. Look at your blue eyes! I bet you can wind your dad right round your little finger.'

'You must be Elsie. You're so delicate, just like a little fairy.'

'Hi Dorry! What are we having for lunch today, hmm? I hope it's your favourite meal.'

'Hello Jonnie. I'm longing to meet all your family, especially Zebby.'

'Come and sit on my lap, Phil. I'll give you a ride up and down the path in my wheelchair. We'll go as fast as a car and you can pretend to be the driver.'

In less than five minutes we felt as if we'd known and loved Helen all our lives. We all clamoured to talk to her. Dad had to help manoeuvre her wheelchair into the house and park her in the living room by the big sofa, so we could all squeeze on to it and chatter properly. The littlies kept running to fetch their favourite treasures to show her. Jonnie of course dragged Zebby

174

down from her bedroom and Helen stroked him solemnly and admired his stripes. Dad and Izzie sat with us and attempted proper conversation with Helen. They tried to shoo us away several times, but we were determined to stick to Helen's side.

Izzie got up reluctantly to go to the kitchen to start preparing lunch.

'I'll help, Izzie,' Helen said immediately. 'I'm surprisingly good at chopping vegetables and mixing salads even though I have hopeless hands, and I love stirring sauces. Please let me come.'

We ended up all trooping into the kitchen, even Dad, because we didn't want to miss a moment with Helen. Clover and I usually whined and made a fuss if we had to help Izzie, but now we rushed around happily like little under-chefs. Helen suggested Elsie set the big kitchen table for everyone, as she knew she'd be really careful with the china and glasses.

So Elsie started laying the table, with Jonnie and Dorry in charge of the knives, forks and spoons. Phil wanted to help too, though he kept getting in the way and dropping things, so Helen eased him on to her lap again and gave him a raw carrot to nibble.

'You don't have to help, Phil, because you're a little rabbit now and you're eating your favourite food,' she said, stroking his curls.

Phil twitched his nose like a rabbit and said, 'I'm Bunnyhop!'

'I think you'd better move in with us permanently, Helen,' said Izzie. 'You've certainly got a magic touch with the children.'

'Ah, but I don't have to be with them all the time,' said Helen. 'I don't know how you cope with six, Izzie, but you're clearly doing a grand job.'

Helen had the knack of paying everyone compliments, but in such a sincere merry way it didn't sound at all smarmy. She was like a splendid fairy godmother waving her wand for all of us.

She even turned a simple meal like fish pie and broccoli into a positive feast. She talked all the while she ate, including the littlies in everything, and she managed to get picky Phil to eat the very first sprig of broccoli of his life and declare it delicious. It was fruit and ice cream for pudding, and she had us all inventing new flavours. Dad and Izzie joined in happily, though we all thought their ideas (single malt and marmalade ice cream?) pretty lame. Dorry invented the most elaborate flavours, as you can imagine. Some were totally disgusting (roast potato and crispy pork crackling ice cream!) but occasionally they had potential (lavender and honey ice cream or banana and plum jam ice cream).

We wanted lunch to go on forever, but Dad said Helen had to have a rest.

'I'm not in the habit of taking a rest, Dr Carr!' she said.

'A rest from all the children, at the very least,' said Dad. 'Izzie's prepared you a room downstairs, and there's a shower in the downstairs loo, so consider it your own personal bathroom while you're here.'

We were curious to see how Izzie had turned the library into a bedroom. I had a peep into the room while Helen was in the loo. Izzie had put several piles of books against the wall, so there was plenty of room for Helen's wheelchair. She'd declared that Phil could sleep with Dorry in Dorry's bed for just one night, and taken Phil's bed downstairs, making it up with the pretty rose-patterned sheets she used for Elsie. She'd put a little table near the bed, with a pretty white lamp in the shape of a lady and a glass vase filled with roses from the garden. She'd cleared two low shelves of books, and set out a stand-up mirror just at the right height for Helen. There were three padded coat hangers hooked on to the other shelf and space for Helen's extra clothes too.

I had to admit that Izzie had done a marvellous job of turning the library into a lovely guest room for Helen. She was good with Helen too, quietly asking if she needed any help lying down on the bed.

'You're totally spoiling me, Izzie. You are a dear,' said Helen, cheerfully accepting her help and making it easy for everyone.

I badly wanted to stay and help as well, but I got shooed away with all the others.

'You can go and play now if you like,' said Dad.

We didn't like. We wanted to be there the minute Helen emerged from her room. Cecy came round, curious to see our visitor too. When Helen came out at three o'clock, hair freshly brushed and smelling of her wonderful orangey scent, we proudly introduced her to Cecy.

'You girls are so lucky to live next door to each other,' said Helen. 'When I lived with my parents there were just elderly couples on either side, and though they tried to be kind to me they were very off-putting.' She did a wicked imitation of them shaking their heads over Helen and clucking their tongues. 'They thought it such a shame I was practically crippled and expected me to be pathetic and saintly, like the little invalids in Victorian storybooks.'

'Didn't you *mind* being crippled?' Elsie asked.

'Elsie! You mustn't say that word!' I said, giving her a shove.

'No, no, it's fine, Katy,' Helen said quickly. '*I* used the word after all. And yes, of course I minded, Elsie. I still do. But I try hard not to think of all the things I can't do and concentrate on all the things I can.'

'Like being ever so clever,' said Clover.

'Well, cleverness is often just a willingness to work hard,' said Helen. 'And I absolutely love reading, so it's no hardship for me to pore over books.'

'We all love reading too – Katy most of all. She even reads some of Dad and Izzie's books now because she's read all her own,' said Clover.

'Then you're obviously very clever too, Katy,' said Helen.

I beamed at her, feeling a great golden glow.

'Oh no she's not!' said Elsie. 'She's always in trouble at school and I know for a fact that her teacher moaned about her to Dad last parents' evening.'

'You shut up, Elsie, you little tell-tale!' I said indignantly.

'Hey, hey, girls! Would you like me to read to you now?' said Helen. She looked round the shelves. 'Where are your own books? Run and bring me your favourites!'

We thought Dad the best storyteller in the world, but Helen proved the best storyteller in the entire universe. She read us picture books first, to keep Phil and Dorry and Jonnie amused, and we found we loved hearing them too. When she read *Where the Wild Things Are* she turned us all into wild things, roaring our terrible roars and showing our terrible claws, and when she came to the wild rumpus part she had us doing a mad dance all around the room.

When she read *The Tiger Who Came to Tea* she pretended to be the tiger and whizzed round the room in her wheelchair eating everything in the cupboard and drinking all Daddy's beer with a great smacking of lips and tigery growls of appreciation that made us all roar with laughter.

Dad came in to see what we were all laughing at, and then he joined in and found an old battered copy of a Just William book, *his* favourite when he was a little boy.

'You read it, Helen,' he said, and he sat cross-legged on the carpet, as if he were still a little boy now.

Helen was exceptionally good at William's voice, magically turning herself into a ten-year-old boy with tousled hair and falling-down socks, but she was positively brilliant at being Violet Elizabeth Bott with her lisp and her ferocious scream.

Izzie crept into the room too, and as soon as she finished the William chapter Helen turned to her.

'Now, Izzie. You have to find *your* favourite children's book,' she said.

'Well, I've always loved *Little Women*,' she said.

Clover and I groaned. Izzie kept trying to make us read it but we'd resisted so far.

'It's such a lame title and it's so goody-goody,' I said. 'I've read the first chapter and it's awful. Those sisters have to give up their entire Christmas dinner to feed a poor family and then the only Christmas present they get is a Bible!'

Dorry gasped at the idea of anyone having to go without Christmas dinner.

'Let me read you my favourite chapter,' said Helen.

She read about Jo, the tomboy sister, writing a story and Amy, the youngest, throwing it in the fire. I listened, my face burning, because Jo sounded quite a lot like me, and Amy seemed as annoying as Elsie. Then there was a very dramatic part where they go skating and Amy very nearly drowns and Jo feels dreadful.

I decided it was actually a really interesting book after all, and when Helen finished reading her chapter I asked if I could have it to read myself. Izzie looked quietly triumphant.

Then Helen asked to go in the garden for a while, so Dad carefully helped ease her wheelchair out through the French windows. She admired all the flowers, making Dad beam, because he loved his garden and spent hours out there pottering about.

She even managed to be complimentary about our children's patch at the end. Dad had cleared a small bed specially for us, and I'd been ultra enthusiastic at first, determined that we'd grow a wonderful red garden, full of roses and poppies and geraniums and salvias and sweet williams and fuchsias and dahlias. I could see them all blooming hotly when I closed my eyes. I wanted them to be there altogether, all at once. I found it boring, digging the earth and then fiddling around with seeds and bulbs and tiny weeny bushes. I didn't always remember to water them all and I didn't see the point of thinning out the little green shoots, because I wanted a mass of flowers.

The littlies lost interest too because they'd wanted to grow food. Dorry was particularly keen on growing bananas, and even I knew that wasn't possible in chilly England. So Izzie suggested they grow mustard and cress on an old flannel. I can't say anyone liked the taste of mustard and cress, even Dorry, but at least their gardening project was a success.

Mine wasn't. Only a few of my flowers *flowered*, and then they got attacked by slugs or snails and wilted, all-over holes.

Dad tried not to say 'I told you so'. He'd given us all this boring gardening advice and we hadn't really listened. But now Helen looked at the sad, weedy patch and the fuchsia that had actually managed to flourish and said she absolutely loved fuchsias with their bright, drooping heads. My own head stopped drooping and I felt pleased that I hadn't managed to kill off absolutely everything in my garden.

We had a lovely tea with egg salad sandwiches, home-made scones and raspberry jam, walnut cake with white icing and chocolate biscuits, all our favourites. Helen declared they were her favourites too, and begged Izzie for her scone and jam recipes.

Then we decided to watch a DVD all together and there was a huge discussion about the right film, but eventually Helen chose an ancient old Disney movie about a little elephant called Dumbo.

We all squashed up on the sofa to watch, but I sat on the arm next to Helen's wheelchair so I could be the nearest to her. I hadn't watched *Dumbo* for ages and ages. I was enjoying it quite a lot, until Dumbo gets separated from Mrs Jumbo. She's put in a cage and Dumbo can't get at her, though there's a heart-stopping moment when they manage to twine trunks.

I suddenly went hot at the thought of little Dumbo's mother torn away from him, and I couldn't stop the tears spilling down my cheeks. We'd drawn the curtains in the living room so it was dark and I managed not to sniff. I hoped no one would notice. But Helen's hand reached out and gripped mine and squeezed sympathetically.

Cecy was most reluctant to go home at bedtime. It took a long time to herd the littlies upstairs, and Elsie tried to hang on to Helen, wanting to curl up on her lap like a little cat. While Dad and Izzie were tucking them up, Helen said softly to me, 'You must still miss your mother very much, Katy.'

'I do, oh I do!' I said.

'I do too!' said Clover.

'Did you know I met her once?' said Helen.

'Really? When? Did you like her?' I asked eagerly.

'I loved her. Your dad and your mum came to visit me in Cambridge. I took them for lunch in the college and then we went for a stroll together. Well, they strolled, I wheeled. Your mum was the most amazing person to go on a walk with. She kept spotting little things that anyone else would miss – a weird gargoyle on an old building, two cats sitting on a windowsill like bookends, a very elderly couple punting on the river, maybe reliving their youth. She make up little stories about everything.'

'Yes, she did, she did! I remember her doing that too,' I said.

'Yes!' said Clover.

'She looked so young too, not really old enough to be married. Your dad clearly adored her. His whole face lit up as he looked at her.'

'I bet Dad misses her terribly too, though he hardly ever mentions her now,' I said.

'It's because he has to be tactful with Izzie,' said Clover.

'It must be hard for Izzie, being a second wife,' said Helen. 'She's lovely too, but in a different way.'

'She's OK because you're here, but she doesn't half nag and moan at us sometimes,' I said. Then I felt mean and oddly disloyal. 'But I suppose she does her best. And we can be a bit difficult. Especially me!'

Helen laughed. 'I can't believe that,' she said.

Clover and I were allowed to stay up half an hour past our bedtime so we could talk to Helen, but eventually we had to go up to bed too.

'I think Helen is my favourite grown-up person in the whole world,' said Clover. 'I wonder if she'd let me have a dab of her perfume tomorrow? She smells so lovely.'

'I love her necklace, the little silver seahorse. I love *her*. Oh, I'm so glad she's staying till tomorrow evening!'

*

I woke up quite early on Sunday morning. I wondered if Helen might be awake too. Perhaps I could take her a cup of tea? I crept out of the bedroom, careful not to wake Clover, and made my way stealthily downstairs. But Izzie was already in the kitchen stirring muesli and chopping fruit.

'Oh! *I* wanted to make breakfast for Helen!' I said.

'What – pancakes?' said Izzie.

I crumpled.

'Sorry, Katy, that was mean,' said Izzie. 'Look, come here and cut the peaches. Only for pity's sake don't cut your fingers off too. I can't face another four hours in A & E.'

I started cutting a peach but Izzie had given me a very blunt knife and I made a bit of a mess of it, practically having to squash the peach into submission. Izzie didn't say anything. She didn't have to.

'OK, I know I haven't made a good job of it,' I said, licking peach juice from my fingers. It then ran all the way up my arm inside my pyjama sleeve.

'Perhaps you'd better eat that one,' said Izzie. She was busy creating a beautiful pattern of fruit over a bowl of muesli with a white Greek yoghurt topping.

'Oh, that looks pretty,' I said, munching.

'I thought I'd make Helen a breakfast tray. Then she can have a little lie-in if she wants, rather than deal with all of us at once,' said Izzie.

She was using the best willow-pattern blue-and-white china on a bright blue enamel tray. She set it with the decorated muesli, a glass of orange juice and a cup of tea.

'Should I put a tiny vase on too, to make it look pretty?' Izzie wondered. 'Run into the garden, Katy, and pick one of the roses. Take the secateurs from the bag hanging on the door so you can cut it off neatly.'

I found the secateurs and went out the back door, on to the lawn. I was barefoot and the grass was wet, but I rather liked the feeling. Tyler was out there, running around happily after being let out for his morning wee. He wanted to play, so I threw an old ball for him until I heard Izzie calling impatiently.

I went to the rose bush – but then saw the fuchsias, Helen's favourites! I carefully cut off a small stem so that she could have a whole mass of bright, drooping flowers. I thought how pretty and original they would look on the bright blue breakfast tray and ran indoors happily.

'Whatever have you got there?' Izzie sounded impatient. 'I sent you out to get a *rose*, for goodness' sake. Can't you tell the difference between a rose and a fuchsia?'

'Yes, of course I can, but I happen to know Helen vastly prefers fuchsias. They're her very favourite flowers. So let's put them on her tray.'

'You don't generally put fuchsias in vases.'

'There's no law against it, is there? Look, they're really pretty.' I stuck the fuchsias in the glass vase. They didn't look quite as pretty as I'd hoped. They were a bit too top-heavy for the small vase. I saw that a single rose would have looked much better, but I wasn't going to back down now. And Helen would see that I'd remembered her remark and be pleased.

I seized the breakfast tray before Izzie could argue with me further. I hurried out into the hall with it, along the passage to the door of the library. My arms ached a little, but I held the tray steady, carefully balancing it so the fuchsia vase wouldn't tip. I didn't have a free hand to knock on Helen's door, so I tapped on it quietly with my foot.

'Come in,' Helen called, sounding wide awake.

I was so eager to see her I didn't set the tray down on the floor to open the door. Tyler had come bounding after me and might put his head in the bowl for a lick of the yoghurt. I held on to the tray with one hand and cautiously reached for the door handle with the other. I got it open, but then somehow the tray started tipping. I jerked it quickly, trying to save the vase of fuchsias, but it teetered and then fell, cold water and little flowers going everywhere.

'Oh!' I cried, so shocked that the whole tray slipped from my grasp and landed with a smash on the floor.

'Oh goodness, is that you, Katy? Are you all right?' Helen called.

'Dear Lord, Katy, what have you done now?' Izzie came running from the kitchen.

I sank down beside the spilt tray and started sobbing.

'I *told* you to be careful!' said Izzie. 'Well, run and get a cloth, for goodness' sake.'

I tried to mop up the mess but the water had sloshed everywhere.

'Look, I'd better do it,' said Izzie. 'You go and apologize to Helen!'

I crept mournfully into Helen's room. She was propped up on her pillows, smiling at me so sympathetically.

'Oh Katy! Were you bringing me my breakfast?'

'The vase tipped! It was the fuchsias – I picked them because you said they were your favourites. Now I've made such a mess. I'm so hopeless!' I wailed.

'Never mind. You were just trying to be kind to me. And anyone can drop a tray. I'm forever dropping things,' said Helen.

'Yes, but that's because your poor hands don't work properly,' I said.

'Well, my arms can still give good hugs. Come here!' Helen held out her arms and I ran to her and wept on her shoulder. I was hugely taller than Helen but in her arms I felt as little as Phil.

'There now. I dare say Izzie will be kind enough to make me another breakfast. Perhaps you can ask for a breakfast tray too and then you can tuck up beside me and we'll keep each other company.'

Izzie made another beautiful bowl of muesli for Helen – and one for me too. 'Though you don't deserve it!' she said, shaking her head.

It was bliss to sit on the bed beside Helen and talk together. I told her a bit about school and she agreed that Eva Jenkins sounded a royal pain, and that Ryan was good fun.

'Will you go to this park with the skateboard ramps?'

'You bet I will, though I'll have to get round Dad and Izzie first, because they confiscated my skateboard. I so miss it. I just love that feeling that you're flying along . . .' I suddenly stopped, realizing I wasn't being tactful.

'Don't look so worried, Katy. I sometimes wish I could do all sorts of things, but skateboarding isn't high on my list,' said Helen, laughing. 'Now, you scoot for a bit while I get myself washed and dressed.'

'Can I help in any way?' I asked eagerly.

'I'll manage. I think you'd better sort out the children. There's a lot of thumping on the stairs!' said Helen.

It was Jonnie in her Spiderman pyjamas dragging Zebby all the way downstairs. Dorry was bumping himself down on his bottom behind her, step by step. Phil was whizzing up and down on his kiddy scooter on the landing, stark naked, with his pyjama trousers on his head.

'Jonnie, are you mad? You're bashing all the paintwork. Take Zebby back!' I said.

189

'No, he wants to come and have breakfast with Helen!' Jonnie insisted.

'Well, he's not allowed.'

'Zebby doesn't like you any more,' said Jonnie, and she poked me with one of his legs. 'There, he's kicked you now!'

'Ouch. Stop it! And Dorry, get up, you'll bruise your bum, you little silly.'

'I'm working out how to get downstairs if your legs don't work, like Helen's,' said Dorry.

'And I'm *being* Helen,' Phil called. 'This is my scooty wheelchair and this is my lovely long hair . . . Look!' He stroked his pyjamas coyly.

'You're all total little nutcases,' I said, but I couldn't help laughing at them.

I was in such a good mood now that I encouraged them all back upstairs and supervised them getting washed and dressed. Clover was awake now and I told her about the unfortunate mishap with the tray.

'But Helen was extra-specially lovely about it and she says I can come back when she's got washed and dressed to help her in any way.' She hadn't exactly said this, but I so wanted her to that I believed it.

'Oh, can I help her too?' asked Clover.

I struggled. I always loved sharing everything with my special sister, but I wasn't sure that included Helen, who in one day had become the most important person in my world.

Clover was gazing at me wistfully with her beautiful blue eyes.

'Of course you can,' I said. 'But just us. Not Elsie or the littlies. There's not room for everyone to cram into her room, and I'm sure Helen wants a bit of peace.'

But when we went downstairs, steering the littlies towards breakfast in the kitchen, we found that Elsie was already in Helen's room, actually brushing her shining black hair with a silver-backed hairbrush.

'Elsie, what on earth are you doing here! You mustn't disturb Helen. Go and get washed and dressed at once,' I said.

Elsie pouted.

'Helen *said* I could come in. She wanted me to. And she likes me doing her hair, don't you, Helen?'

'Yes, I do, darling,' said Helen cheerily. 'You're making a very good job of it too. You're better than a proper hairdresser. I'm so lucky to have three lovely girls at my bidding! Clover, could you possibly find my perfume spray and give me a little squirt on my wrists? And Katy, I know you have nimble fingers. Could you put my little silver seahorse chain round my neck and fix the clasp for me? That would be wonderful.'

Elsie nodded at me triumphantly, brushing carefully. I'd have normally been infuriated, but Helen was too clever at distracting us all. Clover sprayed perfume and was allowed a little squirt herself. She kept sniffing her own wrist ecstatically. The seahorse necklace was very delicate and the clasp a difficult one, but I managed to do it up first time.

'I think I need to take all three of you home with me,' said Helen.

'You're not going home already, are you?' Elsie wailed. 'I want you to stay and stay and stay forever.'

'Well, I'm staying until late afternoon,' said Helen. 'And now we're all such good friends, perhaps your father might drive you all to Cambridge to see me sometime?'

'Oh, that would be wonderful!' I said. 'You ask him for us, Helen. You seem to have the knack of making everyone do whatever you want!'

Helen did ask him, that morning, and he smiled at her happily and said he'd love to bring us all, so long as it wouldn't tire Helen too much.

'And perhaps you can do one little favour for me while you're here?' he said. 'I'd love you to meet a small patient of mine, a little boy called Archie who's been very ill with rheumatoid arthritis. His parents have been pretty despairing. I'd give anything for the family to meet you for five minutes, just so they see you can still lead a full, worthwhile life living with the after-effects.'

Helen agreed happily. We all wanted to come too, not willing to lose even a few minutes of time with Helen, but Dad wouldn't let us.

'It's not fair. I know they'll be much longer than five minutes. Dad always takes ages with his special patients,' I grumbled.

'That's what makes him such a good doctor,' said Izzie. 'Now, I have an idea. Why don't you all use this time to make a special card for Helen, telling her how much you've enjoyed her visit?'

Just occasionally Izzie has good ideas. I got my drawing pad and generously tore out a page for everyone. I even folded it carefully in two for the littlies. Then we all sat at the kitchen table drawing and colouring with Clover's nearly new set of felt tips that she got for her tenth birthday.

Phil finished his card first. It was a portrait of Helen, though it was hard to distinguish her from all the other people he drew. He just did a round blobby body containing eyes and a nose and a smiley mouth, with stick arms and legs – but he added a big scribble of black felt tip on top, to indicate Helen's hair. He can't write properly yet, so inside his card I printed

To Helen,
Love from

and then he scrawled an approximation of *Phil*, with a huge capital P and lots of dots over the i for good measure. Then he commandeered the felt-tip box and rearranged all the colours and got ratty when we needed to use one.

Dorry's card was inventive – and food-orientated. It said down one side

Dear Helen,
I love you
more than . . .

and then down the other side he drew all his favourite foods: turkey and roast potatoes and ice-cream cones and boxes of chocolates and cupcakes and cookies.

Jonnie drew a picture of Helen sitting on Zebby, with a speech bubble coming out of Zebby's mouth:

I only let two people sit on me – Jonnie and HELEN!

Elsie drew a picture of herself and Helen going for a walk together hand in hand, and underneath she wrote in her cramped little writing

We are Best Friends aren't we.

She's not very good at drawing. Dorry and Jonnie are heaps better than her, though they're much younger.

Clover drew an absolutely magnificent card and coloured it in beautifully. She's the only one of us who managed a real likeness of Helen. She even did a perfectly proportioned wheelchair with wheels that looked really on the ground, somehow remembering exactly what it looked like. She didn't try to include herself in the picture, but she did an artful frame all round the card edge of little four-leaf clovers. She wrote inside

To dear Helen,
With lots of love and luck
from Clover

I felt my own card looked very childish by comparison. I'd tried to draw Helen as a fairy godmother, thinking along the lines of Glinda in *The Wizard of Oz*, but my version of Helen looked more like the Wicked Witch. I kept making her nose too long and pointy and then rubbing it out, so that the paper went all smudged. I wrote inside

You are a truly magical person, Helen,
and I've so enjoyed your visit,
Love from Katy xxx

but this seemed a bit of a silly message too. I wondered about starting all over again, but I heard Dad's car drawing up outside and there wasn't time.

The visit had been a big success. Helen had bonded with little Archie, Dad's patient, and had promised to stay in touch.

'You'll stay in touch with us too, Helen, won't you?' said Elsie.

'Of course,' she said. 'I consider all of you practically family. And I've got presents to prove it!'

She'd stopped off at the shops with Dad on the way home and had a bulging carrier bag. There was a big bunch of beautiful blue flowers – irises and agapanthus and blue-pink roses – for Izzie and a bottle of wine for Dad. Then there were three cuddly toys for the littlies, each carefully chosen. Phil had a lion with a smiley face and a lovely soft mane; Jonnie had a zebra cub with big eyes, a baby for Zebby; Dorry had a bear with a big fat tummy that growled when you squeezed it.

Clover and Elsie and I looked on rather anxiously. We were all hoping we might have a cuddly toy too, though I was certainly way too old for such things, and probably Clover was too. The carrier bag was empty. Perhaps Helen thought we were too old for any kind of present.

'I wanted to give you three something special,' Helen said. 'Come into my bedroom with me.'

We jostled with each other eagerly and then stood before her in the library.

'Elsie, I'd like you to have my silver hairbrush. You've got such pretty hair. You brush it every day as carefully as you brushed mine,' said Helen.

I had to swallow hard to stop myself crying out with envy. Helen was giving her beautiful silver brush to *Elsie*! She clasped it to her chest and declared she loved Helen forever.

'Now you, Clover,' said Helen. She reached for her bottle of perfume. 'I thought you might like some perfume. But promise – just *one* squirt each day!'

'Oh Helen, how absolutely lovely! It's the most beautiful smell in the world. And every time I spray I shall think of you,' said Clover, pink in the face with joy.

Helen turned to me.

'Now Katy. What have I got left to give you?' she said.

'You don't have to give me anything, Helen,' I said quickly. 'You can't give away all your pretty things. And I'm hopeless anyway. I'd lose your hairbrush or spill your perfume, you know what I'm like.'

'I do know what you're like. You're a dear, loving girl who can be ultra careful when she tries. Look how deft you were with my necklace. So I'd like you to have it. Can you take it off for me and put it round your own neck?'

'Oh Helen! Oh, I can't take your beautiful seahorse necklace!'

'Yes, you can. I'd love you to have it,' said Helen.

'Then I shall treasure it forever!' I said.

12

I woke early again on Monday morning and lay
happily thinking about the magical weekend with
Helen. I reached out for the silver seahorse necklace
on my dressing table and let it run through my fingers.
I perched the seahorse on my nose, squinting at it,
stroking its little curves.

As soon as I sat up I clasped it round my neck and
went and peered it at in the mirror. It looked so lovely.
I felt a flood of fresh gratitude to Helen. I hoped Dad
would take us to visit her really soon. Meanwhile it was
the start of the summer holidays and I had six glorious
weeks before I had to think of school. I did a little
dance around the room as I made plans, whirling fast
so that the seahorse bobbed up and down, dancing too.

'Hey, you're shaking the floorboards!' Clover murmured sleepily from under her duvet. 'It's too early to get up. Go back to bed.'

'I don't want to! It's the holidays, Clover. I'm making all sorts of plans. Come on, sit up and we'll make a list together of all the things we want to do.'

'Number one on my list is get more sleep,' said Clover, and she wouldn't budge out of her cocoon.

'OK, see if I care,' I said. I decided to make number one on my list a trip to Baxter Park. Only I had to find my confiscated skateboard first.

I went downstairs and started rootling around in the cupboard under the stairs where Izzie sometimes stuffed forbidden things. I sorted through hundreds of welly boots and a toddler trike and a big coil of old washing line and boxes of broken stuff still waiting to be mended, but there was no sign of my skateboard.

'Who's in the cupboard?' Izzie called sharply. She peered inside. 'Oh Katy, I might have known. What on earth are you doing? Those wellingtons were all in neat pairs and now you've mixed them up!'

'I'm looking for my skateboard,' I said.

'We took it away from you. You can't be trusted with it. You really hurt Elsie,' said Izzie.

'I wasn't aiming at her deliberately. She just got in the way,' I said.

'Katy, I'm not getting into an argument at seven o'clock in the morning. You can't have your skateboard back and that's that. Just learn to take no for an answer,' said Izzie.

'But it's *my* skateboard. And I *need* it. I want to go skateboarding with Ryan in Baxter Park,' I said.

'You're not going skateboarding with any boys. You're not going skateboarding at all. Now stop this nonsense and put all the things back in the cupboard. Not like that! *Neatly.* And what have you got round your neck?'

'It's Helen's necklace. She gave it to me, you know she did. You're not going to steal that too?'

'Don't take that tone with me. And stop using ridiculous words like "steal". I'm pleased for you that Helen was so generous – if a little misguided. You know what you're like. You'll either break it or lose it by the end of the holidays. Why don't you keep it carefully in your treasure box and just wear it on special days?'

'I want to wear it all the time because it's so lovely. And today *is* special, the first day of the holidays, and if only you'll stop being so mean I want to celebrate by going to Baxter Park. I'm not taking Elsie with me, so you needn't worry that your precious little darling will get knocked over. I'm not even taking Clover. For once in my life I want to do something by myself. And I'm going to! You can't stop me. You're not my mother!'

There was a little silence. Then Izzie said quietly, 'Sometimes I wish I wasn't even your stepmother.'

She walked away and went into the kitchen. I had one more scrabble in the assorted rubbish but still couldn't see my skateboard. I picked up the discarded washing line, momentarily distracted. The rope was frayed at the ends, but it still seemed reasonably strong. I might be able to fashion some sort of swing for my tree house. I tucked it under my pyjama jacket and smuggled it up to our bedroom.

Clover was getting dressed.

'What are you doing with all that rope?' she said.

'You wait and see.' I sighed dramatically. 'Perhaps I'll hang myself with it. Izzie's being so mean to me. She won't let me have my skateboard back. She won't even tell me where it is. She just wants to spoil all my fun. Well, I'm going to ask Dad. No, wait. *You* ask Dad, Clover. You're much better at getting round people. Would you do that for me? Make out you're desperate to learn to skateboard?'

'So that you can then go off and hang round Ryan Thompson and all those boring boys in your class?' said Clover. 'What do you think I am?'

'I think you're my lovely, sweet, angelic sister who won't mind doing me just this one little weeny favour,' I said, putting my arms round her. 'And you can come with me and I'll show you how to skateboard and you'll probably be a total whizz at it, much, much better than me. Go on.'

'Then promise you'll make bracelets with me this afternoon?'

'Oh Clover, you've got armfuls of those silly bracelets already. But all right. If I must. *If* you get the skateboard.'

So at breakfast Clover nestled up to Dad, telling him how happy she was that the holidays had started. She smiled at him and he squeezed her hand and then sniffed her wrist. Clover had sprayed herself with Helen's perfume. Dad pretended to be overcome by the smell, while Clover giggled.

'I'd really like to do heaps of different things this holiday, really make the most of it,' said Clover. 'I was thinking I ought to take more exercise. Don't you think I'm getting a bit chubby, Dad?'

'I think you're just right, darling, but I'm all in favour of exercise.'

'I want to ride my bike more. Maybe go swimming. And try something new too. *I* know . . . *skateboarding!*'

Izzie stopped wiping Phil's mouth and frowned. But Dad was oblivious.

'That's a good idea, so long as you're very careful, and wear a helmet and knee pads. We've got some somewhere.'

'Yes, we have,' said Izzie. 'We bought them for Katy. And then we confiscated them. And it's perfectly obvious to me that this is a set-up job. Clover's not the slightest bit interested in skateboarding. She's just trying to get the skateboard for Katy. We've already had words about it this morning.'

'Oh dear,' said Dad, looking reproachfully at Clover. 'You little minx! You had me totally fooled. Sorry, girls, I think skateboarding is off limits. But tell you what, I do think swimming is a brilliant idea. I don't have a clinic this afternoon. I'll do my best to be home by two and I'll take you all swimming at the leisure centre.'

Everyone cheered. I was sort of pleased too. I liked swimming and I especially liked it that I was the best at it. I didn't mind playing with the little kids too, giving Phil piggybacks and showing Dorry and Jonnie how to kick their legs and breathe underwater. But it still rankled that I couldn't have my skateboard back. It had been my birthday present. It was *my* property. It was so mean of Izzie not to let me have it back.

I decided I'd go over to Baxter Park anyway and see if Ryan would let me take turns with his skateboard. I wouldn't ask Izzie. She was bound to say no. I'd just slope off by myself. Well, perhaps I'd go with Clover. I wasn't even one hundred per cent sure where Baxter Park *was*, and whether you could walk it or needed to catch a bus. If Clover came too we could figure it out together.

But Clover for once proved obstinate.

'No way! Dad and Izzie would go berserk. They *said* you weren't allowed to skateboard.'

'They said I couldn't have my own skateboard back. That's entirely different. Go on, Clover, come with me. I'll make bracelets with you this afternoon,' I wheedled.

'You're making them with me *anyway*, because I asked Dad for you. And besides, we're going swimming with Dad now,' said Clover.

'Oh please, Clover. We can just slip away. Izzie might not even notice. She'll think we're playing in the garden.'

'Izzie's not daft. She *will* know and then when we come back we'll be in big trouble. We might not be allowed to go swimming. We might not be allowed to do *anything* for the rest of the holidays,' said Clover.

I knew she could be right. But I was now in such a mood that I didn't care.

'OK, I'll go by myself,' I said.

It was easy enough to slip out of the front door while Izzie was doling out Play-Doh for the littlies to model. I did go and call on Cecy though, to see if she fancied coming. She quite liked Ryan, and there would be lots of his mates there too.

But Cecy was all dressed up when she came to the front door, with her hair done in an extremely fancy style.

'Sorry, Katy, I can't come. We're going round my auntie's and we're trying out this new hairstyle for when I'm her bridesmaid in September. Do you like it?' Cecy asked.

I thought it made her look even sillier than Eva Jenkins but I knew it wouldn't be tactful to tell her this. I made some lame complimentary remark and then trudged off down the road. I was starting to wonder if it was a good idea to go to Baxter Park after all. I might have had a much better time playing with the kids at home. I could just go straight back. Izzie would never know I'd gone. But then I'd look such a fool in front of Clover. I needed her to stay thinking I was her big bold sister instead of a silly little wuss who couldn't even go to a park by herself.

I walked on determinedly, swinging my arms to try to make myself feel good. When I was a little kid I loved doing 'soldier' walking, muttering *left, right, left, right* as I marched. But when I got to the shop on the corner I saw what an idiot I looked, like a comedian deliberately doing a silly walk. I tried doing a sexy model walk instead, but that was even worse – and two horrible scruffy little boys yelled 'Wigglebum!' at me. I tried to walk normally, but I seemed to have forgotten how.

I concentrated hard on making up an imaginary game inside my head. I pretended I was a famous celebrity and I was being filmed for a documentary, and people were asking me all sorts of questions about my lifestyle. That was fun for five minutes but even that game got tiresome. So I resorted to my oldest comfort game of all – pretending my mum was walking along by my side, talking to me.

She took hold of my hand, her fingers laced with mine, swinging our arms, and told me that she thought skateboarding was fun, a totally excellent thing for a girl to want to do, and that she'd never ever ever take my skateboard away from me. In fact, she'd beg me to let her have a go too. No, she'd get her own skateboard and then we'd have our own private skateboard championship.

I miss you, Mum, I told her.

I miss you too, my Katy, she said.

Do you know the way to Baxter Park, Mum?

Haven't a clue – but don't worry. We'll just keep walking and I'm sure we'll get there soon.

So that meant neither of us had a clue. I asked several people, but they either didn't know or said we ought to take a bus; and that was no use, because we didn't have any money.

We walked all the way through the town, marching straight past all the shops.

I'm so glad you're you and not Izzie, Mum. She's so boring when we go into town. She wants to drag me round all these awful clothes shops.

Well, she's a drag, full stop, said Mum. *Still, we should be grateful to her, I suppose. She's looking after you and my little Clover. Though I wish she wouldn't keep telling you off. I keep suggesting she should lighten up, but she won't take any notice.*

That's because she can't hear you, Mum. No one else can, not even Clover.

Not even Alistair? said Mum, sounding disappointed.

Just me, I repeated firmly.

Then you're my most special girl, said Mum.

I made her say it a lot. I even hummed it to a little tune I made up. But I still didn't feel quite comforted enough. I was getting tired now and I wasn't even sure how to find my way back into town, let alone all the way home.

I found I was clinging to the little seahorse round my neck, as if it were a tiny talisman.

Which way, which way, which way? Mum and I chanted.

I was so busy talking to her that I started crossing a road without realizing and a car screeched to a halt, almost hitting us. I jerked in terror. I must have given a sharp tug to my necklace because the seahorse suddenly swung free, the broken chain slithering from my neck.

'Oh no! Oh no, no, no!' I exclaimed.

'Oh yes, you idiot girl! Watch where you're going or you'll get yourself killed!' the driver yelled.

I staggered to the other side, clutching the broken necklace tight in my hand. I couldn't see properly because my eyes were all blurry with tears. Mum wasn't with me any more. I didn't have the energy to spirit her back. I couldn't be bothered to look for Baxter Park now. I just wanted to walk backwards ten minutes in time so that my necklace would still be intact.

The seahorse wasn't broken. It was just the delicate links on the chain. I could save up my pocket money and get a new chain. But I probably wouldn't be able to find an exact replica. And it wouldn't be *Helen's* chain any more. I'd spoilt it, just as Izzie had predicted.

It took forever finding my way back again, though I wasn't in any hurry now. I put the broken necklace in my pocket. It was the lightest thing and yet it seemed to weigh me down. I kept thinking of Helen's sweet expression when she gave it to me. It kept making me cry all over again.

But I scrubbed at my eyes and tried to look cool when I got home. I let myself in as quietly as possible with my key. Clover came creeping up the hall to meet me.

'Did she miss me?' I hissed.

Clover nodded glumly. 'Almost straight away. I fibbed for a bit, said you'd gone to play with Cecy, but you know how uncanny Izzie is. She knew straight away I was talking rubbish. She guessed you'd gone to Baxter Park. I'm so sorry, Katy.'

'Oh well. Thanks for trying anyway,' I muttered.

'Was it worth it? Was Ryan there? Did he let you use his skateboard? Did you have a great time?' asked Clover.

I couldn't bear to lose face with Clover. It would sound so lame to admit that I hadn't been able to find it.

'Yeah, truly great,' I said. 'It was super cool to be on a skateboard again.'

'And you could still do it OK? You didn't fall off?'

'Of course I didn't. I was way better than all the boys,' I started, but decided to amend this. Some skateboarding boys were much older than me and able to fling themselves off ramps and turn somersaults in the air *and* get back on their skateboards. Clover might be gullible, but she'd never swallow that. 'At least, better than Ryan and the other boys in my class,' I added.

Then Izzie came out of the kitchen into the hall, wearing her boot face.

'So you've decided to come home, Katy,' she said. 'I gather you went to Baxter Park after all, even though I said you weren't allowed.'

I decided I wasn't going to hang my head and beg her forgiveness. I hadn't done anything really wrong, for goodness' sake. I'd just tried to join some friends in the park. It wasn't the most heinous crime of the century.

'Yes, it was great. Thanks for asking,' I said, trying to sound airy and cool, though I sounded like Dorry in a grumpy mood.

'Well, it's just as well you enjoyed yourself, because you won't be going on any other little jaunts for a long, long time. You are grounded for a whole month,' said Izzie. 'And don't think you're going swimming this afternoon. You can stay at home in disgrace by yourself.'

'Dad will let me come,' I said.

'I very much doubt it. He was very angry when I phoned him at the surgery and told him,' said Izzie.

'Oh, trust you to tell tales on me!'

'What am I supposed to do? I was worried sick. You didn't have a helmet or knee pads or anything with you. You could have had a serious accident.'

'But I didn't, did I?' I said. 'So sorry to disappoint you.' I started stamping my way upstairs.

'Katy? Where's Helen's necklace? Weren't you wearing it this morning? Oh, don't say you've lost it already!' Izzie's tone was sharp.

'No, I haven't lost it, see,' I said, putting my hand in my pocket and bringing it out, careful to keep the broken ends of chain in my palm. 'I was just putting it away for safekeeping.'

I hid it in my treasure box when I was in my room. I held my photos of Mum for a little and had another small weep, but then I put the box away. I just lay on my bed with my head buried in my pillow.

I wished I could start the day all over again. I'd wake up in a sweet mood and be kind to everyone, even Elsie, and when Dad came home he'd put his arm round me and say he was really proud of me.

I heard him come in downstairs. I stayed in my room. I wondered if he'd come up and see me. I planned to fling my arms round his neck and try to explain – but he stayed downstairs.

'Well, see if I care,' I said to myself. I did care dreadfully. I could go running down the stairs, of course, and tell him I was sorry. But I'd have to apologize to Izzie too, and I couldn't bear to do that.

So I stayed where I was, even though I could hear everyone in the kitchen, obviously starting lunch. Then when I did hear footsteps it was only Clover, bringing a tray of food for me.

'It's tomato soup and a cheese sandwich,' she announced. 'And Izzie's made a giant chocolate Swiss roll too, but she says you don't deserve a slice. I tried to smuggle you half of mine, but Izzie saw.'

I said a very rude word to describe Izzie.

'Hmm!' said Clover, giggling.

'Is she still going to stop me going swimming?'

'I'll try to get round Dad,' said Clover. 'Surely going without yummy Swiss roll is punishment enough?'

'You sound like Dorry!' I said.

I ate my soup and sandwich and tried not to care that I didn't have any cake. The children downstairs were quieter now, and I heard Dad's voice talking and talking. I realized he was telling them a story. I felt horribly left out.

Then at last, while the kids were rushing round grabbing old towels from the airing cupboard, Dad put his head round my door.

'Ah. The child doing penance! Dear goodness, what am I going to do with you, Katy?' he said.

'Can't I really come swimming, Dad?' I asked.

'No, I don't think so. Not this time,' he said.

'Just because I went to the wretched park! I thought you *liked* us going out and having fun,' I wailed.

'I do, but not when you've been expressly forbidden to go out. Surely you can see how silly that is. You can't go waltzing off whenever you feel like it. It's a very bad example to the others. *You* might be fine trotting all over the town, but imagine if little Elsie took it into her head to copy you and go out by herself.'

'I wish she would,' I mumbled.

'That's not funny. I'm tired of your silly attitude and your hostile remarks. That's the main reason I'm not letting you come swimming. I can overlook your going to the park, but I'm not having you being so incredibly rude to poor Izzie.'

'She's rude to me,' I said defiantly. 'She's forever nagging at me and telling me I've done things wrong.'

'She's got every right to tell you what to do. She's your mother.'

'*No, she's not!*' I shouted. 'She's only my horrible stepmother and I wish, wish, wish she wasn't!'

Dad shook his head at me and walked away. They all went swimming. They didn't even say goodbye to me.

I sprang up and thumped our bedroom wall in fury, but I just hurt my hand. I prowled round and round the room, muttering wretchedly to myself, and nearly tripped over the big coil of rope in the corner. Then I knelt down beside it, thinking about my tree in the secret garden. I felt instantly calmer.

That was where I was going to go while they were all off enjoying themselves without me! I'd have just as good a time all by myself. I'd make myself a swing.

I wound the rope round and round me in a business-like fashion and strode purposefully downstairs. I seized one of Izzie's sharp kitchen knives in case I needed to cut the rope to the right size. I went out into the garden, down the lawn, past the apple tree to the special burrow under the hedge.

It was hard to wriggle through while all bound up in rope, but I made it. I held the knife carefully, blade away from my body. I could be incredibly careful when necessary. Then I staggered to my feet in the secret garden.

I felt better immediately. I liked being there by myself. I didn't have to sort the littlies out and deal with Elsie. I didn't even have to share with Clover. I could just be myself. I could make up anything I wanted. I could lie in solitary splendour under the willow or dance about the tangled flowers or climb my own huge tree.

I peered up at the tree, holding the rope in both hands now. Yes, there was a long, straight, high branch which would be perfect. I just had to work out how to fashion my swing. I needed some sort of seat, didn't I? I peered round hopefully, looking for a flattish log or a broken piece of fence, but could find nothing suitable. Still, if I were to let any of the others share my swing they might fidget on this sort of seat and end up with splinters in a very uncomfortable place.

I wasn't sure how to attach the rope safely to a seat anyway, and I didn't have anything to drill holes. Dad had a box of household tools but he kept it locked, with the key in his own pocket. I knew, because I'd tried to borrow the odd screwdriver or pliers in my time.

I decided my swing had better have a more elementary design. I could tie one end of the rope to the branch and then let it dangle. I could grasp it and swing backwards and forwards like Tarzan, King of the Apes. *Oh yes!* I felt myself flushing with excitement. It would be marvellous.

The branch was quite high up of course. I'd have to hang on tightly. It would probably be too difficult and dangerous to let the littlies have a go. I couldn't even trust Elsie not to let go and fall. This would be a swing reserved for Clover and Cecy and me.

I wound the rope back round me and started climbing the tree. It was hard work trussed up like the Michelin Man, but I was good at climbing. I got to the biggest branch and straddled myself across it. I felt deliciously dizzy looking down. I was really high up. I was going to have the most fantastic swing. I realized it might be a bit tricky climbing back up again, but I knew how to climb a rope. I'd manage it, easy-peasy, but maybe Cecy would struggle. Clover definitely would.

Well then, this was going to be a swing just for me. I wound the end of the rope round the branch and then set about tying a good firm knot. I knew it should be a reef knot, but couldn't quite remember how to do it. Was it left over right or right over left? But how could you do a reef knot with just one end? I did the best I could, tying one knot, then another, and then another. I tugged hard and it held perfectly.

I breathed out happily, my arms all goosebumps with anticipation. I edged back along the branch to the main trunk, hanging on to the rope. I climbed down just a little bit. My hands were slippy with sweat so I took turns wiping them one at a time on my jeans, then clasped the rope tightly in both hands – and pushed off.

Ooooooh! I swung gloriously swiftly through the air, taking off as if I were flying, further and further, and then I jerked all the way back again in a fantastic swoosh. I went forwards, backwards, higher and higher, learning how to push with my knees and propel myself. It was such a wonderful feeling, soaring and swinging, as free as a bird. I remembered Mum pushing me on the swings in the park when I was very little.

Look, Mum, I'm swinging again! Come and swing with me!

And then suddenly I was jerked sideways, the rope horribly loose, and I screamed as I realized it had somehow come untied. I was flying through the air for real, tumbling over and over, and then I landed with a terrible bone-shaking thud.

13

I woke up and stared up above me in total confusion. The ceiling of my bedroom had disappeared. The entire roof of the house had blown away. I was staring up at blue and green and brown. My eyes were blurred, but after several blinks I sorted out these colours into sky and leaves and tree trunk.

I gazed at them for several seconds, trying to make sense of my surroundings. I could hear something strange too. Something raspy and scared, like some small creature caught in a trap. Was it Tyler?

I tried to call him. The panicky little sobs stuttered and broke. It was *me*. Why was I crying? Was I hurt? Then, immediately, I was aware of the most terrible pain in my head, my neck, my shoulders, my arms, the whole of me. It was as if a hundred giants had marched all over me, smashing and squashing every little piece of me.

Giants? I knew they were only in storybooks. So what had really happened to me? I tried very hard to remember, but there was a roaring in my head and I couldn't manage to grab at any facts. I clenched my fists, trying to will myself to think straight, and realized I was clinging to something. It was long and snake-like and I couldn't make sense of it. I knew it wasn't a real snake because it was lifeless and dry. I felt little fibres with my fingertips and palms. It felt like rope.

Rope! I suddenly remembered flying through the air while clutching the rope. It was my swing. My swing – and it had broken. And now I seemed broken too.

I lay still, feeling my heart thudding violently. I needed help. Why was I on my own? Where were all the others? Had they run to fetch Dad?

'Clover?' My voice worked now, but it came out like a whispery croak. I tried again. '*Clover?*'

I listened. Nothing. I couldn't believe they'd leave me on my own. All by myself. The words echoed in my head. Maybe there was a reason? But my head ached so badly I couldn't remember. I hurt so much. I wanted to crawl back to my own house and lie down in my own bed. I tried to sit up but I couldn't move. *I couldn't move!*

Was it the rope, tying me to the ground? Was something else lying on me? What was happening?

I strained again. My arms flailed but I couldn't get a grip on anything. I tried to dig my elbows into the grass beneath me and lever myself up that way, but my head was too heavy. I started sobbing again, even though this slight drawing of breath made me hurt even more.

I remembered all the times in the past when I'd played dead with Clover and the littlies. It was generally when I'd had a fall like this one, a way of coping with the embarrassment of it all. Instead of groaning and crying I'd lie very still, eyes shut. They'd run to me, calling my name, begging me to wake up. I'd wait until their screams got a little too high-pitched and then I'd suddenly bob up, making them gasp and then pummel me in delighted fury.

I shut my eyes now, pretending to be dead, hoping that when I willed it I'd be able to leap up laughing, but when I tried I was still stuck fast. I seemed stuck in time too. My head hurt too much to think logically, but I knew I was very cold and I certainly seemed to have been lying here on my back for a very long time. *Was I dead already?* Perhaps this was what death was like. No bright lights or beautiful heaven. I'd fallen from the tree and killed myself and now I was going to have to lie here forever, reliving the moment of my death for all time.

But that would mean Mum was trapped in no-time too, but she was a free spirit, watching over me at all times, able to keep me company whenever I badly needed her.

Mum? I don't know whether I said it out loud or simply cried it in my head. She'd been with me while I was swinging through the air. Why hadn't she caught me? Why hadn't she stopped me when I was tying those stupid knots? Why had I done such a stupid thing when I *knew* I wasn't making a proper, safe swing?

Perhaps this was all some terrible dream to help me see the consequences of my actions, a dream that might have been manufactured by Dad and Izzie to teach me a lesson. I'd had really convincing nightmares before, when I'd been left in charge of the children and I hadn't taken care of them properly and awful things had happened to them. I'd wake up sweating, so convinced it was real that it was only when I crawled into bed beside Clover and held her tight that I'd calm down and realize it had just been a bad dream.

This was the realest dream I'd ever had, and yet maybe it was simply my overworked imagination and guilty conscience. Perhaps I was really in my own bed, dreaming after I'd cried myself to sleep. If I only willed it hard enough I could wake up and be back in the ordinary afternoon, and I'd run downstairs the moment I heard footsteps and the children's clamour and I'd be back being Katy again.

I squeezed my eyes tight shut, counted to a hundred, and then made a supreme effort to open them properly. Not to see this static dream world of sky and tree. I must strain back to the real world of my bedroom. I knew

I could do it if I just tried hard enough. I strained and strained, feeling the sweat spring out on my forehead, but the leaves stayed rustling above me.

Please! Please, help me!

Then someone said, 'I'm coming. I'm coming!'

It was a strange, whispery voice, the sort of voice we assumed when we were trying to scare each other playing ghosts.

I listened, wondering if I'd imagined it. Then I heard a weird scraping, tapping, scraping sound, slow but constant: *tap s-c-r-a-p-e, tap s-c-r-a-p-e*. What was it? It was getting closer and closer. I tried to move my head again to see what was coming for me. I saw nothing for a few seconds – and then a metal leg, several legs, and feet, old-lady feet in very old tartan slippers, the sides cut out to accommodate the twin bulges of bunions.

It was such a homely detail I knew once and for all that this had to be really happening.

'Oh my dear!' It was Mrs Burton next door. Well, I *was* next door, trespassing in her garden. I needed to get up and run away, but I was pinned on my back like a butterfly in a glass case.

She was gasping, her paper-white face almost comically horrified. She swayed as she clung to her Zimmer frame, as if she were about to fall herself.

'I'm sorry, Mrs Burton. I didn't mean to frighten you,' I gabbled. 'I'm Katy Carr from next door. I know I shouldn't have been in your garden.'

'I know you're Katy. Oh my Lord! Have you hurt yourself badly?'

'I – I think so. I know it sounds so stupid, but I can't seem to get up.' I struggled again, but she stopped me with a cry.

'No! No, lie still! They always tell you to lie still after a fall. It's was on *Holby City*. I saw you fall. I was so worried when I saw you fixing the rope. I banged on my window but you can't have heard me,' said Mrs Burton. She was so agitated a little froth of saliva gathered in each corner of her mouth and then dribbled. 'Oh dear, oh dear, I should have stopped you! You poor, poor child!'

I was terrified by her reaction. I wanted her to clap her hands and shout at me, tell me to stop play-acting and get up at once. She was behaving as if I'd done something dreadful to myself, something far worse than a few bumps and bruises.

'I must run and fetch your father,' Mrs Burton said.

Poor Mrs Burton couldn't possibly run anywhere, but she manipulated her Zimmer frame with painful slowness to face the other way, and then set off, dragging it at each step. *Tap s-c-r-a-p-e, tap s-c-r-a-p-e.*

'No!' I shouted hoarsely, suddenly remembering. 'Dad's at the swimming pool, with all the others. And Izzie. There isn't anyone at home.'

'Then I will phone for an ambulance,' said Mrs Burton. 'That's what I have to do. Ring 999 – that's the number. Now don't you move a muscle, dear. Keep still as still and I'll go and phone for help.'

'Then will you come back?' I begged her. I knew she was just a sick, helpless old lady but I was so frightened of being left by myself now.

'Of course I will,' said Mrs Burton. She pressed her lips together determinedly, and set off for her house.

I started to shiver, which surprised me because I could feel the sun hot on my face. Perhaps it was because I was scared. Had I really, really hurt myself? I'd always got better before. Dad said I was like a cat with nine lives. I'd had countless falls. I'd sprained my wrist once, broken my ankle another time. It had hurt a lot, but not like this. I'd been able to hobble back to the house. Couldn't I really move at all now? I was desperate to have another attempt at getting up, just to see if I could, but Mrs Burton had been emphatic that I should lie still.

My nose was running because I was crying, but I didn't even dare raise my arm to wipe it. I just lay there, and endless hours seemed to go by. I wondered if Mrs Burton had forgotten all about me by the time she got back to the house. I tried to work out when Dad and the others would be back from swimming. How would they know where I was? Clover would guess, surely. Oh how I wanted Clover now, to hold my hand and tell me I was going to be fine.

I thought of her swimming up and down in the pool, gliding on a float when the wave machine was switched on, turning somersaults in the shallows, with Elsie and all the littlies. And I could have been with them, larking around.

I moaned out loud.

'Oh dear, does it hurt so badly, you poor girl?' It was Mrs Burton returning – *tap s-c-r-a-p-e, tap s-c-r-a-p-e* – calling out to me anxiously. 'The ambulance is on its way. I've left my front door open and told them to come out into the garden.'

'Oh, thank you, thank you,' I said weakly.

'I wish I could sit down beside you, dear, but if I get down on the grass I'll never get up again. My silly old arthritis! If only I could have stopped you swinging on that rope! I'll never forgive myself if you're really hurt. I've always loved to watch you and your sisters and brothers playing all your games in the garden.'

'I didn't know you knew we were there.'

'Mr Burton and I never had any children. All that big house and long garden and no one to play in it! So it was delightful when you kiddies started coming. So many little ones! I get them a bit mixed up, but of course I know you and Clover. You won't remember, but you used to come to tea with Mr Burton and me.' She went on and on, talking about those long-ago uncomfortable visits, telling me what she used to give us to eat, remembering the pink and yellow fancies they gave us for a treat.

It was weirdly surreal, lying flat on my back with rockets still going off inside my head while she stood

223

swaying above me, talking about cake. It was too much effort to keep murmuring politely. I shut my eyes and then I was swinging again, up in the air, and Mum was with me . . .

'Katy? Katy! Don't doze off, dear. It's very important you stay awake. That's another tip I've learned from the telly. You must keep talking to me. What television programmes do you like? I think *Pointless* is a lovely programme; do you ever watch that? What are those two men called? Oh, I always forget a name. Come on, dear, you tell me. I'm sure you know. Or tell me about children's television. Did you know, it was only on for an hour when I was a little girl? And oh how I loved those programmes! *Whirligig* with Humphrey Lestocq and Mr Turnip – now I *can* remember *their* names – and little Jennifer, the announcer. Oh, she talked so nicely! Children did in those days. Do you remember her? No, of course you don't. It was years before you were born; years before your *mother* was born.'

I still had my eyes shut, but I started listening properly.

'Tell me about my mother,' I murmured.

'Oh, a lovely girl, truly a gem. Such a tragedy that she left us so soon. I used to visit her, you know, when she started getting so sick, and she was so brave, chatting away, quite the ticket. But one day she burst out crying and said, "What's going to happen to my poor babies?" It made me cry too. I felt so sorry for her. There . . . I'm getting choked up now. Talk to me, Katy. You remember your mother, don't you?'

Of course she remembers me!

Mum was back, shaking her head in fond exasperation at Mrs Burton's prattling. She knelt beside me.

Come on, poppet, up you get. You'd better come with me. That's the way. My goodness! We're the same height now, you and me.

She pulled me upright and gave me such a hug. It was wonderful feeling her arms round me, so strong, so warm, so undeniably there. I was standing up, the pain was all gone, I was all right after all, perfectly fine.

'Oh Mum, I thought . . . I thought I couldn't even walk!'

'You will walk, Katy, I'm sure you will, but you mustn't try to move now. Keep still. I'm sure the ambulance men will get here any minute.'

Why was Mrs Burton still talking to me? Mum and I had strolled up the garden together arm in arm. I could hardly hear her now.

'There now, love. Keep very, very still. We're just going to pop these foam blocks round your head and neck – that's the way. Oh, what a brave girl.'

What was happening? Who was this? Why were they fussing so? I was fine, couldn't they see? I was with Mum and everything was going to be all right. I didn't want them to keep pulling at me. They were dragging me back.

'Oh Lordy! Has the poor little kiddie broken her back?'

'It's too soon to say. Are you Grandma?'

What were they talking about? As if anyone as old and sad and decrepit as Mrs Burton could possibly be my grandmother! And what were they doing? They were feeling me carefully! And now they seemed to be sliding something hard under my back.

'No, no, don't do that!' I said. 'Stop them doing it, Mum.'

But none of them seemed to hear me now. I couldn't even hear myself. I was flying through the air again, and I couldn't hang on, and I was falling, falling, falling . . .

14

K aty.
   Katy?
   Katy!

So many voices, all of them talking to me.

I felt I was so many Katys.

I was Katy the eldest, organizing all the others, playing games. I was Katy the best friend, giggling and whispering with Cecy. I was Katy at school, chatting to Ryan, sneering at Eva Jenkins. I was Katy with Helen, helping to look after her. I was Katy with Dad; little Katy sitting on his lap. I was Katy with Mum; me in my little red car, Mum running along beside me, laughing. I was laughing too, laughing and laughing.

No, I was crying and crying.

'Poor darling. Here, let me wipe those eyes. There now. We'll give you something for the pain.'

Yes, pain. My head. My back. It hurt so much at the top of my spine that I screamed.

'They've given you morphine, baby. It will make you feel nice and woozy very soon, I promise.' It was Dad, real Dad.

'But you're swimming,' I mumbled.

'Mrs Burton was waiting at her front door to tell us, bless her. God, what a shock you've given us all!'

'Are you very cross with me?'

'Oh darling. No, I'm not cross. Not cross at all. And I'm going to stay here with you now while they X-ray you and give you a CT and an MRI scan,' Dad said, stroking my cheek.

I couldn't understand why he was talking in letters. I didn't know what he meant. But it was enough that he was with me.

'And Mum? Is Mum here too?' I asked.

He paused. He was standing, bending over me so I could see his face. It suddenly creased up, as if he were trying not to cry.

'Dad?' I said, really frightened. I'd never seen Dad cry in my life. I wanted to hug him. 'Let me out of this thing round my head!' I begged, but my words wouldn't come out right.

So I asked Cecy and Ryan, I even asked Eva, because they were all round me, chattering and laughing but taking no notice of me whatsoever, and then they turned into nurses who pushed me in and out of machines. One was a really scary machine like a never-ending tunnel, and I couldn't move, I couldn't see; I could just hear really loud thumps and rattles and I couldn't tell if they were inside or outside my head.

Then at last I was free and in the air again, real air, outside.

'Dad! Dad, am I going home now?' I asked, desperately hoping this was true.

'Not yet, darling. They're transferring you to a special paediatric spinal unit.'

'To a . . . what?'

'A special hospital for children with bad backs.'

'But my back isn't *bad*.' Izzie had a bad back sometimes. She'd hurt it when the twins were little, lumping them in and out of their buggy, and it still played up now. She had a little, hard, black cushion to put behind her back when she sat on the sofa, and when it was really bad she ate paracetamols like Smarties.

'I'm not old like Izzie,' I said.

'Oh Katy. Izzie's not old. Though we're both feeling positively ancient right this minute.'

'Old-man dad,' I said.

'Yes, very-old-man dad. You're a bit out of it, sweetheart, now the morphine's kicked in. Oh Katy, darling . . .' Dad screwed up his face and then bobbed back, out of my sight.

229

'Dad? Dad, don't go!'

'I'm not going anywhere, sweetheart. I'm right here, beside you,' said Dad. His voice was thick. He *was* crying.

'Dad – Dad, I am going to get better, aren't I?' I asked.

He murmured something. I couldn't hear him properly.

'Dad, please! Promise me I'm going to get better,' I repeated.

'They're going to try their hardest to make you better, my special girl,' said Dad. He stroked my face again, outlining my eyebrows and nose and lips as if he were drawing me. I lay still, liking the distracting tickling feel on my face. The roar inside my head had dulled. The pain in my back was still there, but not quite so sharp. I fell asleep, murmuring, 'Better, better, better.'

Then there were more nurses, joltings, a journey, but every time I cried out Dad held my hand and reassured me. Perhaps I was given more morphine when I got to the spinal unit because for a while I felt I was wafting along through the air, several feet above my body, looking down at myself being shunted along endless corridors. Dad was one side of me, Mum the other, and Clover was curled up by my feet, weeping so hard that my toes were quite wet. I was wet and yet my throat was dry, so very dry that my voice cracked when I tried to talk.

'Can I have . . . a drink . . . drink of water?' I whispered.

'Not just now, darling,' said Dad.

'I *want* one,' I said, starting to cry. It seemed incredibly mean to me that I couldn't have a little water when I felt so dreadful, and I hadn't had anything to drink all day long. Or was this even the next day? It felt as if years had passed since I fell from the tree. Time seemed to have stopped ticking sensibly, minute by minute, hour by hour.

'I know, poor girl, but you're going to have surgery on your back now, and we can't risk giving you anything in case it makes you sick,' said Dad.

He bent over me so I could see him. He looked awful, dark circles under his eyes, and his cheeks and chin were shadowed with grey.

'You haven't shaved!' I said, amazed. Dad always took immense care to be softly pink-cheeked and prickle-free.

'I haven't had time, you dodo,' Dad said. 'I've been here with you.'

'You will stay with me, won't you?'

'Well, I can't be in the operating theatre with you, but I promise I'll be there when you wake up,' said Dad.

'Why can't you? You're a doctor!'

'Yes, but not a surgeon. I've talked to Mr Pearson though, and he's a brilliant man, Katy.'

'And he's going to make me better?'

'He's going to do his best. He'll stabilize your back and stop it hurting so much.'

'And then I'll be better. Dad, can I have my skateboard back?'

'What? Darling, you're going to have to take things very slowly –'

'But when I'm better. Promise I can have my skateboard?'

'We'll see,' said Dad.

Then someone injected my arm and Dad gave me my skateboard and I rode it down all the hospital corridors, up the walls and along the ceilings, faster and faster. We were all in a race, but Ryan and I were out in front. I was winning, screaming, 'I'm Katy Carr, I'm Katy Carr, I'm Katy Carr!' as I shot up a huge ramp and then I catapulted off the end, whirling through the air, falling again, falling and falling . . .

I landed with a jolt, and someone was very gently tapping my face.

'Wake up, Katy. That's a good girl. Open those eyes.'

I opened them obediently. There was a nurse bending over me, looking concerned.

'Where's Dad?' I whispered.

'Your dad's waiting to see you, back in the ward. We're just making sure you're all right, honey,' she said softly.

'I'm all right now?' I said. 'So can I go home?'

'Not for a while.'

'Am I still not better?'

'Well . . . Mr Pearson's done a lovely job of your back. It won't be anywhere near as painful now.'

I tried to wriggle. I couldn't manage it.

'Why can't I move?' I asked, starting to panic.

'Shh now. You've only just come round from the anaesthetic. We'll be assessing you later. You've just to be a good girl and stay still,' she said.

'I don't *want* to be good!' I said furiously.

She was looking very sad, but that made her laugh.

'Well, you can be as naughty as you like when you get home, but you have to be a good girl while you're here in hospital,' she said.

'But it's horrid here,' I said. 'You won't even let me have a drink of water!'

'What? No, you couldn't drink before your operation. You can have a drink very soon. Tell you what, I'll get you an ice cube to suck. That will help.' She went away and came back with a cup of ice cubes clinking together. 'There. Pretend it's an ice lolly. What flavour do you like best? I like Soleros – they're less fattening. You know, those orangey-mango ones.'

'I like strawberry. Or raspberry. I like red,' I said indistinctly, my mouth full of ice cube. It felt wonderful in my hot dry mouth. If I tried hard I could imagine a red fruity flavour. 'Mmm, delicious!'

'That's the girl! Let's give your face a little wash while we're at it. You're all-over tear stains.'

'I don't usually cry, you know. I'm not a baby. I'm the eldest. When can I see my sisters and brothers?'

'When you're back on the main ward, dear.'

'They'll find it a bit scary in hospital, even though our dad's a doctor. Phil's only just been to hospital himself, with a cut finger.'

'You sound a very harum-scarum family,' said the nurse. 'No wonder your dad's got grey hair. He's quite a bit older than your mum, isn't he?'

'My mum?' I said, my heart beating fast. I knew I'd only been imagining her, but I wondered madly if she'd somehow really come back to look after me.

'Yes, she's so worried about you. She came while your dad went home for a bit of a wash and brush-up. Lovely lady – she's got hair to die for, hasn't she?'

'Long blonde hair? *She's* not my mum,' I said indignantly. I hated the thought of Izzie coming to see me in hospital. She'd be full of '*I told you so*'s. 'She's just my stepmum. I can't stick her.'

'All right, all right. Don't go working yourself up now. It's all my fault. I chatter on, don't I? There now. Let's see how your blood pressure's doing, pet.'

I let her check me and begged to see Dad again. They let him come to me, though he was all muffled up in strange clothes like the nurse.

'It's just to keep everything hygienic,' said Dad.

'You look weird, Dad,' I mumbled.

The clothes looked silly, and his face still didn't look right, though he'd had a shave now. Then another person loomed beside him, a younger man with a pink, shiny, important face.

'Hello Katy. I'm Mr Pearson. I'm the guy who operated on your back. Now, we're going to do some funny little tests on you – is that OK?'

'Tests? But I still don't think I can sit up,' I said.

'No, you don't need to sit up. You just lie there like a good girl and we'll do the tests on your arms and legs to see how they are.'

'But it's not my arms and legs. I didn't hurt them. I thought you were operating on my back.'

'That's right. I did. But there are lots of little nerves that spread out from your spine down your limbs. We want to see if they're working properly.'

The tests they did were really odd. They touched each arm in turn while I had to close my eyes and call out when I could feel it.

'Yep, you're tickling me!' I said.

They tried hot things and cold things and I had to tell them which was which. They seemed the most elementary tests in the world. Even little Phil could have done them.

'You're doing beautifully, Katy. Well done!' said Dad, as if I'd done brilliantly in my SATs.

Then they started on my stomach. Well, I knew they were poking at it because I opened my eyes a little and peeped. I wondered if they were messing about with me, because I couldn't feel it at all. Maybe they weren't touching me properly this time? It was so strange, as normally when anyone touched my tummy I doubled up laughing because I'm so ticklish there.

Then they moved further down to my legs, pulling off the thin blanket covering them. I tried to lift my head to peer at what they were doing.

'No, Katy, lie still, flat on your back, there's a good girl,' said the nurse.

So I couldn't see what they were doing. I could only watch their faces. They weren't smiling now.

'Are you doing the tests now? What's the matter? Do it harder!' I said sharply.

Then I saw Mr Pearson had a pin in his hand.

'But don't prick me!' I said.

He laughed but he didn't look at all happy. He looked very sad. So did the nurse. And I heard Dad give a little groan.

'Dad? What is it? What's the matter?' I asked, panicking now.

Mr Pearson and the nurse were looking at each other, then looking at Dad.

'Would you like me to have a little chat with Katy?' Mr Pearson asked Dad.

'No. No, I think I'd better do it,' said Dad.

'Well, we'll give you a little privacy then,' said Mr Pearson. He patted me gently on the shoulder. 'There now, Katy. I'll be coming to see you tomorrow and I'll do my best to answer any questions you might have.'

Then he did the oddest thing. He put his arms round Dad and gave him a quick hug.

'Dad? Is he a friend of yours? Why did he hug you like that?' I asked, when they'd left us on our own.

'He's – he's a very nice man,' said Dad. 'And he's stabilized your spine, so you shouldn't have too many problems in the future.'

'So when can I get up properly?'

'Well, that's the thing, Katy.' Dad's face bobbed into focus. He had tears in his eyes. 'I'm afraid you won't be able to get up as such. They'll sit you up soon, and I dare say you'll have to do all sorts of exercises, but you're going to have to use a wheelchair to get around.'

'A wheelchair? What? Like Helen?'

'Yes, like Helen! And she manages beautifully, doesn't she? Of course it will take a lot of getting used to, and I know it will be difficult, but you're a very brave girl, Katy, and we'll all help as best we can.'

'But – but how long am I going to have to use a wheelchair?' I asked, stunned. Wheelchairs were for seriously sick people like Helen, or old, old, old people. Girls like me didn't use wheelchairs.

'I'm not old and I'm not sick!' I said. 'I just had a fall. I'm not going in a wheelchair!'

'I'm afraid you're going to have to, darling, whether you want to or not.' The tears were running down Dad's cheeks now.

'But for how long? When will I be able to walk properly?'

Dad shook his head helplessly.

'Dad, answer me!'

'I – I don't think you will be able to walk, darling. I think you've lost all sensation in the lower half of your body.'

'But I had the operation. You said Mr Pearson had sorted out my spine.'

'He's stabilized it, Katy. But he can't sort out all the nerve damage. It's simply not possible.'

'So when will all my nerves get better?'

'They can't. Well, maybe in the future implants will be possible, who knows. And there are various treatments and devices. But in basic, practical terms it looks like you won't be able to walk at all.'

'But you said I was going to get better! You *said*!' I shouted furiously.

'I didn't, Katy. Maybe that's what you wanted to believe and – dear God! – I want to believe it too. But I don't want to lie to you now. It would be cruel to fob you off with empty promises. We just have to face this awful thing together.'

Dad tried to take my hand but I pushed it away.

'It's not fair! I'm not going to let it happen! I'm going to get better, just you wait and see!' I screamed.

15

I was put in a big room with three other girls. There was a twin unit the other side of the nurses' station with four boys. The girls' unit was painted a wishy-washy lilac, but there was a big painting on the ceiling of purple mountains and flower-strewn meadows and in the foreground a farm with cows and sheep and pigs. There was a fat farmer with a pitchfork attacking a butter-yellow haystack and a jolly soul wearing an apron feeding chickens who was probably his wife. They had children too: a little boy sailing a toy boat on a bright blue pond and a girl making a daisy chain in the emerald grass. I stared at that painting hour after hour. Sometimes I pretended I was a farm child, working hard making hay and feeding chickens like a good elder sister. Mostly though I didn't want any company at all, even from little painted figures. I looked up until my eyeballs ached, staring at the mountains, willing myself up on the peak of the highest one, as far away as possible.

It was so terrible to be stuck here, flat on my back, helpless. Really truly helpless. I'd looked at one of Dad's old children's books at home, about a man called Gulliver. It was written in a quaint old-fashioned way and I couldn't get into the story, but I loved the illustrations, especially one where Gulliver is pinioned on his back, tethered by many small ropes, while an army of miniature people swarm all over him triumphantly. I was Gulliver all right. But at least he had a chance of wriggling free, straining against the ropes and sitting up and squashing all the tiny people between his fingers as if they were flies.

Oh how I wanted to squash everyone around me, even my favourite nurse, Jasmine. She was round and brown and she giggled a lot, but when I cried she'd come and cuddle up beside me, running her fingers through my hair and crooning softly to me. I loved Jasmine and always prayed that I'd get her when it was time for any terrible medical or personal intervention, but sometimes I couldn't help hating her simply because she could walk away, swishing her big bottom, her calves taut and shiny, her white Crocs squeaking on the polished floor.

The nurses alternated, day nurses and night nurses, but they all did the same things. Sometimes these were quite ordinary things like washing us and easing us in and out of gowns. I could actually wriggle in and out of mine because my hands and arms still worked and I could feel down to my waist. Little Marnie could move too, but she was only about three or four so she had to have help anyway.

I wasn't sure if Naveen could move much. She didn't try at all. She lay and cried most of the time, and when her family came to visit her every afternoon they all cried too.

Rosemary didn't cry. Rosemary was a beautiful little girl with caramel-coloured skin and big dark eyes. She came from the Philippines and when she was with her family she chattered in Filipino, but she spoke English to the nurses and to us. She had fallen out of a window and very nearly died, with a fractured skull as well as a broken back. She'd been in a coma but now she was conscious and very lively, talking all the time. She even sang and laughed like any normal eight-year-old, but she was far more badly injured than me. She still had big bandages round her head where she'd had an operation and she couldn't move from her neck down.

When Naveen or I refused to cooperate or had a crying fit the nastiest nurse, Jeannie, would hiss, 'Shame on you. Look at little Rosemary! She's a shining example to us all.'

I dare say she was a truly lovely, courageous little girl, but I wanted to squash her too. In fact I wanted to squash her most of all.

Sometimes the nurses had to do terrible things to us. Terrible for them as well as us. None of us could go to the loo properly. I had to have a catheter for my wee, with an awful little bag, which was bad enough. The nurses had to cope with my bowels. I hated the first session so much that I resolved never to eat again and then I wouldn't need to go. It wasn't too difficult to go on hunger strike. I didn't have any appetite at all and the hospital food was pretty awful anyway. Cereal and soggy toast for breakfast, greasy lasagne for lunch, sandwiches and jelly for tea.

So I didn't eat at all and after a day or so they all started to worry. They had a little conference with Dad. He brought me in a big tub of Loseley strawberry ice cream, my favourite treat. He opened it up and put it under my nose so I could smell its delicate creamy sweetness. I wanted it badly but I kept my mouth tightly shut.

'Oh Katy, what are we going to do with you? Am I going to have to spoon it into you the way I feed little Phil?' Dad said.

My eyes filled with tears at the thought of Philly and the other littlies.

'Oh Dad, I miss them so,' I mumbled.

'And they miss you, darling, terribly. Now that you're more stable I'll bring them all in to see you, just for a few minutes. We mustn't tire you too much. So you need to start eating properly to get strong.'

But I wouldn't eat, and let my ice cream melt into milk. I wouldn't eat the next day either, and just took little sips of water. I heard the staff discussing me. I think they were worried I'd started to become anorexic because of the shock of the accident.

It was dear nurse Jasmine who helped me confide the problem. She was on night duty. She crept round, checking on each bed. When she got to mine and saw I was awake she held up the covers and made a pantomime of peering underneath.

'Katy? Where are you, girl? Oh my Lord, you've faded away so much you've actually gone and disappeared!' she whispered.

'I wish I could,' I said.

'Well, you're certainly going the right way about it, honey. Why aren't you eating, for goodness' sake? You're scaring everyone.'

'I'm just not hungry,' I said.

'Nonsense,' said Jasmine. 'Right. I'll be back in a tick. Don't go to sleep on me.'

She came back a few minutes later with a plate of hot buttered toast cut into tiny squares.

'There now. I've made us a little midnight feast,' she said. 'We'll take it in turns. A square for me, a square for you.'

'No! I said I don't want any,' I said wretchedly.

'Why not, sweetheart? You surely can't think you're fat? Look at you – you're thin as a pin. You need to eat well and build up those muscles. You need to be a strong girl now, especially if you're going to become a wheelchair champion.'

'I don't want to use a stupid wheelchair,' I said.

'Well, I think that's you being stupid, not the wheelchair,' said Jasmine. 'Don't you want to get around under your own steam? Surely you don't want to lie in bed all the time?'

'I don't want to do anything! I don't want to be me any more!' I said, starting to cry.

'Oh darling.' She put her head close to mine on the pillow. 'You're not trying to starve yourself to death, are you?'

I hadn't meant anything as dramatic, but I mumbled yes because I thought she might feel extra sorry for me.

'What a dreadful idea!' she said, suddenly cross. 'How could you think of such a thing! You're already putting your poor family through such torment. And here we are, doing our best to help you too.'

'I know you are,' I said, crying in earnest. 'That's why! I hate what you all have to do to make my bowels work. So I'm not eating so I don't have to go!'

'Oh Katy!' She hugged me tight. 'Sweetheart, you can't carry on like that! We can't have you starving to death!'

245

'Well, maybe it would be a good thing,' I sobbed. 'I don't think I want to live if I can't walk and run and play games any more. Who would want to be a sad, pathetic cripple in a wheelchair?'

She exclaimed when I said the word *cripple*, absolutely horrified.

'Nobody uses that terrible word in this unit! Fond as I am of you I'll wash your mouth out with carbolic soap if you dare say that again!'

I thought she might be joking, but she certainly sounded indignant enough.

'I'm not calling anyone else that word. Just me. Surely I can call myself anything I want?' I said defiantly.

'That's what you think, young lady. There's a young lad called Dexter in the boys' ward and he started letting off steam, effing and blinding enough to make my hair curl even tighter. I soon sorted him out! You can rail all you like against fate – and you wouldn't be human if you weren't very angry – but no swearing and no inaccurate, unpleasant words. Do I make myself understood?'

'Yes, Nurse Jasmine,' I mumbled.

'That's good. Now, let's get your eyes mopped and your nose wiped and sort you out good and proper. Don't let this lovely toast get cold. Try just one little square.'

'But then I'll need help going to the toilet tomorrow and I *hate* that,' I wailed.

'Of course you do. But you're going to need help every single day, so I'm afraid you have to get used to it, sweetheart. It's the same for all of you. Harder for the poor souls who can't even sit up, like little Rosemary. We have to do everything for her but she never makes a fuss.'

'Oh, don't go on about Rosemary. I'm sick of her being everyone's favourite,' I growled.

'What a dreadful girl you are, Katy Carr! And it's not true anyway. *You're* my favourite, though goodness knows why, because you're totally determined to cause me grief.'

'You're just saying that. I bet you tell every single child in the ward that they're your favourite.'

'No, I don't, Miss Smarty Pants. My goodness, you're a trial to me. Still at least you've eaten that square of toast. Come on, be a devil and munch some more.'

I hadn't even realized that I'd been nibbling the toast since I started arguing with her. It tasted so good, warm and comforting and buttery, that I couldn't stop myself reaching for another square.

I ate properly after that, though I still hated the hospital food. Dad tried again with more ice cream, and this time I ate it all *and* scraped my finger round and round the tub. The children brought me a big tin of Quality Street, the chocolates with the purple and yellow and red shiny wrappers that we usually had for a Christmas treat. They'd all clubbed together with their pocket money.

'And we haven't eaten a single one,' said Dorry. 'They're all for you, Katy. Even the purple ones with the hazelnuts that are my special favourites.'

'Oh Katy, when will you get better? I hate you being in hospital. I know your legs don't work now. Dad told us. When you come home you can have Zebby as your special chair if you like,' said Jonnie.

'Don't, please. You'll make me cry,' I said.

'I cried when *I* was in hospital,' said Phil. 'It hurt when they put the stitches in, but now my finger's completely better. Look! Can't you have stitches in your poorly legs, Katy?'

'Hush now. Don't badger Katy so. You'll wear her out,' said Izzie. She looked awful, very pale, and her hair was a bit of a mess for once, scragged back in an untidy knot.

'Won't you ever be able to walk again, Katy?' Elsie asked, her eyes big.

'Elsie! I *told* you not to say that!' said Izzie, so sharply that Elsie burst into tears.

'Oh, don't cry, Elsie! We mustn't cry, you know we absolutely mustn't, because we'll upset Katy,' said Clover, though tears had started to roll down her own cheeks.

'Clover!' I said, and I grabbed hold of her wrist and pulled her close. I was missing Clover so desperately, Clover most of all, because I was so used to her always being by my side, and there all through the night.

She put her arms round my neck and cuddled as close as she could, but stuck flat on my back I couldn't hug back properly. I was like a great big useless baby now. I might still be the eldest, but I couldn't do anything for them any more. I wasn't Katy the fun sister who led them on expeditions and organized wild games and helped them under fences and up trees. I was useless Katy who couldn't do anything. They'd have to help *me* forever and ever and ever.

I was crying now, terrible great wailing sobs.

'Now look what you've started, Elsie!' said Izzie. 'Oh Katy, dear, don't cry so. Shall I take the children away and leave you to have a quiet time with your dad? I wouldn't have brought all of them, but they were pestering me so much.'

It was all topsy-turvy, Izzie trying to consider me and snapping at Elsie. That made me feel worse, if anything. I was the invalid girl now, the disabled person who had to be considered and protected all the time. I cried harder, unable to help it, so Izzie gathered up the three littlies and Elsie and led them out of the room.

Clover stayed, trying so hard to stop crying herself that she made little snorty noises with the effort.

'Don't, Clover,' I gasped between my own sobs.

'I can't seem to help it,' she howled. 'Oh Katy, I know this is all my fault and I feel so terrible.'

'Don't be silly, Clover,' Dad said gently. 'How could Katy's accident possibly be your fault?'

'It is, it is, because I wouldn't go with her to Baxter Park, and if I *had* gone Izzie would have been mad at me too, and then I wouldn't have been able to go swimming, so Katy and I would have been together and maybe she wouldn't have gone to the secret garden with the rope, and even if she *had* maybe I could have talked her out of swinging because I always try to stop her doing dangerous things, and so it *is* my fault, don't you see?' Clover said in a great rush, her words all running together.

'It's not your fault. It's Izzie's, because she wouldn't let me go swimming,' I said. The words just slipped out of my mouth. I saw the expression on Dad's face and I felt dreadful, but I wanted to hang on to feeling that it really was Izzie's fault. Anybody's fault. Because if I faced up to the fact that I had no one to blame but myself, it made everything even more unbearable.

Dad didn't tell me off. He just shook his head sadly.

'You can't blame Izzie. You know that's nonsense,' he said. 'Let's stop all this talk of blaming. It's utterly pointless. Clover, why don't you tell Katy the Circus game you played with all the others yesterday? It was so clever of you to think of something they could do which would distract them a little.'

So Clover started telling me about the game and I tried to listen and say the right things, but it was a terrible struggle. *I* was the one who invented new games, not Clover! And it sounded a good game too, with Clover as

250

the ringmaster, and Dorry and Jonnie trotting round and round the house like ponies, and Phil standing on a bucket roaring his head off being a frightening lion. She even had Elsie being a performing poodle, which normally would have made me laugh delightedly.

'And Tyler was part of the circus too. He's learned a new trick, Katy. When I hold up your old hula hoop he jumps straight through it. Wait till you see him do it!' said Clover, sniffing and wiping her eyes.

I didn't want to see Tyler performing his new trick. I'd been missing him so much: his warm, hairy little body, his big eyes, his waggy tail, his loving licks all over my face. I'd thought he'd be moping round the house, missing me desperately too. It hurt that he was clearly still having fun without me. *I* was the one who taught him tricks, not Clover.

I'd thought that when I got home at last Tyler might creep gently on to my lap and stay by my side as my little guard dog and helper. But he wouldn't want to do that if Clover was rushing round with him, showing him all sorts of fun tricks and making a fuss of him. He'd want to be *Clover's* dog.

'Yes, great . . . it sounds fun. But I think I want to have a nap now. Sorry, but I'm too tired to listen,' I said, and I shut my eyes to make my point.

So Dad and Clover kissed me goodbye and went. I was left feeling worse than ever, hateful inside as well as out.

16

E very day when I woke up I'd keep my eyes tight shut, willing myself to be back in my bedroom with Clover. I listened for the sounds of the littlies giggling on the stairs, Dad walking along the landing humming some ancient old rock song, Izzie putting the kettle on down in the kitchen. I willed myself to smell my own soft clean duvet, the sweet scent of Clover's coconut shampoo, the warm tang of Tyler's hairy coat. I tried to feel him jumping up on the bed and licking me. I wanted to feel the slight sag in my mattress. I wanted to feel my own stomach and hips and legs and feet.

I willed it with my fists clenched, sweat breaking out on my forehead, but I knew I was still in the hospital ward, with Marnie and Naveen and Rosemary snuffling in their sleep. There was a nurse creeping from bed to bed to check on us, and all around us there was the strange clanking sound of the hospital.

Then I started my second struggle of the day. I tried to make my body work again. I knew in my head exactly how to move my legs, to point my feet, to wiggle my toes. I strained to do it now, peering over the thin hospital blanket in the eerie dawn light, looking for the slightest ripple of movement. There wasn't any. The only way I could move my legs was if I sat up slowly and gingerly, because it was still painful, seized hold of them and heaved. They were thin, spindly legs but they felt like massive tree trunks and it was a huge effort to shift them.

I'd been shown pictures of a body's bones and nerves. Mr Pearson had explained how the damage I'd done to my spine had affected all the nerves from my waist down, but it still didn't make sense. My legs weren't broken, I still had strong muscles, I could sit up and feel my taut calves, so why wouldn't they *work*?

The nurses had started getting me out of bed now, which made me feel very sick and dizzy. They supported me so that I could just about stand upright, hanging on to a frame.

'So this is to try to teach me to walk again?' I asked eagerly.

'No, lovey, it's to keep those limbs of yours healthy and supple. When you're a little fitter we'll want you to take your whole weight yourself. We'll have to build up those arm muscles. We'll have you with forearms like Popeye in no time! Though you're such a Skinny Minnie you look more like Olive Oyl at the moment,' said Nurse Jeannie.

I didn't like her, or Nurse Gloria. I hated them teasing me. They'd be furious if I made remarks about *their* size. I could be especially waspish about Nurse Jeannie and her great big bum.

Someone else had done just that. I heard Jeannie telling Gloria, absolutely outraged.

'Do you know what that terrible Dexter said to me when I tried to give him his meds this morning? "You can stuff it right up your great big –" . . . well, that horrible word beginning with an *a*!' said Jeannie with a shudder.

'It's ridiculous him being in a children's unit. He might only be sixteen but he's a right mouthy little yobbo,' said Gloria. 'Poor you, Jeannie.' She sounded sympathetic, but you could tell she was smug that Dexter had never called *her* bottom a rude name.

I liked the sound of this Dexter. I wished I could swap him for saintly Rosemary. Someone had given her a teddy bear almost as big as she was and she spent all day chatting and singing to him. I found it very irritating. Perhaps the teddy found it irritating too, but he was as helpless as she was, unable to put his paws over his ears to shut out the sound of her incessant sweet talk.

When the nurses got me into a wheelchair I soon became tired of wheeling myself round and round the ward.

'Can't I go for a little walk somewhere?' I begged. Then I thought about the word *walk*. I was going to have to use substitute vocabulary for the simplest things now. *Go for a walk. Run and fetch it. Jump up. Leap into action.* 'Can I go on a little trip down the corridor and back?' I amended.

They weren't supposed to let me out of their sight yet in case I slumped sideways or fell forward, because I was still learning the knack of sitting up straight. It was hard work keeping my own skinny a-word in place on a chair now. I struggled to do what a six-month-old baby can manage all by itself.

Jeannie and Gloria wouldn't let me, but dear Jasmine agreed when she was on day duty.

'I'll come with you though. Can't have you escaping!' she said.

'Can I wheel myself and go wherever I want?' I asked.

'Yes, of course you can wheel yourself. It's good practice. You want to be as independent as possible. And you can toddle about wherever you want on this floor, within reason. You can't barge into the boys' bathroom!'

'As if,' I said scornfully.

But I did want to go and have a peek in the boys' ward. Jasmine didn't object. They didn't have the mountains and the farm on their ceiling. They had a racing track with different cars speeding round and round. I stared up at it, imagining myself in the car in front, a red car, a sleek racing-demon version of my long-ago little kiddy car.

Then I peered round at the boys. One boy was flat on his back, peering up at his television set. Two boys about eight or nine were hunched in wheelchairs, totally absorbed in their games consoles. And the fourth boy was propped up in bed, drawing something in a sketchbook. He was wearing a black T-shirt with a skull on it. He was tall and skinny, rather like me, with a very pale face. He had longish, untidy hair that kept flopping in his eyes so that he kept flicking it back impatiently.

'Why don't you let me trim your hair for you, Dexter?' said Jasmine. 'You can't see what you're doing with it hanging in your face like that. Say hi to Katy here. She's paying you guys a little visit.'

'Hi to Katy,' Dexter murmured, not even looking up.

'What are you drawing, Dexter?' I asked.

He shrugged. 'Just stuff,' he said.

'He's ever so artistic, Dexter is. He does all these comic strips,' said Jasmine. 'They're very good, though they're very . . . adult.'

I wheeled myself closer so I could take a peep. I thought he might be drawing rude pictures but I saw a sketch of an old man wearing a hooded cloak, a strange kind of farming implement in one of his gnarled hands.

'Who's he?' I asked.

'Just an old man. Run away, kid,' said Dexter.

'*Run* away?' I said.

'OK. Go and do wheelies somewhere else,' he said, but he looked up at me briefly.

He had surprising eyes. I thought they'd be dark because his hair was black, but they were blue, the sort of eyes that look as if they could see right into your head.

I edged even closer, so I accidentally nudged his bed. His smooth black line wavered a little.

'Now look what you've done!' he said impatiently.

'Sorry! I'm hopeless. I'm always bumping into things. I can't get the hang of this stupid, stupid wheelchair.' I thumped my hand against the wheel in frustration.

'Don't do that. You'll just hurt your hand,' said Dexter, making the old man's cloak wider, past the wobble, and then cross-hatching densely so that it wouldn't show at all.

'I wish I could do shading like that. I don't seem to get how to do it. Show me,' I said.

'Nothing to show. You just draw,' said Dexter.

He carried on drawing. I carried on watching. Jasmine got bored and wandered off to chat to the two boys.

Dexter started on the old man's face. It was difficult to make out under the large hood. The eyes were very

257

large and dark, the nose barely there, the mouth a disconcerting wide grin . . .

'It's a skull, like the one on your T-shirt!' I said. Then I thought harder. 'Hey, I know who it is! What do you call him – the Grim Reaper!'

'Yep, old man Death himself,' said Dexter.

'So who is he going to reap?'

'Well, not quite sure just yet. He's done his best striding through this little patch of the planet, but perhaps his scythe needs sharpening. He's slashed my legs off, and yours, and all these little kids' around us, but he hasn't stabbed us in the heart just yet. He could be having another go after he's had a bit of a rest. He might go at it stealthily, clogging our lungs with pneumonia. Or he could send a little blood clot to our hearts?'

'Hey, Dexter, quit that scary rubbish!' Jasmine called, frowning. 'You'll give Katy the willies.'

'No, he won't. He's funny,' I said. 'Dexter, did you really tell Jeannie to stick your meds up her you-know-what?'

'My fame spreads far and wide,' said Dexter.

'You're awesome,' I said, half teasing, half serious.

'Don't you dare encourage him, Katy. He's a bad boy. He's going to get into serious trouble if he carries on like this,' said Jasmine, coming over to us.

'Yeah, well, would you mind telling me what could be worse trouble than losing the use of your whole body?' said Dexter.

'You could lose the use of your hands too, smart boy. Then where would you be? No crazy drawing for a start. You two moan away about your lot, yet little Rosemary –'

'Oh, blessed little St Rosemary,' said Dexter.

'Oh goodness, do the nurses tell you lot about Rosemary too?' I asked. 'Imagine what it's like for us girls though. We're stuck with Rosemary all the time.'

'You two! How can you mock such a good, sweet little girl?' said Jasmine, pretending to cuff both of us, but she wasn't really cross.

She knew that we didn't really dislike poor, valiant little Rosemary. We just resented her grace and good humour coping with the unbearable, when we were having such a struggle ourselves.

It was wonderful to have found someone darker and moodier than myself. I wanted to stay talking to Dexter all morning, but Natasha, another nurse, called Jasmine back to the girls' ward because Marnie had been sick all over herself and the bedclothes.

'Which means I have to whip you back to the girls' ward too, Katy,' said Jasmine.

'Oh, can't I stay just for a bit? I don't want to go back, not if it all smells sicky. It'll make me be sick too,' I whined.

'You dare!' said Jasmine, and wheeled me off before I could even say a proper goodbye to Dexter.

I came back the next day. I even let Jasmine wash my hair beforehand. I'd just left it in an untidy tangle before. I hadn't even been very cooperative about washing. I hadn't bothered to ask for help putting on the new pyjamas Izzie had brought in for me. There hadn't seemed any point at all. If I was so smashed up that I couldn't even walk, why did it matter what I looked like? I might as well look as hideous as possible and glare at everyone.

But now I had my hair shampooed. It was an awkward business, even though they had a special sink in the bathroom where you could lie backwards, if you were able to wiggle around enough in your wheelchair. I still got shampoo in my eyes and moaned a bit, but Jasmine told me to button it, so I did. Then she dried my hair patiently, which took a while because it's quite long.

I didn't know what to do with it when I brushed it. It sometimes looked halfway decent when it was newly washed, silky and shiny, but now it just hung limply.

'It looks a right mess,' I said dolefully. 'Why's it gone all weird?'

'Perhaps it's because you've had such a shock to your whole system,' said Jasmine.

'Great. I'm a hopeless cripple and I'm going to have a bad hair day *every* day,' I said.

'I've told you about using that word! I'll pour the whole bottle of shampoo down your throat if you dare say it again! Now let's see what I can do. Plaits?'

'They're so babyish.'

'Do *I* look like a baby?' Jasmine had the most amazing plaits, many of them, from the roots of her hair, and then they were all twisted up in the fanciest of ponytails.

'Oh, will you do mine like yours? Please!'

'This is a hospital ward, not a hairdressing salon. It would take forever to do yours properly. But I'll do you the shortcut version if you like.'

She twisted two locks of hair on either side into plaits and then pinned all four to the back of my head. It made quite a difference and stopped my hair flopping forward into my face.

'Oh Jasmine, thank you! It looks lovely!'

'Yeah, it does, doesn't it?' Jasmine chuckled. 'Maybe I'll have a go at plaiting Dexter's hair.'

I asked her to help me put on the new pyjamas. They were pink, the colour I hated most, but they had little dogs like Tyler on them, which I liked. Maybe I could get Izzie to buy me a black pair sometime soon? Or just a black T-shirt, preferably with a skull on it.

Jasmine and I went into the boys' ward mid-morning. The three boys were watching television and playing games in exactly the same poses as yesterday, but Dexter wasn't sitting up drawing. He was lying on his back, one arm over his face.

'Hi there, Dexter. Here's Katy come to have a little chat,' said Jasmine.

Dexter didn't move. He didn't even grunt.

'What's up, pal?' Jasmine said softly.

Dexter didn't respond.

Jeannie up at the other end of the ward shook her head.

'He's been in this mood since last night,' she said.

'Oh Dex. Sorry, man. We'll come back another time when you're not feeling blue,' said Jasmine.

She started wheeling me away.

'But what's the matter with him?' I demanded.

'Oh, come on, Katy. You've had the moody blues too, more than most. It catches up with all of you from time to time, even little Rosemary, bless her,' said Jasmine.

'Can't I still talk to Dexter?' I asked.

'Well, you can try,' said Jasmine.

I wheeled myself back while she went to talk to the younger boy watching television. I tried hard to manoeuvre myself close up to Dexter's bed without bumping it. I didn't succeed. I jogged his bed, but he didn't even twitch.

'Sorry. It's me – Katy. As you must have guessed, seeing as I keep bumping into your bed. Still, at least I didn't muck up your drawing this time.'

I saw his sketchbook was closed, on his bedside locker.

'Would you mind if I had a little look at all your drawings?' I asked, and wheeled myself round.

'Yes. I would mind,' Dexter muttered without moving. 'Push off, Katy.' He didn't actually say *Push*.

262

'Go on. Just one page. I loved your Grim Reaper. Perhaps you could do a whole Grim Reaper family. His wife would be very witchy and if she's got a skull face too she could have make-up all round her hollow eyes and gaping mouth. That would look totally grim, wouldn't it? And then they could have children, little gargoyly kids with tiny toy scythes. They wouldn't be big enough to kill humans; they'd just chase little mice and birds, practising.'

'Katy, I'm not in the mood,' said Dexter.

'I know. You've got the blues. We all get it, Jasmine says.'

'This isn't a wishy-washy *mood*. This is totally full-on despair,' said Dexter. 'For a good reason.'

'Well, yes. You can't walk. I can't walk. None of us can walk.' My own voice went wobbly as I said it. It still didn't seem real.

'Not just that.' Dexter took his hand away from his face. His eyes were red. I felt my stomach lurch. I couldn't bear it that proud, cool, bad Dexter had actually been crying.

'There can't be anything worse,' I said.

'Yep. Much worse. My girlfriend's just dumped me,' said Dexter.

'Oh.' I was floundering now. 'What, she just said she didn't want to see you any more?'

'She came to see me once. She cried all over me. She swore it wouldn't make a difference. But she didn't

263

come back, though I kept texting her. Then at last she texts me back and I feel such a thrill when I see it's a message from her. Then when I open it I find it says, *So sorry, Dex, I can't bear to see you like this, it upsets me too much.* Then she adds one of those gross little emoticons with a sad face. Can you imagine?' said Dexter.

'She doesn't exactly say she's dumping you,' I said.

'It's obvious. And one of my mates texted me to say she's started going out with this other guy anyway.'

'Well, it sounds as if you're better off without her then,' I said lamely. 'I'm sure you'll get another much better girlfriend instead.'

'What are you, a child agony aunt?'

'I'm just trying to be sympathetic.'

'Yeah, well, you're being stupid, because I'm not going to be able to hook up with any other girl, am I – not unless they're totally weird and creepy. Because who wants to go out with a cripple?'

'Watch out. Jasmine goes nuts when you say that word.' I sat silently thinking. Who would ever want to go out with *me* now? I thought of all the teenage years ahead of me. How could I manage at parties? How could I go clubbing? How could I walk hand in hand and kiss under a lamp post? How could I ever have sex? I didn't know much about it, and it had either sounded comical or scary, but I would have liked to try it when I was old enough.

'What?' said Dexter. He was leaning up on his elbows now, watching my face.

'I feel a bit rubbish myself now,' I said, and I wheeled myself back to the girls' ward, not even waiting for Jasmine.

17

I woke up with a start in the middle of the night. Dark, dark, dark all around me. Too dark. I turned on to my side and curled up tight, covers over my head, trying to hide from the dark. Then I realized. My legs! I'd moved my legs! I moved them again, up and down, all over the bed.

I wasn't paralysed any more! I sat up and then slowly, gingerly, slid my legs out of bed altogether. My feet touched the floor, felt the cold, curled their toes. I pressed down and stood up. I stood swaying until I got my balance and then set off walking, left leg, right leg. I could do it! I was walking again.

It was still very dark and yet I could sense people around me. I mustn't let them see me in case they bundled me back to bed. I never wanted to lie in bed again. I wanted to walk and skip and dance and run.

So I hurried along corridor after corridor, dodging round people in the dark. Some of them tried to grab hold of me, some shouted my name, but I was too quick for all of them. Then I got to a big bolted door downstairs and I had to struggle for a minute or two with the lock while the people got nearer, but just as they seized me by the shoulders I forced the door open. I shook them off and ran and ran in the sudden bright sunlight, thudding across the concrete in my bare feet.

I ran across roads and down streets and through the town until I got to the country and then I ran around soft grass meadows, singing for joy because I could walk and I'd escaped.

But then I heard clanking and I was frightened again and ran harder, but the trolley got nearer and nearer, and then – and then –

'Tea or milk, dearie? Cornflakes? One toast or two?'

It was the large lady with the breakfast trolley and I was back in my bed in the girls' ward and when I tried to jump up my heavy logs of legs stayed still, unmoving. It had just been a dream, a cruel hateful dream.

I started crying with frustration and worked myself up so much I couldn't eat my breakfast. I wouldn't even wash or brush my hair. I wouldn't cooperate properly with the horrible toileting. I wouldn't stand hanging on to the stupid frame. I wanted Jasmine but she wasn't on duty today. I decided I hated the other nurses simply because they weren't her. I hated the other girls too, Naveen with her constant peevish wails, Rosemary with her sweetness and cute sayings, Marnie snuffling into her collection of dollies.

I put my fingers in my ears when Mr Pearson came and wouldn't listen to him. After a little while he just patted me on the shoulders and walked away. I heard him talking to the other girls. Rosemary started telling him a story; Marnie burst out laughing; even Naveen stopped moaning.

I covered my face and cried until I went back to sleep.

'Hello, sleepy kid.'

I opened my eyes and peered through my fingers.

'Dexter?' I whispered, my voice hoarse from crying.

'Yep. God, you're in a right state. Snot all over your face. Here.' He wheeled himself deftly round my bed and pulled a handful of tissues from the box on my locker. 'There now,' he said, dabbing at me.

I was mortified and tried to hide my face, but he slapped my hands away.

'Come on, baby, you need to be cleaned up. So. Why have *you* got the moody blues today? Did *you* get dumped?'

I was immensely flattered that he thought I might have a boyfriend, but I shook my head.

'So what's new? Or is it just same-old, same-old?'

I shrugged, not answering.

'Hey, it's not because I said that stuff to you yesterday, is it? You know, about hooking up? Because it's probably different for a girl. And anyway, maybe you'll be a Little Miss Miracle and start walking again.'

'I walked in my dream,' I said. 'I ran. I thought it was real.'

'Oh. I've had one of those dreams. Several. Yeah, it's the pits when you wake up,' said Dexter. 'Maybe there's a particularly malevolent Sandman who sprinkles walking dreams into kids stuck in wheelchairs, just to torture them.'

'You could draw him,' I said.

'OK. I'll whizz back and get my sketchbook.'

'And you'll come back here so I can see?'

'Yep,' said Dexter, and he was as good as his word.

He drew for me all the way through till lunchtime. He even drew for the other girls too, though their pictures weren't stylish black comic strips, they were just ordinary pictures: a portrait of Naveen to give to her parents; a teddy bear's picnic for Rosemary; and a doll's tea party for Marnie.

'My goodness, Dexter, what's come over you?' the nurses cried, thrilled. Even Jeannie looked halfway pleased, though she smoothed her uniform over her big bottom defensively.

'Maybe I've got a fever? Don't worry. I'm sure I'll be as sullen and uncooperative and abusive tomorrow,' said Dexter.

He *was* in a blackish mood the next day, and the one after that, but I didn't mind too much. I visited him and just chatted quietly to him. I even went to see him during visiting hours one day when Dad was late coming to see me. I'd expected to find him on his own, still missing the horrible girlfriend who had dumped him, but his mum was there, and even his granny. They were making a big fuss of him, showing him the new T-shirts and paperbacks and wash bag they'd bought him, acting like it was Christmas. His granny seemed to be treating him like a little boy, ruffling his long hair, even tweaking his nose affectionately at one time.

I stared, fascinated, because Dexter *seemed* much younger with them, going, 'Oh *Gran*, leave it out!' like any boy, and yet grinning at them too, obviously pleased they were there. I hovered shyly, wondering if I should quietly wheel myself back to the ward, because Dexter didn't seem to notice me.

'Who's *this*?' said his granny, smiling at me. She raised her voice and put her head on one side, treating me as if I were much younger too.

'I'm Katy. I'm Dexter's . . .' I didn't know how to finish the sentence. I hoped I was Dexter's friend but it seemed a bit presumptuous to say so.

'Oh, hi Katy,' said Dexter carelessly. 'She's just one of the little kids from the girls' ward.'

My cheeks burned. '*Just*'! And I wasn't '*little*'. My legs might not be able to move but they were still as long as ever. And I was eleven, not a little baby. I spun my wheels so I could turn round.

'Katy? Come and meet my mum and gran,' said Dexter quickly, seeing he'd insulted me.

I hesitated, so the granny sprang up and tried to wheel me over herself. She was being helpful but it was highly irritating.

'So how did you hurt yourself, dear?' she asked. 'Car accident?'

'No, I – I fell,' I mumbled. I hated telling anyone about my fall off my rope swing because it made me sound so stupid, and whenever I talked about it I felt I was falling again and started shaking.

'Dear, dear, you poor little thing,' she said. 'Of course, you know how our Dexter came a cropper?'

I didn't know. I badly wanted to know but I knew he'd hate her telling me.

'Yes, of course,' I said quickly. 'I think I'd better be getting back to my ward to see my own visitors. It's OK, you don't have to push me, I can move the wheels myself. See?'

When I was at the end of the ward Dexter called, 'Bye, Katy. Maybe come back later?'

I gave him a nod and a wave and then I was off. And just arriving in my ward was Dad and the entire family: Clover, Elsie, Dorry, Jonnie and Phil, with Izzie herding them along. They'd bought Cecy too, who peered at me anxiously, biting her lip, looking terrified.

'Hi everyone,' I said.

'Katy! What on earth are you doing wheeling yourself about like that? You know you're meant to stay in your own ward,' Izzie fussed.

'I'm fine,' I said irritably, though I was starting to feel terribly tired and it was an effort to hold myself upright in the stupid wheelchair.

'Shall I help you back into bed?' Izzie asked.

I longed to be lying flat in my bed, but I couldn't bear the thought of the others seeing the whole horrible performance, my useless legs lolling.

'No, I'm fine, I *said*,' I insisted rudely. 'Don't you listen?'

Izzie would normally have told me off for talking back to her like that. Dad would normally be mad at me for cheeking her. But this wasn't normal. They just pretended not to notice.

And I pretended not to notice that Cecy looked as if she wanted to bolt back down the ward, along the corridors and out of the hospital as fast as she could run.

I wanted to run. But I was stuck there.

'Look! We've all made you presents, Katy,' said Clover eagerly, thrusting a carrier bag on to my lap.

Clover had made me a cardboard box, decorating it with stickers and so much glitter that my hands were mottled silver just holding it.

'Look inside,' said Clover. 'See? It's got a special button and ribbon.'

I undid the box and saw Clover had drawn many pictures of us together, a tall stick Katy and a round rosy Clover. We were playing all kinds of games. She'd even drawn us in the secret garden in the cave under the willow tree.

'It's a memory box,' said Clover proudly. 'For you to remember all our happy times together.'

I had to fight not to burst into tears.

Elsie had been busy with crayons and scissors too. She'd made strange little paper replicas of all sorts of things: jeans, Doc Martens, books, CDs, even a mobile phone.

'They're all the things I'd buy you if I had lots of money,' she said.

Everyone was looking at me, ready for me to praise Elsie and tell her I was thrilled. I struggled to find the right words.

Elsie mistook my hesitation.

'Don't you like them? I did make a skateboard and a bike, though its wheels went a bit wobbly, because I knew you'd like them best, but Mum said I mustn't give you them because it wouldn't be tactful,' she piped up.

'Elsie!' Izzie hissed, giving her a little shake.

'Well, that's what you *said*,' Elsie repeated.

'All right, all right,' said Dad. 'Say thank you, Katy.'

'Thank you, Elsie,' I said obediently.

It was easier with Dorry and Jonnie and Phil. Dorry had made me sickly sweet fudge, seven pieces, which made a rectangle with one lump missing.

'I needed to check it tasted OK,' Dorry explained.

Jonnie had made me a loom band bracelet.

'See? It's got red in it, because it's your favourite colour,' she said.

I put the loom band bracelet on my wrist at once and nibbled at a square of fudge to show my appreciation.

Phil gave me a mysterious round newspaper parcel bound tightly with many strands of Sellotape.

'I love using Sellotape,' he told me unnecessarily as I struggled to pick open the many layers.

It took several minutes, and my hands were aching already because I'd had to waggle my fingers about during the boring physio session, but I carried on, smiling gamely, while Phil hopped from one leg to the other. Then when I got to the present at last I was a little bit at a loss.

It was a small round lump of play dough with matchsticks stuck into it.

'Oh lovely! Play-Doh. Great,' I said.

'It's me!' Phil cried. 'I've made you a Philly doll. See? Here's my head and tummy and these are my legs and these are my arms.'

'Of course,' I said. 'Thank you very much, Phil. Thank you, everyone.'

There was a little silence. I saw Clover nudging Cecy.

'I've brought you a present too,' Cecy mumbled. She held it towards me uncertainly. Our fingers briefly touched as I took hold of the carefully folded pink tissue paper. Cecy snatched her hand away, as if paralysis was somehow catching.

I thought of the countless times we'd casually held hands or wandered along with our arms round each other, and this time great stinging tears spurted down my cheeks.

'Why are you crying, Katy?' Elsie asked. 'Cecy's present is the best of all. She's already shown it to us. You'll love it, honestly.'

I bent my head, undid a pink satin ribbon and opened up the tissue paper. There was a black oblong jewellery box inside. I thought of Helen's silver seahorse necklace and felt a stab of shame. Cecy had given me a locket in the shape of a heart. It was inscribed with two words: *Best Friend*.

'Oh Cecy. It's lovely,' I sniffed.

Cecy was crying too.

'Do you really like it? You don't think it's too girly?' she asked anxiously.

But she still stayed her distance and wouldn't help me put it on. I *did* like it, and I knew it must have cost heaps of money. I'd have sooner she'd given me a paperclip necklace and a big hug.

The necklace proved useful during visiting time because whenever there was a little silence one of the

275

littlies would say, 'Can I look inside your locket, Katy?' Cecy had inserted two heart-shaped photos: one of her and one of me.

There were a lot of silences. It wasn't just simple shyness because of the horrible hospital setting. Perhaps it was because so many topics were awkward now. The twins said, 'Guess what, Katy? We learned to skip yesterday.' Then they both put their hands over their mouths, as if they'd said something dreadful. Even Clover did this, starting a tale about some dungarees she wanted Izzie to buy her, and then suddenly stopped, looking agonized.

'It's OK, Clover. I've still got legs, even if they don't work. I can still wear dungarees if I want,' I said.

I meant to reassure her, but the way I blurted it out sounded rude and nasty. Clover looked woebegone. I couldn't bear it. These were my sisters and brothers and my best friend, yet we couldn't seem to talk properly to each other any more.

'I'm sorry,' I said, crying again.

They started to cry too, so Izzie took them all down to the car park because 'We don't want to tire poor Katy too much.'

Poor Katy. Oh God. I was bad naughty wilful tomboy funny bossy Katy, all these things, not *poor*.

Dad quietly took my hand.

'We're sorry too, chickie,' he said. 'It's hard for us all. Especially you. But it will sort itself out. We'll gradually get used to things.'

'I don't want to get used to being stuck in a wheelchair!' I said. 'You wait. I won't have everybody pitying me. I *will* walk again. One of the boys in the next ward can walk a bit already; I've seen him when we go to physio. Up and down while holding on to these bars. I'm sure I could do that if they'd only let me.'

'Perhaps he's got a different sort of injury, darling,' Dad said gently. 'I think the wrong bit of your spine is affected. The nerves don't generally ever start working again. I'm sorry. I hate having to dash your hopes, but I don't want you to get any false expectations and then be devastated.'

'One of the nurses said there's this new research when they take nerves from up people's noses and inject them into the spine,' I said. She hadn't been saying it to me, but I heard her talking to one of the other nurses. 'They could do that to me and then I could learn to walk again.'

'I've read about that procedure too, Katy, and it's very exciting, I agree – but the techniques are still being developed, and we have no way of knowing whether it would work for everyone, or even be practical. Maybe one day it will all be possible, but not now, not for you.'

Then I did a terrible thing. I couldn't bear Dad dashing all my secret hopes. He seemed to be trampling on everything, making it worse, though the sane part of me knew he was trying to be kind. I didn't care. I felt so despairing that I told him to push off. But, like Dexter, I didn't say *push*. I used another word. A word I'd never even said out loud before.

Dad looked terribly shocked. But even then he didn't tell me off.

'You're tired and upset, Katy. Shall I help you into bed? Well, I'll leave you now so you can calm down a bit. I'll be back tomorrow. Goodbye, darling.'

I felt dreadful – so sorry, and yet somehow I couldn't say it. I even turned my head away when he bent to kiss me. I was left slumped in my wheelchair, not able to crawl into bed and pull the covers over my head. I was horribly exposed too. Naveen and her mum and all her aunties and whoever were all staring at me, shocked, because they'd heard me swearing at Dad. Marnie's mum looked horrified too, though she was trying terribly hard to pretend nothing was the matter, dancing Marnie's dollies around her bed. Only Rosemary's parents nodded and smiled at me, as sweet and forgiving as their own little girl.

I sat on, feeling there was a spiked ring of shame all about me. Then Jasmine – oh thank God it was Jasmine – put her head round the door. She drew the curtains round my bed, helped me in, and then sat beside me while I wept. She didn't say anything. She just held my hand, her thumb stroking me gently.

'I said something dreadful to my dad,' I muttered at last.

'Oh well. I expect we've all said something dreadful to our dads. Never mind. You can be extra nice to him tomorrow,' said Jasmine.

I resolved to do just that. I longed to see him, and yet when I saw him coming into the ward I felt sick with embarrassment and almost wished he'd turn on his heel and walk away again. I couldn't look him in the eye as he came up to me.

'How's my girl?' he said softly.

'Oh Dad,' I said.

We gave each other a long hard hug. I breathed in his lovely warm toasty clean smell, loving him so much.

'I'm sorry, Dad,' I whispered into his neck.

'I'm sorry too, darling. Very, very sorry,' said Dad, sounding a little choked.

'What? I was the one who swore at you!' I said, astonished.

'Yes, and don't you ever use that word again, young lady. But I can understand. Oh Katy, I got it all wrong. Call myself a doctor! I should be gently reassuring you, trying to help you be as optimistic as possible – and yet there I was, dashing all your hopes. I just wanted to try to be completely straight with you, but it went horribly wrong. I'm no expert, darling. Maybe you *will* be able to walk again one day. I wanted to help you adjust to things without any false hopes, but that's going to take time. You must still be reeling from the shock of it all.

I know I am. I don't know what to think, what to do. Maybe that's why I'm making such a hash of things.' Dad still held me tight, as if he could never bear to let me go.

It was so strange to hear Dad say this. I didn't really want him to say sorry to me and admit he felt at such a loss. I need Dad to be *Dad*, the person I loved and looked up to most in the world.

He was mumbling something now. I couldn't quite catch what he said.

'What, Dad? What did you say?'

Dad broke away, fumbling for a handkerchief.

'Sorry, Katy. So sorry. I just said something about wishing your mother were here,' he said, wiping his eyes and blowing his nose.

'Oh Dad, so do I.' I paused. 'Dad, sometimes I thought – when I fell out the tree – and then just at first in the hospital – look, I know it sounds daft, I'm sure it was just my imagination, but Mum really did seem to be with me.'

I thought Dad would shake his head and give me some scientific reason why you dream of special people when your body's in crisis – but he just stared at me.

'What did she say? What did she look like?' he asked with desperate eagerness.

This unsettled me all over again. Dad had always been so scornful and sceptical if I ever said I believed in ghosts or any kind of afterlife.

'I – I can't really remember now. It's all so fuzzy and mixed up. But she looked just the same, with her ponytail – remember? – and she was lovely,' I said, my voice wobbling.

'She was always lovely,' said Dad. 'Oh Katy, I still miss her so.'

Dad would never usually talk about Mum, probably because he didn't want to seem disloyal to Izzie.

'I miss Mum too, Dad, so much,' I said.

We sat holding hands, glad to be able to share this moment. Nobody else understand how we felt, not even Clover, because she didn't really remember Mum, though she pretended she did. It was just Dad and me, aching for Mum to come back.

18

I hated it in the hospital, but in a weird way I started to get used to it. I never got used to my new hateful body with its useless bladder and bowels and dead legs, but at least it was the same for all of us patients. I got used to the dreary hospital routine, even the horrible toileting. I got used to the clank and chime of all the hospital sounds and the slight creak of my special spinal bed as the air pumped in and out. I got used to the dreary exercise routines when Vicky, the physiotherapist, held my legs and moved them around so they didn't get stiff. I couldn't really feel what she was doing. It was always a shock when I leaned forward and tried to move my legs with my own hands. They were such sad stick things but they seemed to weigh a ton when I hauled them just a few millimetres.

I got used to transferring from my bed to my wheelchair and back again, though it was nowhere near as easy as you'd think, and if I didn't concentrate hard I misjudged it and nearly toppled over. I *did* fall once and there was a great to-do. I had to be checked all over to make sure I hadn't broken anything, which seemed so stupid seeing as I'd already broken my back.

I even got used to the hospital food, although it was pretty disgusting and the smell of it lurked in the corridors for hours after it was served. They'd show me the menu every day and I'd think, great, macaroni cheese or fish pie, two of my favourites. But when they were dished up the macaroni would be disconcertingly pale with no crispy bits of cheese, and the pasta was so rubbery I'd chew until my jaws ached. The fish pie was even worse, the potato grey and lumpy and hard on top, and the fish so slimy it made me shudder when I swallowed.

I thought longingly of Izzie's macaroni cheese, golden and delicious, and her wonderful fish pie, the potato creamy and fluffy, the fish white and juicy, the little pink prawns tender and succulent.

I went through phases of not ordering hot meals, just asking for salads and sandwiches, although they weren't great either. I got so fed up of damp pink ham or bland tinned tuna that I only picked at them. The dietitian nagged at me, lecturing me about needing protein for my muscles. They even brought some sort of psych-person to 'have a chat' with me. They were clearly worrying about anorexia again, because she kept asking me if I had a voice in my head telling me I was fat. The voice in my head would have had to be totally loony, because I wasn't fat: I was thin as a pin. I didn't *want* to be thin because it made me look gawkier than ever. I just looked like a collapsed giraffe rather than one standing up or striding.

Jasmine was cleverer than any psychiatrist. She got me helping little Marnie to eat her meals. I don't know if Marnie had been dead picky with her food before her car accident, but she was hopeless now, pressing her lips together and turning her head away when you aimed a spoon at her mouth.

'You're a clever clogs, Katy, and so good with the little ones. I suppose it comes naturally, you being the eldest at home. See if you can do a Mary Poppins on Marnie. Otherwise we'll have to feed her through a tube – and you know she'll hate that,' said Jasmine.

'OK, I'll give it a go,' I said, proud that she'd asked me.

So I'd sit with Marnie, our meals in front of us, and I'd make up stories. We had to climb all the way up mash mountain; we had to spear the naughty sausage; we had to count the little green pea beads. Every time I took a bite, Marnie did too. I'd carry on making up this daft kind of fairy story while Marnie and I chewed and swallowed. By the end of the story both our plates were empty.

I also tried swapping to Naveen's special halal food, which was a lot tastier than bland British hospital cuisine, and that was fun for a while too. I became quite friendly with Naveen. She still cried every single day, but when she cheered up she had a wicked sense of humour, almost rivalling Dexter's. We'd whisper funny things about the nurses and the doctors and the dietitian. We were particularly rude about the physios, because they mauled us about so much and kept nag, nag, nagging. We knew they were just trying to help us achieve as much mobility as possible. We hated them all the same because they made us carry on our stupid exercises until we were exhausted, our hearts banging in our chests, our hair straggly with sweat.

Naveen had the most wonderful hair, which she wore in a very long black plait down her back. I got her to do mine like that, but my own hair was so thin and wispy I ended up with a mouse's tail, while Naveen's was a thick glossy rope. I loved Naveen's bangles too, which clanked on each arm. We weren't supposed to wear jewellery in hospital but Naveen said her gold bangles were part of her religion so she was allowed to keep them. She winked at me later and told me she was fibbing, which made me laugh.

So I was friends with Naveen now, friends with Marnie – and I even made friends with little Rosemary. I felt so guilty that I'd disliked her simply because she was so good and patient. I hadn't ever been nasty to her face, but I'd mocked her to Dexter. Now I'd calmed down and wasn't quite so angry all the time, I felt horribly mean. Rosemary wasn't a little prig. She wasn't even being good to get her own way and make all the nursing staff adore her. She was just a sweet, happy little girl, even now, when she was trapped in a body that wouldn't work.

I watched her at physio, her tiny tan face flushing with exertion as they pushed and pulled her. I saw her shrieking with laughter as they splashed her in the little pool. I loved seeing her nuzzling her head against her mum and dad when they came to visit. I heard her sometimes in the middle of the night, muttering away to herself.

One time I managed to do a bold transfer on to the wheelchair beside my bed, even though this was strictly forbidden at night-time, and wheeled myself over to her.

'Rosemary?' I whispered.

She lay quiet, practically holding her breath.

'Rosemary, I know you're awake; I heard you!'

'Are you cross?' she whispered back.

'No, silly! Just curious. What was all that muttering?'

'I was just telling myself a story,' Rosemary said.

'Oh, bless! Look, would you like me to tell you a story?' I offered.

She seemed willing, so I started off on another Marnie-type fairy story. Rosemary loved this, chuckling softly to herself. After ten minutes or so her breathing got slower and steadier and I realized I'd lulled her to sleep. I felt so touched I blew her a little kiss and then wheeled myself back to my own bed as silently as possible.

I got stuck trying to transfer back again, which was nowhere near as easy, and Jeannie came along and whispered at me furiously as she heaved me back into bed – but it was worth it. I often told Rosemary special stories after that. When I ran out of ideas for my own stories I told her variations of 'Goldilocks' and 'Cinderella' and 'The Sleeping Beauty' and she loved them all.

I was friends with all the girls in my unit – and friends with Dexter too. I felt much closer to them now than to Cecy, though she visited several times and wrote me emails when Dad brought his own laptop in for me to use. I was still close to Clover of course, but I couldn't help feeling upset and left out when she told me all the different things she'd been doing with Elsie and the littlies. She seemed weirdly close to Elsie now, starting half her sentences with 'Elsie-and-I'. Clover had always agreed with me in the past that Elsie was a pathetic little wimp who'd tell tales to Izzie if you so much as breathed on her, but now she acted like she was her best friend.

I decided to sort that out straight away the minute I got home. I didn't know when that would be. Naveen had only been in hospital a week longer than me, but

Rosemary and Marnie had been there for months. No one would give me a precise answer. It was always, 'It will depend on your progress,' a pretty useless response.

I longed and longed and longed to go home. It was like a strange, magical land I'd made up long ago. I couldn't imagine myself back there. Sometimes I couldn't even remember the exact details of my bedroom or the bathroom or the library downstairs. They all seemed fuzzy in my mind's eye, as if I was squinting at them through narrowed eyelids. It was hard imagining all the children rattling around inside the house, leading their lives without me.

I remembered that it was still the summer holidays. I felt sure they'd all be going crazy with boredom, because Clover wasn't very good at inventing new games, and Elsie worse than useless.

'Do you remember it's our holiday this Saturday?' Dad said one afternoon while he was visiting.

I didn't understand immediately. 'It's been the holidays for weeks, hasn't it?' I said.

'No, I mean when we go on holiday to Nefyn, to the cottage,' said Dad.

'Oh!' I said. So was I getting out of hospital at last? I imagined myself there, running along the sandy beach, clambering over the rocks, squealing in the icy sea . . . Then I hit both my legs hard with my clenched fists.

'Hey, don't do that! You'll bruise yourself,' said Dad.

'I don't care. I can't feel it, can I?' I said sulkily.

'You have to be extremely careful with paralysed legs. You know that,' said Dad.

'All right, I do know. Look, Dad, I can't wait to go on holiday, but won't it be difficult getting me to the beach? Will I be able to wheel myself along the cliff path? And can you push a wheelchair over sand? And once I'm on the beach I'll have to sit there like a pudding while all the others run about and play games,' I said.

Dad was looking at me as if I were totally deluded.

'Darling, it's simply not possible. Not just now, anyway. Maybe next year. Besides, you have to stay in hospital a few weeks more to build up your upper body and improve your transferring skills and learn to manage your bladder.'

'*Dad!*' I hated it when he said matter-of-fact doctor things, especially about anything personal.

'You do understand, don't you, Katy? I thought about cancelling the cottage altogether, but the children have had such a rough time. They really need a holiday. They've been so worried about you,' Dad went on.

I could hardly take it in. So were they all trooping off to the cottage without me? I had to stay in hospital, while they all went off to have a fun holiday together?

'Katy? I know it sounds so heartless – but you don't want to deprive them of their holiday just because you can't go, do you?' Dad asked.

I shook my head, not trusting myself to speak. I didn't want to deprive them exactly. I suppose I wanted them all to say they couldn't possibly go because it wouldn't be any fun without me.

'Don't worry, love. You're not going to be left all alone,' Dad said, misunderstanding. 'I won't be going. I'll be coming to visit you every day, just as I always do.'

This was comforting, but only to a degree.

'Clover?' I mumbled. 'Is she going too?'

In the old days Clover wouldn't go *anywhere* without me. Cecy might have gone all weird around me, but thank goodness Clover was still the same, hugging me as if she'd never let me go whenever she came on a visit.

'Oh, you know how Clover adores you. She said she couldn't go, not if you weren't able to come too,' said Dad. 'I told her that was nonsense. She has to go. She can't stay home all by herself while I'm out at the surgery. Of course she's going to Nefyn too. She says she'll hate it this time, bless her, but I think when she gets there she'll perk up and enjoy herself.'

I didn't *want* her to enjoy herself, not without me. But that was such a selfish thought I blushed, even though I hadn't said it out loud. I was learning that if I said what I really thought people were shocked and hurt. It was so unfair. Now I was stuck in a wheelchair I was somehow supposed to turn into an unselfish little saint.

I did *try* to be happy for everyone going off on their holiday, but it was a real struggle when they came to see me on Friday. Philly was actually carrying his plastic bucket and spade to show me.

'Look, look, Katy! I'm going to do digging at the beach and make heaps and heaps of castles,' he said proudly, banging me on the knees with both the bucket and the spade for emphasis.

'Don't, Philly! Watch Katy's poor legs!' Izzie hissed, though of course I hadn't felt a thing.

'We're going to make castles too and we're going to swim in the sea,' said Jonnie. 'I can swim a whole length of the swimming pool now, Katy, did you know? I can swim heaps better than Dorry. He can't even do a width.'

'I think swimming's boring,' said Dorry. 'I'm going to have an ice-cream cone every day when we're on holiday. No, I'm going to have an ice cream every morning and another every afternoon and *another* before I go to bed.'

'You're so greedy, Dorry. Mum says you're just a walking stomach,' said Elsie. 'Clover and me are going to collect shells, lots and lots of pretty shells, and then we're going to –'

'Shh, Elsie, it's a secret!' said Clover.

What? I couldn't bear them having secrets together.

'We wish, wish, wish you could come too, Katy,' Clover said quickly. 'It won't be the same without you.'

'I wish I was coming too,' I said, sounding sour.

I forced myself to smile and give them all a hug and a kiss, even Elsie. I said I hoped they'd all have a lovely holiday. But the minute they'd gone I started howling.

I wanted to lie on my front and pull the covers over my head but I didn't have the strength to drag my body round. I just lay miserably on my back with the tears dripping down the sides of my face into my ears.

Naveen and Marnie and Rosemary were all busy with their visitors so they didn't notice. I tried very hard not to make any obvious snorty sobbing noises. I didn't have a tissue handy. I was getting into a horrible soggy state but I didn't care.

'Hey, is it raining in here? You're soaked!' It was Dexter. He'd wheeled himself in so silently I hadn't even heard him approach my bed.

'Oh God. Go away. I look a mess,' I said, trying to hide under the sheets.

'I'll say,' said Dexter. He pulled a few tissues out of the box on my locker. 'Here. Or use the sheet, whatever.'

I wiped my face as best I could and blew my nose several times.

'Better?'

I emerged from the sheet, scarlet with embarrassment.

'Don't fret,' said Dexter. 'Why wouldn't anyone cry in the circumstances? And visiting times are often the worst, aren't they? You look forward to seeing them so much and then it all goes wrong.'

'Well, it's all gone horribly wrong for me, because my lot are all skipping off to the seaside on holiday, leaving me stuck here. Can you imagine?' I said, still snuffling. I didn't add that Dad was giving up his holiday to stay visiting me, as that would have spoilt the effect of my statement.

'Oh, I can imagine all too well. Something we'll have to get used to. Our families go on holiday. We stay Home Alone. Hmm, that's a thought . . . How are we going to cope with burglars in a wheelchair?' Dexter drew himself rapidly, a little cowering creature being threatened by great towering men with striped jerseys and bags marked SWAG.

'Draw me too,' I said.

'No, you won't even be allowed the freedom of the house because you're only a kid. They'll put *you* in the cupboard under the stairs. It's OK – they'll poke in a couple of cornflake packets and some long-life milk to keep you going for the holidays.'

'My dad wouldn't do that,' I said.

'OK. Then he'd hire you a special nanny for the duration.'

'Like Mary Poppins?'

'As if. More like Miss Trunchbull.' He drew her with relish, a massive, muscly, boot-faced creature whirling me about her head while still strapped into my wheelchair. Dexter was obviously expecting me to laugh but I felt like wallowing gloomily for a while.

'Aren't you ever going to cheer up?' Dexter asked. 'Where was this wondrous seaside? Barbados? The Seychelles? Mauritius?'

'Nefyn in North Wales,' I said.

Dexter burst out laughing. 'Oh, a real sun-soaked glamour spot!' he said. 'Come on, you can do better than that. With several flicks of my magic pencil I can transport you on far more interesting holiday jaunts. Where would you like to go if you could choose anywhere?'

I thought hard. We'd only ever been to Nefyn.

'Disneyland!' I said. Half the kids in my class had been to the Disney resort in Florida, or at least to Disneyland Paris on a weekend trip. I'd always wanted to go, but Dad winced at the very idea.

'Disneyland!' said Dexter, wrinkling his nose. 'How old *are* you? Six? Seven? Does diddums want to see Mickey Mouse and all the pwetty lickle pwincesses?'

'You shut up. I bet you've been to Disneyland. You seem like the sort of kid who was spoilt rotten when you were little,' I said sharply.

'Try to be a tad more original, girl.'

I thought hard. 'I know, I know! I don't know the right place, but I'd love to swim with dolphins!' I said.

'Boring,' said Dexter, but he drew me being pulled along on a smiley dolphin's back, a lovely picture that made me sigh wistfully.

'You'd like to swim with dolphins too, I bet you,' I said.

'Maybe. Tell you the animal holiday *I'd* like. I'd like to go trekking in Borneo to see some of the wild orangutans. That would be incredible.'

'Draw it. Go on!' I commanded.

So he drew himself small again, in an ultra-cool wheelchair of his own design like a mini four-by-four. He'd just come across a mother orang-utan with a baby in her arms. He drew the baby half bald, with wonderful sticking-up wisps of hair on his little head.

'Oh, he's so sweet!' I said. 'So where's the dad? I know – he's huge, absolutely huge, and he's striding through the jungle to see who's talking to his wife and he doesn't look very happy. Draw him. Go on, Dexter.'

So he drew a King Kong-size orang-utan with his vast head showing way above all the tallest trees. He had one huge hairy arm raised triumphantly, something small and wriggly clasped in his gigantic paw.

'What's that in his hand? A big spider?'

'No, silly. Look closer.'

I peered at the picture. It was a miniature woman in nurse's uniform. Even though she was tiny she had a very big bottom.

We both rocked with laughter, especially when Jeannie poked her head in the room to see who was being so rowdy.

'What are you doing on the girls' ward, Dexter? You get straight back to the boys' ward, do you hear me?' she said crossly.

'It's visiting time so I'm visiting Katy,' Dexter said.

'You two! You think you can change all the rules to suit yourselves,' said Jeannie, but she let him stay.

We played the Holiday game most days. I sometimes drew the pictures, though I was nowhere near as good at it as Dexter. I thought he'd tease me for my wobbly lines and lopsided figures, but he was surprisingly encouraging because he liked some of my wild ideas.

One day I started drawing both of us racing each other along American highways on huge great motorbikes, but I got a bit stuck, not knowing exactly the position of the wheels or the right shape of the handlebars. Dexter didn't offer to help. He was unusually quiet.

'Dexter? Come on, show me how to draw it. I bet you know all about motorbikes,' I said.

'I know nothing about them. Surely that's obvious,' said Dexter, and he suddenly wheeled himself right out of the ward, leaving his sketchbook behind.

I stared after him, wondering what on earth I'd done to upset him. Then I looked down at my clumsy motorbike sketch.

I waited until Jasmine came into the ward.

'Jasmine, did Dexter have a motorbike accident? Is that how he smashed his back?'

'You'll have to ask Dexter. We're not supposed to give out information like that,' she said.

'Yes, but you know how touchy he is. I don't want to upset him. I just started drawing a motorbike and he went all weird,' I said.

'Well . . . yes, he would do. All right, he *was* in a motorbike accident. Apparently he lost control and went hurtling over and over. It was amazing he didn't kill himself – or anyone else for that matter.'

'But he's only sixteen. I didn't think you could ride a motorbike till you were older.'

'He was larking around with some older lads, desperate to show off – you know what Dexter's like. One of them had a motorbike and Dexter begged to have a go. He was only supposed to ride it to the end of the road, dead slow, but he revved up instead. Idiotically.'

'Oh, poor Dexter.'

'The police have been involved, of course, but I hope they'll think Dexter's been punished enough.' Jasmine shook her head. 'You kids! I don't know why I do this job sometimes. It's heartbreaking.'

I tore the motorbike page into little pieces. I waited till the next day and then put the sketchbook on my lap and wheeled it in to Dexter.

'Hi. You left this behind,' I said.

'Thanks.' He didn't smile, he didn't even look me in the eye, but at least he wasn't lying on his back with his hand over his face.

'Dexter, I didn't know. About the motorbike. But Jasmine told me,' I said haltingly.

'Right.'

'I know how you feel.'

'No, you don't!'

'Yes, because my accident was all my fault too. I tried to make a swing and I didn't tie the rope properly to

297

the tree branch. It wasn't even a real swing; it was just a stupid piece of rope. I was supposed to be staying indoors in disgrace because I'd disobeyed my stupid stepmother, but I wanted to show them that I didn't care, that I could have fun on my own. It drives me mad sometimes, thinking about it. I see myself tying that rope over and over again. I try and rewind that bit in my head, getting the right sort of knot, which is totally crazy, because it's happened and here I am. It makes it worse that it's all my fault. So see, I *do* understand.'

Dexter looked at me at last.

'OK. Agreed. Stop being so wise and mature when you're just a squidgy little kid.'

'I'm not squidgy. I'm tall. Very tall. I bet if we could both stand I'd be much taller than you. It's so weird being hunched up all the time. It's as if someone really has chopped my legs off. I wish they would. Useless things.' I punched them again.

'You're not supposed to do that. You'll hurt them without realizing.'

'I know. They all keep nagging me about it. But sometimes I want to hurt them.'

'Yeah, me too.'

'See. You understand me. We're a pair.'

'We are.'

'We belong together.'

'What? Are you asking me to hook up with you, little girl?' said Dexter, laughing.

I punched him on his shoulder. 'Shut up! You know I didn't mean that. I meant we're mates. Aren't we?'

'Yes, we are. True mates,' said Dexter. 'And we'll make a pact. We'll keep in touch when we're out of this dump, and when you're old enough we'll go on holiday together, you and me doing wheelies up and down the prom or whatever, OK?'

This seemed a blissful idea to me. I almost stopped minding that Clover and Elsie and Dorry and Jonnie and Phil were all whooping it up on the beach without me.

At least I had Dad coming in every day. He was trying to make an extra fuss of me, bringing me special presents each time: a box of four expensive truffles; a rosy cake of soap; a little toy felt mouse; a paperback of Anne Frank's diary.

I started reading the diary straight away. We'd learned about Anne Frank in Year Six and read a couple of extracts, but I didn't realize how good the whole diary was – and how terrifying and upsetting too. I got Dad's point. Anne hadn't lost the use of her legs, but she was equally imprisoned in that secret hiding place in Amsterdam during the last world war, unable to walk about freely for years.

I started to feel tremendously fond of Dad. He'd never given me special presents just for me before. I looked forward to his evening visits enormously. So it was a surprise – and a huge disappointment – to see *Izzie* walk into the ward on Thursday evening.

'Izzie? How come you're back? I thought you were all on holiday till Saturday? And where's Dad?'

She sat beside me on the bed. I loved it if Dad did that, but I hated the slight weight of her pulling the covers. I fidgeted irritably.

'I've brought you a present from Wales,' she said, handing me a carefully wrapped parcel, shiny red paper with a red satin ribbon.

It perversely annoyed me that she remembered red was my favourite colour. I unwrapped the parcel quickly. It was a white T-shirt with a picture of a red Welsh dragon, and red-and-white striped socks to match. There was also a pair of soft black jogging bottoms too, carefully styled, not too baggy.

These were good presents. I was running out of things to wear now that I was in a wheelchair. The physios didn't like me wearing my jeans because they said they were too tight. I mustn't have anything too restrictive that could cut or chafe without my realizing. I'd been making do with old joggers that were washed-out and hideous, and I hadn't bothered with my T-shirts, wearing the same one day after day.

'Thank you, Izzie,' I said, not bothering to sound properly grateful. 'So, come on, why are you here instead of Dad? Why did the holiday end early?'

Perhaps the kids had all moped about, not bothering to dig sandcastles or go paddling. *It's no fun without Katy*, they'd whine. *We miss Katy so.* Day after day. So eventually Izzie grew fed up and bundled them all back home two days early.

'The children are still in Wales, Katy. They're there till Saturday,' said Izzie.

'But who's looking after them if you're here?' I asked.

'Your dad,' said Izzie.

'What? But he has to be here, he has to come and see me,' I said.

'He's been seeing you every day and he's getting thoroughly worn out. I persuaded him to swap with me for the last couple of days. He drove to Wales last night in the Nissan and I drove back in it this morning.'

'Oh,' I said flatly.

'Don't look like that, Katy. He's just got two days! He needs a proper break. Haven't you noticed how thin he's been getting? And he's been having terrible headaches. He stays up half the night poring over medical stuff about spinal injuries on the internet.'

'He's looking for a cure? But he said there wasn't one, not yet.'

'Yes, but he's checking everything out even so, and wondering about other rehabilitation centres, different treatments, anything that could improve your quality of life.'

'And meanwhile I'm stuck here in this dump and I don't get a holiday at all,' I said.

'Well, we think it might be time for you to come home. Mr Pearson says your back wound has healed nicely. You can manage your wheelchair. The nurses say you're very independent. You've learned how to transfer yourself in and out of it. Your arms are strong even though you're so thin. You've obviously got good muscles.' Izzie leaned over and gently squeezed the top of my arm.

'Don't!' I said, trying to lean away. I couldn't stand her touching me.

'So anyway,' said Izzie, trying not to look rebuffed. 'We're wondering about you coming home next week.'

'Next week?' It was hard to take it in. I'd begged to go home every day, but in the way little Phil begged to drive Dad's car. It hadn't really felt possible, not yet. 'But who will help me shower? Or do all the stupid boring exercises with me? Who will put me to bed? And – and what about the toilet stuff? Will I have to have my own special nurse at home?'

'We're hoping that someone trained will come in mornings and evenings just at first. But I'm sure I'll soon get the hang of it, Katy,' said Izzie.

'*What?*'

'Do stop saying that. It sounds horrible.'

'But I don't want *you* to do it!'

'Who else have you got in mind?' Izzie asked sharply.

I struggled to think of some other solution. I couldn't bear the thought of Dad helping me either. Or Clover. But for it to be *Izzie*! She'd fuss and boss me about and I'd be so helpless, reduced to infancy with a mother figure that I couldn't stand.

I thought of my own mum and wept bitterly, longing for her more than ever. I dreamed about her that night. We were both in wheelchairs but we didn't care. We raced along the streets together, hair flying, going so fast that we flew into the air and bowled along the blue sky.

19

I went up and down the ward saying goodbye to Naveen and Marnie and Rosemary. They all three cried, even stoic little Rosemary, and that upset me most of all. And it was worse going to say goodbye to Dexter.

'It won't be the same without you, kid,' he said, in an American gangster accent.

'Perhaps I could come and visit sometimes?' I said hopefully.

'Are you mad? You can't come back here!'

'You'll be going home soon yourself anyway.'

'Yes, that's going to be a bundle of laughs too.'

'And you've got my email address. You'll keep in touch, won't you, Dexter?' I clutched his arm. 'Promise?'

'Promise.'

Then Jasmine came to take me away. I clung to her too, wishing I could stand up and have a proper hug with her. It was so hard being stuck at waist level now.

'I'll miss you so, Jasmine,' I said into her stomach.

'I'll miss you too, chickie.'

'Even though I've been grumpy and difficult sometimes?'

'Incredibly grumpy. Incredibly difficult. But very lovable. I'm going to miss you heaps,' said Jasmine.

Then Dad and Izzie arrived to take me down to the car.

'Where are all the others? Didn't they want to come too?' I asked.

'They're back at school,' said Izzie.

That was a bit of a shock. The whole long summer holidays had been and gone and I'd missed it all. And now all my year, Cecy and Ryan and Eva and everyone, had gone off to secondary school without me. I'd missed the first day, the most important time, when you made sure you were sitting next to your best friend, and you checked out everything together, and you visited the girls' cloakrooms in a pair just in case all those silly rumours about ducking new girls' head first in the toilets happened to be true.

I thought about going to school in a wheelchair – and I felt sick.

It was even scary going down in the hospital lift and along all the corridors, past the busy cafe and over to the main exit. There were so many people everywhere, rushing and jostling, all of them towering above me. And they stared. Some did it discreetly, with quick little sideways glances. Others did it blatantly, peering at my useless legs. One old woman shook her head and tutted.

I felt myself going as scarlet as my T-shirt. I'd been insistently wheeling myself, but I was glad when Dad took over and got me away from them all. It was a nightmare transferring from my chair to the car seat. I'd practised this a hundred times with a dummy car seat back in the hospital, but it seemed so much more difficult with a real car. I so wanted to be independent, but in the end Dad had to get in the driver's seat and pull me in, while Izzie clutched at my legs and hauled them into place. She tried to do up the seat belt for me too, as if my arms didn't work either.

'Off we go. Home sweet home!' said Dad, in a determinedly cheerful voice.

'Hurray,' I said flatly. I felt like bursting into tears. I didn't understand. I'd so longed to go home but now I wanted Jasmine to come rushing out of the hospital, insisting that I was far too ill to go anywhere.

Dad squeezed my hand. 'It's a bit of an ordeal, isn't it?' he said softly.

I nodded, shutting my eyes to keep the tears under control.

We set off. Dad usually hated the car radio but he turned it to a music station and actually tried to hum along to the tunes in an attempt to lighten the atmosphere. I stared out of the window. It was so odd being outside. The streets didn't seem real somehow. The whole town looked like images on television. *I* didn't feel real either. I wasn't me any more. I was this sad invalid girl sliding uncomfortably around on the front seat, my wheelchair clanking about in the back.

Then we turned into our street and I shrank down further in my seat, my head bent, suddenly terrified that someone would see me. I couldn't stand the thought of them shaking their heads pityingly, trying to talk to me in a baby voice as if I'd lost my senses as well as the use of my legs.

It was a terrible performance transferring out of the car back into my wheelchair, with Dad and Izzie fumbling and pushing all over again.

'Oh dear, maybe we've taken you out of hospital too early, Katy,' said Izzie.

'Nonsense. We'll soon get the hang of it all,' said Dad. 'Katy will do so much better at home, won't you, darling?'

I didn't know. I didn't think I was going to be able to cope *anywhere*. I felt so tired and weak and awful that I just wanted to lie down. But Dad and Izzie commanded me to look up, and I saw the children had put a big banner up over the front door saying WELCOME HOME,

KATY! I was appalled that it was there, because that meant everyone in the whole street would have seen it, and maybe they'd come knocking and peering and I couldn't bear it. But I managed to give a grim little smile.

'How lovely,' I said.

'They're all so excited that you're coming home at last,' said Izzie. 'It was a really hard job getting them into school this morning. But I thought it might be a bit much for you if they were all clamouring at once.'

I didn't want her to be so wretchedly thoughtful. I didn't want to be grateful. But I managed to stay smiling as they wheeled me up a new little ramp to the front door.

'We didn't want to have to jolt you up the steps each time,' Izzie said.

Then we were in the hall. I looked at all the stairs.

'So how am I going to get up there?' I asked.

'Well, we'll probably get a stairlift installed. We've had discussions with Social Services, but it's going to take forever being assessed and filling in all the paperwork and I doubt we'd qualify for help anyway, so maybe we'll manage everything ourselves,' said Dad.

'Yes, but how am I going to get up to my bedroom *now*?' I said, and I couldn't stop myself wailing petulantly.

I so longed to be up in my own bed at last, with all my things around me and Clover close by.

'Well, we thought for the moment, until we can make all the right changes, you'd be happier in the library,' said Izzie. 'It worked very well while Helen was here. Come and look. We've made it as nice as we can.'

'Izzie's worked so hard to make it look special,' Dad murmured. 'And you've always said the library is your favourite place in the house. Think how lovely it will be to have all the books around you all the time.'

But they were all *Dad's* books, not mine. There were a whole load of medical books, some of them really old, with weird pictures of people's insides. Clover and I used to giggle over them in secret, but they weren't books I could ever read. Then there were Dad's yellow cricket books, and they were beyond boring. He had a lot of novels too, but not the sort I liked, with easy stories and lots of drama. I didn't mind his old children's books – some of them were my favourites too, like the big Orlando picture books and *Wind in the Willows* and the Narnia stories and *The Hobbit*, but I'd read all these already.

The bookshelves took up all three walls, and the fourth was mostly window, so I couldn't have any of my posters up. My bed was now stuck in a corner, with my bedside table beside it, but neither looked as if it belonged. There were strange new ornaments arranged on the table, all of them made out of seashells. There were three shells with inked-on faces and stuck-on woolly bits.

'The children all made you presents when we were at Nefyn,' said Izzie. 'Dorry and Jonnie made spider shells; Phil says his is an octopus. But to be truthful I can't tell them apart.'

I looked at the spiders and the octopus without comment. There was also a little box studded in seashells. The shells were carefully arranged in a pretty pattern. I reached out and ran my finger over the wavy shells.

'Clover and Elsie worked together for ages. They hardly needed any help. Haven't they done it splendidly?' said Izzie. 'It's a jewellery box. It's so you can keep your mother's watch and your special locket and Helen's seahorse necklace in it. Incidentally, I can't find it. You must tell me where you keep it, Katy.'

I thought of the broken chain hidden in my treasure box and I started sobbing.

'Oh darling, don't cry so. You're just tired out,' said Dad. 'We'll get you into bed and you can have a little nap.'

He left Izzie to yank my jogging bottoms and knickers off and stuff my legs into pyjamas. I cried all the way through this awkward procedure. I'd never let Izzie dress or undress me before and it was terribly humiliating having her help me now.

It was also another desperate struggle to get into bed itself. My arms seemed to have lost all their strength and I'd forgotten the knack of swinging myself round.

By the time I was lying flat I was trembling with exhaustion.

Izzie drew the curtains to shut out the sunlight. She ruffled my hair as if I were one of the littlies and then went out of the room. I was left there, alone in my new room that didn't belong to me at all. I cried and cried, muffling my sobs as best I could because I didn't want Dad or Izzie to come back. I wanted my mum more than anything, but I couldn't conjure her up.

It was a long time before I could go to sleep, but then I dozed most of the day, just waking up at lunchtime to have a bowl of tomato soup. It was Izzie's own home-made soup and it tasted especially good after the hospital's watery variety, but I couldn't bring myself to compliment her.

Then suddenly there was a lot of shouting and banging of doors and I realized the children had come home from school. I thought they'd come bursting in on me at once, but I heard Izzie hushing them severely and whispering that they must be very quiet and only stay with me a few minutes because I was very weak and tired.

'No, I'm not!' I shouted. 'Come here! Come and see me! Quick!'

So they all came rushing in, Clover and Elsie and Dorry and Jonnie and Phil. The littlies climbed right up on the bed and Clover took one of my hands and Elsie the other. They all talked at once.

'Careful, careful!' Izzie commanded, but they took no notice, and Dorry heaved himself hard on to my lap so that there was very nearly a nasty accident.

'Hey, big lump, shift yourself!' I said quickly, terrified I might wet myself.

Dorry rolled right off the bed again, looking hurt.

'I'm not a big lump. You mustn't call me that even though you're ill,' he said mournfully.

'Sorry, sorry. You're a big boy, that's all, a fine big boy. And I'm a useless lump and you can call me that all you like, because it's true,' I said, reaching out to take hold of his hand and squeeze it.

'Did you like our spiders, Katy? Mine is the one with the smiley face. I didn't want it to look too fierce in case it frightened you,' said Jonnie.

'Did you like my ockypus?' Phil demanded. 'I know it has to have eight legs, Mum told me, but I don't think I've quite managed eight.'

'Our shell box is the best though,' said Elsie. 'Clover and me made it and we were *soooo* careful, choosing all the shells the right size and setting it out just so. We wanted it to be truly special, didn't we, Clover?'

'It is special. All your presents are very, very special and I love them,' I said.

'Oh Katy, I can't believe you're home at last!' said Clover, hugging me, but very gently. 'I've begged Izzie to let me have my bed down here too, but she won't let me.'

'So I go in Clover's room because she's missing you so,' said Elsie happily.

I hated the thought of Clover and Elsie cuddled up together. I hated feeling so helpless while the littlies clambered all over me. I was so used to romping with them and giving them piggybacks and tossing them into the air until they squealed. I hated not feeling in charge of everything. The children were all talking at once again, telling me things about school, and it was hard not to feel muddled.

'Mr Robinson sent his particular best wishes to you, Katy. He's so worried about you,' said Clover. 'He kept me back at playtime to ask all about you. Oh, he's such a lovely teacher, isn't he?'

It felt so strange that he was no longer *my* teacher. I didn't go to Newbury Road Primary any more. I didn't go anywhere. My head ached just at the thought of doing lessons again. My brain seemed to have stopped working as well as my legs.

'Come on now, children. You've got juice and cookies in the kitchen. Give Katy a bit of peace for now,' said Izzie.

They all protested, even Dorry, who usually charged kitchenwards at the first hint of a cookie. I protested too, but I was secretly glad when Izzie shooed them all away nevertheless. I was left by myself. I lay back, exhausted, feeling all the blood jangling in my head and down my arms and my heart thumping in my chest

313

as if I'd been running hard. I felt absolutely nothing in my stomach and hips and legs. It was as if I was only half a person now, a dreary old granny figure who had to be left to have her nap.

I felt tears dripping out of my eyes again and I reached up and slapped my face hard, because I so hated this weak, wailing, self-pitying creature who had taken me over. I longed with all my heart and soul to be Katy again. My family loved me dearly but they didn't *understand*.

I longed to be back in hospital where everyone understood. Especially Dexter. I wanted to send him an email. Dad's laptop was in my suitcase from the last time he'd lent it to me, just before I came out of hospital. The suitcase was on the other side of the library. I heaved myself up on my elbows, trying to work out how to get hold of it. I'd have to transfer back into my wheelchair and then ferry myself across the room, reach down for the case, struggle with opening it, get myself all the way back to the bed while trying to balance the laptop on my knees, then put it on the bed where it wouldn't be nudged off, and then haul myself and my dead legs back on to the bed, under all the covers.

It was exhausting even thinking of it. I could call Izzie or Clover and they'd fetch it for me. But I didn't *want* to be reduced to calling for help every single time I needed to do anything at all. I wanted to do everything for myself.

I remembered how I'd struggled to be independent when I was very little, after Mum had died. When Izzie arrived she had tried to take over. Clover had been too small and biddable to protest, but I had thrown a tantrum any time Izzie attempted to brush my hair or button my coat or do up my shoes.

'*I* do it!' I'd yelled again and again, so I went round with my hair hanging over my face, my coat lopsided and my shoes falling off.

Then I heard a ring at the door and Cecy's mum talking, and Cecy herself, sounding high-pitched and anxious. It didn't sound like she was very keen to see me. Maybe her mum had insisted. There was Izzie again, ' . . . I'm not sure . . . Katy Katy . . . very tired . . .'

'No, I'm *not!*' I shouted.

I felt scared of seeing Cecy in case she was all weird again, but I couldn't bear Izzie thinking she knew best all the time.

So she ushered Cecy and Mrs Hall into the room, opening the curtains again. The daylight made me blink. I'd thought hours had gone by but clearly it had only been a matter of minutes.

Cecy was wearing her new Springfield uniform, white blouse, navy-and-red tie, navy skirt. It suited her.

'Hello Katy, dear. Oh, you look lovely and comfy in here,' said Cecy's mum brightly.

'We'll try and make it a bit prettier if this is going to be Katy's room permanently,' said Izzie. 'Luckily we've already got a shower in the downstairs loo. And we'll get a stairlift for the stairs . . . that'll make life a lot easier.'

'Oh goodness, Izzie. It's turned your life upside down, hasn't it?' said Cecy's mum. 'I feel so sorry for you.'

What??? *I* was the one who'd had the accident and was stuck in bed unable to do the slightest thing for myself, *I* was the one who couldn't run or dance or play properly with the littlies, *I* was the one who couldn't go to secondary school with all the others, *I* was the one who'd get pointed at and ridiculed or pitied, *I* was the one who'd never be able to have proper mates on an equal basis, *I* was the one who'd never get a boyfriend, *I* was the one who couldn't ever have a proper career, *I* was the one who couldn't ever manage in my own house, *I* was the one who would have to be treated like a helpless baby forever.

I didn't say any of this, but perhaps it was plain what I was thinking, because Izzie steered Cecy's mum away to the kitchen for a cup of tea. 'So that the girls can talk.'

Well, that was a stupid thing to say. Cecy and I just stared at each other. Both of us swallowed hard, but any words stayed stuck in our throats.

At last Cecy stammered, 'H-how are you, Katy?'

I stared at her. It seemed such an incredibly stupid question. So silly that I actually burst out laughing.

Cecy looked startled – and then started giggling feebly too. Then we carried on laughing until we were gasping and heaving and snorting, and it felt so good to be having a mad giggling fit just like we'd done in the old days.

'You nutcase!' I blurted out, between bursts.

'I know!' said Cecy. 'But I couldn't think of anything else to say!'

'Oh Cecy. I've missed you!'

'I've missed you too, so much.'

'You didn't come to see me in hospital! All that time and you only came once!'

'I'm sorry. I was so busy in the summer show. I did write to you. And email. But – but it was so scary seeing you stuck there. And I'm so squeamish. I hate hospitals, you know I do.'

'I hate them too!'

'Oh Katy.' Cecy sat down on the bed beside me and grabbed my hand just the way she used to. 'Was it really, really bad? Were you in a lot of pain?'

'Well, I was for a bit. From the wound thingy in my back, after the operation.' I paused. I decided to torture her. 'Shall I tell you what they had to do to stabilize my spine? They cut right down and –'

'No! No, don't! Shut up!'

'OK, OK, but think what it was like for me, actually having to have it done.'

'You mean you were fully conscious? They didn't give you any anaesthetic?' Cecy's voice grew high with horror.

'Well, of course they knocked me out first, but then think what it was like for me when I came round and I still couldn't walk at all.'

'And – and you still can't now, not even a little bit?' Cecy's eyes swivelled fearfully to the long mound my legs made in the bed.

'I'll show you,' I said, pulling at the duvet.

'No, don't!' said Cecy, panicking again, as if I were trying to expose something hideous and suppurating.

'It's OK, you nutter. They just look like legs. Perfectly ordinary. Just useless.' I pulled until my legs were exposed from the knee down. Cecy peered at them anxiously.

'Now, tickle under my feet.'

'What?'

'You know how ticklish I've always been, *especially* on my feet. So give it a go.'

Cecy reached out and tickled.

'More. And then poke them. Twiddle the toes backwards and forwards. Stick pins in them, anything.'

'*Pins?*' said Cecy, but she started manipulating my toes busily.

'Can't feel a thing,' I said.

'God, that's weird.'

'Yep. You could pour boiling water on them and I wouldn't flinch.'

'Really? Do – do you want me to do that?'

'No, of course not, because I'd still burn and blister. I just wouldn't be able to feel it. It's like the bottom half of me has turned into a statue.'

'Wow. It's like you're in a myth or a fairy tale. People are always getting turned into statues or trees or whatever in them. Or you're like one of those old-fashioned children's classic books. There's lots of people who can't walk in them.'

'And if they're ever so good and patient and get lots of fresh air and pray heaps then they're up and walking by the end of the book. Yuck.'

'Yeah, double yuck,' said Cecy uncertainly.

'Me and my friend Dexter are maybe working on a new book about death and disease and all that kind of thing,' I said proudly.

'Dexter?'

'He was one of the boys in the other ward. Well, not really a boy; he's sixteen.'

'And he's your *boyfriend?*'

I hesitated. I was desperate to get things back to normal – with Cecy being a little bit envious of me all the time – but my friendship with Dexter was so precious to me I didn't want to pretend at all.

'He's not my boyfriend. He's my *friend*.'

'Half the girls in my class say they've got boyfriends. But I'm not sure I believe them,' said Cecy.

'What's it like, Springfield?'

319

'It's a bit scary. It's so big. And it's horrible not having you there. I have to sit next to this lumpy girl called Alice who's incredibly boring.'

'Who else is in your class? Is Ryan?'

'No, worse luck. At least he'd be a laugh. He's in 7A. Still, the good news is that Eva-so-up-herself-Jenkins is in 7A too.'

'So who do you hang out with?'

'There's no one really special. I don't actually reckon any of the girls. Some of them are a bit scary. They act ever so old and wear make-up and do weird things with their eyebrows. They've all got boyfriends, or at least they say they have.'

'Aren't there any who like reading or art, stuff like that?' I asked.

'I wish! Well, there's Celia, this girl who has her head in a book all the time, but she's a bit . . . she's got a funny hand and does this limpy thing. The eyebrow girls are having a go at her already.'

I sat still, staring at Cecy.

'*I* don't mock her,' she said.

'But you don't want to be friends with her.'

'Well . . . So? I want to be friends with *you*.'

'Yeah, but if you didn't know me, and I was starting at Springfield now, then would you go, "Well, there's Katy, this girl who has her head in a book all the time, but she's a bit funny and cripply"?'

'No! Don't joke like that, it's horrid.'

320

'Well, even if you didn't say that, think what those eyebrow girls might say. I'm not going to Springfield!'

'You're not?'

'Well, how can I, like this?'

'So where will you go?'

'I – I don't know.'

I hadn't even talked about it with Dad. I had some dim expectation that I'd have to go to some special school for disabled kids. The thought made my stomach churn.

I was disabled now, forever and ever. And I hated it.

20

'Y ou need to rest,' Izzie kept saying.

But I couldn't rest. I was rest*less*. I tossed my head and flung my arms about so much that I kept pulling muscles. It was as if I wanted to escape my own lower half and run away on non-existent legs.

Izzie tried to make me do my exercises when I was in this mood, but I didn't want to do pathetic physio stuff. I wanted to run and jump and cycle and skateboard.

'Where *is* my skateboard?' I said fretfully.

'Oh Katy. What do you want with your skateboard now?' said Izzie.

'It's mine. It was my birthday present. I want it back, even if I can't use it,' I said. 'You were so mean to hide it away from me.'

'Don't start,' said Izzie.

But I couldn't stop. 'And if you *hadn't* been so mean, if you'd said, "Yes Katy, of course you can go skateboarding with your friends. Off you go," then I'd have gone off and had a lovely time all morning, and then in the afternoon we'd all have gone swimming together and the accident would never have happened.'

'So you're still saying it's all my fault?' said Izzie quietly.

'I'm just saying that *if* you hadn't confiscated my skateboard then none of this would have happened. Probably.'

Izzie didn't argue with me. She went to her room and I heard her rootling around in some cupboard. She came back with my skateboard and put it down beside me on the bed. Then she walked away without any further comment.

I was left holding my skateboard. I stroked it for a while, spinning the wheels. I remembered exactly how it felt to hurtle along the ground, gathering momentum, to go up a ramp and fly . . .

Then I took the skateboard and hurled it with all my strength at the wall. It took a chunk out of the plaster under the window. Izzie must have seen it but she ignored it. She didn't speak to me and I didn't speak to her for the rest of that day.

Some days were like that. On other days Izzie tried desperately hard to be friends and chatted non-stop.

They were worse. I could only cope with Izzie having to do all the hateful toileting stuff if we were both silent, pretending it wasn't happening. I could only accept this new diminished life if I could feel Izzie was my cruel jailer, my hateful enemy. I resented it when she bought me special new paperbacks, a drawing pad and new felt tips, more T-shirts, more pyjamas.

I even started to find it tiresome when the children kept making me more and more presents: little wobbly paper people, clay angels, felt mice. It was so sweet of them, but I started to get tired of pretending that all the ornaments and tiny toys wobbling about on my bedside table were making me feel much better.

They brought me their own toys too. Jonnie even insisted I take ownership of her beloved Zebby chair, which got in the way horribly when I tried to wheel myself about. The others kept donating their favourite cuddly toys until there were so many tucked into bed I hardly dared move my arms or else I'd send half a dozen fluffy teddies flying.

I drew the line when Elsie came skipping into my room with her entire menagerie, even the filthy cuddle blanket she'd dragged round everywhere when she was little.

'For God's sake, Elsie, it's just a load of dirty old junk,' I said. 'If you've grown out of them then take them to an Oxfam shop, but don't dump them all on me,' I snapped.

Elsie peered at me, stricken. She mumbled apologies, scooped them all up in her arms and scurried away. I heard her howling when she was upstairs.

I felt bad then, really bad. I waited for Izzie to come stomping in and berate me for upsetting her own precious darling, but she kept away. Somehow that made me feel worse.

I sent a heartfelt email to Dexter.

Am I the worst person in the world??? I've just been so mean to my little stepsister and now she's blubbing away and no one will even tell me off, because I'm the poor, helpless cripple. Why do I have to be so mean?

I spent a long time deliberating on how to sign off. I was too shy to put *Love, Katy*. It seemed too silly and formal to put *With best wishes*, let alone *Yours sincerely*. In the end I just typed my name. I added one x, then removed it, then at the last second put it in again as I sent it.

I got a reply in a matter of minutes.

Definitely Poor Crip Girl is second-worst person in world. You're still a total amateur in meanness next to the warped and evilly twisted Mad Crip Guy. I just reduced Jasmine to tears – lovely Jasmine, the sweetest of them all. If I'd bad-mouthed old Jeannie Big Bum it wouldn't be so bad.

Don't beat yourself up about it. How are you
doing anyway? They're talking about me going home
soon too. Can't say I'm looking forward to it, with
parents fussing and fretting. But it's totally crap
here too, especially since you went home. No one fun
to talk to!
Dexter x

He'd sent me a kiss too! And he'd made it plain he
was missing me! I felt so cheered that I yelled out to
Izzie and Elsie that I was sorry, and acted like St
Katherine for the rest of the evening – but the next
morning I felt as mean and mad as ever.

When she came back from ferrying the children to
school Izzie tried to get me interested in her stupid
handbags. They were made of very soft suede or leather,
with appliquéd flowers added on top. They were much
too posh and girly for my taste, but Izzie sold quite a
few at craft fairs.

'I want to do a special wintry design with sprigs of
holly and mistletoe instead of flowers. I think they'll
sell really well at the big Christmas craft fair at the
garden centre,' said Izzie. 'Do you think you could help
me with them, Katy?'

'What, you want me to come along and act like a
Victorian waif? I'll be the pathetic little crip girl in her
wheelchair: "Oh please buy my stepmummy's handbags
so I don't have to sell matches on the street."'

'Katy, don't! I didn't mean that at all, though if you wanted to come I think you'd quite enjoy yourself. No, I meant perhaps you could help me make my bags.'

'What, use your machine?' I did get vaguely interested then. Izzie wouldn't ever let any of us go near her special sewing machine.

'No, not my machine – well, not unless I give you lessons with lots of supervised practice first. Would you like to learn to use it?'

'Not really,' I said, just to stop her getting all eager.

'Anyway, what I'd *really* like is for you to cut out some of the leaves and berries for me. I'll make a template and then all you have to do is cut round it. It's quite hard cutting leather, but I've got very good scissors.'

'*Oooh*, cutting out! And I'm to be trusted with real scissors! Are you sure you can trust me with them? Perhaps I'd better use Phil's plastic ones with the rounded ends? We don't want the little crip girl to cut her fingers off too, do we?'

'For God's sake, what's the *matter* with you, Katy?' Izzie said, her face flushing.

'What's the matter with me? Oh, let me see . . . Could it possibly be because I'm stuck here in a wheelchair being nannied by my stupid stepmother and my whole bloody life is ruined?' I said.

'What about *my* life?' Izzie shouted. '*I* don't want to fuss round you all day long. You act like a spoilt little cow the entire time. You're hateful to me; you're hateful to your brothers and sisters; you're hateful to everyone. I know you're desperately unhappy, of course you are; I'd give anything to make you better. But I can't. I know you don't like me, Katy. We've never got on – though I've tried and tried. You think I'm trying to take your mother's place, but I don't want to do that. I just hoped we could be friends, get close somehow. Fat chance of that! Don't help me with my bags then. Don't do anything. Just sit there and be spiteful.'

She ran out of the room. I sat there, shaking. I'd never seen Izzie lose her temper before. When she was cross she generally became even more controlled. It was shocking to see her shouting, with spittle on her lips, tears in her eyes. I could see just how much I'd really hurt her.

I told myself I didn't care. I wanted to hurt her. She was right: I didn't like her. Why should I have to try to love her just because she'd married my dad?

But I still felt dreadful. She was right. I *was* spiteful. I could feel the spite in me, bubbling away. I wanted to hurt everyone because I was hurting so.

I thought Izzie might leave me alone all day. I wouldn't have blamed her. I heard her in the living room, talking to someone on the phone. I went cold all over. She was telling Dad how mean I'd been. Dad was still the only member of the family I tried hard with, apart from Tyler.

Oh Tyler! He had been so excited to see me come home, had licked me all over for a full five minutes, and I had cried with joy to be with him again. I'd had visions of him becoming a special assistance dog who would sit on my lap all day and run and fetch me things when I commanded him. Tyler ran – but he didn't come back. He jumped up on me frequently when I was in bed or stuck in my chair, but then he bounced off again and stood staring at me with his head on one side, clearly wondering why I wasn't jumping up to play with him. He was fine when he was sleepy and would come for a cuddle, using me like a favourite old pillow – but when he was wide awake he made it plain I was no fun any more.

I still tried hard, inventing new games and treats, but he hung out with the other children when they were home, treating me very much as sixth-best.

Izzie's voice was still murmuring away. I strained to hear what she was saying. I knew she was talking about me; I heard her say 'Katy' several times. Then she said something like, 'Thank God you're coming to see her.' She *was* talking to Dad! She'd summoned him home from the surgery, something that only happened in dire emergencies. What if she'd said she couldn't look after me any more? I didn't *want* her to care for me – but who else would do it if she wouldn't?

I sat despairing, hearing her go into the kitchen. Then she came into my room with two cups of tea.

'I think we both need to calm down a bit,' she said, giving me one.

'Were you phoning Dad?' I asked.

'No!' she said.

'Really? I know you were going on about me. I could hear a bit.'

'Yes, but I wasn't talking to your father. He's worried enough about you already. Now drink your tea,' said Izzie.

She'd brought me a couple of Party Rings biscuits too, my favourites. I nibbled and sipped. I started to try to think of a way of saying sorry that didn't sound too sickening. I went hot with embarrassment but I knew I had to give it a go.

'I – I didn't really mean what I said,' I mumbled.

'Yes, you did,' said Izzie. 'And I meant what I said too. We're both worn out with trying to cope. I suppose it's only natural we get fed up with each other.'

'I do like you. Sort of. It's just . . .'

'I know.'

'And you don't actually like me. You can't do. Because I'm so difficult.'

'Yes, you are difficult. Bloody difficult,' said Izzie. It was the first time I'd ever heard her swear. 'But I do like you, Katy, a lot of the time.'

'Not always.'

'Well, I'm not a saint,' said Izzie.

'Who *were* you talking to?'

'If you must know, it was Helen.'

'Oh goodness!'

'I was a bit worried about phoning her in case she was in the middle of a tutorial or something, but luckily term hasn't started yet so she had time to talk. I thought she might have some advice. Maybe she could think of some way of helping you learn to cope.'

'She didn't ask to speak to me?' I said, feeling disappointed.

'She's coming to speak to you in person,' said Izzie. 'She said she'll cancel a couple of things and come tomorrow.'

'Oh goodness. To stay?'

'No, she's making a day trip. Driving all the way from Cambridge to see you and then going back again after a couple of hours. She really cares about you, Katy,' said Izzie.

'Oh.' I swallowed. 'Izzie, thank you. Thank you for phoning her. It was really thoughtful of you.'

I felt almost happy for the first time since the accident. Fancy Helen coming all that way to see me. Just me.

Dad grew fussed about it when he came home from work. He was in a bad mood anyway, because his receptionist had been a bit high-handed with his patients and they'd had a row. Now it looked as if another row was brewing.

'You might have talked it over with me first, Izzie. Why on earth did you pick tomorrow? I've got several case conferences. I'm not going to be able to take any time off at all.'

'Well, Helen will be coming to see Katy, not you,' said Izzie.

'And haven't you thought about Helen's workload? I'm sure she's desperately busy too. It's a bit much to expect her to drop everything,' Dad said.

'She sounded as if she really wanted to see Katy,' said Izzie.

'But you could have asked her to phone or email – or what about Skyping?' said Dad. 'I don't see why you're so worried about Katy anyway. She's doing fine. She's getting her strength back, she can manoeuvre her wheelchair about brilliantly, she'll be ready for school soon. She's starting to adjust; she's always reasonably cheerful and positive –'

'With you,' said Izzie. 'Not with anyone else. There's no need to tell me off like a naughty schoolgirl, Alistair. I'm trying to do what's best for Katy. Helen made a wonderful impression on her. And I thought as Helen herself has come to terms with her own disability she might be able to help Katy.'

'Katy's only met her once. And so have you. Why didn't you wait to ask me to phone her? I've been her doctor all these years.'

'I know she's your special star patient, Alistair, but when she came to see all of us she became a family friend. Why are you being so awkward? I don't see why

I have to consult you over everything. I'm the one who looks after Katy. I haven't heard *you* offering to give up your job to care for your daughter.'

'Don't be ridiculous. You can't compare making a few handbags to my profession!'

I sat listening, holding my breath. I'd always wanted Dad and Izzie to have a real fight. Normally I'd have been one hundred per cent on Dad's side. But he was being really unfair to Izzie. I was scared she might tell him just how difficult I'd been with her ever since I came home from hospital, but she didn't tell tales. She went into the kitchen and slammed the pots and pans about, while Dad went into the living room and shouted at Jonnie and Dorry because they were playing Shipwreck, turning half the chairs upside down.

They came trailing into my room, very indignant.

'Dad was very mean to us, Katy. He stopped us playing Shipwreck and yet he always let you and Clover play it,' Jonnie wailed.

Oh, those long-ago imaginary games! Clover and I had pretended so vividly that we actually saw turbulent turquoise water instead of beige Axminster, and Dad's big armchair was the tragic sinking *Titanic* and the cushions our life rafts. I wished I still had that power so we could play the Katy-Walking game.

'We went to tell Mum but she was cross too and she wouldn't let us stay and do cooking, even though she knows it's my all-time favourite thing,' Dorry whined.

'You don't like cooking, Dorry; you like tasting,' I said. 'Look, why don't I read you two a story? What would you like?' I peered at the old children's books on the library shelf. 'I know, let's read a *Mary Poppins* chapter.'

I read them my favourite 'Topsy-Turvy' story. I wished Mary Poppins really could have the power to whisk me up to the ceiling. Not being able to walk wouldn't be so bad if I could bob about above everyone's heads whenever I fancied.

I felt very proud of myself, diverting my little brother and sister, and I happily let Phil come for the story time too, though he fidgeted an awful lot and kept singing garbled versions of 'A Spoonful of Sugar' and 'Let's Go Fly a Kite' because he only knew the *Mary Poppins* film.

I hoped Clover and Elsie would come and listen too, and then it would be just like old times, but they were up in my bedroom playing their own games. They didn't come down until Izzie called that supper was ready.

'I'll wheel you into the kitchen, Katy,' said Clover.

'I can wheel myself,' I said. 'So what have you two been up to?'

'Oh, we've been having such fun, Katy. Clover and me were being pop stars and we have our own dance routine to our music. Do you want to see?' said Elsie, flushed with excitement. 'Listen: *We are the dancing girls, twirl, twirl, twirl* –'

'Stop! You're doing my head in already,' I said. The Pop Girls game had been one *I'd* made up, and Clover and I were a singing trio along with Cecy. I'd even invented that embarrassingly stupid song. I didn't want to play Pop Girls now – I felt far too old – but I didn't want *them* to be playing it without me either, especially when the littlies forgot all about me and Mary Poppins and wanted to be in the Popchicks band too.

So there were three of us in a bad mood at supper. I left half of mine, even though it was fish pie and I usually begged for seconds, especially the crunchy, cheesy topping.

'You see? Katy's not even eating probably. She's thin as a rake,' said Izzie.

'She's always been naturally thin,' Dad snapped. 'Leave her be.'

'And *I've* always been naturally big, so why won't you leave me be and let me eat heaps of everything?' said Dorry.

Dad and Izzie would have usually laughed at this, but they both sat there po-faced and didn't respond.

Clover nudged me. 'What's up with them?' she mouthed.

'Izzie asked Helen to come tomorrow and Dad's all narked because he didn't want to bother her,' I whispered.

'Helen's coming! Oh hurray!' Clover exclaimed.

'Oh great, great, great! I can't wait to show Helen my diary. I've kept it every day, just like she said I should,' said Elsie.

'I got bored keeping my stupid old diary – but I'll show her my special secret recipe book,' said Dorry.

'Perhaps I can borrow Zebby back just while Helen is here, Katy. I know he'd like to meet her again,' said Jonnie.

'Helen, Helen, Helen! She reads better stories than you, Katy!' said Phil.

'You'll only see Helen for an hour or so. If that,' said Dad. 'She'll have to go all the way home again, and if she's got any sense she'll leave long before it gets dark. She'll be exhausted doing that journey in a day.'

He looked at Izzie reproachfully and she tightened her lips and did her best to ignore him. When she helped me settle down for the night I suddenly took hold of her hand. We'd never kissed goodnight, not even when I was tiny. I always flinched back if Izzie's head came anywhere near me. But now I hung on to her hand and squeezed it tight.

'Thank you,' I whispered, meaning thank you for calling Helen, thank you for not telling tales about me, thank you for everything you do for me every day.

Izzie didn't speak, but she squeezed my hand back and for a few moments we stayed clasping each other, closer than we'd ever been before.

336

Because he was in such a bad mood I wondered if Dad would even bother to duck in to say goodnight, but he came in quietly a few minutes after Izzie had switched my light off.

'You still awake, pet?' he whispered. I loved it when he called me *pet*. It made me feel so small and special.

'Of course I am.'

'I've just come to say goodnight. And to say sorry I've been so grumpy.' Dad sighed heavily and sat on the side of my bed. He stroked my tangled hair. 'I know I've been horrid, especially to poor Izzie.'

'Why don't you want Helen to come and see me, Dad?'

'I do, I do. I just don't want her to get exhausted. And – I don't know – I suppose I like to think she's *my* special friend, which is ridiculous, I know.'

'Oh Dad!' I understood entirely. I always wanted Clover to be *my* special sister, Cecy to be *my* special friend, even Tyler to be *my* special dog.

'And I was annoyed with Izzie for making this cry for help, because we're doing all right, aren't we, Katy? I know Mr Pearson was very pleased with the way you've bounced back from the physical trauma. That's why they let you out of hospital so early.'

Dad seemed desperate for reassurance, so I gave him a hug.

'So you're doing fine physically, managing everything you need to do. But Izzie thinks you're not so good mentally,' Dad went on.

337

'Oh well. You know me, Dad. I've always been a bit mental,' I said, trying to joke.

'Oh darling! Obviously you're going to feel very upset and angry at times, but do you feel absolutely despairing about everything?' Dad asked, sounding almost fearful.

Of course I feel absolutely despairing! I wanted to shout. *I feel it's the end of my world. I'm never going to be me again. I can't do anything any more. I'm so miserable I can't stand it.*

But I knew Dad couldn't bear to hear that.

'I suppose I'm OK, Dad,' I mumbled. 'But I really would like to see Helen.'

'Of course you would, pet. Well, I hope you have a lovely time together.'

I felt so excited the next morning. For once I didn't moan during the long washing, dressing, toileting, breakfasting process when Izzie was back from taking the others to school. I was happy to wear one of my new T-shirts and my smartest joggers. I even let Izzie fiddle around with my hair and tie it up in a topknot.

'Where's that lovely seahorse necklace that Helen gave you?' Izzie asked.

'Oh! I – I'm not sure. Never mind. It'd look a bit odd with a T-shirt, wouldn't it?' I said quickly.

'I think it would look lovely. And Helen would be touched to see you wearing it,' said Izzie. 'It's not in your shell box? Well, it'll be upstairs in your old bedroom. I'll run up and have a look for it.'

I took a deep breath.

'I've got something to tell you,' I said.

Izzie looked at me. 'Oh Katy, don't tell me you've lost it!'

'No. But – but I broke it.'

'Oh no! And you were so proud to have Helen's lovely necklace,' said Izzie.

'I know,' I said. 'I'm hopeless. Nag at me all you want, Izzie, I deserve it.'

But for once Izzie didn't nag.

'Where is it? Let me see if there's any way I can mend it,' she said.

'I can't even remember properly where I put it. It was the day of the accident. I tugged at the chain without meaning to and it broke. Everything was awful that day.'

'I'll find it. I've got to know most of your hiding places,' said Izzie.

She was as good as her word. She ran up to my room and came back within a minute with my treasure box.

'You have a look. It's your special box. I think you might have tucked it in here.'

I opened my box silently, brought out the necklace and handed it to Izzie.

'The seahorse isn't broken; it's just the chain. We can easily get that mended, you silly girl. And meanwhile

339

you can use the chain on Cecy's locket. Let's see if we can thread your seahorse on to it,' Izzie said.

The chain threaded through the link on the seahorse easily.

'There you are!' said Izzie, doing up the clasp round my neck. 'And don't go tugging at this chain!'

21

I hugged Helen when she came. She only had short arms but mine were long, so we could both lean forward and embrace. I started crying again and then scrubbed at my eyes furiously, embarrassed.

'I'm sorry. I don't know what's the matter with me. I've blubbed like a baby practically every day since the accident,' I sniffed.

'Of course you'll cry, Katy! Who wouldn't be sad? You've had your whole life turned upside down,' said Helen.

'Yes, but it was all my own fault,' I wailed. 'Did Izzie tell you how it happened?'

'Yes, she did. It must seem so horribly unfair. A little swing from a tree! I bet a hundred thousand kids

341

have swung from a tree just like that without falling. And if they *did* fall, very few would have the bad luck to hurt themselves so severely. A broken arm, a broken leg, and then they'd be as right as rain in a few weeks,' said Helen.

'Whereas I'm stuck like this forever and ever,' I said.

'Well, as far as we know. They might find some way of helping people walk again in ten or twenty years – who knows.'

'And then we'll *both* be able to walk!'

'I don't think so. My poor little legs have gone for a burton. I've had replacement hips and knees and yet I can only walk one or two steps like a clockwork soldier, then I fall over – *clonk*.'

'Have you been stuck in a wheelchair ever since you were a baby?' I asked. I hadn't liked to ask the last time Helen came; it seemed much too rude and intrusive to bombard her with personal questions. But now we were both in the same situation it made everything seem different.

'I was fine when I was really little. In fact, my mother says I was one of those toddlers that never kept still. I ran round and round the garden until I got dizzy and then I'd fall over, shrieking with laughter. But then I developed rheumatoid arthritis when I was three or four and I was in and out of hospital for most of my childhood.'

'How did you get to be so brave? You never ever complain. Dad thinks you're an absolute angel,' I said earnestly.

'Oh, that's hilarious! I'm anything but. But how sweet that your dad sees me like that. I think *he's* the angelic one. He's always been so kind to me. My own father's a bit withdrawn and has always been a bit awkward with me. I think my disability embarrasses him, though he'd never admit it. I used to fantasize that your dad was *my* dad. You're so lucky to have him, Katy. I know he's always taken time to play with all of you, and he reads aloud, doesn't he? And he always talks to you sensibly and explains everything carefully. Whenever I cried as a little kid, because I hurt and I was scared of having injections and operations, he was always so gentle and understanding,' said Helen.

'Yes, I suppose I am lucky. He is a lovely dad. But actually he's been a bit weird with me since the accident. He tries ever so hard, but he gets grumpy sometimes too. And he hates it when I get really upset. He keeps making out I'm doing splendidly, when I'm not,' I said.

'I think that's because he loves you so much. He probably feels incredibly frustrated because he's a doctor and yet he can't cure you. He's not even in charge of your medical care. He's just a dad and he feels helpless.'

'Yes, that's it exactly! You're so wise, Helen! Why can't I work things out like that?'

'Because you're eleven and I'm more than twice your age,' said Helen. 'What about Izzie? How is she reacting?'

I cocked my ear, making sure Izzie was still in the kitchen getting lunch ready. 'Well. She's been weird too. Before, she used to nag, nag, nag me all the time. We were always arguing. I could never do anything right. But now she's horribly patient with me all the time.'

'Horribly?'

'Well, it sort of gets on my nerves. I don't want her to be nicey-nice with me. I don't want to have to feel grateful all the time.'

'Oh yes. I understand that. It's the great trial of the disabled: having to be bloody grateful when we can't help ourselves and have to get people to do things for us,' said Helen.

'We had a big row yesterday, Izzie and me. I said horrible things to her. She did get angry then and say stuff back. But then she phoned you, which was lovely of her. I suppose I'm pretty horrible to her a lot of the time. And I'm mean to the others too, especially Elsie. It's awful, Helen. I didn't used to be such a nasty person, but now I can't seem to help it.' I was nearly crying again.

'It's because you're angry. You go through all these stages when you've had a serious life change like your accident. You're sad, you're angry, you're resentful, you're depressed. Oh, it's a right bore for you, and for everyone else!'

'Did you go through all these stages?'

344

'I'm sure I did when I was little. But it all happened more gradually for me. And now I can't really remember ever being so-called normal. I've grown up different. Maybe it's easier for people like me.'

'But you've been ill longer.'

'Yes, but I've grown up being used to it. This *is* me, this little person in her wheelchair, bowling along. Whereas I bet you don't feel like you're the real Katy any more.'

'Yes! Oh, you're the only person who really understands! Apart from Dexter. He's this boy in the hospital. He used to say dreadful things to the nurses and do these really dark, wonderful, cartoony things. Dexter is the coolest boy I've ever met, but he's kind of scary too. He emailed me once after I got home,' I added proudly.

I'd emailed him back – one, two, three times – but he hadn't responded further.

'It's amazing how close you can get in hospital,' said Helen. 'You find yourself talking about real things, not all the trivial stuff.'

'Yes, exactly. Like us! I feel like I've changed so much since the last time we met, when I just wanted to burble on about our silly games,' I said.

'You can still play games now. You can do all sorts of things. Those are my two favourite words, Katy. *Can do!*'

'Well, that's a bit daft,' I said, then blushed. 'Sorry, I didn't mean to be rude. But how can I do anything now? I can't do a blessed thing!'

Helen looked at me earnestly. She reached out and took hold of me by the shoulders, though it was a great stretch for her.

'I think that's maybe the big difference between those of us like me who've been disabled ever since they can remember and people like you who have become disabled overnight. You're thinking right now of all the things you can't do. But maybe soon you'll be able to start thinking of all the things you *can* do. Maybe new, fantastic things you'd never have thought of before.'

'Like what?' I said, and it came out more rudely than I meant. But Helen wasn't the slightest bit fazed.

'Like travelling, especially when you're older and can do it under your own steam. Like writing – I've done all sorts of articles for newspapers and magazines. Like acting – I've seen groups of people with all sorts of disabilities putting on fantastic shows. Like educating – I've given lots of talks in schools to try to show what it's like to be disabled, and I tackle all the weird stuff that people say about us. Stop wincing, Katy! You hate that word *disabled*, don't you?'

'Yes, it's horrible. I don't want to be it!'

'But you are, sweetheart. And it's not necessarily a bad thing. I'm proud to be the way I am.'

'Yes, but it's OK for you.'

'Why?'

'Well, you're so clever. You're an academic, aren't you? You *can* do all those things.'

'How do you know you're not clever too? I bet you did well at school.'

'I was always mucking about.'

'Well, you can still muck about now. The main thing is to get you back to school,' said Helen. 'You must be getting bored out of your mind hunched up here at home day after day, and you're probably driving poor Izzie crazy into the bargain.'

'Yeah, but which school? Dad went and looked at this special school somewhere, but they don't do proper GCSEs, and they haven't got any spare places anyway.'

'Which school were you going to go to?'

'Springfield. It's where Cecy and all my friends from my old school have gone. But I'm not going there, not where some of them know me. And anyway, I can't go there. Dad's phoned up. They haven't got any lifts, so I wouldn't be able to go to any of the classrooms upstairs.'

'But you'd be able to go to the classrooms *down*stairs – and lobby hard to try to get them to put in a lift! I think that's the first step you need to take, Katy.'

I stared at Helen. 'But how would I manage? You know. The toilet stuff. Izzie does it all for me.'

'You can certainly learn to look after most things yourself. And maybe it's time to be more independent at home. Do you shower and dress yourself?'

'Well. Sometimes. But I'm so slow at it now.'

'That's because you're out of practice! You'll get much quicker and learn little tricks for doing things.

Of course it will always be quicker if someone else helps you – but you want to do it by yourself, don't you?'

'Yes, I do. But – but I still don't see how I could manage at Springfield. What would all the others say? Some of them can be really mean. What if they laugh at me?'

'Then you have to laugh back. Or swap insults. Show them you don't give a stuff. Show them that you're still Katy Carr and they can't mess with you. Right?'

'Right!' I said.

'That's the spirit.' Helen smiled at me and then picked up the little seahorse round my neck. 'It looks great on you, Katy. It was my lucky charm, so I hope it brings you lots of luck too.'

Izzie called that lunch was ready and we sat together in the kitchen, just the three of us. Helen and I stopped talking about special things and just chatted generally, but it was still very enjoyable with no children butting in every second. Izzie had made a lovely lunch too, a special home-made asparagus quiche with three different salads, and then my favourite Eton mess for pudding – meringue and cream and strawberries. She'd used the special blue-and-white willow-pattern china and put some late roses and a few Michaelmas daisies in a pretty jug.

'This is lovely, Izzie,' said Helen. 'You'll have to give me the recipe for this quiche – it's wonderful. Katy, why don't you get Izzie to give you a few cooking tips?'

I waited for Izzie to start telling her the tale of my disastrous pancakes, but she just smiled and said, 'That's a good idea.'

When we were all nibbling Turkish delight Dad came dashing in, having come all the way home just to snatch a precious half-hour with Helen. He practically ignored Izzie and me. I rolled my eyes and Izzie smiled at me.

I realized just how special Helen was. We all vied with each other to talk to her. It didn't matter in the slightest that she was in a wheelchair and couldn't walk. Maybe I could get to be a special person too.

Dad told Helen more about little Archie. Helen told us about the book she was writing. Izzie showed Helen some of her handbag designs. I started thinking of Helen's *can do* approach.

I could help small children come to terms with being in a wheelchair. I could write a book: not an academic discourse, naturally, but maybe a storybook for younger children. I could make something: perhaps not a boring old handbag, but some kind of toy or soft sculpture. I thought of all my old hopes and plans. I could still have my big house, only I'd be stuck on the ground floor. *No! – can do, CAN DO!* I could install a lift. That would be the coolest thing ever, to have a lift in the house. Then I could swoop right up to the top floor and down again, keeping an eye on all the children. Well, they wouldn't be children then. Maybe they'd have children of their own, and I'd be Auntie Katy, and they'd all cluster round my wheelchair and I'd devise games for them and let the winner have a little ride on my lap, and then when they were tired I'd read them all a bedtime story. Even the very littlest would listen entranced to *Mary Poppins* . . .

'You're quiet, Katy,' said Dad, suddenly squeezing my hand. 'Why don't you make the most of Helen while she's here?'

'I have been, Dad. We've talked and talked,' I said.

'I've been preaching at the poor girl,' said Helen. 'I bet she can't wait to see the back of me.'

'That's not true!' I insisted. 'It's been lovely to see you. I only wish you lived nearer. I want to see you every day!'

'Well, I'll second that,' said Dad. 'In fact, my cup runneth over right this minute. I'm with my favourite patient, favourite daughter, favourite wife.'

Then he started, because he realized exactly what he'd said. Favourite *wife*? Any other time I'd have kicked off royally in defence of my mum. But I knew why he'd said it. He'd simply got carried away. He'd told Helen she was his favourite, but he wanted to include Izzie and me too. I knew *I* wasn't actually his favourite daughter. He either said he didn't have any favourites or insisted we were all his favourites, but even so I was pretty certain Clover was his actual favourite. Just as I was certain Mum was his favourite wife, always and forever, but it would be unkind to say that in front of Izzie. For the first time in my life I didn't want to be unkind to Izzie either.

Dad was glancing at me anxiously but I just reached for another little white-dusted delight and popped it in my mouth. Izzie smiled at me and Helen did too.

Dad had to dash off back to work. Helen and I took a little nap together in the library, both of us lying on top of my bed. It took quite a bit of manoeuvring for us to get there, and Izzie did have to help, but it was somehow fun being gently pushed and shoved together. We didn't actually do any proper napping. We just lay there with the curtains drawn and I spoke into the dark and told Helen that I knew I was still me, but I wanted to be a new version too. I intended to be totally mature and thoughtful and everyone would think me as heroic as Helen and marvel at my fortitude. This resolution only lasted till we transferred back to our wheelchairs and Clover and the littlies came home, fetched by Mrs Hall.

They all clamoured round Helen. Elsie was so eager to get to her that she tripped over the wheels of my own chair and literally landed in my lap. I might have been fantasizing about having a child on my lap an hour or so ago, but in reality it was alarming, even though I couldn't properly feel Elsie's weight.

'Get off, you numpty! You know you're not allowed to do that! You could really hurt me,' I yelled.

'I'm sorry! Oh Katy, I'm truly sorry! Have I really hurt you?' Elsie gasped.

I saw Helen looking at me and felt terrible.

'No, I'm OK,' I mumbled.

Helen reached out to give Elsie a reassuring hug and she was happy again. I felt ashamed. I watched Helen talking to all my sisters and brothers, careful to pay attention to each one, cleverly diverting their attention if they got too shrill or boisterous, and I felt even worse. I'd never had that patience with them. Before the accident I'd controlled them easily enough, but that was because I was the biggest. I could run faster, I could think quicker. Now I couldn't run at all and I couldn't even seem to think properly any more. My brain seemed to be turning to jelly inside my head.

After ten minutes or so Izzie called them all away to have their juice and biscuits.

'Phew!' said Helen. 'They can be quite full-on, can't they?'

'You're so good with them all,' I said.

'It's easy for me. I'm the novelty. But I'm not sure I could be Miss Sweetness and Charm if I had to cope with all of them every day,' said Helen.

'I seem to be Miss Snarl and Bite. Especially with Elsie,' I said ruefully, lowering my voice. 'I don't know what it is about her. She's just so whiny and needy and clumsy.'

'Poor little Elsie,' said Helen. 'It's funny . . . I think she's the one I'd make into my special pet. Why don't you try making an extra fuss of her? She'd love that. She really looks up to you, Katy.'

'No, she doesn't! She's all over Clover now. They're total best friends,' I said. I heard the whine in my voice and blushed. 'That's a good thing of course,' I added.

'Oh Katy. You're the one who matters most to all of them,' said Helen. 'And you matter to me most too. I was so worried after Izzie's phone call, but it seems to me you're doing all right, truly. Just get back to school and get on with your life.'

'I'll try,' I said. 'I wish you lived nearer, Helen. I think I need you to come and sort me out every single day!'

'I'll phone. And email. And I'll be thinking of you all the time,' said Helen.

I had another strange dream that night. I was with Helen and we were out together, the two of us dressed up. We were sitting hunched, legs dangling, as if we were in our wheelchairs, but there weren't any wheels or even chairs – we were just suspended in space. We were moving forwards at a great rate as if we were riding on the air itself.

'Follow me!' Helen cried, and she sped right up into the sky.

'Helen! Come back! Wait for me!' I cried.

'You come and join me,' she called.

I didn't know what I was doing. I didn't even have anything to cling to. I just had to will myself upwards. I jerked backwards and forwards, straining desperately, and just as I was about to give up I suddenly juddered upwards, just a few inches above the ground.

353

'That's it. That's the way!' Helen called.

I soared upwards until I joined her way above the rooftops and we raced along together, both of us shouting for joy.

When I woke up I still felt joyful, even though I was imprisoned in my bed. Well, I wasn't quite a prisoner. I'd just got into the habit of lying there, waiting while Izzie got up and made breakfast and organized all the children and got them off to school. I always felt desperately tired in the morning, as if I hadn't slept at all, and transferring myself out of bed seemed like far too much effort. But today I heaved myself about and managed to get myself into my wheelchair, though I almost toppled on to the floor in the process. Then I wheeled myself quietly into the shower and did the whole transferring process all over again on to the shower seat.

'Katy?' Izzie was knocking at the door, sounding anxious. 'Katy, are you all right? Have you had an accident?'

'For goodness' sake,' I muttered, because she was treating me just like Phil. 'I'm fine,' I said louder. 'Don't worry so, Izzie. I just thought I'd get myself up for once.'

'Are you sure you're OK?' she called. 'Shall I just come in and –'

'No!' I said. Then I took a deep breath. 'No, thank you, Izzie. I can manage.'

354

And I *did* manage too, though it took me ages and ages to get my pyjamas off and then there was a kerfuffle turning on the shower, trying to get it not too cold and not too hot, and then I realized I was clutching the shower gel but not the shampoo, which was way out of my reach over on the windowsill. So my hair got washed with gel and actually it didn't seem to make any difference whatsoever.

Izzie came back twice to check on me, and the children banged on my door too before Mrs Hall took them all to school. I called back to each of the children. Elsie knocked last, breathless because she'd been hunting hard for her school shoes ever since she got up (it turned out Philly had turned them both into boats and taken his two tiniest teddies for a sail in them on his bed). She knocked so loudly that my eyes jerked open and I got shower gel in them, which stung a lot. I'd normally have yelled at her but I somehow stopped myself.

'Bye, Elsie,' I called. 'Have a good day. Don't worry if Mr Peters shouts at you. He's grumpy with everyone. If he has a go at you just stare back at him and imagine him stark naked, all big fat pink belly, and then you won't be scared of him. That's what I used to do when I was in his class.'

'Really!' said Elsie. 'Big fat pink belly! Oh Katy, you are funny.'

'*Elsie!* Mrs Hall's waiting for you – and I've found your shoes,' Izzie called distantly from the front door.

'Coming! Just saying goodbye to Katy. Goodbye, Katy! See you later, alligator!'

This was a silly saying of Dad's, something that *his* dad used to say to him when he was little. I generally found it so daft I didn't respond, but today I called, 'In a while, crocodile!' in a deep, alligator-ish voice, which made Elsie giggle.

There, Helen! I said inside my head.

I was exhausted by the time I'd finished and turned the shower off, but I couldn't just flop back into my wheelchair soaking wet. I had to towel every bit of myself and dry my hair too. Then I had to wheel myself back into the library, naked and shivering, wondering how on earth I was going to get my clothes out of the cupboard when I was so bone-shakingly tired. I found Izzie had laid my underwear and T-shirt and jogging bottoms out on my bed, easily within reach. It was a dreadful struggle to get them all on. I had to inch things up, and everything stuck to me because I was still damp. My joggers were all twisted, and I couldn't face bending over to fix my shoes, but I was more or less dressed. I'd done it!

Izzie knocked on the door and came in with a cup of hot chocolate with a cap of white frothy cream.

'Here – I think you need this!' she said. 'Well done, Katy.'

'I'm so tired I feel like going back to sleep,' I said. 'This is a bit mad. I'm going to take all day getting myself up, and then as soon as I've done it I'm ready for bed.'

'It'll get easier with practice. Oh Katy, I'm so proud of you. But I don't mind helping if it makes it easier for you.'

'Well, perhaps you will have to help me at first when I go back to school,' I said.

'School?' said Izzie. 'So would you like to go and see some schools with your father?'

'Well, I was thinking ... maybe I should go to Springfield after all,' I said.

'But you were so adamant that you couldn't bear it,' said Izzie.

'Yes, but I talked it over with Helen and now I think maybe I'd like to give it a try.'

'I think that's a good idea. And Cecy will be there. She'll look after you,' said Izzie.

I bristled. 'I won't need looking after.'

'That's true. You'll manage splendidly,' said Izzie hurriedly.

I licked the cream from the top of my hot chocolate. 'Sorry. I didn't mean to snap. It *will* be good to have Cecy there. And she'll help me catch up. Izzie, do you *really* think I'll manage?'

'Yes, I do,' said Izzie.

'And at least I'll be out of your hair if I'm away at school every day.'

'Well. You never know. I might miss you,' said Izzie.

'Rubbish!'

'I said *might*.'

So it was decided. I was going back to school.

22

Dad made an appointment with Mrs Matthews, the head teacher, and we went to see her the next morning. I'd seen her already when we all visited Springfield during my last term at primary school. She was large, with longish curly hair and floppy purple clothes and lots of big beads and clanking bangles. She looked like one of those soft, soppy nursery teachers who show you how to do finger painting in Reception class. I expected her to simper at me and say, 'Hello, what's happened to you, you poor little girly?'

Nothing of the sort.

'How do you do, Dr Carr, Katy? Do come and sit down,' she said briskly.

Dad sat on a proffered chair. I was clearly already sitting.

'It's good of you to see us immediately, Mrs Matthews,' said Dad, in his most doctorly voice. 'But Katy has made a good recovery and feels she's ready to go to school now.'

'But I thought you felt Springfield was unsuitable. When you phoned earlier –'

'I know. Katy felt she needed to make a completely fresh start, at a school where she didn't know anyone, given her circumstances. But now –'

'Now I've changed my mind,' I said, though actually inside I was still wavering. I kept thinking about Eva Jenkins and her cronies imitating me, calling me names; about Ryan looking at me pityingly and backing away from me. But Helen had given me courage. I would cope with them. Somehow.

'The trouble is, I've already given your place to someone else,' said Mrs Matthews smoothly. 'So it's going to be a bit of a problem. Did you put Katy's name down at another school in the interim, Dr Carr?'

'No, we didn't. I went to look at several schools, but none seemed suitable,' said Dad.

'I wonder if you looked at Manor Road? I believe they have several disabled pupils at their school and have all sorts of facilities – a lift to the upper floor, a special disabled lavatory. I think Katy might find it easier there,' she said silkily, giving me a little smile.

'I did look at Manor Road, but it's so far away from us. It would be a forty-minute journey, maybe more in the rush hour. And, to be frank, Manor Road doesn't have the academic reputation that Springfield has,' said Dad. His tone was equally pleasant, but firm. 'Katy's very bright, Mrs Matthews.'

'Oh, I'm aware of that, Dr Carr. Her report from her primary school makes that plain,' she said. 'That's partly the difficulty. We like to introduce our pupils to as wide a range of subjects as possible. We feel that the sciences are particularly important. Unfortunately the science labs are all on the first floor, so I don't see how Katy could access them.'

'Is there no possibility of having a lift put in?' said Dad.

'Well, certainly that would be an ideal solution. It might well be possible – but, as I'm sure you realize, we can't simply install a lift overnight.'

'Could Katy not meanwhile study the science textbooks somewhere else downstairs, just until the lift *is* installed?' said Dad.

'Well, that is an option, though far from ideal. And then there's the question of lavatories. I'm afraid our girls' toilets all have small, narrow cubicles. I went to check earlier on. I simply don't think it would be possible for Katy to manoeuvre her wheelchair in and out,' said Mrs Matthews.

'Oh,' said Dad. 'Well, I'm sure it would be possible to install special disabled facilities. But I can see perhaps we'll have to wait until that's the case.'

I was thinking hard. I thought about the toilets at my old school. The girls' toilets. The boys' toilets. And the special, nicer toilets just for the teachers.

'What about the staff toilets?' I asked. 'They're bigger, aren't they?'

'Yes, I suppose so,' said Mrs Matthews.

'Big enough for my wheelchair?'

'Perhaps. But I'm not sure they're still suitable and there's only one on the ground floor anyway.'

'One's surely enough?' said Dad. 'Just until you get a proper disabled lavatory installed.'

'Dr Carr, I've only got a limited amount of money in my annual budget. I can't work miracles. These are old premises. It's not as if it's a new-build.'

'Yes, I understand it's going to be a bit of a problem, but I'm sure there are special grants, given the circumstances. And as I'm sure you're aware, schools do have to make special provision for disabled pupils nowadays,' Dad said.

Mrs Matthews looked at him. She looked at me.

'I can see you're both determined that Katy should attend Springfield. Very well. We'll do our level best to welcome you here, Katy. Perhaps you'd like to start next Monday?' she said.

Dad and I waited till we were out in the corridor and then high-fived each other.

I wrote a long, triumphant email to Helen that afternoon. I also tried Dexter again, showing off a little, boasting that I'd bulldozed my way into the school of my choice.

Helen replied that evening, a wonderfully long email that made me glow all over. And Dexter replied too, though without any words. The subject on the email said *SuperKaty*, and he'd sent a photo of a page from his sketchbook. He'd drawn me looking even taller, with *SK* inscribed on my T-shirt, sitting in a wheelchair like Boudicca's chariot, with iron spikes sticking out from both sides. I was charging my way into a school, with staff and pupils alike running in all directions and shrieking and cowering.

I laughed out loud, and showed it off proudly to Clover and Cecy when they came to see me after school.

'So you're really coming to Springfield after all, Katy?' Cecy asked.

'Yep, it's all arranged. Mrs Matthews tried to put us off, but we soon fixed her,' I said airily.

'My goodness! You argued with *Mrs Matthews?*' said Cecy, sounding incredibly impressed. 'She can be really scary sometimes. Good for you! Oh Katy, it will be wonderful having you at school with me. I do hope, hope, hope we'll be in the same class. You mustn't worry about a thing. I'll push you everywhere you need to go.'

'I won't need to be pushed; I'll wheel myself,' I said. 'But thanks anyway, Cecy. It'll be great to be with you.'

'And *I'll* be at Springfield next year and I'll watch out for you then,' said Clover fiercely. 'Is it true that the big

363

girls grab hold of you in the toilets and stick your head down the loo?'

'That's rubbish, Clover. No, they're mostly all fine. And the boys are OK too. There's this really cool guy in Year Eight – Richie – and he bumped into me in the corridor and sent all my books flying –'

'What?'

'He didn't mean to; it was a total accident. Anyway, he helped me pick them all up and now every time we see each other in the corridor he says hi and makes a little joke about it. All the girls in my class are dead jealous because he's making a fuss of me and yet he's thirteen already,' said Cecy proudly.

'Katy's got a boy of sixteen interested in her,' said Clover.

'Really?' said Cecy, not sounding convinced. 'Who's that then?'

'He's called Dexter,' I said. 'He sent me an amazing cartoon. Wait till you see it!'

'Oh, he's just that boy you met in hospital. You told me about him,' said Cecy, unimpressed.

'You mean he doesn't count because he's in a wheelchair?' I asked.

'No, of course I didn't mean that,' said Cecy hurriedly – but maybe she *did*.

Didn't she think *I* counted now because I was in a wheelchair? And if my best friend thought that then what would everyone else think of me?

I started to wish I hadn't insisted on going to Springfield after all. Cecy was ultra apologetic and asked to see Dexter's cartoon. She went on about how marvellous it was, but she wasn't fooling me. I didn't pick a fight with her, because she was still my best friend, and I was certainly going to need a good friend at Springfield whether she pushed me round or not. All the same, it was a relief when she went next door to have her tea.

It was good to be left with Clover. The littlies came into my room too, and Elsie told me a long, involved tale about Mr Peters and how she wasn't remotely scared of him any more. 'All because of you, Katy,' she said, throwing her arms round my neck.

'Oh Elsie,' I said, and I pulled her – carefully – on to my lap.

'I don't want to hurt you, Katy!' she said anxiously.

'No, I'm fine. Just don't wriggle too much. But I want a proper cuddle,' I said, smoothing her funny fringe and rubbing her soft cheek on mine.

'Oh Katy, I do love you!' she said.

I wondered how I could have been so mean to poor Elsie all these years – and why she was so wondrously forgiving. I made yet another resolution that I would always, always, always try to be a proper sister to her.

I wanted to be a proper sister to *all* my siblings. They were all talking excitedly. Dorry was going off on a riff about school dinners.

'It's absolutely the pits. The dinner ladies say we can't have seconds any more. I think they just want to munch all those lovely chips and pizza triangles themselves. And they give such stingy servings even though I keep telling them I'm so hungry I've got a pain. And they want me to try eating mad stuff like salad, which is just boring green leaves – and who on earth would like that?'

'Zebby absolutely loves green leaves. And grass. And dandelions,' said Jonnie.

'Zebby doesn't really *eat* them. He just pretends. I know, because he hides them under his legs, and the greens end up all brown and withery, and Mum gets cross,' said Dorry, unwilling to indulge Jonnie's maternal fantasy for once.

'I have lovely food at nursery. Yummy fish fingers, much, much nicer than that boring real fish Mum gives us. And baked beans, lots and lots of baked beanies. They're my favourite. We never ever have to eat leaves. I don't want to go to big school if it's leaves. Is it twigs too?' said Phil.

They could all three witter on in this vein for hours. They usually drove me mad, but now I seemed to have turned into little St Katherine. I told Clover to get my sketchbook and asked each child in turn to list their all-time favourite foods and then drew them in a spiralling pattern across the page.

'So what's *your* favourite food, Katy?' Elsie asked.

'Oh, a big salty packet of chips from a proper chippie,' I said, and added without thinking, 'I love walking home with Cecy after we've been to the shopping centre and sharing our chips.'

Then there was a little silence. Even Philly realized what I'd said. Clover quickly put her arm round me.

'You can still go to Flowerfields with Cecy,' she said. 'She could wheel you.'

'I can wheel myself,' I said.

'Yes, but it's too far,' said Clover.

'Well, we could get a bus,' I said.

They stared at me.

'How could you do that? Cecy couldn't pick you up in your wheelchair and lift you on to the bus, Katy,' said Elsie. 'What if she dropped you!'

'She wouldn't need to pick me up. Buses have ramps for people in wheelchairs,' I said. 'Yeah, maybe I'll ask Cecy if she wants to go with me this Saturday.'

Saturdays were a bit bleak. I couldn't get into the secret garden now and the others shied away from it as if it were a terrible, haunted place. The littlies generally went off and played their bizarre pretend games. Their current favourite was a variation on Zoos. Dorry was the zookeeper and he kept nagging Izzie to give him real food for all his exotic animals, though he mostly kept it to feed himself. Zebby and various teddies stood in for a full menagerie, and Philly was a real lion who roared himself hoarse.

Clover and Elsie were too old for such nonsense, so they sat doing girly things, making bracelets and drawing fashion outfits and experimenting with Izzie's old lipsticks and eyeshadows. I wasn't interested in those sorts of activities either so I was generally left to my own devices.

I read, and that was absolutely fine, but it did feel a bit lonely. I was wildly excited at the thought of going into town with Cecy and wandering round the shops just like a normal person. I phoned her up on my mobile and asked her if she'd like to go with me straight after her dancing lesson.

'We could have lunch in McDonald's. On me. I've got heaps of pocket money because I haven't been able to go out to spend any of it. Oh God, my mouth's watering just at the thought of a Big Mac and fries!' I said excitedly.

'Yes, that would be great,' said Cecy, but she sounded uncertain. 'So is your dad taking us?'

'No, of course not. We'll go on our own. We're allowed now,' I said.

We'd been into town twice on our own during the summer term. Izzie and Mrs Hall had reluctantly agreed, although they'd fussed terribly and made us promise not to talk to any strangers and only cross the road at the traffic lights, as if we were tiny tots.

'Yes, I know we're allowed – but that was before,' said Cecy.

'Before what?' I said sharply, though of course I knew what she meant.

'Well, you know,' Cecy said awkwardly. 'But hey, yes, let's. It'll be such fun. We could walk there and I could push your wheelchair if you get tired.'

'We can get the bus,' I said.

'Yeah. Fine. Right. It's a date,' said Cecy.

But ten minutes later I heard Izzie's mobile ringing in the kitchen and a long conversation. Then she came into my room. She looked at me worriedly.

'I'm going,' I said fiercely. 'You mustn't fuss. I'll be all right.'

'I know,' said Izzie. 'But Cecy's mum isn't at all happy about it. She says no.'

'Oh, for goodness' sake!'

'She thinks it might be too much responsibility for Cecy. And, to be fair, I can see her point,' said Izzie. 'I'm sorry, Katy. I can see how much you were looking forward to it.'

I bent my head so she couldn't see my teary eyes. I clenched my fists. I wanted to howl and lash out. I waited, fighting for control. Izzie came and stood beside me and gently rubbed the back of my wrist.

I sniffed hard. 'Could you come too then, Izzie? That'll reassure Mrs Fusspot Hall.'

'Well, she said that they had plans for Saturday afternoon anyway, some visit to a friend or an aunt or someone,' Izzie said uncomfortably.

369

'A fictitious friend or aunt?' I said.

'Perhaps. How do we know?'

'Izzie, could I go with Clover? I'd *sooner* go with Clover.'

'I think I'm going to do a Mrs Hall on you, Katy. Clover would love it, of course she would, but she's only ten, and quite young for her age. I think she'd panic a bit if there was any slight hitch. But I could accompany both of you. I'll walk way behind so that no one will know I'm keeping an eye on you,' said Izzie.

'Oh, you're a darling,' I said, and I really meant it.

We set off on Saturday, Izzie and Clover and me – and Elsie. I decided we might as well ask her along too.

'Oh Katy, yes please! I'd love to come! I'll bring all my pocket money and I'll buy you the bestest present ever, Katy. This means I'm one of the big girls, doesn't it? I'm not one of the littlies any more, am I? I'm truly big, aren't I, Katy?'

'You're almost as big as me,' I said. 'In fact, you're bigger now I'm stuck in my wheelchair. You tower over me. You're the big girl and *I'm* the littlie.'

'You'll always be the biggest, Katy,' said Clover. 'You're still the boss of all of us.'

'Even me,' said Izzie.

So on Saturday we went shopping while Dad stayed at home looking after Dorry, Jonnie and Phil. He did offer to drive us into the town centre – we could just about all squash in if I transferred into the front seat and we collapsed the wheelchair and stowed it in the boot.

'It's sweet of you, darling, but I think we'll have a girls-only trip,' said Izzie. 'We're going to shop until we drop.'

'Do you want to go with them then, Jonnie?' Dad asked.

'No fear! I hate shopping,' said Jonnie.

'I like it. I especially like that food court at the Flowerfields shopping centre,' said Dorry. 'You lot could go shopping and leave me in the food court if you like.'

'I think not, chubby chops,' said Izzie, fondly squeezing his cheeks.

Dad suggested that the littlies might like to go for a special hike in Oxshott Woods.

'I don't think I like hiking,' Dorry whined.

'But you will like a little picnic in the sandpit when we've had our exercise,' said Dad. 'In fact, you can be in charge of making the picnic, Dorry. I bet you'd like that.'

We left them preparing a mound of exotic sandwiches invented by Dorry: traffic light ones of strawberry, lemon curd and greengage jam; cream cheese and banana and honey; and ham and apricot jam.

Izzie, Clover, Elsie and I set off down the road for the bus stop. It felt so strange to be going along the pavement again. The curtains twitched next door and I saw Mrs Burton's pale moon face peering out. I waved

371

to her. She shut the curtains quickly, but when we were down the road a bit we heard her calling.

'Mrs Carr! Katy! Little girls!' Her voice was squeaky, as if it needed oiling. Perhaps she wasn't used to talking to anyone.

We stopped politely and went back to say hello.

'Oh my goodness, it's good to see you up and about,' she said, patting my knee with her little claw hands.

'Well. I'm not up. But I am about,' I said.

'I've been so worried about you. Dr Carr came round to reassure me. He said you've made splendid progress, but oh dear, oh dear, you're still having to use a wheelchair! Does he have any idea when you'll be able to walk again?' she asked anxiously.

There was an awkward pause. Clover and Elsie exchanged glances, looking agonized. Izzie cleared her throat, ready to say something, but couldn't seem to get any words out. It was up to me.

'It doesn't look as if I'll ever be able to walk again,' I said flatly.

'Oh my Lord, you poor little lamb,' Mrs Burton gasped. 'Crippled at such a young age!'

'Still, Katy's managing wonderfully,' said Izzie. 'We're very proud of her. Well, we'd better be off. We have a bus to catch.'

We set off again. Clover and Elsie were still looking at me worriedly. I was smarting, but I knew old Mrs Burton didn't mean to be offensive.

'Baa!' I said. 'Baa, baa, baa.'

They looked at me as if I'd gone mad. Then Clover chuckled.

'You're being a poor little lamb!' she said.

It was a silly joke but they all laughed heartily with relief. It was awkward waiting at the bus stop. Several other old ladies looked at me pityingly, shaking their heads and tutting to themselves, and a little kid Philly's age said loudly to his mum, 'Why is that great big girl in a buggy?'

She hissed at him to be quiet, which made him ask it even louder. Then a girl in Clover's class at school joined the queue with her nan and stared at me, open-mouthed.

'What's up with your sister, Clover?' she asked right in front of me, as if I couldn't hear what she was saying.

'Nothing's up with her,' said Clover, going pink. 'She's just had an accident, that's all.'

I was getting a bit sick of all this attention. When the nan wasn't looking I pulled a ferocious face at the Year Six girl, crossing my eyes and lolling my tongue. She veered away from me, panicking. It cheered me up a little.

'Here's the bus coming at last,' said Izzie, sounding relieved. 'I'd better go first, girls, and ask the driver to let down the ramp thing.'

But the driver sucked his teeth at her. 'Hmm, don't think it's possible, love,' he said.

'What? You must have a ramp,' said Izzie.

'Oh yes, I've got one all right, but I've no space inside the bus, see. I've got three buggies crammed in already. You'll have to try the next bus,' he said.

'But that's ridiculous. Can't the buggies be folded up? Surely my daughter takes priority here?' said Izzie indignantly.

'Sorry, love. It's first come, first served. There'll be another bus along in ten minutes,' he said.

'This is outrageous. I shall report this!' said Izzie.

'Report all you like, dear,' said the bus driver. 'Come on, folks. On you hop.'

So they all filed on and we were left helpless at the bus stop.

'What a *whatsit*!' said Izzie. She used another word beginning with w instead of *whatsit*. A word that was strictly forbidden in our family. Clover and Elsie giggled in astonishment. 'Well, he is,' said Izzie. 'He should have insisted those mums collapse their buggies. They could easily have their babies on their laps. What are *we* supposed to do? I can't very well sit with you on my lap, Katy, now can I? And what happens if the next bus is full of buggies, and the one after?'

'Well, if they won't let us on the next bus then we'll just have to walk,' I said.

'But it's too far for you to wheel yourself. Your hands won't hold out. You'll get blisters,' said Izzie.

'Then maybe you'll all have to take turns wheeling me,' I said, though I'd always wanted to show I could wheel myself independently.

'*Oooh* yes, Katy! Let me wheel you first!' said Elsie, though her little stick arms could barely make me budge.

But it didn't come to that. The next bus had a much nicer driver, though he kept up a stream of patter that was annoying to say the least, but I made myself smile because I could see he meant well.

'Oh, here comes little Queenie in her chariot. Hold your horses, madam, and I'll roll out the red carpet for you,' he said.

He operated his ramp and I managed to shunt myself up it by myself, though I was a bit scared I might tip backwards. There were buggies in the wheelchair space in this bus too, but a mum immediately darted forward and collapsed hers so I could just about squeeze into the space. I was horribly aware of people staring at me. It seemed so awful that I couldn't go anywhere anonymously any more. People would always be peering at me, even if it was simply in sympathy. I felt my cheeks burn. I didn't want anyone's pity. I wanted to go back to being ordinary Katy again, where no one gave me a second glance – or if they did it was because I was mouthing off, or had a fit of the giggles.

I even felt suddenly angry with my own family. I didn't want Izzie to be so gentle and forbearing with me all the time, patiently ignoring me when I was tetchy or mean. I didn't want Clover and Elsie to treat me as if I were an angel on a pedestal. I wanted to laugh and scrap and boss them around and I wanted them to argue and moan at me. I just wanted to be *me* again.

'Are you all right, Katy?' Izzie said anxiously. 'You don't look very comfortable. You don't feel travel sick, do you? This bus is very jolty.'

I shrugged. I *was* starting to feel a bit sick actually. If I were Dexter I'd draw myself vomiting copiously over everyone on the bus. It was a tempting thought.

We got to the town centre at last and had to wait for everyone else to troop off the bus before I could wheel myself down the ramp.

'Have a good time, Queenie. Don't mow too many people down with your chariot,' shouted the bus driver. He saw some other wheelchair user in the distance. 'Look, look, another chariot! You can have a race!' he yelled.

My smile wavered. What a total idiot! Izzie thanked him coolly and gathered us together.

'Sorry, Katy. I suppose he thinks he's being friendly, making all those fatuous remarks. Take no notice,' she muttered.

I was looking at the other wheelchair user. He was a teenage boy, propped upright in an awkwardly rigid position. I saw that he was quadriplegic, unable to move any of his limbs. As we got nearer I heard him grunting and groaning incoherently. I couldn't tell if this was his way of making conversation or if he was just making random sounds. His mother was pushing him – or maybe his grandmother, it was difficult to tell. She was grey and stooped and she looked exhausted, but she was chatting away to her boy in a cheery tone, making his responses for him.

Izzie was looking at them too. I squirmed. I didn't want to acknowledge that I was very lucky compared to that boy. I thought of little Rosemary in hospital, forever stuck on her back like a stag beetle, but never complaining. I hated feeling ashamed.

Izzie glanced at me.

'I know, I know. I just don't feel like counting my blessings, OK?' I said rudely.

'I know that too,' Izzie said quietly. 'Are you tired? Would you like me to push you for a bit?'

'No, let me push Katy!' said Elsie.

'I'll push myself,' I said obstinately, though I was starting to feel horribly weary.

'We'll walk either side of you then, Katy,' said Clover. She was looking round, glaring at anyone who was staring at us. I knew she was suggesting this to protect me, but I found that irritating too.

'No, don't. I might barge into you. Don't keep fussing,' I said sharply.

Clover didn't reply but she went pink.

I felt horrid. What was I doing, being so mean to Clover and Elsie and Izzie, when they were trying so hard to be kind and let me enjoy a shopping trip? I took a deep breath.

'Sorry, sorry, sorry,' I said quickly. 'Look, I know it's early, but let's go to McDonald's right this minute and have something to eat. Then I'll get my strength back and won't be so ratty.'

'Good idea,' said Izzie heroically, because she hated McDonald's with a passion.

So we all sat and ate Big Macs and fries, even Izzie.

'Oh, this is so yummy. Isn't it, Katy?' said Elsie.

'Won't Dorry be furious if he finds out!' said Clover.

'It's totally yummy, yes.' Then I looked at Izzie. 'But not quite as good as your cooking.'

'Oh, come on, Katy. You needn't go that far,' said Izzie, laughing.

'OK, not as healthy as your cooking. How about that?' I said.

I felt a lot better afterwards. I even managed to stay calm and serene when Izzie took the two girls to the loo. A mother with two squirmy toddlers came and plonked herself down at my table and started talking to me in that soppy, emphatic way people use with three-year-olds.

'Oh, you poor dear! You're surely not here all by yourself? Here, let me go and order you some food,' she said. 'Don't worry, I'll help you.'

I was quite tempted to say yes please and scoff another burger – but I just smiled at her.

'It's OK. I'm with some people. They'll be back in a minute,' I said.

'You're such a good girl to wait patiently all by yourself,' she said. She poked her arm towards me and I thought for a moment she was actually going to pat me on the head like a little dog, but she chose my shoulder instead. 'Good girl,' she repeated.

I squirmed but managed to stay smiling. She kept on chatting to me till Izzie and the girls came back at last.

'Sorry, Katy, there was a long queue in the ladies',' said Izzie.

'The poor little mite's been such a good girl,' said the interfering woman. 'We've been keeping her company.'

'That's very kind,' said Izzie briskly. 'Come on then.'

I happily took off my brake and wheeled myself round the table to the exit.

'Good Lord, she's leaving the poor kid to wheel herself,' the woman muttered.

'Did you hear that, Izzie?' I said.

'All too clearly,' said Izzie crisply. 'Why can't some people mind their own business?'

But that was the last of the hassle. We went all round the shops in the centre with no problem at all, going up in the glass lifts between floors. We went in Topshop and Zara and New Look. When we were in Primark

Izzie let Clover and Elsie dress up in anything they fancied. Elsie was particularly thrilled to squeeze into a tiny tight skirt and a sparkly top. She came running out of the dressing room to show me.

'Look at me, Katy! Don't I look sexy!' she shouted.

Izzie winced but didn't tell her off.

'You must dress up too, Katy,' said Clover.

I rolled my eyes, because it would be far too much of a performance to wriggle out of my joggers and into a silly little skirt.

'Not my style,' I said.

'You could maybe do with a new outfit,' said Izzie.

'You only just bought me one,' I said.

'Yes, but I think it was more my taste than yours,' said Izzie.

She led the way to a really funky shop playing heavy metal music.

'Let's see if we can find you a T-shirt more to your fancy,' she shouted above the din.

There were some amazingly cool designs. Clover wanted me to have a black T-shirt with a bright psychedelic design. Elsie preferred a blue T-shirt with a huge green chameleon. I liked both, but then I saw a black and grey T-shirt with a skull, the exact same design as Dexter's. I had to have it.

Izzie treated Clover and Elsie too, taking them to Claire's and letting them choose whatever they wanted. Clover went for a little pot of flamingo-pink nail varnish and Elsie fell in love with a ridiculous purple feather boa which she insisted on wearing immediately.

Izzie treated herself to a couple of Anne Tyler paperbacks in Waterstones, and she bought several Beatrix Potters for the littlies.

I was getting really, really tired by now, and my hands hurt and shoulders ached from manoeuvring my wheelchair. I didn't object when Izzie started pushing me, and I didn't moan when she suggested we make tracks for home.

The bus ride went without a hitch and we were home in half an hour. Clover and Elsie wanted me to dress up in my new T-shirt straight away, but I was too tired. I went straight to my room. My arms felt too weak and wobbly to do a proper transfer, so Izzie helped haul me out of the wheelchair and get my heavy legs up on to the bed.

'There now. Have a little nap,' she said.

'Thanks, Izzie. Thanks for everything,' I murmured.

When I was alone I punched the air with one trembly arm, because I'd managed the bus ride and the shopping trip. Then I fell fast asleep almost immediately.

23

'Are you absolutely sure you're ready to go to school, Katy?' Izzie asked.

'Of course I am,' I said fiercely.

'Don't you think you'll get desperately tired going for a full day?' Izzie persisted.

She didn't need to remind me that I'd been exhausted after a couple of hours in the shopping centre. I'd still been tired all day Sunday, flopping in my chair, scarcely able to wheel myself about the house. The thought of the noise and clamour of a new school made me feel sick and trembly, but I knew I had to go through with it. If I backed out now, or just attended in the morning or afternoon, I'd be giving Mrs Matthews ammunition, and she'd persist in suggesting I go to a different school.

So on Monday morning I set my alarm an hour early and got out of bed before anyone else was up. I felt grimly virtuous as I laboured to get washed and struggled into my school uniform. Izzie had bought it right at the beginning of the summer holidays, before my accident. It was five times harder to get into than my usual T-shirt and joggers. It was especially hard trying to get my feet into the tight new socks. I was gasping and swearing at them when Izzie put her head round the door.

'My goodness, you're an early bird. You've done really well, Katy. Here, let me,' said Izzie, deftly twisting the sock and getting it easily over my heel.

Then she bent down and helped with my shoes. It was strange seeing Izzie with her hair unbrushed and straggly and her face pale without her careful make-up. She looked much sweeter and softer.

'Are any of the others awake?' I asked.

'Not yet.'

'I'll get them organized if you want to start breakfast,' I offered.

We hadn't sorted out a stairlift yet but I could shout to the kids easily enough.

'The first small Carr to reach me, properly washed and dressed, will get a whacking great present,' I called.

It worked a treat. Phil came running down first. He wasn't technically fully dressed: his T-shirt was on back to front, he'd forgotten his shorts altogether, and his shoes were on the wrong feet, but he was still first.

'Well done, little Philip Pirrip,' I said, giving him a hug. 'Here you are, here's your reward.'

I gave him a Milky Way I'd kept from yesterday.

'Don't eat it before breakfast though!' I said, as he started tearing the wrapper off.

'That's not fair! Phil's only in his pants!' Dorry complained bitterly. '*I* should be first – I'm dressed properly. Don't eat that Milky Way, it's mine!'

'Your shoes aren't done up and you've got hedgehog hair,' said Clover, running up, her own hair brushed and glossy, her clothes neat, her patent-leather shoes shiny. 'I think that Milky Way belongs to *me*!'

They were still arguing over its ownership at breakfast.

'Now look what you've started, Katy!' said Izzie, but she was smiling. 'Come on, eat up. You're going to need plenty of food in your tummy to get you through the day. Would you like a boiled egg?'

I didn't want an egg. I didn't want cereal. I could barely chew on one quarter of a slice of buttered toast. Then breakfast was over and the others were scurrying to clean their teeth and go to the loo and wailing about lunchboxes and mislaid homework. I sat on at the table, feeling sick.

Izzie stopped clearing dishes. She came up to me and tentatively put her arm round my shoulders. She didn't say anything. She just stood still and held me. I let myself lean against her for a moment.

'Right, Katy?' said Dad, coming back into the room.

He was taking me to Springfield in his car, while Izzie ferried the rest to school and nursery. Cecy came with us. She was fizzing with excitement.

'This is *sooooo* great, Katy,' she kept saying. 'I can't believe you're actually coming to school with me. You mustn't worry about her, Dr Carr. I promise I'll look after her.'

'I don't *need* looking after, Cecy,' I said. I couldn't help being irritated, even though I knew she was just being sweet and protective. I remembered all our old experiences of school together, and how *I'd* always been the one to look after shy Cecy.

'Cecy's simply trying to reassure me, Miss Prickle,' said Dad. 'Thank you so much, Cecy. It's a great comfort to me to know that you'll be looking out for Katy.'

'Look, we're not venturing off into some weird *Pilgrim's Progress* land, all Vale of Despair and Mountains of Gloom, with giants and ogres attacking us night and day. I'm simply going to school, like every other eleven-year-old,' I said.

But as Dad drove the car through the Springfield gates it looked like the Castle of Despond, overrun by tribes of terrifying teenagers, each and every one of them capable of towering over me now I was stuck in a wheelchair.

385

'Look! Look!' Cecy cried suddenly, making me jump. 'See that boy there? The one with the floppy hair. Oh, he's waving to me, look!'

I looked. I saw a perfectly ordinary, gawky guy, a bit spotty. He gave one brief salute with his hand and then carried on chatting with his mates.

'I take it that's Richard?' I said.

'*Richie!* Yes, isn't he fantastic?' said Cecy ecstatically. 'And he *waved* to me!'

'Big deal,' I said, and then worried I sounded too sour. I didn't want Cecy to think I was jealous. Perhaps I was. I wanted to be back in an old life where I might have been thrilled if some random guy waved at me. Though even then I don't think Richie would have affected my happiness quotient one way or another.

Dad was looking amused. We shared a quick glance and he raised his eyebrows slightly.

'Now, Cecy, calm down and tell me where I can park,' he said.

Cecy tried to direct him to the visitors' car park but Dad actually took no notice and drove right up to the main entrance.

'I don't want you and Katy fighting your way through all that rabble,' said Dad. 'Now, you sit tight, Katy, while I get your chair sorted.'

He sprang out of the car and started struggling with the chair, opening it up and putting the seat pad in place. Then he pushed it right up beside the car so I

386

could transfer into it. I noticed Cecy looking away uncomfortably while I was panting and heaving, as if I were doing something indecent. I made a complete pig's ear of it and had to abandon the attempt and sit gasping like a fish before I had enough breath to give it another go. Dad hovered, not sure whether to intervene or not. I tried again and almost missed the chair altogether, but I got a corner of buttock in the right place and hauled hard. I made it at last, though I was damp under my arms, my new school blouse clinging to me. I had a horror I might have started smelling sweaty. Maybe I was going to be labelled the *Smelly Cripple Girl*?

'Now, I think I'll come in and see Mrs Matthews, make sure she's got everything in place for you,' said Dad.

'No, honestly, I'll be fine, Dad,' I said.

I didn't feel fine at all. I felt as lost and helpless as a little kid starting in the Infants, but I was scared of being mocked, the girl who couldn't go to secondary school without her dad.

'Don't you worry, Dr Carr,' said Cecy. 'I'll show her the way. Here, I'll carry your school bag for you, Katy. Gosh, it's heavy, and you haven't even got any home-work yet. Whatever's in it?'

'Oh . . . just stuff,' I mumbled. 'It's OK. I'll have it on my lap.'

I had packed it with spare everything – LoFric catheters, change of pants, change of skirt, just in case

387

I had a terrible accident – plus a pencil case full of new pens and pencils, and my phone in case something awful happened and I needed to call Izzie quickly to come and get me.

I said a quick goodbye to Dad, willing him not to kiss me, because I'd feel an idiot if anyone was watching – though in actual fact I wanted him to give me a huge hug. He understood and just patted me once on the shoulder. When I looked back he was staring after me, busily blowing his nose.

There was a little ridge to get into the main door. I approached it at full speed, trying to jerk myself over, but ground to a halt. I backed up and tried again, but no luck.

'Perhaps you could push me over this stupid bumpy bit, Cecy?' I asked.

'Oh, sure. Sorry! OK then,' said Cecy, flustered.

She seized hold of the wheelchair and tipped it alarmingly.

'Not quite so much!' I gasped.

'Sorry, sorry! Hang on. I'll just . . .' Cecy jerked again and the chair and I skittered forward. 'There! Wow. I think I'm getting the knack now.'

'Thanks.' I sped down the corridor, needing to show I was still independent.

'Slow down, Katy. I can hardly keep up with you,' Cecy panted, scurrying along beside me. 'We'll go and report to Mrs Matthews and then I'll take you along to our classroom. I'm going to see if Alice or Liz, the girls either side of me, will move somewhere else so we can sit together. That would be great, eh? What will you do, Katy? Stay in your special chair or sit on one of the school ones?'

'Stay in my wheelchair. It'll be easier,' I said. I was getting a bit out of breath because I was speeding so. People kept passing us in the corridor and staring. Then we got to Mrs Matthews' office at last. The door was shut.

'Oh help. What are we meant to do – knock or what?' Cecy whispered.

'What do people usually do?'

'I haven't got a clue. I've never been to Mrs Matthews' office before. You only get to go if you've done something brilliant or something outrageously bad,' said Cecy.

'I expect I'll be in the latter category then,' I said, and I edged my wheelchair right up to the door and knocked smartly, pretending I wasn't the slightest bit afraid.

The door opened and there was Mrs Matthews, all pink and lavender drapey clothes and scarves today, with a matching set of pink and purple bangles. It's a wonder she hadn't given her blonde hair pastel highlights to match.

She smiled at me.

'Ah, Katy! I was expecting you. Do come in, dear. Caroline, well done for showing Katy the way.'

She held the door open and I ushered myself into her study. Then I stopped dead, so that Cecy barged straight into my chair. Mrs Matthews wasn't alone. Eva Jenkins was sitting demurely on a chair, giving us her butter-wouldn't-melt smile with her perfect rosebud mouth.

'I believe you and Eva are old friends, Katy,' said Mrs Matthews.

'Well,' I said, not trusting myself to say anything further.

'I know you were in the same class at primary school so I thought it would be nice if Eva looked after you for the first week or so, took you around and showed you where to go,' said Mrs Matthews.

'But that's what I'm going to do, Mrs Matthews!' said Cecy, dodging round in front of me, so indignant she forgot to be frightened.

'It's very kind of you to offer too, Caroline, but that wouldn't really be practical, as you and Katy are going to be in different classes,' said Mrs Matthews.

My head was spinning. It was all going horribly wrong.

'But Mrs Matthews – I so hoped I was going to be in Cecy's – Caroline's – class. We're best friends and neighbours,' I gabbled.

'Well, that's lovely, dear, but I'm afraid it's not possible for you to be in 7T. We've taken on two more pupils and that class is full to bursting, whereas 7A has a convenient space as someone dropped out. Don't look so downhearted. You'll still be able to see Caroline at

390

break and lunchtime – and meanwhile Eva will befriend you, as I said.'

I burned at the word *befriend*. I especially didn't want Eva to do it. She wasn't my friend. She'd always been my worst enemy. Although she was simpering away at me, batting her little-doll eyelashes, I knew she was still my enemy now. But what could I do? I'd been a fool not to let Dad come into school with me as he'd suggested. He might just have been able to make Mrs Matthews change her mind.

'The bell's due to go any minute,' said Mrs Matthews. 'So run along, girls.'

I caught her eye. I didn't say a word but I knew my face was saying *run?* She went a little pink to match her floaty scarf and I felt a tiny triumph.

Outside her door Cecy and I looked at each other.

'I'm sorry,' Cecy said desperately.

'It's not your fault, Cecy,' I said, because of course it wasn't.

'Don't worry about Katy. I'll look after her,' said Eva. 'Shall I push your wheelchair?'

'No! I can do it,' I said gruffly.

Eva shrugged. 'Suit yourself.'

She marched ahead and I had to follow her. Cecy and I pulled agonized faces at each other.

'I'll be waiting outside your classroom at break, promise,' said Cecy, and then she scuttled off in the opposite direction.

I had to follow Eva down a maze of corridors. I tried hard to memorize where we were going, so I would stop being dependent on her, but after chanting *left, left, right* inside my head I got muddled, especially as Eva kept turning round and saying, 'That's the library,' and 'We go in the hall for lunch,' and 'We go through that door to get to the playground,' and 'There are the girls' toilets.'

'Where are the staff toilets?' I asked.

'What? Haven't a clue,' said Eva.

'Well, I'll need to find out, because I'm going to use them,' I said.

Eva paused, looking curious. 'So can you still go to the toilet then? I mean properly?'

'Mind your own business,' I said curtly. I certainly wasn't going to discuss my toileting with Eva Jenkins.

'And your legs – you can't even walk a little bit?' she went on.

'Oh, actually I can run around and dance and do all sorts. I've just got this weird compulsion to sit in a wheelchair,' I said.

'What? Oh, joke. Ha ha,' said Eva. 'What's it like then, Katy? Being . . . you know?'

'What do you think it's like?' I said fiercely.

'No need to be so grumpy. We were all *soooo* sorry for you when we heard,' said Eva.

'Yes, well, I don't need your pity, thanks,' I said.

'OK. *Be* like that,' said Eva.

392

'So where is this poxy classroom then? I thought you were meant to be showing me.'

'It's here,' said Eva, and she dodged inside the next door.

It slammed right in my face.

'You . . .' I muttered a very rude word. It was partly to stop myself bursting into tears. If only Cecy could have stayed with me. Oh, how I wished Dad had stayed. Or Izzie. No, it wasn't really them I was wanting. It was a fiercer, more desperate need. I wanted my mum. I wanted her so badly.

I couldn't often summon her up now. It was as if the accident had chopped through my imagination as well as all the nerve endings in my spine. I couldn't make her up. Whenever I tried I just saw shadowy images like old photos. I couldn't make Mum real any more.

I thought back to my very first memory, sitting in the red toy car, with Mum running along beside me, her ponytail swinging.

'*I'm Katy Carr!*' I said inside my head.

I was *still* Katy Carr, even if I couldn't walk any more. Katy Carr wasn't a little wimp who kept dissolving into easy tears. Katy Carr was tough. And bold. And fierce. And she'd never ever let a girl like Eva Jenkins get the better of her.

I strained forward and struggled with the door handle. It was slippery with use and it was hard to get a proper grip on it because I was at an awkward angle.

Then I had to back up because the wretched door opened towards me, so it was all a tremendous effort, but I did it, I got it open, and I wheeled myself in.

There was a classroom of mostly strange kids, all of them staring at me. And there was Eva Jenkins with her two cronies, Maddie and Sarah, all three huddled together, eyes bright, all of them pink in the face.

'Oh, here, Katy. Let me help you! Hey, I'm so sorry – I didn't realize the door would be such a struggle for you,' Eva lied, rushing to me.

'I'm fine,' I said. 'Don't fuss.'

They were all staring, staring, staring. I wanted to go to my desk and hide myself away, but I didn't know which wretched desk was mine. I forced myself to stare back. Oh God, there was Ryan, looking at me with such shock and horror on his face. I couldn't bear it. I gave him a ferocious glare that made him turn crimson – but he came up to me all the same.

'Katy?' he said, as if he barely recognized me.

'What?' I said rudely.

'Katy, what happened to you? I mean, the wheelchair.'

I stared at him.

'You really don't know?' I said, thinking he might be winding me up.

'Well, Mrs Slater said there was a girl called Katy in a wheelchair joining our class – but I didn't realize it was going to be *you*. Did you – did you break your leg?'

'I wish. I broke my *back*, Ryan.'

'How did you do it?'

'You're not meant to ask about it, Ryan. Mrs Matthews says it's not polite,' said Eva. 'I'm in charge of Katy.'

'No, you're not. *I'm* in charge of me. So shove off, Eva Jenkins,' I said.

'Well, there's gratitude,' said Eva. She raised her little arched eyebrows at Ryan and shook her head in a pitying gesture at me. I would have died if Ryan had raised his eyebrows back. But he didn't. He was barely listening to her.

'I kept on wondering why you never came to Baxter Park during the holidays. I thought about getting in touch, but then I worried you might be avoiding me. Then when I started at Springfield someone said you'd gone to some other school. Nobody said anything about an accident. Did you get run over?'

'Nope. I fell from a tree. I made myself this rope swing but I suppose I didn't tie it properly and I suddenly went flying. The doctor in hospital said I was very unlucky.' My voice went a bit wobbly. I still hated talking about it.

'So how long will it be till you can walk again?' Ryan asked.

Trust Ryan not to beat about the bush.

'I won't,' I said. 'Still, who needs legs when you've got wheels?'

It just sounded pathetic. Then thank God the door opened and a teacher walked in.

'Oh, Mrs Slater!' said Eva, rushing back to my side. 'This is Katy. She has to use a wheelchair. Mrs Matthews says I have to show her round.'

'Hello Katy,' said Mrs Slater. Thank goodness she said it in a perfectly ordinary way, not as if I were a toddler in a buggy. She was a plain woman, thin and tall, with a long horsey face and horsey teeth too, but I liked her because she was brisk and no-nonsense. 'Now, where shall we sit you?'

'Please, Mrs Slater, she'd better come and sit with Maddie and Sarah and me so we can look after her,' said Eva.

'I don't need looking after,' I said through gritted teeth.

'No, you look like a girl who can look after herself,' said Mrs Slater. 'I think we'll put you at the front, so you don't have to go barging up all these narrow aisles.'

I used to hate sitting at the front under the teacher's nose. I was often put there as a punishment for messing about in class. But I'd much sooner be stuck under Mrs Slater's long nose than squashed up with poisonous Eva and Maddie and Sarah. Our first lesson, maths, was right there in our classroom, because it was Mrs Slater's subject.

She gave me a textbook and an exercise book, and then started explaining some new kind of problems, writing stuff on the whiteboard. I stared at it, my heart thumping. I'd always been good at maths, generally second or third in the class. Swotty Simon always came effortlessly top. He'd gone to some posh private school now, so I'd secretly hoped I had a chance of coming top at Springfield. That would show them that I might have rubbish legs but I still had a brain in full working order.

Ha! And ha again. I couldn't understand a word of what Mrs Slater was saying. I strained my ears. I could hear her all right, I just couldn't make sense of it. I looked at the board but all the numbers and squiggles were meaningless hieroglyphics. I peered round at the rest of the class. Perhaps they were finding it incomprehensible too. Half of them were barely paying attention. Eva and Maddie and Sarah were whispering among themselves. Ryan was yawning and cracking his knuckles. Yet when Mrs Slater wrote another sum on the board and told everyone to try and work it out, they all started scribbling busily in their exercise books. Everyone except me.

Mrs Slater was watching me. She came forward, bending down near my ear.

'Do you have problems writing, Katy?' she whispered.

Oh God. Perhaps she thought I was quadriplegic. It was tempting to pretend that was the case.

'No, I can write OK. I just don't know what to write. I – I don't quite get it,' I said, and I blushed, because I so hated to sound stupid.

'Don't worry. You've missed a lot of schooling. You're bound to be a bit rusty,' she said cheerily. 'Here, I'll go over it again for you.'

She went through it all again, doing it quietly and discreetly, but of course it was obvious to everyone in the class that I needed extra help. I knew it was important to concentrate, but my mind skittered all over the place. Mrs Slater tried giving me a little refresher course, going back to stuff I'd learned in Year Six at primary school – and at last something went click in my brain. I could follow what she was saying and relaxed a little, but every time she tried to edge me forward towards learning something new I went blank again.

'Don't worry. It'll come,' she said. 'You just need to get your brain in gear. I've seen your reports, Katy. I know you're a bright girl.'

I could have thrown my arms round her and kissed her.

I didn't feel a bright girl though, especially not in the next lesson, French. The languages classrooms were right the other end of the school and it was a long trek, following in the wake of Eva and all the others. My arms were aching horribly already and my hands felt like they were getting blisters.

'Are you all right? I mean, would you like a push?' Ryan asked, hovering.

I *would* have liked a push, but I shook my head fiercely.

'She's determined to be independent, Ryan,' said Eva, looking round. '*I'm* supposed to be pushing her, but she won't have it.' She walked along beside him, abandoning Maddie and Sarah. 'So, did you go up the park on Saturday? I didn't see you there.'

'No, I had to help my dad take some stuff to the tip,' said Ryan. 'Sorry if you went specially.'

'No, it's fine. I was there with all my mates,' said Eva. 'Still. I'll come again next Saturday.'

'Yeah. Well. OK,' said Ryan.

I felt a terrible pang. *I'd* been going to meet him at Baxter Park the day of the accident. And now I was the girl in the wheelchair and no one was ever going to hang out with *me* down the park. Ryan was looking at me anxiously and I gave him another glare, daring him to feel sorry for me. Let him trot round after pretty, poisonous Eva. See if I cared.

I sat at the front again in the French classroom. We called the teacher Monsieur Brun, but he was no more French than I was, though he rabbited away in French all the time. I didn't understand a word. He was quite nice though, spending time chatting to me and giving me special lists of vocabulary. I felt they'd all think I hadn't a clue and always needed tons of support.

He encouraged me to join in the conversation, so I mumbled, '*Je m'appelle Katy*,' and managed to tell him my age correctly. Then he wanted to know what hobbies I had. I was a bit stuck there. In the end he helped me say that I liked to read, which sounded pretty lame.

Then it was break time and Cecy came dashing up, as she'd promised. We went out into the playground together and sat in a corner for a bit, chatting. Some of the girls in Cecy's class were messing around copying the dance moves from a music video. I saw Cecy's foot tapping away and wondered if she was wishing she could be with them.

'Can you do that dance?' I asked.

'Well. Sort of. It's easy, actually.'

'Not for me,' I said.

Cecy gave a little shudder.

'I'm sorry,' she said.

'No. No, I meant I've always been useless at dancing. You know I have,' I said.

Cecy took a deep breath. 'You can do wheelchair dancing, you know.'

'What?'

'There was this programme on telly once. It showed all these wheelchair dancers. It was beautiful. They were ever so graceful.'

I pulled a face. 'OK. I'll do a wheelchair tango, shall I? I'll stick a rose in my teeth and then I'll whizz right across the floor and run Eva Jenkins over. Yep, that would be fun.'

'Is she being hateful to you?'

'No more than normal. But listen, I need you to help me find the staff toilets on the ground floor. I'll die if I have to get Eva Snotnose Jenkins to help me. Can we go and check it out now?' I asked.

We went back inside the school, though Cecy was looking anxious.

'We're not really supposed to be indoors before the bell goes,' she said.

'Stick with me, babe. We'll break all the rules,' I said, in a silly American gangster voice.

Halfway down the first corridor a teacher came clip-clopping along in high heels.

'What are you two girls doing in school? You know you're supposed to be in the playground,' she called.

'I'm taking my friend to the toilets. She's got special permission,' said Cecy.

'Oh, yes, I see. Sorry, girls,' said the teacher, and walked on.

Cecy and I did a high five behind her back.

She waited for me outside the staff toilets. It was harder than I'd thought to squeeze the wheelchair inside and get the door locked. I managed to sort myself out OK, which was a relief. There was a big mirror that went almost down to the floor. It was weird seeing myself properly. All the mirrors at home were too high for me now.

I didn't look like myself. It wasn't just the wheelchair. My face had changed too. I was paper-white now, though I'd always been lightly tanned, even in the autumn. I was too thin. I'd always been skinny but now my face looked peaky, my eyes much too big. I was like some terrible bug, all eyes and stick limbs. Even my hair looked wrong, scraped back in a childish ponytail. I'd hoped it made me look fun and bouncy like Mum, but I just looked sad and old-fashioned.

What was I doing, imagining that Ryan might still like me a little bit! No wonder Eva and Sarah and Maddie had a good laugh at me.

'Katy? Are you all right? You haven't locked yourself in, have you?' Cecy called anxiously.

'No, I'm fine. Just coming,' I said. I pulled a hideous face at myself in the mirror and then unlocked the door.

The bell went suddenly, practically deafening us.

'I wonder where I'm supposed to go now?' I said. I looked at the timetable Mrs Slater had given me. 'Double science. In the lab on the first floor. Upstairs. So I can't get there.'

Cecy looked at me. 'So – so shall I try and pull your wheelchair up the stairs?' she asked.

'No, you daftie, you'll pull your arms out of their sockets. They said I'll have to study by myself. But I don't know where.'

'Oh Katy. Shall I ask someone?' Cecy looked round worriedly.

'I'll ask. It's OK. Go on, you don't want to be late for your lesson. I'll see you at lunchtime, right?'

'Oh Katy,' Cecy repeated helplessly. 'No, I'll stay with you.'

'I'll be fine. Truly. Go on, scram,' I said.

So Cecy trailed off reluctantly and I was left in the corridor. I wondered about holing up in the staff toilets. If I'd had an interesting book on me it might have been a good idea. I patrolled the corridors instead. There was a flurry of pupils dashing to classrooms and then sudden silence. It felt so weird wandering aimlessly, not really having a clue where I was going. The emptiness everywhere was disconcerting. I'd seen too many films where the hero walks down endless empty corridors and then suddenly some monster/serial killer/zombie leaps out at them.

I heard scurrying footsteps behind me and I whipped my head round so quickly I nearly cricked my neck. It was Eva! *She* was my monster/serial killer/zombie. I burst out laughing.

'What's so funny?' Eva demanded breathlessly. 'Where have you been? I've been searching all over for you! Here. Miss Dean says you've got to start reading some textbook in the library. She's going to come and see you when she has a minute. Come on, you know where the library is, don't you? I did show you.'

'Yeah, well, I've forgotten.'

'It's this way – turn left at the end of the corridor. OK? Do you want me to come with you?'

'No thanks.'

'OK, suit yourself, but don't you dare tell Mrs Matthews I haven't been helping you. I don't want her getting mad at me.'

'Don't worry. You can stay a little teacher's pet, Eva Diva,' I said, and I dodged round her in my wheelchair and bowled down the corridor.

It wasn't quite as simple finding the library as she'd made out, but I got there eventually. It was hard work getting the wretched door open again, but I managed it. The library was a surprise. I was expecting a cubbyhole in an ex-store cupboard like the one at my old school, but Springfield had a huge room absolutely crammed with bookshelves all round the walls, with many free-standing units too.

'*Wow*,' I said softly.

'I love a girl who says *wow* at the sight of books!' A cool, short-haired woman in a black shirt and black jeans bobbed round the shelves and stood smiling at me. 'You're Katy, aren't you? Miss Dean said you were coming. I'm supposed to supervise you during your science studies. So you settle yourself at a table with this incredibly boring textbook Miss Dean has left for you – and if you study for forty minutes for the first session then I'll let you have a good browse round the real books. Bargain?'

'You bet!' I said. 'So are you a teacher?'

She looked so young and super-cool I thought she might be a sixth former.

404

'I'm Miss Lambert, the librarian. I don't teach but I do a few reading sessions with some of the kids who need extra support. It's my mission in life to turn everyone into bookworms. So, Katy, what's your favourite book just now?'

'I don't know . . . there's heaps. I love the three *Hunger Games* books.'

'Good choice. Have you read *The Knife of Never Letting Go*? Even better. With the best dog in all literature. I think there's a copy on the shelves. If not, I'll reserve it for you if you like. And you can take out two more. But look, get your head stuck in *Introductory Science* first before you tackle dystopian science fiction. Do you know what *dystopian* means?'

'Sort of. When people write about the future but it's all weird and dangerous?'

'Exactly. Opposite of *utopian*. Oh, you're a sharp girl. I can see we're going to get along,' said Miss Lambert, grinning at me.

I set to with the science book. It was deadly dull, but I made myself learn how to write up experiments. I read about magnets and iron filings and bell jars and candles and vacuums, so when Miss Dean materialized for five minutes I was able to parrot what I'd learned.

'Well done, Katy. I look forward to having you upstairs in my class as soon as it's possible,' said Miss Dean.

Miss Lambert gave me a thumbs-up sign. She was busy the second session supervising two boys who had problems with their reading and writing. She didn't give them proper books or make them write out stuff. She gave them each an iPad and had them read out a passage about some violent war. There were lots of swear words but she didn't seem to care. The boys stumbled over some of the descriptive passages but they were spot on with the cursing. Then she had them pretend to be soldiers and they had to write a dialogue together. They used a lot more swear words, but as long as they spelled them accurately she praised them.

When Mrs Matthews herself put her head round the library door both boys had the wit to switch to reading some poem about war with no swearing at all.

Mrs Matthews nodded approvingly. She gave me a little nod too.

'How are you coping, Katy? Eva's looking after you properly?'

'Yes, though I don't really need her to. And I saw Cecy – Caroline – at break and I'm meeting her at lunchtime too.'

'Excellent. Well, I'm applying for a grant for a lift, but I can't promise we'll be able to install one immediately. Still, I'm doing my best.'

'Thank you, Mrs Matthews.' Perhaps she wasn't such an old bat after all. And Miss Lambert was brilliant. I had a wonderful wander round the bookshelves. I was going to choose some more dystopian books, but then I came across a golden-oldies section marked *My Special Favourites* so I thought I'd choose a couple to show willing. I didn't want her to think I was sucking up to her the way Eva did with all the teachers, but I liked it that she seemed happy with my choices.

'*The Member of the Wedding* and *I Capture the Castle* – both great reads. If you're inspired, do write me a review and I'll stick it on the library noticeboard.' She handed me my three books. I struggled to fit them all into my school bag, which was already crammed full.

'Hey, I've got a better idea.' She had a whole collection of canvas bags with book-related slogans on them hanging on a peg by her desk. 'I'll give you one of these and you can hook it over the back of your wheelchair as a book bag.'

'Thanks so much, Miss Lambert.'

'You're very welcome, Katy. Come back any time, not just when you're mugging up on science. And let me know how you get on with your books.'

'Will do.'

I *loved* Miss Lambert. I decided to ask Izzie for new black jeans. They would probably be a trial to wriggle into but I didn't care. I wanted to look cool too.

I wheeled myself out of the library, wondering how I was going to find my way to the hall. I couldn't remember if it was left or right from the library. But then Cecy came puffing down the corridor one way and Eva came sashaying along from the other direction, both intent on steering me towards lunch.

'We don't need you, Eva. I'm Katy's friend and I'm taking her,' said Cecy.

'Yes, well, Mrs Matthews told *me* to look after Katy, and if I don't I'm the one who'll be in big trouble, so you push off, Cecy Hall,' said Eva, but then she started simpering and smiling at someone behind me. Ryan.

I rolled my eyes at Cecy, knowing I'd be forgotten now – but Ryan barely paid her any attention.

'I thought I'd kind of escort you in, Katy. The other kids can be a bit rowdy. I'll keep them out your way, OK?' he said, blushing. 'You can come and sit with me and the boys. We'll look after you.'

'Oh Ryan, you're so sweet. But Katy doesn't need you fussing round her. She's not an invalid,' Eva cooed. 'And she's going to sit with Maddie and Sarah and me.'

'No, I'm not. I'm sitting with Cecy,' I said. 'Thanks though, Eva. And thanks, Ryan. You're very kind.'

Eva went off in a huff, but Ryan still hovered.

'You come and sit with us too, Cecy. And tell you what, Katy – you say what you want to eat and I'll go and fetch it for you. You don't want to have to wait in a queue and it'll be hard for you balancing a tray,' he insisted.

He wouldn't take no for an answer so we sat with him and three of his mates. They'd all been at primary

408

school with us, so it wasn't too awkward. They were typical daft boys. Cecy seemed to think they were all a bit childish and jokey compared with her Richie, but I didn't mind them messing about and flicking food at each other. I felt so much better sitting at the end of the table, my wheelchair scarcely visible. They laughed and messed around as if I were still the old Katy.

Ryan did his best to bring me exactly what I wanted in the way of lunch. He hadn't chosen a very big baked potato, it had grated cheese instead of melted, and he'd piled my plate with coleslaw and lettuce when I much preferred tomatoes and grated carrot – but it didn't really matter.

'I've brought you pudding too. I didn't know what you wanted, so I got you an apple pie *and* a strawberry yoghurt. You choose which you like best. Or you can have both, I don't mind,' said Ryan.

'Those boys are so childish,' said Cecy, when we went off together after lunch. 'Typical Year Seven. Still, Ryan's OK. He's clearly nuts about you.'

'Don't be daft. He wouldn't be, not *now*,' I said.

'I think he still fancies you,' said Cecy. 'I think it's great, especially as Eva's after him.'

'Well, yes, I think it's great too then, though I still think you're imagining it,' I said.

Still, it was fun to play with the idea even if I didn't really believe it. I felt almost my own self again. I stayed feeling good the first lesson after lunch, which was

English. Mrs Levy was the exact opposite of cool Miss Lambert. She was old and grey-haired and she wore bright red lipstick, not a good combination with large tombstone teeth. She wore a prim blouse and a skirt that sagged at the back and sensible shoes with stumpy heels. I hated the way she read out poetry, all trilling and faux sincere, but I was fine when it came to analysing a poem ourselves. It was 'Adlestrop', one of Dad's all-time favourites. He read it to all of us when we were still at nursery-rhyme stage. We used to chorus it together with enjoyable emphasis:

YES, *I remember* AD-LE-STROP –

all the way through to

all the birds
of OXFORDSHIRE *and* GLOUCESTERSHIRE.

I might be too fuzzy-brained to cope with maths, but I knew 'Adlestrop' backwards, and I wrote two pages about it, even though it's a really short poem. Mrs Levy was clearly one of those teachers who can't be bothered doing much marking, so she got a handful of us to read out our essays. Some of the comments were pretty dim:

This is a poem. It's about a train station. Nothing much happens. It's in the country.

410

Then she picked on me, so I started rattling through my first page. And then the second. I heard Eva give a loud yawn. Some of the others got a bit fidgety. I knew it probably wasn't wise being all showy-offy. I'd get labelled an insufferable nerdy teacher's pet. Still, I'd sooner this than be the poor dumb wheelchair girl who could barely add two and two together.

It looked like I was certainly going to be Mrs Levy's pet.

'Marvellous, Katy!' she said, smiling widely, lipstick all over her two front teeth. 'You've got such a sensitive appreciation of poetry. Well done! It's going to be a pleasure to have you in my literature class.'

Someone made a muffled vomiting noise. I can't say I blamed them. But I didn't care. OK, maybe I was useless at maths now, but I could manage all the other subjects. I was coping. I was still Katy Carr.

Then the bell went and I looked at my timetable. Double PE. Oh God. How could I possibly do any sport now? I'd already had two science lessons I'd had to miss. Now I'd have to sit out these two PE lessons too. Still, I wouldn't mind going back to Miss Lambert in the library.

I wheeled myself to the classroom door and set off library-wards. I knew the way now.

'Hey, you. Little Miss Suck-up Sensitive,' Eva called. 'You're going the wrong way. We go across the playground and over to the changing rooms for PE.'

'Yeah, but I can't play wheelchair footie, can I?' I said.

'Obviously. But Mrs Matthews says you've got to go to PE all the same. Mr Myers is going to help you do exercises or something,' said Eva.

What? Oh God! It would be like physiotherapy all over again – and in front of everyone else. I went hot all over.

'I'm not coming,' I said.

'You've got to,' said Eva.

'You can't make me,' I said.

'Maybe I can't. But Mrs Matthews can,' said Eva. 'Do you want me to fetch her?'

I wondered what punishment Mrs Matthews might inflict. She'd wag her finger at me in remonstration, her bangles all a-jangle. Which would be worse: Mrs Matthews treating me like a naughty toddler, or this Mr Myers inflicting useless exercises on me? I couldn't decide.

'Come on, Katy,' said Ryan. 'Come with us lot. You'll like Mr Myers. He's good fun.'

I could picture him already, a great hearty bloke in one of those pale grey tracksuits, all-over sweat stains, with a whistle bobbing about on his big hairy chest. I shuddered at the thought, but I gave in and wheeled along beside Ryan. When we went down the corridor near Mrs Matthews' room Eva insisted on hanging on to my wheelchair handles and pushing me herself.

'Get *off*, Eva,' I hissed.

'Why do you have to be so horrid all the time?' said Eva, in a teeny-tiny voice, her chin quivering. She went to join Maddie and Sarah, her head lowered. She wasn't *really* upset, she was just play-acting to get sympathy. It worked too.

'Poor Eva,' said Ryan. 'She was only trying to help.'

'Then why don't you go and console her?' I snapped, because that was exactly what Eva was after.

Ryan stayed walking beside me, frowning. 'You aren't half grumpy sometimes, Katy.'

'Wouldn't you be, if you were me?' I said.

Ryan shrugged. 'Perhaps. Though you were always a bit fierce even before your accident.'

'Rubbish!'

'Some of the kids were a bit scared of you.'

'Were you scared of me, Ryan?'

'Petrified,' he said, pretending to shake with fear.

'Well, watch out now then,' I said, making out I was aiming my wheelchair at him.

He laughed and started running. 'Can't catch me!'

'Yes, I can!' I shouted and I wheeled myself as fast as I could, dodging madly round half the class.

We reached the doors to the playground together, both of us pushing and shoving.

'Ryan Thompson! I can't believe it! Were you really shoving a *girl in a wheelchair* out of your way?'

It was Mrs Levy, her whole face as red as her lipstick. 'Katy, are you all right? You could have tipped her right over, Ryan! What were you thinking!'

'I'm sorry, Mrs Levy,' said Ryan, looking upset.

'It wasn't Ryan's fault, Mrs Levy, honestly. We were just having a race, that's all. *I* was pushing *him*. Truly,' I said. 'Don't worry, I think I could hurt him far more than he could hurt me!'

Mrs Levy blinked at us both. Perhaps she was upset that her little sensitive wheelchair girl could fight back.

'Well, I still think it's not gentlemanly behaviour, Ryan, treating Katy like that. I shall be keeping an eye on you,' she said. 'Now open the door for her properly and help her out into the playground.'

'Yes, Mrs Levy,' Ryan muttered.

I let him take hold of the wheelchair and edge me outside.

'There's a little gent, Ryan,' I said softly.

'You're a total mischief,' said Ryan. 'Watch it, or I'll tip you right out.'

We both laughed. Eva peered round and looked upset. Hurray!

It was hard work going all the way over to the PE block on the uneven asphalt and I was already exhausted. Perhaps I could tell this Mr Myers I was much too tired to do any stupid exercises. There wasn't any point anyway. No exercise in the world would get my legs moving again.

Ryan and I had to part company at the PE block while we went to our separate changing rooms. I didn't know what to do. I didn't have any PE kit to change into, and even if I had, I wouldn't have struggled into it in front of everyone for the world. The PE lesson would be practically over by the time I'd got myself sorted.

So I just sat in my wheelchair gazing at my lap so I wouldn't be staring at any of the girls. Though I couldn't help peering every now and then, feeling such painful envy. Everyone was moaning about their figures, sucking in their stomachs and slapping their thighs disgustedly, but I'd have traded places with the fattest, wobbliest girl because she could move about, she could bend over, she could stretch up, she could sit on the bench and kick her shoes off and wriggle out of her tights.

Eva came strutting up, looking wonderful in her little T-shirt and shorts. She put her hands on her hips, tight-lipped.

'You do know Ryan's my boyfriend now, don't you, Katy?' she said.

'Yeah, well. Whatever,' I said.

'And you do also know that he doesn't really *like* you. He's just being kind because you're . . . you know.'

I swallowed. 'And your point is?' I said, hoping my voice wouldn't go wobbly.

'I just needed to spell it out to you,' said Eva. 'So you don't get the wrong idea.'

'So *you're* being kind to me. Have I got that right?' I said.

'Well. In a way,' said Eva.

'Because we're such good friends, like Mrs Matthews said.'

'You always twist things,' said Eva.

'That's me. The twisted girl,' I said.

'Come on, you girls,' someone shouted from outside. 'The boys have been ready for a full five minutes.'

The someone was clearly Mr Myers. I followed all the other girls, though I was tempted to lurk in the changing rooms. I found myself in a huge, brightly lit gym, with girls and boys rushing round bouncing balls all over the place. And then Mr Myers himself came bouncing up. He wasn't the hearty, sweaty old guy I'd imagined at all. He was young and dark and fit, with thick, curly dark hair and brown eyes, a bit like that male model who advertises underwear. He clearly had an effect on all the girls, because they pranced about and squealed and giggled as they fetched balls and started bouncing them too.

'Hello. You must be Katy,' said Mr Myers. He held out his hand and I shook it warily.

'So how long have you been using a wheelchair?' he asked.

'Since the beginning of the summer,' I said, praying he wouldn't ask all about the accident. Eva's words still echoed in my head. *Ryan's just being kind.*

Well, she would say that, wouldn't she, because she was hateful and we were worst enemies. But I believed her all the same. Cecy had been crazy to say that Ryan still liked me. I'd been even crazier to believe it.

'So, not long at all,' said Mr Myers. 'Yet you've got brilliant wheelchair skills. You must be worn out though. It's your first day back at school, isn't it?'

'Yes,' I said, and I realized I was aching all over now and my head felt fuzzier than ever.

'Don't worry, I'm not going to be too hard on you,' said Mr Myers. 'Let me just get the others organized and then we'll see what you can do, OK?'

He clapped his hands. 'Right, everyone. I want two mixed teams for a game of Myball. George, you pick one team; and Eva, you pick the other.'

Oh God, so he was another teacher who thought the world of Eva. I went off him right away. But I was curious about this new game.

'Myball?' I muttered.

'I'm Mr Myers and it's my invention – hence Myball. It's like a mixture of netball and basketball – with bigger teams and two balls in play at the same time and everyone can have a go at shooting a ball through the net.'

I watched once the teams were picked. Eva's first choice was Ryan, needless to say. Myball looked fun. No, it actually looked *great* fun, with everyone running round and balls whizzing all over the place. I'd have loved to play. I'd have been good at it too, really good. I could dodge and catch a ball and I'd always been the best at shooting because I was so tall.

Mr Myers appointed a ref for each team and then came over to me.

'What do you think of Myball?' he asked.

I thought his question was tactless under the circumstances. I just gave a shrug.

'Do you want to try your hand at shooting hoops?'

I stared at him. 'I thought you were going to give me exercises?'

'Well, I can if you want. I just thought shooting would be more fun. Do you think you're any good at it?'

'I'm the best!' I said.

He laughed. 'OK, show me,' he said, walking over to a hoop at the end of the gym. He threw me a ball and I caught it easily enough. I aimed at the net and waited for the ball to soar through the air and fall with a satisfying little whisper through the net. Only it didn't. It fell short by a mile. I stared as if I couldn't believe it.

'Have another go,' said Mr Myers, retrieving the ball.

I had six goes in a row – and I was useless, the ball failing to reach the hoop each time.

'Try again,' said Mr Myers.

'There's no point. I'm absolute rubbish now,' I said, nearly in tears. 'I don't get it. There's nothing wrong with my arms. Why won't the wretched ball go *in*?'

'What did you used to do?'

'I don't know! I just used to aim and throw and in it went. I didn't really even think about it. It just happened.'

'Would you have still been able to dunk the ball in if I'd lengthened the pole so the hoop was right up by the ceiling?'

'Well, obviously, no.'

'Think about it. You're sitting hunched up in a wheelchair. It makes you half the height you used to be. So, let's experiment.' He fiddled with the hoop, sliding it halfway down. 'Now try.'

The ball still didn't go in, but it was a near miss. I had another go. That didn't work either. But the third time the ball actually went through the hoop.

'Yay!' said Mr Myers, grinning. 'And again. Come on, girl. You've got it back. Keep going.'

I did. There was a dispute with one of the Myball teams and Mr Myers went to sort things out. I carried on shooting, chasing my own ball. It was hard work bending down and trying to scoop it up. All the muscles started twanging in my arms and shoulders but I carried on.

'Excellent,' said Mr Myers, running back. 'Ten more goes. See if you can get ten out of ten.'

I got eight out of ten, which annoyed me, but Mr Myers high-fived me and said I was brilliant.

'Yes, but it's cheating, isn't it? I mean, no one plays with the hoop right down there,' I said.

'This is training. Carry on at this height today. Then next session we'll put the hoop up a bit. You'll soon get your eye in. It'll take several weeks, but we'll have you scoring goals by the end of term.'

'Maybe,' I said doubtfully. 'But what's the point? I can't actually play, can I?'

'Who says?' said Mr Myers. 'This is Myball, my invention. I make up all the rules. If I say you can play, then you can.'

'But I'm in a wheelchair. I can't run.'

'You can whizz about easily enough. And I think the chair works to your advantage. I'll let you get away with a bit of mild barging and bumping as long as you don't seriously injure anyone. OK?'

I stared up at him. 'Oh wow. It's more than OK!' I said.

I tried another ten balls. I only managed seven goals this time but I didn't get downhearted.

'You wait till next time,' I said. 'I really will score ten out of ten, you'll see.'

24

I was so tired when I got home that I went straight to bed. I just hauled myself on to the bed, not even bothering to pull off my shoes. Clover and Elsie both started talking to me at once, asking me endless questions about my day. Tyler came and jumped on my bed, licking my face passionately because he'd missed my being at home with him all day. I could barely raise my hand to stroke him.

'Come on, everyone. Let Katy have a little nap,' said Izzie, shooing them all away.

She came back two hours later, telephone in her hand.

'So sorry to wake you, but it's Helen on the phone, wanting to know how you got on,' said Izzie.

I did buck up a bit then, and I told Helen proudly about my day. I didn't moan about the awfulness of Eva or all the staring and whispering wherever I went. I focused on the positive and Helen was full of praise and told me I was splendid.

Dad and Izzie and all the children told me I was splendid too, making a huge fuss of me. I was Katy the brave, the bold, the magnificent. I basked in all this adulation, though I knew I didn't deserve it. I went back to bed straight after supper, still desperately tired. Clover came with me and lay down carefully beside me to keep me company.

'Oh Katy, I do miss you being upstairs in our bedroom together. Izzie says there isn't room for me to sleep in here with you, but I'm going to curl up with you every night so we can have all our old chats and games together,' she said.

'That'll be lovely,' I murmured, but my eyes were already closing and I couldn't keep awake even for Clover.

I don't know when she gave up and crept away. I didn't hear either Dad or Izzie come in to say goodnight because I was in such a deep sleep. But then I woke up at four o'clock in the morning, absolutely wide awake, aching from all the extra exercise. The events of yesterday were going round and round in my head: the silly little slights, the things I couldn't join in with, the sheer struggle of it all. I couldn't concentrate on the positive now. I trembled with pointless rage because I was stuck in a wheelchair and all the ordinary everyday things in life were going to be a struggle forever. I desperately wanted to moan to someone, but not Helen or any of the family; not even Clover.

I struggled out of bed into my chair and wheeled myself over to the little table that was now my desk. I opened up the laptop and started writing a long email to Dexter. I knew he was much older than me and we didn't really have anything in common apart from being paralysed, but he seemed the only person in the world who would truly understand.

I wrote about Mrs Matthews with her steely smiles and her artificial kindness. I wrote about feeling different all the time. I wrote about the panic of not knowing where I was going or if I could even fit through the wretched doors. I wrote about the agony of being dependent on a hateful little show-off like Eva. I wrote about the shame and embarrassment of knowing deep down that she was right: Ryan was only paying me attention because he was sorry for me. I wrote that some things had been OK, and that I liked Miss Lambert and Mr Myers; but I knew all too well that in my old life I wouldn't have been one of the lame, weedy kids wanting to take refuge in the library, and I wouldn't have needed special concessions in PE; I'd have been the star of the top team, no problem.

It felt great to heave it all out of me. After I'd sent the email I felt that wonderful feeling of peace you get when you've been violently sick. I didn't even have the strength to haul myself back on to the bed. I fell asleep slumped sideways in my wheelchair.

Izzie discovered me in the morning and was appalled.

'I think it's all too much for you, Katy. It would be madness to go into school today. You need to stretch out in bed and have a proper sleep. Perhaps wait a couple of weeks and build up your strength first,' she fussed.

'No way! It would be like starting as a new girl all over again. I'm fine, really I am,' I protested.

'Well then, how about mornings only for a while?'

'Definitely not. I especially need to go in the afternoons,' I said. I'd looked properly at the timetable. All the PE sessions were in the afternoon.

'You're the most obstinate girl in all the world,' said Izzie. 'But maybe that works in your favour now. Your dad and I are very proud of you.'

So I went back to school on Tuesday. And Wednesday and Thursday and Friday. I stayed desperately tired and I ached all over and I developed dreadful blisters on my hands from all the wheelchair-pushing, but Izzie bought me fingerless leather gloves that actually looked incredibly cool.

Mrs Slater gave me special maths tuition whenever she'd set the others work. I still couldn't get my head round these new problems so she went back over sums I'd learned in Year Six, even Year Five, and at last my mind whirred into action. It was as if she'd given the batteries in my brain a good shaking to get them working again. Then when I could whizz through all the old sums she started adding a few new ones, and I coped with them OK. She seemed as pleased as I was when I started getting them right.

I managed all the other lessons too, and especially enjoyed 'science', when I chatted about books half the time with Miss Lambert. I did well in Mrs Levy's class too, but my favourite lesson was PE. I kept practising with Mr Myers, who raised the net a little each session – and soon I was scoring goals when it was nearly at the proper height.

Mr Myers started bouncing the ball near me to see if I could stop wheeling, catch it, and then hang on to it until I was ready to pass it to someone else or try shooting myself. It sounded easy enough, but it was incredibly difficult to get the rhythm right.

I kept trying but I simply didn't have the knack. I found it especially humiliating when the Myball teams were having a half-time break and watching me. I knew Eva and Maddie and Sarah were all smirking as I missed the ball again and again.

'Katy, if I helped you, could you manage to sit on the floor with your back against the wall?' Mr Myers asked softly in my ear.

'Well, yes, I suppose so. But I don't think it'll help me much, so what's the point?' I said.

'You'll see,' he said.

425

He lifted me very carefully and sat me down on a gym mat, making sure I was safely propped up.

'Right, I want a volunteer,' he called. 'Who's one of the best at Myball?'

Lots of them waved their hands in the air – including Eva.

'OK, Eva, you go first,' said Mr Myers.

He wheeled my chair into the middle of the floor.

'Right, Eva, hop in. Let's see how you can manage Wheelie Myball.'

Eva went pink. 'Oh sir, do I have to? I don't want to sit in Katy's wheelchair!'

'Give it a go. Be a good sport,' said Mr Myers. He said it lightly, but there was an edge to his voice.

So Eva climbed into my wheelchair, grimacing as she did so, as if she thought I'd wet the seat. Mr Myers threw her a ball and she caught it.

'There! I can do it, easy-peasy,' she said.

'Yes, any fool can catch the ball if they're stationary,' said Mr Myers. 'Try wheeling and then I'll throw it. And then have a go at shooting. See how you do.'

Oh joy! Eva couldn't catch it once. She dropped it again and again. She couldn't control the wheelchair at all. And then when Mr Myers made her try shooting she was useless at that too, and couldn't get the ball anywhere near the net.

'There. It's not actually as easy-peasy as you'd think,' said Mr Myers.

426

I wanted to throw my arms round him and kiss him. It was a moment of total triumph. And suddenly half a dozen people wanted a go in my wheelchair, and they all found it difficult to manoeuvre and lost all their ball skills. Ryan tried too, and was equally useless.

'Wow, this is impossible. You're a real star, Katy,' he said.

I didn't point out that I'd had ages to get used to my chair and I'd been practising with the ball for a long time too. I just smiled.

'So, next lesson I think it's time you joined in a game of Myball, Katy,' said Mr Myers. 'Do you fancy having a go?'

Did I ever! I was nervous at first, wondering how it would work out, whether I'd be overwhelmed – but it was wonderful. The others were nervous of me, scared they might bump into me or somehow knock me out of my wheelchair, so I could dart among them and score yet another goal while they hung back.

'We're just being nice to you because you're disabled,' Eva puffed, her face a mottled salmon pink.

'Good!' I said. 'Because my team's winning!'

I was in Ryan's team. He'd picked me first! We were both the highest scorers, five goals each! So we high-fived each other and everyone in our team cheered.

My email to Dexter was in bold capital letters that night. I never got any reply from him, but I kept on writing. It was as if I were keeping a diary just for him.

Perhaps he didn't even bother to read it. But if he did, I knew he'd understand.

The games of MyBall helped change my status in class, especially with the boys. I was Katy the ace Myball player, not Katy the girl in the wheelchair. We even played our own version of Myball in the playground at break, and they always asked me to join in.

They were sometimes a little rough now and Izzie exclaimed at the bruises on my legs, the scratches on my arms.

'For goodness' sake, Katy!' she said, dabbing at me with Savlon. 'You must stop all this rough-housing. You know you have to take particular care of your legs. One of these cuts could easily go septic without you realizing.'

'They're *scratches*, Izzie. Don't fuss!' I said.

She did fuss though, and made me show my legs to Dad.

'You're still my harum-scarum tomboy, chickie,' said Dad. 'Don't go too mad. But I'm glad you're having fun.'

But the fun was over soon enough. In one game of Myball I happened to wheel straight into Eva. It was an accident. OK, maybe it was accidentally on purpose, but she was deliberately blocking me, stopping me aiming at the net. So I barged forward and knocked her out the way. She overbalanced and sat down on her bum. She wasn't really hurt at all. She just looked a bit silly. I couldn't help it if some of my team laughed. Me especially.

She didn't say anything much at the time. She just sloped off after the game, muttering darkly to Maddie and Sarah.

I forgot all about it until the next PE lesson. Mr Myers came up to me. For once he looked awkward, his dark eyes not quite meeting mine.

'I thought maybe you and I could practise hitting a ball with a rounders bat, Katy. Would you like to do that?' he said.

'Well, yes, I suppose so. But can't I play Myball?'

'Not today.'

'Why not?'

'Mrs Matthews has had a word. She doesn't think it's a good idea. She's treating it as a health and safety issue.'

'What? But I'm fine, you know I am. And even if I tumble out of my wheelchair it doesn't really hurt,' I protested.

'I think maybe Mrs Matthews is worried about other pupils being hurt,' said Mr Myers.

He didn't look in Eva's direction. But I did. She was smirking triumphantly. She'd told on me. Perhaps her wretched mother had emailed Mrs Matthews. I hated Eva, I hated her mother, I hated Mrs Matthews.

Mr Myers did his best with me. He bowled me balls and tried his hardest to turn it into our own private game, but we both knew it was a poor substitute for a proper game with everyone else. I'd so loved being part of a Myball team and now I couldn't take part any more.

'Never mind,' said Ryan. 'You can still play games with us in the playground.'

But I wasn't even allowed to do that. The teacher on playground duty came over and said apologetically, 'I'm so sorry, Katy, but I don't think you should be joining in. Someone might get hurt.'

I wrote a long and desperate email to Dexter that night. I said I'd never go back to Springfield again because they wouldn't let me be an ordinary pupil and I couldn't stand always having to be an isolated onlooker. But in the morning I dragged myself up and got ready all the same.

'Where are you going, Katy?' Cecy asked, when I set off determinedly down the corridor as soon as we got to school.

'I'm going to see Mrs Matthews,' I said fiercely.

'Oh goodness!' said Cecy. 'Are you sure? You're not really supposed to see her without a proper appointment and she's always very busy before school starts.'

'I don't care,' I said. 'I'm seeing her.'

'Look, I know you're really angry, and it's ever so unfair, though I don't quite get why you want to be in a Myball team so much. It's crazy – I'd give anything to get out of having to play. I hate it. It's so rough and

430

everyone barges into you, and last time someone threw the ball right at my head and it really hurt.'

'Oh, poor Cecy,' I said. 'But that's exactly it: Myball is a rough game and people do get knocked about a bit. I'm going to tell her that. I'm going to make her change her mind.'

'I don't think anyone can change Mrs Matthews' mind,' said Cecy anxiously.

She was right. The head frowned at me when I bowled straight into her study without waiting for her to call me in.

'Ah, Katy. I'm very busy, dear. Can you come back later?' she said, peering at various reports, her glasses right on the end of her nose.

'No, I'm afraid I need to talk to you now, Mrs Matthews,' I said, trying hard to keep my voice polite. 'Why have you banned me from taking part in Myball?'

Mrs Matthews put the reports down and hitched her glasses up her nose so she could focus on me properly. Her frown had deepened.

'I haven't banned you exactly, Katy. I just don't think it's very wise for you to take part. You could easily get hurt – or indeed you could unintentionally hurt another pupil,' she said.

'It's because of Eva, isn't it?' I said. 'I bet she complained. She's always got it in for me.'

'Don't be silly, Katy. I don't like your tone. And I thought Eva was your friend?'

431

'No. That's just it. You *thought* Eva was my friend. She's never ever been my friend,' I said, not quite as polite now.

'Well, I don't have time for this childish nonsense. I've made a decision. I don't want you joining in any contact sports either in PE or in the playground. I have to think of the safety issues.'

'But anyone can get knocked over by anyone else. Look at rugby! Or you can get whacked about the legs playing hockey. It's so unfair! Everybody else can join in and take a risk. Why can't I?'

'You know why, Katy. Now stop this silliness and run along.'

'I wish you wouldn't keep telling me to *run* when it's obvious I can't. And I'm sure there's some regulation that says you have to treat disabled people the same as everyone else,' I said.

'And there's also a regulation that says the head teacher can discipline or indeed exclude any pupil being persistently difficult and disruptive,' said Mrs Matthews briskly. 'I don't think you realize how hard we are all trying to accommodate you. So please stop this silly arguing and go to your classroom.'

So that was that. I couldn't win. And I couldn't play Myball any more.

Mr Myers tried very hard to keep me feeling part of each PE lesson. He devised a game where I stayed sedentary and batted the ball while one person bowled at me and two others fielded, but it wasn't anywhere near as exciting as Myball.

'Here, Katy,' said Mr Myers at the end of PE. He handed me a piece of paper with a name and phone number. 'I've made a few enquiries and this guy here runs special wheelchair basketball sessions at a health club in Markover. It's held on Friday nights. I know it's a bit of a journey, but maybe your dad could drive you over. I think you'd find it fun.'

'Thank you, Mr Myers,' I said, because he was really trying to help me, but I tucked the paper in the bottom of my book bag and didn't make any attempt to get in touch with this guy. I didn't want to do 'special' basketball with a load of disabled strangers. Probably most of them were old and helpless and they were just chucking balls about as gentle therapy.

I didn't want to define myself as disabled. I wanted to be *me*.

School didn't get any easier. I still had to get up much earlier than anyone else to manage my washing and dressing – and I could see it would get harder the older I got. Eva and co. were already experimenting with elaborate new hairstyles and make-up. If I tried to fiddle around like that I'd have to start getting up at four in the morning.

School itself was mostly OK, but it was still exhausting keeping up with all the others, showing

433

them I was just as good as they were. I was still absolutely exhausted when I got home every day. I didn't always have to go to bed straight away but I certainly couldn't stay up much later than supper. Izzie gave Jonnie and Dorry and Phil their bath while Clover and Elsie helped me into my pyjamas and got me tucked up in bed.

'And then we'll read you a story, Katy. You'd like that, wouldn't you? Can *I* read it to you? Mum says I'm good at reading aloud. Did you know that, Katy?' Elsie babbled. She laid all her favourite books in a line on my bed as if she were playing Patience. 'Go on, choose which one you want.'

I didn't really want to choose any of them. I'd have much sooner Elsie buzzed off so I could have a peaceful chat with Clover just as we used to. But somehow I couldn't be mean to Elsie now.

'Oh, *Winnie-the-Pooh*. I absolutely love those stories,' I said, knowing that they were the ones Elsie liked most. 'Could you possibly read me a chapter, Elsie?'

So Elsie sat cross-legged on the end of my bed each night, reading me chapter after chapter. She *did* read aloud well, and she had different voices for each of the characters. She had a jolly, fat voice for Pooh; a tiny, squeaky voice for Piglet; a sad, sighing voice for Eeyore; and she even tried to do Australian voices for Kanga and Roo. Sometimes Clover and I got the giggles listening to her, but we simply pretended we were laughing at the story, which satisfied Elsie.

434

They always settled me down carefully, tucking me up under the duvet and switching off my bedside lamp, and then they'd tiptoe away with elaborate care. I'd sometimes sit up again and write another email to Dexter. More often I'd fall asleep straight away – but I'd nearly always wake up in the middle of the night.

That was the worst time. All my courage and resolution leaked away. I just lay uncomfortably in the dark, so sad and angry and resentful, feeling like a half-person whose life had finished already. I cried sometimes, which was always a mistake, because I'd end up with a splitting headache and red puffy eyes. I could cry Niagara Falls and it still wouldn't make any difference. The accident had happened. I couldn't walk.

I did walk sometimes, in my dreams. I ran, I danced, I swam – and then I'd wake up and maybe for a second or two I'd forget and try to jump out of bed. Each time I remembered, it was sharply painful.

School days were hard work but in a way they were better than Saturdays. We obviously didn't go to the secret garden now. Dad and Izzie tried harder to do things with the children rather than leave us to our own devices. Dad often went swimming on Saturday mornings with the littlies, which they loved. Izzie found a pottery class for children and took Clover and Elsie and me there. It was mostly for little kids Elsie's age or even younger. Clover didn't seem to mind and loved messing around with the clay, taking immense pains painting her little pots once they were fired, but I felt much too old. I wasn't much good at it either. My own pot went horribly lopsided, its lid didn't fit properly and the rays of all my painted suns were too watery and dribbled down the sides.

I stopped going. Clover immediately offered to stop going too, but I knew how much she loved the pottery classes, and she and Elsie wanted to make lots more pots for Christmas presents for the whole family.

'OK, I'll drop you two off at pottery and then Katy and I can go shopping,' said Izzie.

It was OK the first time. We went round the shopping centre and Izzie bought a new scarf and treated me to a stripy sweatshirt, and then we hung out in McDonald's until it was time to go and collect the girls. But we couldn't buy stuff every week and it was a bit pointless going round and round the same shops anyway.

'Let's just go home,' I said the third week.

So that's what we did. It was very quiet in the house, just Izzie and me. She settled down to her boring old handbag-making, setting up shop on the kitchen table with all her bits of suede and leather.

'You come and keep me company at the other end of the table,' said Izzie.

I got my homework out and tried to concentrate. I juggled all my books, swapping from maths to English to history. I still had so much catching up to do. Most of the teachers set me extra work now. I knew it was simply to help me, not a punishment – but it felt like one.

I couldn't seem to concentrate no matter which book I picked up. I tried for fifteen minutes, until all the lines of text started wriggling about like worms, and then I lost it altogether, threw three books on the floor and burst into tears.

In the old days before the accident Izzie would always have had a right old go at me if I lost my temper. But now she picked my books up, gave me a box of tissues, and made us both a mug of hot chocolate. She went the whole hog with whipped cream and tiny marshmallows. I couldn't help cheering up a little.

'I'm sorry,' I said, sipping. 'I just feel so hopeless. It's so awful, being stuck here.' Then I blushed, because I realized I was being tactless. 'I didn't mean stuck with you. You're being ever so kind. It's just . . .'

'I know,' said Izzie. 'Why don't you take a little break from all that schoolwork? Do something else.'

'I can't think of anything else,' I wailed. 'I feel so stupid and useless. Maybe I should have stuck it out at the pottery classes. Then at least I'd be making my Christmas presents like Clover and Elsie. Though you'd have to be pretty weird to be grateful for one of my wobbly pots. But what else can I make?'

'Well, I know it was a bit of a disaster the last time I suggested you do some sewing with me . . .' Izzie said cautiously. 'But I've got lots of little offcuts from my bags. How about making purses for the girls?'

I didn't really fancy the idea at all, but I agreed to give it a go because Izzie was trying so hard to be kind to me. She spread out all the odd pieces of suede and leather and gave me a special needle and thread. She showed me how to make a simple fold-over purse. It was actually a bit too simple.

'Could I perhaps design my own?' I asked.

'Of course,' said Izzie, though she looked a little sceptical.

It was a piece of green suede that had set me thinking. I sketched out a design on a piece of paper first, not wanting to cut into the suede and muck it up. Izzie watched me drawing four loops and looked interested. I pinned the paper to the suede and cut round it carefully twice.

'Oh, I get it!' said Izzie. 'It's a four-leaf clover!'

'Do you think Clover might like it?'

'I think she'll love it!' said Izzie. 'What a great idea.'

It was hard work stitching round the loops and I had to do it very carefully to make the stitches even. I wanted a little zip inserted in one of the loops, and that was way beyond me, so Izzie stitched it for me on her machine.

'There!' she said, giving it to me. 'One present solved.'

'I'll start on Elsie's purse next,' I said. I thought hard. What on earth would Elsie like? I sifted through the offcuts. There was a piece of white leather and a little scrap of pink suede. I had a sudden idea. I started another drawing and then started cutting out a white shape.

'OK, I'm guessing again,' said Izzie.

'It's going to be a daisy with a pink centre,' I said.

'I love the way you're cutting the petals out so carefully,' said Izzie.

'Let's hope it doesn't go too wonky. I want it to be special for Elsie.'

'Katy, she'll love it,' said Izzie. 'She'll especially love it because you've sewn it for her.'

I didn't have time to finish Elsie's purse that morning. I worked on my purse project every Saturday morning after that. Jonnie was next. I used more of the white leather and stuck some narrow black strips on it.

'Zebra stripes!' said Izzie, laughing. 'A perfect choice for Jonnie.'

I knew Dorry would like a purse too. It was easy to make a design for him. I used yellow leather and the white, and then a piece of red suede, and fashioned a cake with a lot of cream and a cherry on the top. Philly wouldn't want to be left out, so I made him a yellow duck purse with an orange beak.

I had to make Cecy a purse as well. I used pale blue suede, fashioning her a high-heeled shoe with a crystal button sewn on the front.

I needed to send Helen a present too. As soon as I picked up a scrap of silver leather I knew what I was going to make: a seahorse purse. I copied the design from my necklace and stitched the little face very carefully, giving him a green glass eye.

I wanted to make a proper wallet for Dad. Izzie had to help me a lot, especially with the complicated folds inside. I stitched Dad's initials on the front piece of leather. They went a little bit wobbly, but I hoped Dad would think it was just an artistic style of writing.

That left Izzie. I didn't want her to see what I was making. I collected up various scraps of lilac and grey suede and purple leather and made her own purse in secret in my room. It was a miniature handbag, copying her most popular style, the bag she used herself: a deep purple leather with lilac and grey suede roses appliquéd on the front. Of course I couldn't make it look totally professional, and I didn't attempt the little pockets or the grey silk lining, and I had to fasten it with four little buttons cut off an old baby dress of Jonnie's because I couldn't manage to sew in a zip, but I was still pleased with the way it turned out. I hoped Izzie would be too.

She was certainly very complimentary about my other purses.

'They're brilliant, Katy! I know you've always rather despised my handbags but if you ever wanted to do something similar in the future I'm sure you'd be a great success,' she said.

'A suitably genteel occupation for a poor little crippled girl,' I said. I meant it as a silly joke, but Izzie winced.

'I wish you wouldn't talk like that, Katy,' she said. 'I didn't mean that at all. And you know you can do just about anything if you set your mind to it. Look at Helen.'

'I know, I know,' I said – but I *couldn't* do anything I wanted. I couldn't be a sporting champion, playing football or running or racing cars.

There was something else I couldn't do. Dance. Well, I'd never really been much cop at dancing, but I'd been able to jig about to pop music. There was a Springfield Christmas disco for all the Year Sevens and Eights. Mr Myers was arranging it in the gym and it was already a big talking point.

'Don't get too excited, folks. It's not a prom, so keep your fancy dresses in your wardrobes, girls. It's going to be very low-key. A good old-fashioned school disco like you had at primary school, with fruit punch and crisps and chipolata sausages, and I'll be the DJ playing the sort of Dad music to make you groan. OK? But it'll be fun, I promise you.'

Cecy certainly thought it would be fun. She was so thrilled that the Year Eights were going to be there too.

'Do you think Richie will ask me to dance?' she asked for the hundredth time.

'I don't know,' I said, shrugging. 'Why don't *you* ask *him* to dance?'

'I'd never dare! What if he said no?' said Cecy. 'I'd feel such a loser.'

'Well, I think you should sort it out with him before the disco to make sure you've got someone to be with,' I said.

Cecy stared at me. 'Well, I'll be with you, won't I?'

'I'm not coming,' I said.

'But you've got to. Everyone's coming. Even the truly geeky boys who can't dance for toffee.'

'Yeah, well, I can't dance for toffee either, can I?'

'I talked about it with my mum and my nan, and Nan said when she was young she used to do this hand jiving. She showed me how to do it. Look.' Cecy waggled her hands in the air as if she were wearing invisible puppets. 'Shall I teach you, Katy?'

'Cecy, I dare say you and your nan mean well, but I'd sooner gnaw my own fingers off than do a hand jive,' I said. 'I'm not coming to the disco, full stop.'

'But it won't be any fun if you're not there,' said Cecy. 'Please come. Oh Katy, please. You liked the leavers' disco, didn't you?'

'Not really,' I said – although that dance with Ryan had meant a lot. Fat chance of that happening again.

I wouldn't go, even for Cecy. Very weirdly, it was Maddie who made me change my mind.

I was stuck with her and Sarah and horrible Eva one English lesson, when we were supposed to be making up a play together set in the First World War. They

442

were all three hopeless, without an original idea in their heads, though Eva acted like she was Shakespeare.

'I'll be one of those valiant Red Cross nurses, saving all the wounded soldiers,' she said. 'And the really dramatic scene will be me holding the hand of a dying soldier and comforting him.'

'While he spews up blood all over you?' I said.

'Trust you to be revolting, Katy Carr,' said Eva. Her eyes glistened. 'I know, *you* can be one of the wounded soldiers, seeing as you're in a wheelchair already.'

Sarah giggled but Maddie looked uncomfortable.

'You shouldn't be mean about Katy's wheelchair, Eva,' she said.

'Why not?' said Eva. 'Katy's mean to me. She's always been mean. Why should it be any different now?'

'Well, it's sad for her that she can't do things any more,' said Maddie.

'Look, I'm right here. Don't talk about me as if I'm deaf,' I said, but they weren't listening.

'What are you on about, Maddie?' said Eva, frowning. 'Do you want to pal up with Katy? Is that it?'

'No! It's just . . . well, she can't do PE like us, and she can't get up stairs, and she can't wear cool shoes, and she can't go to the disco, and —'

'*Yes I can!*' I said, irritated beyond measure. 'OK, I can't do proper games in PE because of you, Eva-whine-to-her-mummy-Jenkins, and I can't get up the stairs yet because they haven't got a lift, but I can wear

443

any shoes I want. I just can't stand stupid high heels. And I'm going to the disco, so there.'

They stared at me.

'But you can't dance,' said Eva.

'Lots of people go to discos and don't dance a single step. I bet half the boys won't dance. I'll hang out with them,' I said.

Eva's eyes narrowed. 'Well, don't think you're hanging out with Ryan. He's *my* boyfriend, not yours.'

'So you keep saying. We all know you're mad about him. But he doesn't seem to give you a second thought,' I said fiercely.

'You wait and see,' said Eva.

I knew she was probably right. And I didn't want to go to the wretched disco at all, but I seemed to have committed myself.

Cecy was thrilled when I sheepishly admitted this to her.

'That's brilliant, Katy! I'm so glad you've changed your mind. So, what will you wear?'

I shrugged. 'I don't know. My T-shirt and jeans.'

'You can't, not to a disco!'

'Mr Myers said it was casual.'

'Yes, but not T-shirt and jeans casual. You need to wear something special.'

'OK. Well, last time I looked in my wardrobe I did spot a pink Cinderella dress, with a low neck and puff sleeves and flouncy skirt and all-over sequins. I shall have to fold the skirts up uncomfortably under me so they don't get stuck in the wheels of my chair, but still – a girl's got to suffer to look beautiful.'

'Have you really . . .?' Cecy started. 'Oh Katy, stop kidding! Seriously though, you need to wear something kind of partyish. I've got this new skirt Mum bought me. It's wonderfully short and tight and I'll wear it with my blue top which sort of puckers a bit so it makes me look as if I've got a figure.' Cecy sighed. 'I wish I *did*. I keep doing all these chest-expanding exercises every morning but nothing's happened yet.'

'You're nuts,' I said, but fondly.

'Will you wear your red flared skirt with the black sparkly top? You looked great in that at the leavers' disco,' said Cecy.

I pondered. 'Cecy, if I wore that short flared skirt in my wheelchair I'd be flashing my knickers at everyone,' I said.

'Well, you'd probably attract a lot of boys then,' said Cecy.

I talked over the clothes problem with Clover and Elsie but they weren't much help either. They were both very young for their age. Elsie's idea of partywear was a Princess Elsa costume, and Clover's favourite outfit in all the world was a purple net ballet skirt.

I asked Izzie's advice.

'How about a nice corduroy pinafore dress with a white frilly blouse?' she said.

I stared at her, appalled – and she fell about laughing.

'I'm teasing you, Katy. I wouldn't take too much notice of Cecy. I think you'll be fine in your black jeans and that weird skull T-shirt. But maybe we'll get you new shoes. Those black plimsolls with the sequins are too small for you now.'

It was weird – my feet had carried on growing, even though they couldn't move.

'I hate shoes. I just want trainers,' I said.

'I've got an idea,' said Izzie. 'What about Doc Martens?'

'Oh *yes*!'

'They'll be expensive, but they can be an early Christmas present from me,' she said.

'Oh Izzie, you're so great! Can they be really bright ones? Red?'

'I don't see why not,' said Izzie.

She knew my size so she went to the shops and bought them for me.

'They say I can return them if they don't fit,' she said, showing me the wonderful scarlet shiny Docs.

They fitted perfectly and they meant the world to me. I couldn't walk or run or dance in them, but there they were, making a statement on my feet, telling everyone I was still Katy Carr, a girl to be reckoned with.

That girl felt very small and shy and stupid the evening of the school disco. I wondered why on earth

I'd opened my big mouth and insisted that I was coming. Even Cecy was in a total dither, flapping about her hair and forever fussing with her skirt, trying to pull it down an inch or two.

'Tell me honestly, Katy. Does it make me look fat? Are my legs skinny enough? And what about my bottom? Does it stick out too much?' she kept asking anxiously, as Cecy's mum drove us both back to school.

I hesitated. *Yes, no, yes* might have been the honest answer, but I swore blind that Cecy looked skinny and fantastic. She in turn told me that my red Docs were brilliant, and Mrs Hall echoed this, though I knew for a fact that they both hated big clumpy boots.

Mrs Hall wasn't as bold as Dad and didn't like to drive right into the school and she couldn't find anywhere nearby to park the car. All the other parents were just slowing down and letting their children jump out, but of course this was beyond me. We ended up in a side road three streets away, and then there was a great fuss because Mrs Hall didn't put the brake on my wheelchair and it skittered away when I tried to transfer into it. Luckily I hung on to the car door and she managed to catch it and get it back under me, but we were both hot and sweaty by the time I was safely sitting in the wretched chair.

'I'll walk with you to the school, girls,' she said breathlessly, but we were both adamant that we would manage fine by ourselves. I was determined to wheel

447

myself, but the kerbs were scarily high when we went to cross the road, so I had to ask Cecy to bump me down. We just about managed, though in bending over to manoeuvre me Cecy showed so much thigh that a bunch of passing Year Eight boys gave delighted wolf whistles.

'Oh my God!' Cecy gasped. 'I do hope they're not Richie's mates. I feel such an idiot!'

It felt strange approaching Springfield in the dark and seeing everyone out of school uniform. Some people looked just the same but others were scarcely recognizable. And when we got to the gym, transformed with Christmas decorations, music already blaring, the teachers looked so different too. Mr Myers seemed surprisingly fit in tight jeans and a white T-shirt, but Miss Lambert was the coolest, in a short black dress cinched in at the waist and high-heeled boots up to her knees.

'Look at Eva!' Cecy said.

Everyone was looking at Eva. We expected her to be wearing something sexy and outrageous, but she was clever enough to go the other way entirely. She was wearing a white broderie anglaise dress with a full skirt, and she had her long fair hair partly tied back with a white satin ribbon. I suddenly remembered way back in the Infants when we performed a Nativity play. Eva was the angel Gabriel in a long white sheet and gauzy wings. She had exactly the same breathtaking effect now. It was extraordinary how such a mean girl could manage to look so angelic.

'Well, no one's going to be looking at *us*,' said Cecy. She looked round the room and gave a little start when she saw Richie. Then she sighed. 'Even Richie's staring at her. Oh, I'll absolutely die if he asks her to dance.'

'Don't be daft. He'll ask you, just you wait and see,' I said.

Nobody was doing any dancing at that moment though. People were helping themselves to drinks and food and laughing and joking in little clumps. Wonderfully, some of the boys in our class came over and chatted. Including Ryan. He went specially and brought me back a glass of fruit punch with a twirly straw. Cecy had already fetched me one, but I hid that behind my chair to be tactful.

The boys all admired my Docs.

'You're all prepared now to give someone a good kicking, Katy,' one boy laughed.

Then there was a little pause as everyone took in what he'd said. I laughed hurriedly.

'Yeah, well, I wish,' I said, and then I quickly blew bubbles with my twirly straw. This started a bubble-blowing competition until Ryan got so enthusiastic his bubbles overflowed and he had to go off to the changing rooms to mop his shirt.

Eva waylaid him on his way back. She actually hung on to his arm, pulling him into the middle of the room.

449

She was clearly cajoling him to dance with her. He'd gone very red in the face. *Say no, Ryan!* I willed him. *Say you don't fancy it. Say you don't fancy **her**. Oh please, please come back to me.*

Ryan took no notice of my silent pleas. He danced with Eva, jigging about while Eva twirled in her white skirt. They looked good as a couple. They were practically the same height and they were both good at dancing. They encouraged the others. The gym floor suddenly got crowded, with other couples and a little clump of girls dancing together, plus a group of Year Eight boys doing modified breakdancing. Some of Ryan's mates got up to dance too. Still, I still had Cecy to chat to. Cecy, my best friend in all the world.

But she wasn't being very talkative. She was peering round – and when she caught Richie's eye she dared give him a little wave. He hesitated and then came over to us.

'Hey, guys,' he said, as if he were in some stupid American High School movie. He was even trying to talk with an American accent. He nodded at Cecy. 'Fancy a spin?'

I struggled not to burst out laughing then, he sounded so ridiculous. How could Cecy possibly have a crush on him? He was absolutely pathetic. Surely she'd come to her senses and fob him off. She was staring up at him, her whole face shining.

'Yeah, that would be great,' she breathed. But then she glanced at me anxiously. 'Is that OK, Katy?'

No, no, it's not OK. Don't dance with this idiot! Stay with me!

I took a deep breath.

'Of course it's OK,' I muttered.

So Cecy rushed off with Richie and I was left on my own. And it was awful. The music seemed to get louder, the lights brighter, the laughter more mocking. My eyes had gone blurry, so I couldn't tell if people were staring at me pityingly or not. It didn't matter. I felt they were. I'd been mad to come. I *knew* this would happen. If only I could be back at home. I looked down at my red Docs, wishing I could click them together like Dorothy and be safe at home in an instant.

'Cool boots!' It was Miss Lambert, smiling at me.

I sniffed and did my best to smile back. 'You're the one with the cool boots,' I said.

'They're a bit over the top, aren't they? They're my clubbing boots. I don't know why I wore them here. I'm hardly going to be dancing with any of Year Seven or Eight,' she said, sitting down beside me.

'You could dance with Mr Myers,' I said.

'Hmm. We're good mates but I don't think that would work. Anyway, you lot would all laugh at us.' She peered round. 'Do you think everyone's enjoying themselves?'

'I suppose so.'

'What about you?'

I shrugged. 'Dances aren't exactly my thing.'

'Dances are always a bit weird, especially at first. If it's any comfort, all the best literary heroines don't go a bundle on dances. Look at Jo March in *Little Women*. And Elizabeth Bennet snubbed by Darcy in *Pride and Prejudice*. And have you read Rosamond Lehmann's *Invitation to the Waltz*? It's an adult book and it's pretty dated, but you might like it. The girl in that has a terrible time – only leery old men or losers want to dance with her.'

'Yes, but Jo and Elizabeth and the Waltz girl *can* still dance,' I said.

'That's true,' said Miss Lambert. 'Point taken. Sorry.'

'It's OK,' I said, because I liked her and she was just trying to be friendly. But it wasn't OK. And the evening didn't get any better. Cecy came back to sit with me, but Richie came too, and the three of us had to make stilted conversation together.

Ryan came back three times, bringing me more fruit punches. It was sweet of him, but I had to keep hiding them because there was a limit to how much liquid my bladder could hold nowadays. He didn't just dance with Eva. He danced with lots of other girls too, but he danced *most* with Eva. Then she got up to do a showy-offy dance routine with Sarah and Maddie, and Ryan came hurrying over to me again.

'Can I get you another fruit punch, Katy?' he asked eagerly.

'No thanks.'

'There's still some food left. Shall I fetch you a plateful?'

'No, honestly, I'm fine.'

We sat still and silent.

'Are you OK?' said Ryan.

'Everyone keeps asking me that. Do I look a right grouch?' *Well, you're acting like one.*

'No. No, you look great. Love your boots.'

'Thanks. Like we said, great for giving people a good kicking. If I could.' *Will you stop it! It's like you're begging for pity.*

Ryan laughed uneasily. The music switched to that 'Happy' song and everyone started bouncing about. Eva waved at Ryan. He seemed not to notice. She gestured again.

'Your girlfriend's beckoning you,' I said. *Now you just sound petty and jealous.*

'She's not my girlfriend,' said Ryan.

'She says she is.'

'Yeah, well, she's not.'

'Don't you like her any more?'

'She's OK. She's very pretty. She makes all the other boys jealous of me,' said Ryan. 'But I'm not really into that boyfriend–girlfriend stuff.'

You once asked me to be your girlfriend, back in Year Six, when everything was different. You probably don't even remember.

'Though I did want you for my girlfriend once,' said Ryan, as if he were reading my thoughts. 'Only you didn't reckon me.'

'I did. I mean . . . it was just, well, I'm so tall and you're . . .' *Don't say it!*

'And I'm so small,' said Ryan.

'No, I didn't mean that,' I said quickly, though we both knew I did.

'Tell you what – I'm taller than you now,' said Ryan, standing up. 'See? I practically tower over you.'

'So you do,' I said.

'I wish we could have a dance together, Katy. Remember the leavers' disco? We had a fantastic dance, didn't we?'

'Yeah, we did.'

'Look, how about you sit in your chair and we hold hands and you whirl me about, like you're the man and I'm the girl. I could dance all round you, see?' Ryan said.

'We'd look weird,' I said. 'It's OK, Ryan. You don't have to be kind to me.'

'I *want* to dance with you, you nutter. Come on, let's give it a go.'

'No.'

'Come *on.*'

'People will laugh at us.'

'Let them. What do we care? Go on, Katy, I dare you.'

That was it. I always had to accept a dare, no matter what. I wouldn't wheel myself into the middle of the floor. I stayed right on the edge, hoping that somehow – miraculously – no one would notice us. But Ryan was a flamboyant dancer. I tentatively spun him round and he immediately got into this new way of dancing and put his whole heart and soul into it, jumping about and waving his free arm in the air. I could see people nudging each other and staring. Some people actually stopped their own dancing to watch. I got so hot with embarrassment my hand was almost too sweaty to keep contact with Ryan – but somehow, by the very end of the track, I'd got into the rhythm of the music, and was kind of bobbing about from my waist up.

When the music stopped there was a sudden cheer and clapping. Mr Myers, Miss Lambert, Cecy, lots of other Year Sevens, all of them clapping us. Not Eva. She was flouncing about, raising her eyebrows and obviously saying something catty to Sarah and Maddie. And did I care? No, I didn't!

'I was thinking, Katy,' said Ryan, when we were all saying goodbye and wishing each other a happy Christmas. 'Me and the lads still go to Baxter Park and skateboard. Could you get yourself over there some day in the holidays?'

'Well, I had a hard job finding it even before I was stuck in a wheelchair. And it might be OK for a bit, but it's too cold just to sit and watch you guys having all the fun,' I said.

'No, I wasn't meaning watch us skateboard. I know you're not that sort of girl. But I could ask some others in our class too. We could get up our own teams for Myball. And you could join in.'

'Hmm.' I thought about it. 'Are you going to ask Eva too?'

Ryan laughed. 'Do you think I'm daft? Then you wouldn't come, would you? Give us your mobile number and I'll get it all fixed up and give you a date. Right?'

'You bet,' I said.

25

It was nearly Christmas. Dad bought old-fashioned do-it-yourself paper chains and we all sat around one afternoon, slotting each chain into place. Even Phil joined in, though he licked his chains so thoroughly they wouldn't stick.

I couldn't help with the hanging of the chains and I couldn't decorate the top of the Christmas tree this year, but the littlies and I made a brilliant job of festooning the lower branches while Clover and Elsie finished off the top. They both made felt angels with yellow sewing-thread hair and sequined wings and then told me I must choose which angel was the nicest to go at the top of the Christmas tree.

It was obvious whose angel was the most splendid. Clover's had a sweet smiley face and dainty limbs and a golden trumpet fashioned from a Quality Street toffee wrapper. Elsie's had a lopsided face with squinty eyes and was altogether very squat and plain.

Clover couldn't help looking triumphant. Elsie looked desperately hopeful all the same.

'Come on, Katy, you've got to choose,' they chorused.

'I can't possibly choose,' I said. 'They're both beautiful. Why don't we have them as sister angels and they can squash together on the topmost branch?'

Clover didn't mind too much and Elsie was ecstatic. Izzie mouthed *thank you* at me over their heads.

Then on Christmas Eve we all made mince pies together, with Izzie supervising Phil very carefully just in case he took it into his head to start chopping again.

'No, Phil is going to be chief mixer,' I said, scooping mincemeat from the jar into a bowl. It didn't *need* any mixing at all, but it kept him gloriously busy, holding on to the wooden spoon with both hands and muttering, 'Mix, mix, mix,' with great satisfaction.

Izzie put all the ingredients and the scales and measuring jug on the big table instead of her high worktop, so I could reach to weigh everything out. She showed us how to rub the butter into the flour and we all had a go, even the littlies. Dorry was surprisingly good at it, his pudgy little fingers working the pastry very deftly.

'I think you might well be a cake baker when you're grown up, Dorry,' I said.

'Dorry couldn't be a baker because he'd eat up all his cakes himself,' said Jonnie, laughing.

'When do we do the tossing bit?' Phil asked eagerly.

'No, darling. You don't toss mince pies; that's just for pancakes,' said Izzie. 'Katy's speciality,' she added drily.

I might have fussed at this once, but now I just laughed along with the others. We were allowed one mince pie each for supper and then I read all the children the last lovely Christmas chapter of *Nancy and Plum*. Then they all went to bed and I changed into my pyjamas too, but I was allowed to stay up with Dad and Izzie, wrapping everyone's presents and filling little Christmas stockings with sweets and satsumas and small sets of crayons and notebooks and tiny teddies and whistles.

'I think those whistles are going to be a big mistake, Alistair,' said Izzie. 'They'll be blowing them at five o'clock in the morning.'

'Oh, let them have a bit of fun,' said Dad. 'Maybe you can organize them into a band, Katy?'

It was strange. Our family seemed to have regrouped now. The littlies were still a small threesome, but now Clover and Elsie came together, while I seemed to have joined up with Dad and Izzie. Or maybe I was one on my own now.

No, I was part of my own little gang now. People who understood, like Helen and Dexter. Helen had sent us all Christmas presents. They were laid out neatly under the tree. We'd all felt them carefully, trying to work out what they were, because Helen gave such good presents. Mine was a slim, flat rectangle. It was definitely a DVD. I wondered which one she'd chosen for me. I hoped it might be the second *Hunger Games*.

Dexter had sent me a Christmas present too! I was utterly amazed. He had never replied to any of the emails though I'd been writing to him ever since I started at Springfield. I'd been so disappointed at first, but after a while I stopped expecting any response. Writing to him was just like writing a diary. I'd have been startled if my diary started writing back to me, after all.

But then, in the middle of December, he *did* reply. Tersely.

What's your address?
Dexter. x

I got tremendously excited, thinking he might be coming to visit me. I emailed back at once with my address and full instructions how to get here. He didn't come – but a few days before Christmas a jiffy bag arrived addressed to me. On the back someone had written *Happy Christmas* in beautiful black printing. I knew that writing from those weeks in hospital.

'Oh my God, it's from Dexter!' I said, starting to tear at the bag.

'Don't use that expression, Katy!' said Izzie. 'And leave that bag alone! Wait till Christmas Day!'

'But I must see what it is!'

'No, wait!' said Izzie, and she snatched the parcel from me.

'Oh, don't be so mean! We don't know for sure it *is* a Christmas present. Let me just have one peep,' I begged.

'Absolutely not,' said Izzie, and she wouldn't relent.

I wondered if she and Dad were giving me a Christmas present as well as my red Docs. I'd looked carefully under the tree. There were smallish presents for Clover and Elsie and an enormously huge parcel addressed to Dorry and Jonnie and Phil – but nothing for me.

'Aren't I getting anything this year?' I asked.

'You'll just have to wait and see,' said Izzie – and she and Dad exchanged a sly little glance.

I let them sleep for an hour or so while I supervised the children on Christmas morning. They came running downstairs to my room with their stockings and all crowded into my bed. We ate our sweets and satsumas and swapped toys and then started up the Carr Family Whistle Band. None of us could play the simplest tune but we had a lot of fun trying. Our cat Sally mewed in protest and whisked out of the room, but Tyler joined in enthusiastically, throwing back his head and barking.

'I know what *I* want for Christmas,' said Izzie, putting her head round the door. 'Ear plugs!'

She made our usual festive breakfast of bacon sandwiches. We ate them in the living room and then everyone started opening their presents. I picked up Dexter's jiffy bag but Elsie said quickly, 'Oh Katy, open mine first! I tried making you a pot but it went all wrong, so I did this specially and it took *ages*.'

So I opened her parcel and discovered a little handwritten book called *The Story of My Special Big Sister Katy*. It had a picture of me on the front looking like a daddy longlegs. I had one long spidery arm round a little Elsie who was smiling from ear to ear.

Elsie's story was heavily illustrated inside too. There were pictures of us in the secret garden, pictures of me climbing my tree, pictures of me spreadeagled on the ground with my eyes crossed and my mouth open, looking very dead. Then there were hospital sketches and eventually portraits of me in a very wonky wheelchair.

The last page took me by surprise. I was standing upright.

AND THEN KATY GOT BETTER AND COULD WALK AGAIN. HURRAY!

Elsie had written that part in large triumphant capitals.

I swallowed hard. 'It's a lovely story, Elsie,' I said. 'I'm not sure the last bit's going to happen though. Still, wouldn't it be great if it did?'

Then I opened Clover's present. She'd made me a beautiful big blue pot, perfectly symmetrical, with tiny underwater creatures swimming round it.

'Do you see what they are, Katy?' she asked eagerly. 'They're little seahorses like the one on the special necklace Helen gave you. Do you like it?'

'It's lovely, Clover. The best pot I've ever seen. I'll keep it on my bedside table,' I said.

Dorry gave me a box of cherry chocolates. I peeped inside but he hadn't sampled any of them, bless him.

'I didn't eat even half of one,' he said proudly. 'And they look ultra yummy.'

'Try one now,' I said, offering him the box.

Jonnie gave me a red knitted square with several dropped stitches.

'Did you know I can do knitting now, Katy? Izzie showed me how. I was going to make you a shawl but it took too long. I thought you could use it as a winter hankie. It *is* your favourite colour,' she said earnestly.

I hugged the twins and then turned to Phil. He gave me a soft squashy parcel tightly bound with probably an entire roll of Sellotape.

'I wrapped it up all by myself,' he told me unnecessarily. 'Wait till you see what's inside. I bet you'll never ever guess.'

As a long floppy ear and several paws were poking through the wrapping paper it wasn't too difficult. Phil had given me Bunnyhop. The others all laughed when they saw and told Phil he was silly.

'You don't give away your old toys as Christmas presents,' Clover told him. 'Especially not Bunnyhop, because he belonged to Katy in the first place.'

'But he's my best thing,' said Phil, his face clouding.

'And he'll be my best thing now,' I said, resolving to lend him back to Phil at bedtime.

'Wait till you see what Mum and Dad have got you. *That* will be your best thing,' said Elsie. 'Oh Mum, can I go and fetch it for Katy now?'

'In a minute, darling. Why don't you open your present from us first?' said Izzie.

They'd given Elsie her own mobile phone.

'Oh wow! I'll be able to text everyone and join in all the big-girl secrets now!' Elsie said joyfully.

Clover had new shoes, purple suede with straps and small blocky heels.

'They're the most beautiful grown-up shoes ever,' she said, cradling them as if they were two small purple babies.

Dorry and Jonnie and Phil all got to share their present. They each took a turn at ripping off the wrapping paper. It was called Magical Zoo: a wonderful zoological garden with a grassy meadow for unicorns, a turquoise pool for mermaids, a dark cave for baby dragons, an ornate aviary for a splendid phoenix and a wild prairie for assorted dinosaurs.

'Oh, you lucky things!' I said, wishing I was little enough to share their present.

Dorry and Jonnie hunched down, looking at it with awe. Phil was more hands-on, grabbing at the zoo inmates.

'This is *my* horsey, *my* fish lady, *my* little monster, *my* birdy, *my* Tyrannosaurus rex!' he said, clutching them to his chest.

We all laughed that he was spot on identifying the dinosaur.

'They're magic creatures, Phil. The white horse is a unicorn – see his great long horn? Perhaps he'll let you ride him. And this is a mermaid. She'd like to go for a swim with you. This is a baby dragon. He looks very docile, but be careful not to make him angry or he'll breathe fire all over you. And this isn't any old bird, he's a phoenix, and I think he grants wishes,' I said.

'What do they all like to eat?' asked Dorry. 'I'm the chief zookeeper and I do all the feeding.'

'Will you play zoos with us, Katy?' said Jonnie. 'Oh please! We can put the zoo on the kitchen table so you can reach comfortably.'

'Yes, you always get the best ideas and make it real,' said Dorry.

'Play now! And can I have all the dragons?' said Phil.

'Play later,' said Izzie firmly. 'I shall want to set the table for Christmas dinner. Now Elsie, go with Dad and help fetch Katy's present from the garage.'

'But I've already had my Christmas present: my lovely red Doc Martins,' I said.

'Well, just this once we're giving you another present too,' said Izzie. 'Shut your eyes, Katy.'

I shut my eyes obediently.

'Wait till you see, Katy!' Elsie called triumphantly.

'Can you guess?' said Clover, putting her arm round me.

'Give me a clue,' I said.

'Well, it's got wheels,' said Clover, giggling.

For a mad moment I thought she meant a new skateboard or a bike. And then I realized. It would be a new wheelchair. I felt painfully disappointed. My own wheelchair wasn't quite right for me. It was an adult one because I'm so tall, but it was very heavy and clunky, the bog-standard sort. Dad and Izzie had been conferring for ages about getting me a lighter model. It was very kind of them, and generous, because fancy wheelchairs were very expensive, but who in the world would get excited about a wretched wheelchair as a Christmas present?

Me! Elsie told me to open my eyes and she proudly pushed the most amazing wheelchair into the room, shiny and light and streamlined and *bright red*. It even had dyed crimson sheep's wool on the seat for extra comfort.

'Oh, I love it, I love it!' I said.

Dad took hold of me on one side and Izzie the other and they carefully lifted me into my new chair. It was like getting into a Ferrari after months of driving an old banger.

'*Wheeeee!*' I went, wheeling myself at top speed round and round the living room.

'Hey, hey . . . you'll knock us all over!' said Dad. 'So is it really comfy? It certainly looks the right size for you. We had to take such a chance ordering it, but we wanted it to be a surprise.'

'And it's a wonderful surprise. I absolutely love it. Thank you *soooo* much,' I said, giving him a hug and then Izzie one too.

'Let's all go for a walk with Katy in her new wheelchair!' said Clover.

'Later. After dinner. Come on, we've still got lots of presents to open,' said Izzie. 'I've got one from Katy. I wonder what it is?'

She seemed to love her little buttoned purse. Dad liked his wallet and immediately transferred his cash and credit cards into it. Clover and Elsie and Dorry and Jonnie and Phil liked their purses too. Dad gave them each a shiny silver fifty-pence coin to keep inside them.

Then there was a further flurry of present-opening. We'd bought Sally and Tyler their own little stockings. Sally had a packet of Dreamies and a toy catnip mouse in hers. She had five Dreamies as a special Christmas treat and then retired to the back of the sofa, her mouse in her mouth. Tyler wasn't very interested in his doggy chews or his new ball, but he loved the growing pile of wrapping paper. He kept jumping in it and tearing it and rolling in it, barking excitedly.

I had two presents left. I was a little bit disappointed in Helen's present. It was a DVD of the Paralympic Games.

'What a thoughtful present, Katy, especially as you're such a sporty girl. Helen's so clever,' said Dad proudly.

It was almost *too* thoughtful. I didn't want to watch any softie sports specially for the disabled. I was sure it would be very boring. I tossed it to one side and picked up Dexter's present.

It was a book, my very own book, *Katy Superwheels*. It wasn't just one cartoon; it was a whole graphic novel about a girl in a wheelchair who goes to school and stands up for herself. Every time she argued with the head teacher her wheels grew so that she rose six feet in the air. She had many battles with an infuriating pretty girl – Dexter drew an absolutely perfect likeness of Eva even though he'd never seen her. The story ended with the school disco. Dexter had someone spiking the fruit punch with alcohol and everyone getting drunk. There were hilarious portraits of the teachers, and Katy Superwheels herself veered tipsily around, pursued by the handsomest boy in the room. They had a dance together, exactly like Ryan and me, only they ended up under a big sprig of mistletoe. The last picture was in the shape of a heart and there was a silhouette of a couple kissing.

'Oh my God!' said Clover, who'd been peering over my shoulder, reading along with me. 'Did you and Ryan *kiss?*'

'No! And nor did I get drunk!' I said.

'Why are you blushing, Katy? Let me see that book!' said Izzie, sounding anxious. 'What's all this about drunkenness and kissing?'

'It's all fantasy, Izzie. A cartoon version of my life. Dexter always twists things about,' I said.

Izzie and Dad came to have a look.

'He's done it beautifully,' said Dad. 'This is the weird young man in the hospital, right? He's actually very talented.'

'And it's so detailed, page after page. He must think a great deal of you, Katy,' said Izzie.

There was a little card too, but I didn't show it to anyone. It was just for me.

Dear Katy,

Glad things are working out for you. You've made me consider going back to school myself. I'll need A levels to get to art college.

This book is my reply to all your emails. Keep them coming, kiddo.

Love Dexter x

It was so strange – this was somehow turning into the best Christmas ever. Izzie cooked a wonderful turkey dinner. Dorry ate ten roast potatoes with his and then had two portions of ice cream and begged for more.

We helped Dad do the washing-up and then we all went for a walk to the park and back. I wheeled myself at a gentle pace, children all around me, but on the way home, the downhill stretch, I raced by myself, faster and faster.

I'm Katy Carr, I'm Katy Carr, I'm Katy Carr I shouted inside my head and I felt Mum running along beside me, the way she had when I was tiny, pedalling my red car. She was still there. She always would be.

When we got home Dad and Izzie dozed in front of the television while all us children played with the Magical Zoo. I made up all kinds of adventures for the creatures. We got so involved it felt as if we had unicorns pawing the living-room carpet, mermaids singing in the bathtub, dragons blowing fiery breath to warm our toes, phoenixes flying round the paper chains and dinosaurs sticking their vast leathery heads through the windows.

When I went to bed that night I turned the pages of Dexter's book again, relishing all the little details. I was still wide awake, so I slotted the first disc of Helen's Paralympic DVD into the computer. I only planned to watch it for ten minutes but it was surprisingly riveting.

The competitors were all so brilliant. This wasn't softie sport – this was the real thing! I'd had no idea that people with all kinds of disabilities could achieve so much. There were only snatches of the men's and women's basketball but I replayed them over and over. It was real, competitive, skilled sport – and oh how I wanted to have a go!

Mr Myers had given me the name and phone number of the guy who ran the basketball club. It was still scrunched up in the bottom of my book bag. I'd ring him as soon as the holidays were over. Maybe even sooner. I was desperate to start.

I was fizzing with excitement. I played another disc, the opening ceremony this time. It was incredible: an imaginative recreation of *The Tempest* and a brave new world where everyone was equal, everyone was included, everyone had a chance to star as themselves. There was an amazing young woman in a wheelchair playing Miranda. She had fantastic blue streaks in her short hair and wonderful red sequin jeans. I watched her, spellbound. At the end everyone was dancing and singing and laughing – and I joined in too, alone in my room.

I was Katy Carr. My life wasn't over. A new life was just beginning.

'A wonderful story' Jacqueline Wilson

What **KATY** Did

Susan Coolidge

I loved *What Katy Did* when I was a child. It's such fun and very easy to read, even though it was written in the nineteenth century. I especially liked naughty tomboy Katy in the first part of the book, forever getting into scrapes. I found the accident scene in the middle very dramatic, and I was fascinated by Katy's time as an invalid before she eventually recovers.

It wasn't until I was grown up and reading *What Katy Did* to my daughter Emma that I started to feel uncomfortable. Saintly Cousin Helen tells Katy after her accident that she should try to be very good and patient and tidy and act like a little mother to her brothers and sisters. Katy does her best – and is eventually rewarded by learning to walk again.

I didn't think this seemed very fair or likely. I decided to write about a modern Katy, still very much a naughty tomboy. I mirrored a lot of the adventures in the original book. My Katy has a similar dreadful accident – but then my version of the story changes. I try to show what it's really like to suffer a severe spinal injury. I have my Katy going through a despairing stage in hospital and then at home, but eventually she learns to deal with her new life. She's tough and determined and stands up for herself, and is courageous enough to go back to mainstream schooling. She fights battles and often wins.

She's certainly not a little saint in my modern version but she's a remarkable survivor. I feel she'll still have a great life even if she can't walk.

I love my Katy and I hope you do too.